LEEDS HOUSE

a novel by
T/JAMES REAGAN

LEEDS HOUSE

LEEDS HOUSE

A *RiverVerse* Novel. First Edition: November 16th 2014
ISBN-13: 978-0692330500 / ISBN-10: 069233050X
Copyright © 2014 by Tom Reagan

On The Cover:
Photograph by Andrew Lorrie

Contact the author:
tjamesreagan@yahoo.com
http://tjamesreagan.com
@t_jamesreagan

Also Available by T/James Reagan:

Lovetrust
Beach House Burning
Famous For Nothing
Empire Waste
Neon Blacktop
Southland Tales: The Complete Saga
Miss Julie 2020

Table of Contents

"One day the angels came to present themselves to the Lord, and Satan also came with them. The Lord said to Satan, Where have you come from?' Satan answered the Lord, 'From roaming through the earth and going back and forth in it.'"

~Job 1: 6-7

"The curtain rises on a vast primitive wasteland, not unlike certain parts of New Jersey."

~Woody Allen

LEEDS HOUSE

FOR:

Kyle, Rob, Mike, Steve and anyone else who joined us on 5 for $5 VHS movie night.

Rob, again, for taking me to my first basement show and exposing me to music that didn't exclusively revolve around shooting people.

LEEDS HOUSE

I. Foundation.

We're all born to a home. We can't choose the location where we'll enter this world, but as soon as we arrive, we create a divot there. We'll spend the rest of our lives returning back to that divot, either to fill it in, or to dig down deeper.

Some of us may want to preserve our first home with a clear seal of weatherproof varnish so that everything can remain exactly as we remember it, while others may want to level the entire place to the ground for revenge.

Even if we were to engulf our home in flames, the foundation would likely remain. The first step in building a house is the last to be destroyed. If only we could extend that solid foundation to the roof, then everyone's childhood could crackle forever. This would ensure that there was always a definitive marker that could be visited, if not for closure, then for acceptance.

As you can see from the cover of this novel, we're about to go into the woods. Of course we'll find a house in those woods, and this house will change things.

Despite this novel's setting, and despite this novel's title, it could be argued that what we're about to experience isn't a story about a house at all.

This is a lesson about a *home* from which there is no escape.

There's a very distinct difference between a house and a home.

You probably don't understand.

Yet.

This story, like a house, starts at the foundation.

Covering the walls of this foundation are various high school art class still life drawings of pumpkins and bowling pins.

Pushed to the perimeter walls, we see tables covered with CDs, bumper stickers, and small black T-shirts.

Inside this basement, near the door that leads out into the backyard, we notice a pack of 20 teenagers standing, nodding their heads.

In front of that group, we find more kids- they're pushing each other without malice. Skinny over-privileged teens crash into each other,

expending all their pent up rage stemming from when Dad bought them a
Jetta instead of a Lexus, or when their little sister spilled nail polish all over
their room, or when their girlfriend gave a blow job to their lab partner.

Moving further forward, we find more kids. They're facing the crowd.
They're playing instruments. They're "Lies As Language," a space-metal
Christian metalcore band. This excessive genre description is what happens
to a band that dares to defy the rigid conventions of the metalcore genre.
While sonically ambitious, at their most basic, Lies As Language are simply
five guys pouring out their souls on stage.

It's the intimacy that strikes us. This concert experience isn't happening
in a rock club built for commerce- we're in Scott Trunkett's basement. Most
of the venues that previously supported and showcased the local hardcore
and metalcore bands in Connecticut have now closed. The previous
generation spoiled all the fun for the millennials that are crowded around
us tonight in this basement. It was the suburban neighbors who didn't like
the noise that accompanied people smoking cigarettes outside a bar that
willingly agreed to stop selling alcohol on all-ages night. It was the teen
with the heart condition in the mosh pit who collapsed and the subsequent
lawsuit served to the venue in a desperate attempt to assign blame for the
early passing of a girl with a genetic defect handed down from two guilt-
ridden parents. It was the explosion of EDM music where profit margins
were exponentially higher because the entire under-aged clientele arrived
totally fucked up on pills and needed to stay hydrated at the price of $7 per
bottle for water.

At the old venues, everything was structured to make money. The more
structure you have, the more money you can make, and the more money
you can save. Having this show in a basement means this rigid structure is
abandoned for a pure escape from the pressures of relentless capitalism.
We didn't need to buy a ticket online to enter this basement; we just
needed to show up and hand over $5 at the door. No one was turned away,
and everyone came together, then proceeded to share an experience that
will be imprinted on this home, and this crowd, forever. The ghosts of this
crowd will haunt this basement, and the reverberation of their energy will
create a lingering presence.

The passion contained within the foundation is contagious. Connections
are passing like an electrical current and even with the strobe effects and
colored lighting that was set up to enhance the mood, everything in this
basement feels bright, and clear, and illuminated.

Teens who are still figuring out where they belong in this world feel at
home here. It's all escapism- a night away from those overbearing parents,
a vacation in someone else's house. It's like a sleepover, but everyone will

leave here before they fall asleep. There's the excitement of staying up late, with a bunch of people just like us, and we're all looking in the same direction, except for the band.

The band is easily identified by their instruments, by their microphones, by the fact they're facing us, sometimes even looking us in the eyes. Lies As Language's songs don't sound exactly like they do on that little file on our computer, and we like the noticeable difference. The music isn't perfect, and that makes us even happier. There's a human element to this performance; there's a reflection of our presence in the songs. We genuinely believe that our attendance tonight was the introduction of the imperfection. *We* are the cause of the slight sonic difference. Sometimes, we're called upon to sing the song- filling in missing words, eking out high notes, gang-vocaling dramatic choruses. Even though we aren't pretty like the lead singer, even though we aren't facing in the right direction, a microphone is held out toward us, and if we sing loud enough, our voices will be bursting from the speakers, rendering us both singer and audience. As soon as Kyle, the lead singer, brings the mic back to his mouth and continues with the song, his absolute power is restored. We're familiar enough with these songs to sing them, which means we're familiar enough to know that this current song will be over in 40 seconds, 30 seconds, 20 seconds...

Lies As Language's final song wraps up in that epic, self-indulgent manner that only rock bands are egotistical enough to end their shows with. We yell, howl, and clap with approval, while simultaneously fighting the tide of reality that is crashing against the basement door.

Mike Connor shakes his Robert Smith inspired, dyed black hair back and forth, while his bass hangs around his neck. His hands are wrapped around a microphone that he screams into with a throaty growl.

Rob Martin, a big nosed, Charlie Manson haired kid with vacant eyes, slams the keys on his keyboard, trying to overpower the crowd's screams.

Wil Chapman sets his guitar down on the basement floor, then lights a cigarette. A young, attractive, ghostly Elvis, Wil's hair is styled in a black pompadour, his outfit is a pure white dress shirt, and his skin is a nearly matching pale white with the only color coming from his haphazard tattoos. Wil's entire identity seems like a hodgepodge of different eras, yet he remains distinctly captivated with the present. He's not focused on us though. He's focused on his cigarette. It's possible he doesn't even see us here.

Jody Lennard, the somewhat overweight, slightly over 30, goateed older brother to the band's lead singer, throws a black towel into the audience, then frantically smashes his drumsticks across every drum splayed out in front of him. Jody is out of place, yet necessary. He bought the keg that sits in the backyard. This aluminum distraction allowed each band the time to set up their own equipment, and prevented the drummers from being forced to use the same kit. The audience would go outside, have a beer, then return when the next band was ready. While waiting for his set to start, Jody played bartender, cutting off lightweights and bragging about the Jersey gig. Ms. Trunkett, owner of this home, and mother to the organizer of this show, turned a blind eye to all of this. She also actively avoids eye contact with Jody because he'll wink at her anytime the opportunity presents itself. Jody is well regarded by all, and not just because of his casual stance on liquor laws.

Kyle Lennard sweeps his angled bangs away from his eyeliner blasted eyes, then his fingerless black gloves strangle the mic as he belts out the final lyric to the final song of the night. As soon as words leave his lips, the crowd reaches for Kyle and there's no barrier to stop their hands and hugs. Kyle accepts this outpouring of love. He appreciates the warmth, as sweat cuts down the artfully dipped bridge of his nose. Two years ago, so many of the people in this crowd ignored Kyle as he made his way to his locker. Then a hidden talent went public, and Kyle was no longer invisible. This sudden acceptance arrived with no resentment on Kyle's part.

After our hugs have been reciprocated and our hands have been grasped, Kyle gently puts the mic on the concrete basement floor. He backs up a step, so that he's directly in front of his brother's drum set, then he places his gloved hands together and bows.

When the mood lights go off and the house lights come on, Kyle picks the mic back up, and tells the crowd, "I'd like to thank Ms. Trunkett for the iced tea, sandwiches, free parking, and most of all, the stage."

"Misses! Trunkett!" the crowd cheers in unison, "Misses! Trunkett!"

We look to our left, waiting for the coolest mom in Connecticut to make her signature appearance. Tonight's crowd is exclusively composed of children who would willingly admit that they'll likely spend the first 30 years of their life relying on the patience and support of the Empire generation that Mrs. Trunkett has the privilege of being a part of. Arriving to acknowledge the crowd's chants, Ms. Trunkett descends a few stairs holding a glass of wine, looking like an aged Jackie O. Eyeing Wil, she points at him with a long smoldering cigarette, then says, "No smoking in the house, Wilem."

Wil, reverting back into a little boy for a moment, looks down, embarrassed, then regaining his rock star persona, puts the cigarette out on his leather watch band.

Scott Trunkett, the yellow t-shirted boy we saw moshing next to us a song ago, takes the mic from Kyle. Scott is slightly embarrassed that everyone has just been reminded that 'The Basement of Doom' shows do, in fact, take place in the basement of his mother's upper-middle-class Connecticut home. Regaining control of the crowd, Scott says, "That was Lies As Language! Thank you for coming out tonight and I'd like to thank all the bands for putting on a great show. If you liked what you heard, buy some T-shirts and CDs, I'm sure the bands will appreciate it."

Lies As Language collectively take this moment in. They want this to be the last time that they walk onstage and already know the first name of every person in the audience.

II. Merch.

We stand. No. We *shiver*, as we wait outside on an unusually cold early November night. The Lies As Language merch table has been set up on the side of a long driveway that's been converted into a shanty town of SUVs borrowed from nervous parents. These luxury cars have to be returned by midnight, as though everyone in attendance was Cinderella, but with a maid or mother who takes care of the chores.

People we just saw perform are now desperately hawking merchandise. So many out-of-town bands are struggling to break even tonight. Most music now resides intangibly in the cloud, so anyone making a CD purchase here is doing so as a small show of support, like a contribution made to an art museum so that the paintings don't end up in storage just because hi-res scans can be easily accessed via a simple Google image search.

A $10 bill is placed in Rob Martin's palm. We last saw Rob in front of the keyboards, and now he's in front of a banquet table covered in T-shirts and CDs.

A skinny, bald (by choice) boy points at the Lies As Language debut album. The cover is all white, except for a two-tiered gray rectangle that looks like this-

LIES
LANGUAGE

"I torrented the album..." the bald boy admits, "...but once I heard how good it is, I had to buy it. Honestly, I'm feeling a little guilty."

"For torrenting it or thinking it's good?" Rob asks, then sports a wide, crooked smile.

"Maybe a bit of both," the bald boy says with a small laugh. He picks up the CD, looks at it, then glances back up at Rob.

Rob holds up the cash to confirm the clean transaction, then says, "Gas money."

"So you're driving down to the Starland tomorrow?" the bald boy asks.

"No," Rob says, and he hopes that the tension in his jaw will be obvious enough that additional questions won't be asked.

"Oh, you're playing The Stone Pony?" the bald boy asks.

Rob shakes his head no.

Slightly less impressed with this "big break," the bald boy stumbles through the customary, "Oh. Well. Good luck, man," then hands over a little cash to get the band a couple miles closer to the first real Lies As Language concert. Rob knows that if tomorrow goes well, The Stone Pony will be next; Starland will be next. The next time this bald boy finds Rob at a merch table, Lies As Language will have played those venues, and so many more. The underground clubs might be gone, but the bigger venues are a realistic future for Lies As Language. No more basements. Tomorrow there will be a sound check, a bar that isn't illegally stocked by Jody, and security will be provided- in more ways than one.

The next boy in the merch line is a kid in a green sweater and khaki pants. He appears incredibly out of place, but he makes up for it in enthusiasm, "I can't believe I'm going to miss you guys opening for Sullen Wishes this weekend."

"Only if we can figure out all the traffic circles in Jersey," Rob says, and a smile doesn't follow this comment. The one time that the band let Rob drive the van, it ended poorly. It was late and Rob offered to drive while the rest of the band slept. When the guys woke up, they were parked on the edge of the highway, the van was clam-baked, and Rob was giggling, watching conspiracy theory videos on his phone. Wil, hardly the band's most responsible member, had to remind Rob that an important part of driving was, "Not being really high," and, "Moving forward on the road toward the destination." They haven't let Rob drive since.

"In no time you'll be leaving all your friends in Connecticut, huh?" the boy in the sweater asks, holding up a twenty to show that this is a comment that arrives with gas money.

Rob snatches the bill from the boy, and says, "Yes, freeze in hell."

The boy in the sweater reaches down to pick up a real, actual, band t-shirt. The guilt that Rob is feeling about the fact he'll almost certainly be stealing this money from his bandmates is placated by the excited look on sweater boy's face. Rob just changed a life. He altered the course of this kid's existence. If someone changes your life for only twenty bucks, you got a damn good deal.

At the precise moment that the boy in the green sweater finds his true self, Punchcunt Love- a once relevant hardcore band- finds the rest of Lies As Language by the keg.

Punchcunt Love, for a short period of time, had the honorable distinction of being the single most buzzed about band in the Connecticut scene. Their relentlessly aggressive first EP ended up in the hands of some of the biggest celebrities in the world after one of the top trainers in Hollywood used it to score his high priced, fast paced workout sessions. When River White mentioned Punchcunt Love on the celebrity blog *Famediet*, a mass of people flocked to iTunes to pick up Punchcunt's record. Time has passed, and the generally disagreeable nature of every member of Punchcunt Love has sent them back to the basement circuit.

It could be viewed that Lies As Language have stolen the buzz that Punchcunt once relied on.

We all know who closed The Basement of Doom tonight.

We all know that egos bruise easily.

We all know that a band full of guys who now shave their heads because their hairlines began betraying them must despise a band full of long haired, heavily made-up kids, no matter how old their drummer looks.

Jody, Mike, Kyle, and Wil nurse their beers and make small talk with fans, as Punchcunt Love approaches. "Well, look who it is... Jody and the Pussygoths," barks Punchcunt's very drunk lead singer, Abaddon Cold (Real name Fred Daniels).

Wil lights another cigarette, then asks the lead singer of Punchcunt Love, "Was that a dig at our clothes?"

"Certainly was," Abaddon says, his arms crossed, his band behind him.

"You're wearing all black too," Mike points out in his conversational voice, which is meek, and this creates a startling dichotomy from the powerful screams we heard during the Lies As Language set.

"These jeans aren't black, they're dark navy, you emo jerk off," yells Bloodsnake (real name unknown) (nick-named after a snake tattoo that wraps around his neck.) (The snake is biting his Adam's apple) (Was it Biblical?) (No. Probably not.)

"How'd it feel to play under us, bitch?" Jody taunts.

Kyle sighs. Jody has been incited. This will end poorly.

"I asked all your moms the same thing last night," Bloodsnake says. Bloodsnake is either Mexican or he goes tanning frequently.

"All our moms were at a PTA meeting last night. You guys went to a PTA meeting?" a confused fan asks.

"You goth retards, you have no idea," Abaddon says.

"Is he implying there was a gang bang at the PTA meeting last night?" another fan asks, also confused.

"More like a T&A meeting," Jody says, then holds up his hand for a high five that never arrives because his comment helped Punchcunt Love's pathetic assault. Jody continues, undeterred, suddenly angry, "This is disgusting. When we played the high school prom, they wouldn't even let us play 'Madeline,' because of the lyrics, 'I lie in you, it dies in you,' sounded like they encouraged teen abortion, but now it's okay to have a gang bang at the PTA meeting?"

"I'm saying that I fucked your mom. Not the PTA kid's mom. I don't know who his mom is... so..." Bloodsnake mumbles, a little uncomfortable, now less focused on hurting Jody and more focused on just clarifying things for the fans.

Jody's bizarre anger has taken all of the tension that Punchcunt was working to build and transformed it into general confusion.

Respecting their elders and dismissing them with equal flourish, Lies As Language start their walk across the lawn, toward the merch table, away from Punchcunt Love.

"That's right, run away, faggots," Abaddon yells.

Jody and Kyle Lennard, without looking at each other, both turn around and head back toward Punchcunt Love.

Someone inside the garage at the end of the driveway clanks together three bottles and screeches, "Grown men in women's jeans, come out and play-ay." This statement is punctuated by the smacking sound of Jody's fist connecting with Abaddon's face.

Bloodsnake, and whoever plays bass for Punchcunt Love, both tackle Kyle. The men punch Kyle's body because it already looks like someone blacked his eyes and this whole fight started because a hardcore band didn't want to be associated with eye makeup.

Jody pounds his fist into a trembling Abaddon. Primed after 30 years of fighting- first with the family dog, then with his best friend Steve Greenblat, and most recently with his brother- Jody is a skilled warrior who's camouflaged by his poor physique.

Ever since the moment Kyle learned to speak, he's watched Jody's fighting talents develop... as Jody kicked his ass around their childhood home. Kyle has become a pro at using his skinny frame to slip away, and he shows this talent to the growing backyard crowd. Kyle is skinny, but he can defend himself. Tonight, outnumbered, he isn't interested in testing his limits.

Kyle is able to wriggle away from Bloodsnake before sustaining any substantial rib injuries that would affect his singing, and once he's extricated from the mess, he looks down at his stained hoodie, and he realizes that he has a choice. As the frontman, it's Kyle's responsibility to either bring this fight to a screeching halt or he can elevate it to one of those epic stories that will become part of Lies As Language legend.

Still unsure of his plan, Kyle rushes to the edge of the driveway, then pops open a long, fat bottomed, skinny necked, black case. After picking up Bloodsnake's guitar, Kyle yells, "Hey, cunts!" and he acquires center stage again.

Jody temporarily stops beating Abaddon senseless and takes note of the raised guitar reflecting the porch light. "Dude! No!" Jody calls out in a momentary plea for mercy. "You're crossing a line breaking a man's instrument."

Jody releases Abaddon from his grip, and the pummeled man crumbles to the ground like a sack of rocks being dropped.

Cutting across the yard, the drummer of Lies As Language approaches the lead singer.

The Lennard brothers will face off once again.

"Give me the guitar," Jody demands, zeroing in on his younger, much skinnier brother.

"Why? They called me a fag so I'll show them what a-" Kyle is unable to finish his sentence before Jody lunges forward and starts beating his brother to keep the music alive.

Bloodsnake runs over and grabs his guitar off the ground, then brushes the dirt off its body. Pleased with the unblemished condition of his gear, Bloodsnake goes back and gets a beer, then watches the Lennard brothers beat the living shit out of each other.

 **. Round II.**

We cruise through the quiet Connecticut suburbs in the black Lies As Language van. Kyle drives, while Jody sits shotgun, treating the swelling on his forehead with a sock full of ice (compliments of a disapproving, but mildly entertained Ms. Trunkett). Mike, Wil, and Rob fill the middle bench seat, and behind them is their carefully secured equipment.

Sock to his face, Jody plows through one of his signature one-sided conversations, "-a kick ass red stripe. If we give this van a red stripe, everywhere we go people will be like, 'Oh shit, it's the A-Team reincarnated as a metalcore band! Let's either book them for a gig or, you know, stop running coke and become more responsible with our free time.'"

Rob is energized by this fantasy, and adds, "We'll be like, 'Hand over the coke. Allow us to take possession of it. We'll stash it in our pockets... for safe keeping,' then we'll get super coked out and save kittens or expose people as racists so we can gain us the internet's favor."

In this alternate universe, Jody would drive a striped version of the Lies As Language van, while Rob did bumps of coke off his house key.

"Maybe we don't need to trick people into thinking we're the A-Team. Maybe they'll just be like, 'Oh shit, it's Lies As Language.'"

"I bet if we made the stripe rainbow colored, you'd change your tune," Jody says.

"If the Lennard brothers can't play nice we're going to have to separate you two again," Wil growls.

Mike adds, in his little voice, "Of course it will be a temporary separation because without enough money for a hotel room in Jersey tomorrow, we're going to be spending a lot of time together."

"Hit me with the numbers, Cliff," Jody says, using Mike's birth name, only because Mike hates this name.

"Well," Mike says, "I figure it takes about three hours and twenty minutes to get to South Jersey. That's seven total hours of gas, which, in short, is all the money we made tonight. We get $1,500 for the show, and whatever we make off merch, minus the venue cut. I'll split up the take in the van after the gig, then I'll give you the official numbers." Mike takes a deep breath, then announces, "Before we go, I'm stealing as much food as I can from my house. I suggest you all do the same."

"Mike, unlike you, we don't live with our parents so we can't steal food from home. We'd be stealing from ourselves," Wil says.

"You get none of my mom's sugar cookies," Mike states plainly.

"You know I didn't mean it," Wil says, with a rare apology. "So, I get some of the cookies right?" he asks after a beat of silence.

The big black van stops. The door swings open. Mike gets out. He's home.

Standing in the street, his arms pinned to his sides, Mike says, "Yes, I'll bring you a ziploc of cookies because you seem repentant regarding your comments."

Mike doesn't move from his frozen position, so Rob gives him a friendly wave, then slides the van door shut.

"Fuck the cookies, I just want whatever mood stabilizers he's on," Rob states casually.

IV. The Connor Home.

We stand under a giant bear that rears over us on its hind legs. The bear doesn't eat us. It doesn't do much of anything, beyond peacefully co-existing with a fox, some birds, and portions of two deer. We're in Mike Connor's living room. No. We're in Mike Connor's *mother's* living room, and a taxidermied animal kingdom surrounds us. This gutted, stuffed, glass eyeballed crowd was the first once-live audience that Mike had ever performed for.

Lois Connor, Mike's mother, stands in her nightgown in the dimly lit living room. "Did they like your songs, hon?" she asks. It's obvious she stayed up to make sure that Mike returned home safely.

"Yeah, I guess," Mike says in his little voice, while he organizes the mail on the coffee table into a symmetric mosaic.

"Who was there?" Lois asks, determined to get some sort of conversation out of her son.

"I don't know. Kids. It was... good."

"So, are you all ready for South Jersey?"

"Noon," Mike responds.

"Is that when you're leaving?" Lois asks. She doesn't receive a response. This is typical, as Mike has never been a fan of conversation, nor has he been particularly skilled at it. He likes being with his comics, or with his laptop, or with his guitar. He also likes to hunt with his father, a man he hasn't seen in three years. It's been a long time since Mike went hunting. At least he was able to stuff enough memories to keep himself company in this dark living room.

"Okay... well," Lois says, turning to leave, but then she relents to her idle thoughts, and mentions, "I was talking to Mrs. Stephens today, and I learned some things about Rob Martin. Will he be there?"

"Yes," Mike says, without emotion, "He's in the band. He helped form the band."

"I recall now. Well, please don't get mixed up in anything you'll regret," Mike's mother requests, lightly, in an echo of Mike's tone of voice.

Fulfilling one requirement from the modern mother handbook, Lois moves on to another, as she says, "Goodnight. Love you. Knock their socks off, kiddo."

V. Round II. Part II.

We sit in the big black van, still. The ice has melted in Jody's sock, and he's changed topics, "Take a final look around at the simple life, boys. This may be the last time you see it. At the show tomorrow, some music exec will be dragged to the gig by their daughter and we'll fall madly in love." Jody pauses, reviewing his own statement, then says, "I mean, I'll be in love with the daughter, not the executive. Don't be stupid, how could there be a woman executive anyway? We aren't playing this gig in fantasy land."

No one in the van laughs at this. They might be shaking their heads in disappointment, or maybe the van just hit a couple of bumps.

"Then again, the music industry is in the shitter so maybe women did take everything over?" Jody says, then laughs gleefully at his joke. When we don't join him, Jody continues his rant, "Regardless of gender politics, this executive's rich, beautiful daughter, in a desperate attempt to keep the untamable Jody Lennard around longer, will get her father to sign us to a record deal. He'll have no choice because it's the only way he can satisfy the whims of his naughty little daughter. His dirty nympho, virginal-"

"-I swear, if you start touching yourself again, Kyle will let you out right here and you'll have to walk home," Wil interjects from the back seat.

"I live on this road. My house is like 50 yards from here," Jody points out.

"He's touching his dick," Wil says, sticking his head between the seats.

The brakes slam on the big black van, and Wil's head almost strikes the parking brake when he's thrown forward by the sudden stop.

"Since you only live 50 yards away, it'll be a short walk," Kyle says.

"Dude! I wasn't masturbating. I was checking for lumps. These cell phones turn our dicks into zombies so you have to pulse-check them from time to time," Jody says, acting as his own attorney.

Rob nods at this, merely because it supports some of his conspiracy theories.

The big black van doesn't move. The individuals in the van seem to be confident that there's nothing wrong with Jody's balls.

"Fine assholes. Fuck you all for the next..." Jody looks at his digital watch, "... nine hours. I hope each of you has the worst nine hours of your life. I'm putting a pox on all of your houses- Shakespeare style."

"Really?" Kyle asks, equipped with the knowledge that Jody always folds when questioned further regarding his plans, "What does the pox do?"

"Uh. You guys.... are now... all fuckin' poxed with..." Jody stares out the window. The parked van is silent, until Jody perks up in his seat and declares, "I've poxed you all with the 9-hour butt herpes virus. I'm sorry it had to come to this."

No one responds. Jody opens the door, hops out of the van, then slams the door behind him.

The black van pulls back into traffic and drives away.

Walking home, Jody immediately starts texting his bandmates.

"I've made a donation to the 9 hr butt herpes foundation in ur name," is sent to Wil.

"Sorry 2 hear abt ur butt herpes. Tell ur roommate to get tested," is sent to Kyle.

"Don't let ur butt herpes define u. UR more than ur 9 hr disease," is sent to Rob.

And, "FYI- Besides us, the rest of our band has butt herpes 4 the next 9 hrs. Don't get near their butts until 10 hrs from now," is sent to Mike.

Jody receives only one response to his string of texts- it's from Mike, and it reads, "Okay. Thank you for the warning."

After a strenuous two block walk, Jody keys into his house and immediately passes through the living room to the kitchen. He grabs a beer, then returns to the living room and checks his cell phone. He sees no new responses to his diagnosis so he sits down on the sofa, ready to relax.

Leaning forward, Jody picks up a red notebook and searches for where he left off.

BAM!BAM!BAM! Three quick, loud knocks interrupt Jody from the task at hand. He drops the notebook, and his attention refocuses on the noise that cuts through the quiet house.

Approaching the door that's shaking with a steadily slamming *BAM! BAM! BAM!* Jody prepares to grant mercy on his bandmates and lift the pox. He swings the door open, then says, "Listen. If you didn't want butt herpes, you shouldn't have put a herpes penis in your exit area."

Jody quickly notices that it's not one of his band members at the door, but instead a sweaty black boy who's no more than 12 years old. The boy tries to push his way into the house, but Jody's large frame bounces him back. "Whoa. I don't think so, OJ," Jody says, holding out a hand to stop the boy.

"Please, we have to get inside now!" the sweaty boy begs.

Jody's eyes become slits, "Did I just catch you in the middle of a ding-dong-ditch?"

"What?" the boy asks, confused, "No. No. He's after me!"

Jody peeks his head outside, "I don't see anybody, kid."

"At least let me use your phone. We need to call the cops," the boy begs.

"You're a tweenage boy. You expect me to believe that you don't have a cell phone?" Jody questions, appointing himself sheriff.

"It exploded," the boy says.

"Let me see it. That sounds awesome," Jody says, finally showing some interest.

The sweaty boy digs his hands in his pockets, then gulps, "I dropped it when he was chasing me. I had to escape."

"Okay, kid. I'm going to go on the internet and look at videos of people with real problems, not this made up stuff," Jody says, beginning to shut the door.

"You have to help me," the boy responds with desperation.

Jody continues closing the door, but he offers some advice, "The 'ditch' is the most important part of the gag."

"No!" the kid screams, but the screams are much quieter once the door is shut.

VI. Round II. Part III.

We're staring out the window of the band van, as the passing blur of trees creates a stasis that eases us off the pure adrenaline we pumped with tonight at the concert, and again during the fight, but before we can level out, Rob begins screaming, "Stop, stop!"

The brakes slam on the big black van and equipment crashes forward in an off-key punctuation of the rapid deceleration of the vehicle and rapid increase of our heart rate.

"What! What?" Kyle asks, frantically searching the road for the child he was about to run over or the closed bridge that could lead to our watery demise.

"Dude, can you drop me here?" Rob asks casually.

"Here? In front of Cari Simmons' house?" Kyle asks, craning his neck to see if the lights are even on in the house- they aren't.

"Yeah, that's where I'm staying tonight," Rob says.

"Are you fucking Cari Simmons?" Wil asks, then considers it, and admits, "That's an upgrade for you."

"No, she just hooks me up- lets me stay at her place," Rob stumbles, replacing the truth with a lie.

Kyle catches the slip, and asks, "You haven't started using aga-" but before he can finish, Rob slides open the door and gets out of the van. Standing in the street, he rages, "-I don't need this. Fine. Okay. I'm fucking her. Feel better?"

"Why would that make us feel better?" Wil asks.

Rob thinks about it, then says, "Because you want to support your friend."

"Come on, you know me better than that," Wil says, almost as though he was offended that allegations were being made regarding him being a supportive guy.

"Tomorrow, 9 AM- be here, at the curb, ready, sober," Kyle says. He makes sure to push everything three hours earlier than the real departure time because he knows Rob too well.

Rob nods his head once to confirm he accepts Kyle's plan, then Wil slides the door shut.

The van pulls away from Cari's house, and an uneasy vibe seems to arise, then expand, so Wil climbs into the front passenger seat.

Kyle and Wil sit together, accepting the quiet as they move through the sleepy residential streets of Connecticut.

"Do you think he's...?" Kyle starts to ask.

Wil lights a cigarette, then with a hard exhale, he says, "Cari Simmons wouldn't fuck him."

Kyle accidentally inhales Wil's exhale, then croaks, "It's not a person that I'm worried about him doing."

Wil looks over at Kyle, but can offer no assurance regarding Rob's conduct.

The silence returns, humming until the big black van pulls into a dreary parking lot drenched in yellow light.

Kyle parks the van, then closes his eyes and lets out a strained breath. "I'm beat. Literally," he says, lifting his shirt slightly to show his giant yellow and purple bruises.

"Do you need me to help you out?" Wil asks, lightly touching a particularly gruesome looking patch of discoloration. "Will it hurt to sing?"

Kyle lets his shirt drop, then pops open his door, and asks, "Do you want the metalcore answer to that or the emo answer?"

Outside the van, Kyle and Wil move in a circle, going around to each door, then pulling on the handle to ensure that the gear is secured. They take every precaution to make sure that their future will not be robbed from them.

Even after the security check is complete, something inside Wil prevents him from leaving the van. Maybe it's the idea that things are so close to working out, he's unable to believe that tomorrow will go smoothly. In a life populated with a trail of near-misses at happiness, something bad *will* happen, and it becomes about decreasing the chances of failure. Lingering by the van, Wil asks, "Could I have the keys? I want to bring her home tonight."

"We're leaving in a couple hours. She'll be fine," Kyle says.

"I don't want anything to happen to her. Your parking lot is..." Wil looks around, "...dark. Just let me get her out."

Kyle, in an effort to end this night as soon as possible, tosses the keys to Wil.

Quickly, the back door of the van is thrown open and a black guitar case is removed from the stack of instruments that were jostled during Rob's emergency stop.

"Is that the acoustic?" Kyle asks, as the van is sealed and double checked again.

Wil nods, then hands the keys back to Kyle.

"Working on a solo project?" Kyle asks, surprised that Wil grabbed a guitar that isn't used on any of their tracks.

"Nah, I'm sticking with you," Wil assures him.

In the lull that always balloons when the thrill of the performance has evaporated, the two men walk across the parking lot in silence. Wil studies his friend in the dull light, "You're cut above your eyebrow," he tells Kyle.

"I know, Jody got me good, and I would have done something about the swelling, but Scott didn't have any more clean socks."

Wil lets out a laugh, then a beat of silence resets the moment, and he asks, "Why do you and Jody still do that shit all the time?"

"I don't know. I think he's mad at me. Or I'm mad at him. Or maybe, at the time, it was the only way to stop the fight between us and Punchcunt before it got too big. It's obvious that they started that fight with us so we'd miss tomorrow's gig," Kyle says, then touches his eyebrow. He checks his fingers for blood, but they come back clean; there's dried blood on his fingerless gloves, but very little of it is his own.

"Do you want me to fix you up?" Wil asks after a beat of silence, then the silence continues.

Kyle looks to Wil, who nods once, hitting reset on the moment again.

Wil backs up, watching as Kyle opens the door to the apartment building.

"Tomorrow," Wil says.

Kyle looks over his shoulder, and confirms, "Tomorrow," then walks inside his building.

Exhausted, Kyle shuffles his black Converse across the tan carpet until he reaches the end of the hall. When he keys into his apartment, he's met with the familiar smell of pot and cake. Slowly closing the door behind him, making sure it doesn't slam- the light shrinking until it is only a paper thin sliver- Kyle lets the darkness wrap around him, and he takes inventory of his pain. He's thankful for the darkness; he doesn't want to get hurt again tonight.

Using his cell phone to light up his tiny apartment kitchen, Kyle drifts over to a piece of paper on the counter. "Sorry I missed it," reads the top of the note, then lower he finds, "I left the light on for you," which is crossed out and, "Light too bright. Must sleep," is written as a replacement. "Also, cake," is written at the bottom in tiny letters, then an arrow points toward the fridge.

Kyle walks down the hallway, then turns off the screen of his phone before entering the bedroom. It's warm in the bedroom; it's home in the bedroom.

Sliding into bed, sensing the steady rise and fall of a chest without bruises, Kyle realizes that this moment is the best part of his day. He makes sure to remember this feeling because it will ensure he makes the right decisions in the future.

When the most important person in your life is going to miss the most important night of your life, you hate them, but when they keep the bed warm for you and make you cake, you love them.

VII. The Ghost of Hendrix.

We're walking through a dark so complete that every step on the cold asphalt is like diving deeper into the depths of the ocean.

All of the streetlights on this stretch of road have been claimed by some surprisingly accurate beer bottle tosses during Wil's many drunk departures from Kyle's apartment. Wil is an angry drunk, but only on the walk home. Luckily, the suburban neighbors are always tightly tucked in bed by the time Wil makes his climb up the hill toward a lifeless house that receives no visitors, unless Lies As Language are practicing in the living room. Wil inherited this house in a way that makes it a burden instead of a gift. He anticipates that in the next two years he'll lose the property because he can't pay the ridiculously high taxes that he's been assessed. Sure, he'll make money off the sale, but who wants to sell their childhood home?

Tonight, the walk feels longer, darker, steeper. Then, suddenly, brighter. The darkness begins to flee faster than we can climb.

A roaring engine sends us dashing to the side of the road, as a tan van blows past us, tearing up the hill, then stopping with a screech like there was something in the road.

Wil squints up the road, and something momentarily flickers past the red eyes of the van's tail lights. Maybe it was a bat... are there still bats out in November?

With a reaction that feels almost instinctual, Wil lifts his guitar case and glass instantly shatters across the black shell in a violent spray.

In the moment, his instincts failing, Wil lets his guard down to indulge his curiosity. He bends down and carefully picks up a piece of curved glass off the ground, then studies it.

In our periphery, we notice another glimmer of glass. We take a step back, then a clear beer bottle hits Wil directly on the crown of his head. He yelps, and the still intact bottle rolls down the incline of the road until it disappears into the ditch on the shoulder.

Wil drops his guitar case to hold the warm gash that has opened on his head. Disoriented by the moment, he has a fleeting thought that the streetlights are fighting back in the truest form of street justice.

As his vision clears, Wil looks up the road to see a tattooed arm extend out of the idling van and launch yet another bottle. This time, he's prepared. This time, Wil dodges the bottle, while keeping his hand pressed against his split scalp.

The van begins to climb the hill again, the lights getting smaller, closer together, dimmer- like Punchcunt Love's fan base. It's obvious what happened, even with the disorienting strike rendering Wil's thoughts foggy and incomplete. The street lights are not possessed- tonight's assault is courtesy of a group of men searching for what Wil is about to find. This attack was about spotlights, not streetlights. The aging men of Punchcunt Love seemed to have fulfilled their need to cause yet another scar on a young rocker destined for the cover of *Kerrang!* or *Alternative Press,* and the night returns to the cold silence it had operated in after the Basement of Doom backyard brawl.

Wil studies his guitar case for any new dents or gashes. When he's sure that his case fared better than he did, he resumes his walk, his head tilted back so he doesn't get blood in his eyes. Unsure of what a concussion feels like, Wil takes out his cell phone and debates calling for help. He doesn't want an ambulance; what he really wants is to walk back down the hill so he can stitch up Kyle, then Kyle can return the favor, but he's afraid to be turned away at the door, again.

Staring at his phone, Wil begins to type out a text to Jody, informing him that his curse worked. With his left hand holding the handle on his guitar case, and his right hand texting, Wil has too much to focus on, and he doesn't notice the engine noise from the van as it bears down on him, returning back down the road.

We're unable to judge how close the van is because its headlights are off, so we immediately step down into the dipping gutter at the side of the road, then breathlessly watch as the van swerves toward Wil.

Once again, tapping into an instinctual ability, Wil spots the vehicle at the last moment and despite his quick dodge, the grill of the van hits Wil's guitar case, sending it tumbling across the hood, then spider-cracking the windshield on impact.

The abused streetlights look down at this accident, unable to illuminate the hazards that are about to beset Punchcunt Love's van.

We listen to the squeal of tires on edge- the sound of a futile attempt to correct the van's swerving path. We watch the wobbling taillights traverse from one side of the road to the other, then we hear the thud of a van lipping the low shoulder. The wheels spin hard, until the right front tire gets enough traction to pull the van back onto the road abruptly.

It's quiet for a moment, but after the quiet comes the crash, as the driver of Punchcunt's van over-corrects to such a degree that the van tips onto its side, then the momentum, combined with the gradient of the hill, continues to carry the toppled vehicle forward. Grating across the jagged asphalt, the right side of Punchcunt Love's van illuminates the dark scene with a trail of sparks.

Wil watches the van until it grinds to a stop. Witness to the quickest act of karma ever carried out in the universe, he briefly considers calling 911, but eventually settles on snapping a picture of the crash. Reviewing the picture on the screen of the phone, he shakes his head, then deletes the macabre image.

After turning on the flash, Wil takes another picture. This second picture is much better, but before he can send it to his bandmates with the message, "Next album cover?" Wil remembers that his guitar was what originally caused the van's path to career off course, and he begins a frantic search.

After panning across the surrounding area with the light of his cell, Wil spots the top of the case peeking out from the ditch to his right. Worried that he'll be cradling a broken neck, Wil ignores the disabled van and makes his way to his guitar.

Moving the glow of his phone across the ditch, Wil sees the case is badly damaged. The black cover has been gouged and the wood underneath is visible and splintering, but the guitar might be fine because the hard shell case was built for this type of abuse. Wil assumes that the same is true for the members of Punchcunt- their van is in bad shape, but the band is probably only shaken up, and that's why their cries sound so piercing- the shock of it all. Wil's wet collar dampens his sympathy toward the men who now perform a very different version of their screamed gang vocals.

After taking a deep breath, Wil pops the locks to the case, which reveals, sitting on the red velvet, an acoustic guitar in near perfect condition. He picks up the guitar, then turns it over, revealing a jagged crack in the otherwise smooth body. Wil's bloody hand runs along the splintered damage. The mouth-like crack becomes painted with a crimson lipstick.

Wil's performance will not suffer from this- it will be enhanced. As his mind focuses on revenge, Wil gently places the guitar back down, then he clicks the case shut.

Taking his time, moving slowly like the blood that drips down his neck, Wil approaches the screams that beg for his help.

Stopping 50 feet away from the van, Wil removes his pack of cigarettes from the front pocket of his white dress shirt. After lighting a Pall Mall, he continues his walk down to the front of the van. He can't talk to Punchcunt Love from the driver's side, because the driver's side is currently pressed against the asphalt of the road, while the passenger side is aimed toward the heavens. Providentially, the guitar had splintered the windshield enough that the men in the van could hear Wil ask, "Was this part of the plan?"

One of the bald babies whines, "Listen, Wil. We're sorry. What we did was fucked up. We were aiming for you, not your guit-"

"-oh, so you were just trying to run *me* over, not my guitar. I suppose that makes your actions okay?" Wil responds, his head tilted, dripping.

"We just wanted to spook you. Please don't let this happen," someone else in the van yells.

"I guess you win," Wil says through the spider web crack.

"You win! You win!" someone in the van yells back.

Wil nods, then, sniffing the air, remarks, "I love the smell of gasoline in the early morning."

"Please help us. We could burn alive," a person who might be Abaddon says from inside the van.

Wil exhales a cloud of smoke, then confirms, "Yes, you certainly could."

"Please help us. Please. You have to," a desperate sounding Bloodsnake begs.

"Do I though?" Wil asks the broken window. "Is that truly my responsibility? To help you? I'm not sure what rule book you go by, but then again, I'm not much of a reader anyway."

As though someone turned a gas burner on, a flame appears from under the hood of the toppled van.

"Help!" is screamed in a chorus that will not repeat for much longer.

"Here, look, this is me trying to put out the fire," Wil says, then spits at the broken window. "You watched those Lennard brothers beat the shit out of each other over the fact that you don't f.ck with a man's instrument. And, unfortunately for you, you didn't understand the moral of the story."

"You can't just leave us here!" Abaddon screams.

Wil thinks about it for a moment, then says, "The thing is... yeah, I can. Bye, cunts. Love, Lies As Language." Wil flicks his still lit cigarette in the air and it lands perfectly inside the open passenger side window facing toward the heavens.

After retrieving his guitar case, Wil resumes his walk home.

Once again, a flying beer bottle has plunged the street into new depths of darkness.

VIII. Tour.

We're sitting in a van that's currently upright, doing about 60 MPH, not on fire. Kyle is back in the driver's seat, while Wil, Rob and Mike have returned to their respective places in the back seat. Jody, in the front seat, decides he'll share his blessed news. "I was going to save this information until we were backstage, but this drive is boring as fuck so, gentlemen, I would like to announce that I was visited by a young Afro-American boy last night."

"Like a young black version of the ghost of Christmas past?" Rob asks.

"No, Rob. He was obviously a young Afro-American version of the ghost of tomorrow's future, which is today, but yesterday it was tomorrow..."

"Can we stop saying Afro-American?" Mike asks politely.

"Sorry, Grand Dragon. We can't," Jody dismisses the request.

"It's not that. It's that you're reducing the boy's existence to a dated term. People don't like that," Mike explains.

"Know what they don't like for sure? A van full of cracker ass honkies telling them what they do and don't like," Jody responds.

"What did the boy want?" Wil asks, hoping to move past a no-win discussion.

"He was like, 'Help me. You have to let me in your house. A man is after me,' and some other stuff that was basically a reworded version of that original premise."

"So who was chasing him?" Mike asks.

"I don't know, dude. I didn't let the little bastard in my house, what if it was all a ruse to steal my laptop?"

"I thought you were telling us this story because you interpreted his presence as a sign," Kyle sighs, hoping to find some meaning in this conversation.

"Correct, Kyle. The young Afro-American was sent as a preview of what being famous will be like. We'll have Afro-American kids, white kids, hell, maybe even a couple Mexicans trying to see how rock stars live. I felt very blessed as I turned away the little harbinger of our enviable lifestyle to come."

Everyone in the van is quiet and they try not to deconstruct Jody's story.

"Know what guys?" Jody comments brightly, "I think I just figured out who chased that boy to my home."

"Please don't ask him who it was," Kyle requests of his bandmates.

"No need to ask," Jody says, "I'll freely share. I believe our little Afro-American was delivered to my doorstep by none other than Mr. Destiny himself."

IX. The Show.

We stand in a much larger crowd, at a much larger venue than the last show we were at, and we're impressed that this is where we're witnessing Lies As Language perform. There's no exposed piping in the ceiling and there are no gaps of open space in the crowd. The fans who came to hear Sullen Wishes have arrived early and they've been slowly won over by this young, energetic band.

Lies As Language finish their set with the same flair they perfected in Scott Trunkett's basement. They finally feel themselves arriving, right before they have to leave the stage.

Kyle's fingerless gloves wrap tight around the mic, then he purrs out, "New Jersey. We love you. Do you love us back?"

The audience roars with approval.

"Do you love us enough to let us park our van in your driveway and sleep at your house tonight?" Kyle asks, exaggerating the seductive tone of his voice. The girls in the audience shriek. Kyle looks around and points to a girl in a black tank top with hummingbirds tattooed above her breasts.

"You, Hummingbird. Can we sleep in your garage?" Kyle asks.

"Yesss!" Hummingbird celebrates in excited convulsions. Kyle had been watching her. She knew all the words to every song so he's sure that Lies As Language has been invited into her home on a nightly basis.

Following a beckoning flick of Kyle's exposed fingers, security begins to help Hummingbird onto the stage. The girl stumbles over, obviously drunk, and hugs Wil, then runs over and grabs Kyle for stability.

"We need a place to stay and she clearly needs a designated driver, so we'll see you later, New Jersey," Kyle says, then drops the mic.

Despite the bruised ribs, Kyle scoops up Hummingbird in his arms, merely for practical purposes.

Each member leaves the stage exactly the way that they had pictured it in their fantasies.

Tonight, Jody kept his drumsticks instead of launching them into the crowd. His black towel is still on his shoulder. These items will be keepsakes of this amazing night, and also Jody figures that he can make a boatload of cash by autographing this shit and selling it on eBay in a couple of years.

X. Directions.

We're standing in a cold, teen-filled parking lot, as everyone waits for their parents to come pick them up.

The men of Lies As Language momentarily stop loading equipment in their van so they can take pictures with two girls wearing homemade Lies As Language tank tops, then each member autographs the official Lies As Language T-shirts the girls bought after the set. After the venue cut, Lies As Language sold $400 in merchandise tonight, despite the fact that no one was at the merch table. The shirts and CDs were left unattended, with a giant sign that said, "You stole our music behind our backs, please don't do the same with our shirts." This was Mike's idea. "You can sell almost anything with enough guilt tacked on," he explained, and it made sense, so they committed to the idea. Plus Jody didn't want to overcrowd the van with a merch guy. "We need room for babes," he proclaimed.

Jody views the girls with the homemade tank tops as children, and he lets them scurry away after they get their pictures. The girls are already on their phones, bragging to their friends who bailed on the concert.

Two other girls, slightly older than the teens in the custom shirts, wait at a distance, watching everything, but pretending as though they're busy in conversation. One of these girls is the fan that Kyle carried off stage. She's bleached blonde, shivering, drunk, and hummingbird adorned. Over her black tank top, she wears a tight black hoodie that thankfully doesn't have the name of a high school or "Punchcunt Love" screen printed on it.

The second girl is rosy-cheeked, unsure of herself, and chubby. She has very straight shoulder length black hair, complemented by black eye makeup that wings out from her eyes to make them seem longer. Her gray peacoat causes her to closely resemble some of the mothers in this parking lot who are searching for their kids. She's visibly excited and further afflicted by overt nervousness. This combination makes the girl with the hummingbird tattoos look almost sober in comparison.

"Come on, Hummingbird! Bring your drunk ass over here and take us to the promised land," Rob yells, then he slams the back doors of the van shut.

"I still have a semi-full bottle of Bacardi in the garage that we can drink when we get home!" Hummingbird shrieks gleefully, then skips toward the van.

The boys get ready for what they hope will be a short drive. Now is not the time to drive back to Connecticut. Lies As Language are "on tour" not "on a day-trip." Rock bands call their loved ones from the road and tell them they miss them. Rock bands have to search for kind strangers with available showers. Rock bands sleep with their groupies.

The drive home can be done tomorrow; tonight is about celebrating. Tonight is about leaving people wanting more. Tonight is about leaving with the hot drunk girl who probably has Doritos and other cool snacks at her house.

Before rushing to the van, Hummingbird asks, "Can we bring Morgan too?"

Jody hangs his head out of the van, looks back at the shivering Hummingbird, then asks, "Is Morgan a dude?"

"No, Morgan is a ladyyy," Hummingbird says, then curtsies for some reason.

"A lady or a girl?" Jody asks.

"A girl who is a ladyyy," Hummingbird responds, her teeth chattering from the cold.

Jody begins crunching the numbers on general automobile safety, then cross-references this with the odds that he'll get a hand job tonight. "Okay, she can come," Jody decides.

"Morgan, come ooon!" Hummingbird yells with the long "O" of a horribly unattractive South Jersey accent.

Jody, still hanging out the window, spots the chubby girl approaching the van, then quickly amends his invite, "Oops. I meant Lauren. You can bring your friend Lauren. Definitely not Morgan. We need to save room for the merch guy. Steve. Steve, the merch guy. Great on merch, bad on getting back to the van on time."

"I don't have a friend Lauren," Hummingbird says, then scrunches her nose at Jody.

"Alright, case closed, let's hit the road," Jody says, relaxing back into his seat, then rolling up his window.

A second Lennard brother has been watching this exchange and studying Morgan's confused pause.

"Come on," Kyle says, waving his gloved hand to get Morgan's attention.

Morgan bites her lip. She looks at the van rocking as the boys fight for who gets to sit next to Hummingbird. Morgan shakes her head, then says, "No. It's so cramped in there... and..."

Kyle begins to make his way across the parking lot to a girl who was hanging on his every word tonight. The way Kyle sees it, the only difference between Morgan and Hummingbird is their confidence levels.

"I'm not leaving some random girl in a parking lot in South Jersey. Karma will definitely catch up with me," Kyle tells the hesitant girl.

"You believe in karma?" Morgan asks.

"Gotta believe in something," Kyle says.

"Yeah..." Morgan responds, blushing. She seems unsure if this moment is really happening.

Kyle, in that low whisper that he uses to begin some of his songs, assures Morgan, "I want you to come with us tonight."

Morgan's entire face turns red, then she flips up the collar on her coat.

"Will you join me?" Kyle asks, searching Morgan's face from under his bangs. Kyle points to the van, then says, "Your friend is in there, and she's drunk, and she's with band guys, and she has a giant tattoo on her chest which is proof positive that she has poor judgment, so it's your responsibility to keep track of her."

Morgan giggles then puts her Mia Wallace hair behind her ear. She says, almost in a whisper, "You're right. Her parents wouldn't come looking for her if you guys stole her. And my parents don't know I'm here... they're the worst. They wouldn't let me go to this show and they wouldn't even let me get a dove tattooed on my foot." After a pause, Morgan shakes her hair out from behind her ear, like she was trying to swat her who-cares stories away.

Kyle patiently leads Morgan toward the van with short steps, and easy conversion, "When we get to Hummingbird's house, I'll make Wil show you all of his regrettable tattoos, and that way, when you get home to Mommy Morgan, you'll thank her for her wise body art restrictions."

Morgan smiles at this, then Kyle walks ahead of her and opens the sliding door on the left side of the van.

Rob leans over and whispers to Morgan, "Okay, Jody is a little crazed about vehicle safety. He's in the middle of a story, so just find a place in the back where you aren't sitting on our gear and if you're quiet until we get on the Parkway, this will all be a success."

Morgan climbs inside the van, then slides the door shut. She can hear Jody ranting in the front seat, "I looked out into the crowd and I saw every person as a young Afro-American boy. I mean, yes, they were almost exclusively white people, but they *became* Afro-American boys tonight."

Morgan doesn't question this statement; she just scrunches up her legs so she doesn't get footprints on anything.

Lies As Language, and their accommodation sponsors, take to the road, crammed into the big black van. Hummingbird lies across Mike, Wil, and Rob in the back seat, and she drunkenly mumbles, "Oh no, we forgot about Steve the merch guy."

"So... Hummingbird... where do you live?" Kyle asks, directionless on Parkway South.

Hummingbird giggles, "My names not Hum-"

"-easy on the sass, Hummingbird. We need a location," Jody says.

Time is of the essence now, and Jody is ready to celebrate his triumphant conquering of South Jersey. To make sure everyone is visually aware that it's time to party, Jody pops open the glove compartment, then takes out a special piece that will complete his wardrobe.

Hummingbird laughs, "Is that a cowboy hat?" as finger points at Jody's new black headgear.

"Of course it's a cowboy hat. If you visit the south, you wear a cowboy hat. It's like how if you go to Niagara Falls, you wear a plastic bag, or if you go to Detroit you wear a machete strapped to your chest so you can fend off the residents trying to steal your riches," Jody explains.

Hummingbird laughs, then assures Jody, "It's cute."

Kyle, almost losing his cool, demands, "Hummingbird, focus, directions."

"How are you guys brothers?" Hummingbird asks, in an extremely high register.

"You're going to want to stay on the Parkway, then it will be about an hour South until the exit," Morgan yells up toward Kyle.

Jody leans over and whispers, "How do we know she's not just leading us to a Burger King?"

"Thank you, Morgan," Kyle says, then winks at her in the rearview mirror.

"You drove an hour to see us," Mike says, to Morgan, not to Hummingbird.

"Yeah! It wasn't that bad though, I was drinking all the way on the train so the time passed quickly," Hummingbird butts into the conversation.

"You've been drinking? I never would've guessed," Wil snarks.

"I know, I'm a good drunk," Hummingbird says, then follows it up with a cooing drone, "I'm tired. I'm sooo tired."

Hummingbird's eyes flutter like the wings of a...

XI. Suspects.

We're in the middle of an argument. Everyone in the van is screaming at each other.

Hummingbird pops out of her blackout and looks around the van.

"-someone make a fucking decision, okay?" Wil growls.

"What's going on? I fell asleep, where are we?" Hummingbird asks, confused.

"Good question. Let's have Morgan answer that," Wil says, turning around, "Morgan, where are we?"

Kyle hops in, "South! I've been driving south, just like she said to."

Hummingbird looks out the window and sees a green sign reading "Atlantic City - 45 Miles" then she ekes out, "Oh no."

Mike immediately looks over to Hummingbird, and still in his meek voice, he says, "Oh no? Please tell me you are, 'Oh no-ing' because you need to puke and not because we're lost. I can deal with a smelly van that has a destination. What I can't deal with is being lost in New Jersey."

"I could puke in here if you want, but I was, 'Oh no-ing' the fact that we went way too far south."

"Fuck," Kyle whispers.

"Shit," Rob says.

"Sheittt," Jody echoes.

"Typical," Wil says.

"Turn," Hummingbird says.

Kyle leans over to turn down The Cure CD that's blasting over the speakers, as he mumbles, "This is just-"

"Turn!" Hummingbird screams.

We look to Hummingbird, who points up to the road. We follow her finger, which gestures to something... bobbing... in the air?

What the fuck is that?

We don't get a good look, but we get enough of a look before the large black and white floating object crashes onto the Parkway, then spits up red onto the windshield.

Kyle swerves to avoid the... what the fuck *was* that?

Everyone besides Kyle looks back as soon as the severe turn is sliced. We look past Morgan at... a bloody, dead cow in the road? The big black van screams as it cuts across two lanes and takes an exit pushing 80 miles an hour. The wipers streak red across the windshield, while Kyle bobs his head, using the clear patches in the carnage to find out where he's headed.

"It was floating," Mike states, casually.

"It was dropped," Morgan adds.

"Slow down, my tummy," Hummingbird warns, as the van vaults off the asphalt for a moment, then bottoms out.

Rapid crackling begins as an unpaved road replaces the smooth asphalt.

"We're going to be okay... we just need to..." Kyle says, disjointed and unconvincing, revising his plan in split-second intervals. He keeps glancing in the rearview mirror. Morgan would like to think that Kyle couldn't keep his eyes off her, but Kyle's eyes are not looking at her, but instead *past* her.

Jody laughs, "You guys are such pussies. It was a cow in the road with some fucked up optical ill-" but he's interrupted by a raking screech, as though a pair of claws are slicing across the top of the van. "What was that? What the fuck was that?" Jody shrieks.

"Drive," Wil screams at Kyle, who was already complying with this demand before it was made.

Rocks spit up as the big black van blasts deeper into the woods. Anytime Kyle's foot leaves the pedal to steady his nerves before a sharp turn or to consider which fork in the beat up road should be taken, another long screech vibrates on the roof, but never penetrates the interior of the van.

Jody yells, "Our paint job is fucked!" and his bandmates question if this is all part of an elaborate plan masterminded by Jody so he can get an A-Team paint job.

The van sails over the rough waves of dirt, while weaving around tree branches that reach into the road like arms.

"I don't think we're in New Jersey anymore," Mike says, watching the branches melt by in a dark blur.

"Where do I go? How do I get rid of it? What the fuck is it?" Kyle asks begging for assistance.

Morgan sobs in the backseat as she's struck by jostling equipment.

When the reactionary screams melt into preemptive fear, Kyle's foot lets up on the pedal.

Everyone looks up toward the ceiling of the van.

The scratches don't resume, and Kyle allows the van to coast.

Rolling to a crackling stop, everyone checks the lock on their door to make sure it's engaged.

"Alright, pussies," is how Jody addresses the terrified van full of people, "Let's get out and see how fucked our paint job is."

"I'm not getting out," Morgan says, wiping tears off her face.

"Cool," Jody responds, then pops open his door.

The band follows Jody's lead, and we get out of the van, leaving the door open for whoever wants to follow or rush back to safety. We're curious to look at the sky because, on the clearest night of Lies As Language's existence, the sky rained cattle.

We walk between the beams of the van's headlights and we watch Jody hoist himself onto the hood so he can form a ridiculous hypothesis about what might have dropped the animal, about who attacked the van, and how this is all Morgan's fault for throwing off the weight distribution that was carefully calculated prior to the trip.

Jody cautiously avoids the red splatter on the edges of the windshield as he peeks at the roof damage.

We're not completely confident that whatever caused the scraping sound has truly left.

The rest of the band is dealing with the attack in their own way. We watch Hummingbird follow the smell of Wil's cigarette, as Mike spots Jody to make sure he doesn't slip. Kyle talks to himself as he slides through various screens on his phone. Morgan has refused to leave the van. Rob has agreed to honk the horn if he sees anyone coming up in front or behind us on a road that more resembles a path.

"Son of a bitch," Jody says, stomping a dent into the hood, "What kind of careless douchebag damages a band van with reckless actions like this!?"

"You," Mike observes, too quiet for Jody to hear him.

"There are huge gashes in the top here," Jody says, slapping the roof and providing information that was common knowledge even before the van stopped.

Kyle doesn't look at Jody. He peers into the screen on his phone, but he can't focus on his GPS App. He keeps playing the moment over. The animal levitating. The animal dropping. The scraping sounds on the van. Kyle is careful to keep his cell phone in his gloved palm. He's sure to remain in the glow of the headlights.

On the back bumper of the van, between the tail lights, Wil and Hummingbird share a Pall Mall.

"If I wasn't so fucked up right now, I'd be really shaken up," Hummingbird says casually.

"Me too," Wil says, exhaling a cloud of smoke that dissipates into the red tinged night.

"You play drunk?" Hummingbird asks.

"No. I just meant generally fucked up. Tonight's little moment of madness doesn't even break the top five of what-the-fuck moments in my life."

"But what was it?" Hummingbird asks, snatching the cigarette back.

"Mike!" Wil yells to the boy who is carefully listening to Jody's verbal field study on the damage. "You've shot a lot of animals, what animal kills cows?"

Mike takes one last look at Jody to make sure that he won't fall off the hood of the van, then walks, arms pinned to his side, back to where Hummingbird and Wil are. "Coyotes," Mike announces, the taillights coloring him red.

"I love coyotes. They have a bad reputation only because of that shirt where they are howling at the moon," Hummingbird says.

"No. Those are wolves. Although, if you were saying that wolves also eat cattle, you're correct," Mike tells Hummingbird.

"So. You're saying it was super-wolves that did this?" Wil asks.

"Werewolves!" Hummingbird shrieks.

"The super-werewolves are invading? Is this correct Cliff?" Jody yells across the length of the van.

"Why did he just call you Cliff?" Hummingbird asks.

"It's Mike's real first name," Wil explains.

"Your parents named you Cliff?" Hummingbird asks, in the way you'd ask a child if they skinned their knee.

"Yes," Mike admits.

"Aw. Mike-"

"-please stop analyzing Cliff and spend a little more time analyzing the theory that aqua-peoples committed this act," Jody demands, yelling across the van.

"No one was discussing aqua-peoples," Wil yells back.

"They don't exist," Mike says definitively.

Almost instantly, Jody appears next to Mike, ranting, "The greatest trick the aqua-peoples ever pulled was making you believe they don't exist."

Hummingbird giggles, then gleefully repeats, "The aqua-peoples."

"Wouldn't the aqua-peoples, oh, I don't know... live in water?" Wil asks.

"That's why it's a perfect plan, bigots like you have these stereotypes about aqua-peoples so when they destroy my property and throw livestock in the air like fuckin' confetti, they always get away with it."

"You don't own livestock," Mike points out.

"I wonder why," Jody says, then points out into the woods.

"And how did we come to this conclusion that it's the aqua-peoples' fault?" Kyle asks, joining everyone at the back of the van. The only reason he's seeking the comfort of Jody's totally incorrect theory is because it will distance him from the confusing reality he's been wrestling with.

Hummingbird, already bored by the once-enchanting idea of the aqua-peoples, starts drunk texting people things like:

"u awake?"

"hey. U dwn 2smoke l8r?"

"u awake?"

And, "i got kidnapd in a vvan. kyle lennard did itfuk hes hot."

Jody looks at the glowing phone, then says, "Hummingbird, I hope you're texting people to let them know how Lies As Language puts on such an incredible live show that the aqua-people rose from the seas to force us back to the venue for an encore."

"Jody, where is this aqua-peoples thing coming from? It makes less sense than your story about the Afro-American boy who visited you," Wil says.

"Didn't you see the signs?" Jody asks.

Everyone is silent, even the surrounding woods.

"What signs?" Hummingbird responds, looking up from her phone, feeling the atmospheric turn the night has just taken.

"The signs for Atlantis City. We drove by a bunch of them," Jody says, pointing back in the direction we came.

Everyone exhales a depressed sigh.

"The aqua-peoples live right by here. If they're gonna start fuckin' with humans, it would definitely be in... Hummingbird, where are we?"

"I'll check on my phone," she says, then goes back to texting her friend, providing a running commentary, "Mermaids destroyed ourvan. How fckd."

"Jody, Atlantic City and Atlantis are two totally different places," Mike advises carefully.

"Dude, I know that," Jody scoffs, "Atlantic City was built to get us accustomed to the aqua-peoples so they could infiltrate our society."

"Virtually all the information you've provided just now is unquestionably incorrect," Mike notes, without judgment.

"Well, yeah, it's incorrect now that the aqua-peoples have gained the ability to take to the air," Jody says, placing his index finger to the sky. "Frankly, I knew there would be doubters questioning my accident reconstruction, but I never fathomed you would be one of them, Cliff."

"The only thing that makes less sense than the sky raining cows is mermen making the sky rain cows," Wil says.

"Don't be sexist. We didn't see any merdicks floppin' around on our windshield, this could be the work of a merwoman," Jody says.

"Mermaidsss," Hummingbird coos, then puffs the last of the cigarette and flicks it away. She curls her hands up inside her sleeves, covering her scars, shivering in the November cold.

"Be realistic. Maids aren't smart enough to plan a raid like this," Jody tells Hummingbird, "This was like Mer-Seal Team 6 type shit."

Mike shakes his head, then says, "If we're discussing theories, I'd like to throw one out there."

Wil and Hummingbird direct their full attention to Mike now that their coping mechanism- that calming cigarette- has been extinguished in the sandy soil.

Mike, in his quiet voice, says, "Before my dad left me, he took me on this hunting trip to Texas. He was really interested in hunting javelina."

"Your father shot Mexican border jumpers?" Jody asks. "Not very PC, dude. I told you you're better off without him."

"I'm not going to even pursue your thought pattern on that one," Mike says.

"Because they throw the Mexicans over the fuckin' fence like a Spanish javelina," Jody says, and more than one person audibly asks, "What?"

"A javelina is a new world pig," Mike says.

"Whoa there. Relax your bigotries, Cliff," Jody says, holding up a hand, "This type of racism is learned so I still blame your father."

"Javelinas are warthogs, Jody," Kyle says.

"Right," Jody says, then turns to the woods and cups his hands around his mouth to announce, "Hear that, aqua-peoples! Don't try to drop warthogs on us or Cliff will shoot them out of the fuckin' sky!"

Ignoring the disturbing fact that flying pigs are now a generally accepted possibility in Jody's reality, Mike continues his story, "We were hunting the javelinas with a Mexican guide, and he started telling us about the legend of the chupacabra. Now, before Jody can say something racist, I'll tell you why I think we're dealing with one here- cattle mutilation is the chupacabra's calling card. The way the beast was described to me, the chupacabra feeds on the Mexican cattle, literally sucking them dry of their blood."

"El chupacabra must have seen Morgan in the back window," Jody says, then he smiles at everyone, his eyes glimmering as he waits for the uproarious laughter.

Unanimously, everyone decides to go back inside the van to warm up with Morgan and Rob.

XII. Good Thing We Have Cell Phones.

We're back in the van, but we felt safer outside.

Outside, things were silent and we could talk to each other without yelling; the last time we were in the van, we were attacked.

Kyle turns the key and we close our eyes, expecting the van not to start.

When the engine immediately roars to life, everyone releases the breath they weren't aware they were holding.

Morgan looks at the map on her phone and she tries to figure out how she could have messed up the directions to her own town. She briefly considers calling her dad to come pick her up, but she's supposed to be at Hummingbird's house, doing sleepover things like looking up boys' Facebook profiles, or dusting off a Ouija board that's gone untouched since middle school.

Listening to three different electronic GPS voices, all giving conflicting information, Kyle drives deeper into the woods, searching for a way out, hoping he doesn't receive any answers as to what chased us into these woods in the first place. The road is too narrow for us to turn around, and the pines are too close to the van for maneuvering, so forward is the only option, despite what the GPS voices suggest.

After five minutes of driving, Kyle reaches another fork in the road. He rolls down his window and listens for the sounds of passing cars, while Jody quietly searches for a sign.

We hear nothing and the glow from the phones gives a blue tint to everything in the van.

"Go left," Jody says, at the same time Morgan says, "Go right."

"Uh oh," Mike says, quietly.

"What provider do you have?" Jody asks Morgan.

"Verizon."

"I have AT&T."

"Both of those companies are equally untrustworthy," Mike comments, keeping the stalemate alive.

"Just bear left. Anytime you have the option, choose left. It's New Jersey, we'll come upon a house on this road soon," Hummingbird says, soberer now.

"I don't mean to be rude," Wil begins, and everyone knows something rude is about to follow, "But can I suggest that Mike checks where we are? I'm sorry, but the last time Hummingbird gave us directions, she passed out, then mythical creatures from Jody's subconscious spawned into reality."

"Hummingbird is from South Jersey so I'm going to listen to her," Kyle decides.

"That seems like precisely not the reason to listen to her," Wil argues.

"Hummingbird is drunk and only has one shoelace on," Mike points out.

We all look at Hummingbird's feet, and it's true, she's missing a shoelace in her Chucks. She's wearing colorful blue socks depicting a moon whose face is creased with a creepy smile.

"Can anyone give me some insight as to where the fuck we are?" Kyle yells, and it earns him our attention. "There are like ten people in this van, everyone get on your phones and form a plan."

"We must be in Pennsylvania. New Jersey is way more polluted than this," Wil says, looking away from his cell phone, out the window, to the trail of trees repeating with no variation.

"We're in the Pine Barrens," Morgan announces, and everyone is quiet. The way Morgan said, "We're in the Pine Barrens," didn't indicate that it was a place with good strip clubs that are perfect for celebrating a career-making main stage performance.

Wil looks back at Morgan, then responds, "Okay, that's awesome, now how the fuck do we get out of the Pine Barrens?"

"I don't know! Just because I live in Jersey doesn't mean I have some divine knowledge of where we need to go," Morgan says, turning off her phone, which happens to be filled with div:ne knowledge of where we need to go.

Everyone is silent again.

"We need to call someone," Hummingbird suggests.

"Who?" Mike asks.

"I don't know... AAA. They can come out and tell us where to go."

"Do you have the money for that, Hummingbird?" Kyle asks.

"No. I spent all my money on the ticket for your concert. Don't you guys have money for towing and stuff? I mean, you're rock stars."

"No. We're not rock stars. Rock stars don't rely on drunk fans for lodging," Wil says. "Rob's phone only works on WiFi. That's not very rock star."

"What's the WiFi password for the woods?" Rob mumbles, struggling to take his phone out of the pocket of his tigh: pants.

"Hey!" Jody barks, "We *are* rock stars, and I don't have a robust data package on my phone, but I've gone ahead and used the internet excessively even though the data surcharge will buttfuck me hard."

"Wait," Rob calls out, finally freeing his service-less phone from his pocket.

"You know how to get us out of here?" Mike asks.

Rob's fingers move slowly across the screen of his phone, then he grunts, "...listen."

The cell phone plays a clip of an electronic pop song.

Everyone stares at Rob with silent disdain.

The song clip ends.

Kyle shakes his head, then begs, "Let's just-"

The song interrupts Kyle as it starts on a loop.

Rob fiddles with the phone. "It sounds... so good," he says, half asleep. Everyone in the van listens to the song for one and a half more loops before Rob finally finds the button to turn it off.

"Rob is high," Mike says atonally, then looks down at the cell phone in his lap, and declares, "We're going in the wrong direction."

"Finally," Kyle responds, slamming on the breaks. Quickly throwing the van in reverse, Kyle guns it, knowing that we're the only people on the road at 2 AM in the middle of the Pine Barrens.

"You can't just reverse for 20 minutes," Morgan says.

"Watch me," Kyle says, but a split secord later the van bounces with a crunch-thump, jostling the band, the instruments, and the girls.

We might be the only vehicle on the road, but now the question becomes, are we the only *people* on the road?

"What the fuck was that?" Kyle whispers.

Everyone in the van pauses, waiting for an animal yelp or a human moan; neither arrive.

"We have to get out and look," Mike says, with curiosity, not concern, and this causes Kyle to ask, "What?"

"We're not getting out, let's just go home," Wil says, "We're on a road that's barely a road, are you surprised it's bumpy?"

"We drove over something, and it crunched," Kyle processes the moment, replaying it in his head.

"*You* drove over it, because *someone* insisted on reversing," Hummingbird slurs, her intoxication seemingly waxing and waning as the night progresses.

Jody is silent. He doesn't want to enter this conversation. This was supposed to be the night Lies As Language became rock stars. Everyone else who's Jody's age is filling their lives with fender benders and tense conversations in overcrowded vans, and Jody is unwilling to become one of them. He was exactly like them for an entire decade at that stupid job.

"Fuck this," Jody says, popping open his door, determined to bring things back to an adrenaline hyped mania.

"Jody!" everyone in the van yelps.

"Yell, 'Drive' if you see any scary shit out there," Hummingbird requests.

Kyle doesn't follow his brother, he merely looks across the passenger seat, then waits for Jody's reaction. Wil has his hand on the door handle and he begins weighing his options, searching for courage. Rob is asleep. Morgan is in the fetal position, next to the drum, her heart mimicking the percussive noise from earlier tonight.

Accessing the necessary mix of confidence and annoyance required for action, Wil yanks the van door open, then slides out from under Hummingbird.

Joining Jody at the side of the road, Wil fixes the collar on his white dress shirt, then yells, "Everyone up and out."

No one moves.

"Get out of the van," Wil barks, and for some reason, this time, we listen. Maybe it's that realization that if something is under the van, we don't want to be trapped inside. We want a running start.

Everyone besides Rob assembles just outside the van, but no one lowers themselves to check and see what we hit.

"We're all going to look under this van," Wil informs us, "If we don't find anything, we'll continue reversing down this road and you'll be given the following jobs- Mike, you'll have the directions on your phone the entire time. Do I make myself clear?"

Mike's eyes dart around the woods, then he says, "Yes. Understood."

"Rob-" Wil continues.

"-Rob is high on drugs in the van," Mike interrupts.

Wil shakes his head, then says, "Hummingbird. Okay, Hummingbird. You have to slap anyone who suggests we stop the van again. Does everyone agree that Hummingbird can-"

Jody drops to his knees and shines the light from his phone under the van, unable to accept anyone's plan but his own. Tilting the light carefully to review the sandy road under the van, Jody feels confident that it was just a turtle or a mound of dirt that we struck. As the cell-light stretches to the far front tire, a shadow breaks the beam, and Jody pops backward. Everyone points their phones toward the front of the van and, in the combined light of numerous flashlight Apps, a tall shadowy figure hobbles away, its long limbs appearing to grow, as though it was pulling itself into the darkness, becoming the darkness. The image of this figure burns into our being- it was the shape of a person, but wasn't a person per SE- it was an exaggerated outline moving on an injured, but incredibly fast tilt. Its feet made no noise on the sandy road as it fled... or maybe it was just repositioning itself...

"What the fuck was that? What the f-" Morgan screams, but Hummingbird drops her phone to the ground, then covers Morgan's mouth to silence her.

"Shut up. Shut the fuck up or it will come back for us," Hummingbird whispers loudly.

Mike, still holding up his phone, turns it to illuminate the two girls, and we see the reflection of a tear as it blinks out of Hummingbird's left eye.

Jody is slumped on the ground, silent. His black cowboy hat sits next to him. Even the one member of Lies As Language who's equipped with an incredible imagination cannot resolve what we just witnessed. It was a shadow, but when the shadow caught the light, it was illuminated. It was an absence of light- a void- yet this particular shadow also reflected light. Jody sits perfectly still, trying to divide by zero, trying to imagine nothing, trying to hold onto hope. What we witnessed should not have happened, yet it did.

Morgan is the only one not frozen. When Hummingbird releases her, she runs to the van and dives inside. A smaller girl would look like an action hero; a bigger girl resembles a charging rhinoceros. The van door slides shut, sealing Morgan inside with a version of Rob that's distinctly elsewhere for the time being.

We stay outside of the van, with a group that has excited themselves to the point that sweat glistens on their foreheads and perfumes the cold air.

"I filmed it," Mike says in his little voice.

"What?" Kyle whips around, looking into the camera on Mike's raised phone.

"I have video of the shadow hobbling away," Mike says calmly, still filming.

"Replay it," Kyle demands.

Mike taps his glowing screen, then lowers the phone and begins the playback. We watch the perfectly steady footage that begins with Jody jerking away from the van, then the camera pans up to where the shadow, flanked on either side by headlights, hobbles away. We watch this being melt into the darkness. The phone redirects and, "What the fuck was that? What the f-" can he heard, an echo of Morgan's fear forever captured by the mic on Mike's phone. What appears next on the video sends a chill rocketing down our spine. In the final four seconds of Mike's video, he turns the phone back to the path and the headlight beams are breached again, as the shadow begins to limp back toward the van.

Mike drops the phone, aware that the shadow is looming.

When the phone hits the ground, the light moves across the darkness and we choose to run because we don't want to see what may be revealed.

Fleeing with severity, boy and girl alike abandon the van in an all-out sprint.

We run in the dark, from the dark.

XIII. The Disconcerting Fact We Saw Nothing.

We're doubled over, pulling in desperate breaths, searching our surroundings to make sure that everyone has escaped safely. There's Jody- his cowboy hat once again on the ground. It must have been knocked off by his hands, which are interlocked on atop of his head, his stretched lungs gulping air. There's Mike- squinting into the darkness, searching the path for any ripple, any unnatural movement. There's Hummingbird- sitting on the sandy ground, fixing the tongue on her laceless shoe. There's Kyle- eye makeup smeared, possibly from sweating, possibly from crying. There's

Wil- making noises like the dark is strangling him, but it's clear that Wil's tar caked lungs are responsible for the duress he's under.

"Morgan is missing," Hummingbird says, standing up, then looking back down the road.

"Of course she is," Jody responds. "We ran here."

"I heard the van door open," Hummingbird tells us, but we don't remember hearing this noise.

"How do you know it was Morgan who opened the door?" Kyle asks, then his posture straightens as Morgan's absence becomes more threatening.

We study the darkness, to see if the darkness followed us.

Distinct movement and the *pat-pat* sound of shoes slapping down on the sandy road causes a spike of adrenaline to shoot through us again.

Relief washes the adrenaline away when the approaching figure ends up being Morgan running toward us at full speed- which, honestly, isn't really all that fast.

"Oh no. Oh shit. I think something's chasing her!" Hummingbird says, grasping onto Jody's arm.

Morgan doesn't ever look over her shoulder as she approaches us in a rumbling sprint. When she reaches Mike, she grabs onto his arms. Mike searches Morgan's face. He sees that she's smiling, which makes Mike smile.

"I saw a house," Morgan gasps out, and the group gravitates to this information, "A house with its lights on. It's just off the road a bit," Morgan says, between heavy heaves that make us worried we're misunderstanding her.

"I don't want to walk into the darkness," Hummingbird says. "Let's just go back to the van. We'll all do the jobs that Wil gave us, and it'll be morning in no time."

"Let's walk to the house and see if they have candy, Hansel and Gretel style. There are probably houses built from chocolate chip brownies all over this motherfucker," Jody says, then picks up his cowboy hat.

This was an odd little detour back to childhood.

As a kid, fairy tales taught us lessons.

As a kid, we felt invincible.

As a kid, we were warned against getting inside a suspicious looking van.

As a kid, we weren't supposed to accept candy from strangers, but there was one night when that rule was void.

Tonight, fearlessly, Lies As Language arrived in front of a group of strangers, then won them over. Why would that confidence dissipate just because their stage was removed? Convincing strangers to help a group of boys searching for their place in the world was a success at the merch table, so why can't it be recreated here?

We walk along a cold trail, and Morgan's hopeful smile seems to be reason enough to have confidence in the trek.

Quickly, desperate bonds begin to form. Mike's cell phone was dropped and abandoned; Hummingbird's cell phone was dropped and abandoned. To cope, Hummingbird uses Kyle for his cell-light, and Mike uses Morgan for her cell-light. Morgan's free hand reaches for Mike and he locks fingers with her. She accepts the odd pace of Mike's walk in exchange for the comfort of his curiosity. Jody and Wil bring up the rear of the group, their phones out, as they make sure that no one, or nothing else, sneaks up on us.

Morgan's confidence in the existence of this house never waivers, even as we walk for a longer distance than Morgan remembers running. When Morgan saw us abandon the van, she swung the door open and asked Rob if he wanted to join her. Rob begged her to stay, which she did, for a couple of minutes, but when her desperate attempt at feeling safe just made her feel ashamed, she ran from Rob as well. Morgan was able to run so far, so fast, because she didn't want to be alone.

"There it is," Mike says, pointing with his free hand.

Finally, the pines relent and show us a small dark structure with light pouring from two windows.

Mike, without a cell phone, says, "It's like three in the morning. I'm not sure it's the best idea to start knocking on random people's doors right now."

Everyone looks at Jody for some reason.

"Yeah, what if some crazy homicidal backwoods piney lives there?" Hummingbird asks.

"What's a piney?" Wil asks, then throws up a hand and mumbles, "Great, now we have to worry about something called a piney..."

"If we go through with this, it's going to bring us more trouble," Hummingbird predicts, and this causes Kyle to finally snap, "What do you want to do instead?" When no one responds, Kyle provides the only other option, "Do you want to sleep in the van until the morning and *then* knock on this door to ask for help? We can barely all fit in the van, much less sleep in there."

"Well, Kyle, in that case, you can be the one who knocks on the door and does all the talking," Hummingbird says.

Kyle nods at this, then responds delicately, "Hummingbird, before I do that, can you come here for a moment?"

Hesitantly breaking her bond with the group, Hummingbird walks over to Kyle, because, after all, the lead singer of Lies As Language is practically begging for her intimate attendance. Kyle pulls Hummingbird close, and his lips whisper a warm sentence across her ear, "If you want Jody to do something, just say that the act requires the most qualified member of the group to take the lead."

Kyle announces in a serious tone, "Hummingbird and I just had a quick discussion, and there are now questions regarding if I'm the right man for the job. I think... we need someone truly brave to lead us to safety. This could end up dangerous so we'll want to send the most prepared person, male or female, to knock on that stranger's door. So I guess the question is, who's going to go?"

"Who is me," Jody says, fixing the rim on his dusty black cowboy hat, "I'll go. And you, who are all little bitches, will stay over yonder." Jody points to a spot about ten feet away from the house.

Kyle lifts his eyebrows at Hummingbird, and she stifles a smile.

"Cliff, I'm summoning you," Jody declares.

"I'm not a dragon," Mike says, then flattens his eyebrows with his fingers.

"You're right. Tonight, we will enter like a lamb," Jody says.

Hummingbird shakes her head at this plan, then begins to suggest, "Maybe we should just go back to the van and-"

"-and get butt-fucked by a shadow? No thank you," Jody responds, "Most of the men among us are recovering for 9 straight hours of butt herpes. Don't put their asses on the line again."

Mike's eyes turn to slits, then he starts to question, "How would a shad-

"-come on Cliff, let's let these pussies be pussies," Jody interrupts.

"Psh," Wil spits, "Ever since he joined the band Mike has become the biggest pussy out of all of us."

Jody turns around and points aggressively at Wil, "No he's not. The fact he's coming with me is pretty fucking brave if you look at my track record."

"Thanks, Jody," Mike says.

"Don't thank me... it makes you sound like a pussy," Jody scolds, then he holds out his cell phone for light and walks up to the shack.

After fixing his cowboy hat, then raising his cell phone to the crack of the door like it's a police Maglite at a traffic stop, Jody knocks on the door forcefully.

No answer.

"Woods police," Jody says in a deep voice.

He knocks again.

No answer.

Jody pauses for a moment, then he forcibly turns the doorknob, and lowers his shoulder into the door- which opens easily- and his ramming force is met with no resistance, so he stumbles forward into the darkness. There's no delineation between the inside and the outside beyond the door frame, so Jody needs to keep his cell phone out as he begins his search.

We listen for a scream or a hurried explanation regarding the troubling situation we've found ourselves in. We wait. We wait longer than any of us want to. When the silence begins to buzz, Kyle lights up the path with his cell, and we all walk toward the house.

As we approach the open door, footsteps can be heard inside. They're not casual, they're careful, like an object is being avoided, or someone is trying to move about undetected.

"Check it out," Jody's voice booms, and it causes all of us to flinch.

We hold onto each other, and watch as Jody takes a step back so he's framed in the doorway, then he lifts his cell phone to illuminate the room, and welcomes us with a self-satisfied, "Enter."

Kyle is first to step inside, and we follow behind in a single file line like we're on a field trip. The line moves slowly and we're at the end of it- looking behind us as much as we're looking forward. When we get inside, our complete attention is focused on the floor. Despite being built on a flat stretch of the Barrens, the room slants on an obvious gradient that's highest at the door frame and lowest at the outer wall. It appears the house has no foundation and the sandy soil is slowly swallowing the structure. There are very few items near the front door, because, thanks to the incline, they've all slid down to the far edge of the room. In the electronic glow, we notice that everything at the lowest point of the slant appears to be equipment that people have left at campsites. Mice crawl in and out of the haphazard pile of coolers, lanterns, sleeping bags, backpacks, and clothes.

Hummingbird, possibly forgetting all the other troubling shit that has happened, or maybe she's just been desensitized, merely lets out an airy, "Creeepy," then immediately looks bored and lost because she can't send a picture of this weirdness to anyone, so it has no worth.

Jody walks up the slant to a door that's surrounded by a thin golden frame, then looks to us for permission. No one says, "Jody, no!" so he interprets this as, "Jody, yes!"

Without a knock, Jody swings the door open.

We peer over his shoulder to see what the bright room looks like.

What we find is a warm living room, and at the far edge of the room, an old frail woman sits with her back to the door. We're assuming this is a woman because we can only see her crooked shoulders and long white hair, as she remains seated, leaning over, carefully working on a project. Her right arm makes a repetitive movement that creates an unnerving scratching noise. We all wait to be noticed, but the woman doesn't acknowledge our presence.

Moving into the room, we're able to fully review this pared down home. Stripped sticks lie in piles everywhere, like the frail woman was stocking up on extra clean firewood for the impending winter. It's warm inside this room, but there's no fireplace visible.

Since Kyle has the softest, most empathetic voice out of all of us, he's wordlessly chosen as the speaker. He's only able to get to the "Ex," in "Excuse me," before the old woman lets out a piercing scream. The terrible shriek fills the room like a human alarm.

"I'm sorry!" Kyle says loudly, as he pushes through the screams and approaches the woman. The worst part about this shrieking reaction is that the woman doesn't look back at us, she continues to face the wall.

"We're not robbing you. We're just lost! We need directions! We're lost!" Kyle yells.

The scream of the frail woman continues, slashing through the otherwise tranquil house.

"We're not going to hurt you, we just need your help," Mike says quietly.

Kyle continues moving toward the chair, requesting, "Please. Help us."

The frail woman's scream finally stops and she begins coughing. After she composes herself, she finally turns around.

We take a step back when the woman looks at us, and we don't feel guilty about this because she can't see us. Her milky eyes stare at nothing at all. She nods once, acknowledging the girls' fear, smelling their sweat from a labored night of escaping. The old woman clears her throat and in her weak, grainy voice, she finally speaks, "If you are looking for R.F. Behringer's house, don't waste your time, he's dead."

"Two questions. Who the fuck is that? And where the fuck is his house?" Jody asks.

"He's an author," Morgan says.

Jody rolls his eyes at the idea that being an author is still a profession.

Kyle, in the soothing voice that he used when recording the spoken word intro on "Regretful Me," says, "We're lost, we need to find out how to get back to the-"

"-wait," Jody interrupts, "You're right, we're huge Behringer fans and we're looking for his house so we can put up various signs that inform passers-by that we miss him and he will not be forgotten."

"He's dead, I said," the woman repeats.

"I know," Jody responds, shrugging- a wasted gesture, "That's why the signs are in past tense. We're all holding signs right now," Jody realizes that he can exploit the fact the old woman can't see, and he adds, "My rippling biceps are flexed as I hold up my expertly crafted sign, which is pretty high up because I'm 6'1" with perfect posture... anyway, I just want to see the house. I want to see... where the writer... of famous... fictions... created his... masterful sentences of words."

"No... you don't," the woman informs us.

"Please, I'm a big fan of sentences," Jody says.

The frail woman issues a warning that clearly excites Jody, "You don't want to end up at that house."

Wil steps forward, tired, impassioned, and says, "Yes, we do! Listen, lady. Where's the house?"

Kyle shoots Wil a look, and the frail woman says nothing.

"Where the fuck is Behringer's house?" Wil yells.

Everyone is confused. How did we arrive at this point? This isn't fun. We want to leave.

The frail woman says nothing.

Wil walks over to a short table covered in foot-long whittled sticks. He throws the table over, and the sticks cascade to the floor, then continue rolling, revealing that this room is uneven as well.

"Point me in the direction of Behringer's house," Wil demands.

The frail woman points toward the slanted room.

"How far? How far? How far down the road lady?!" Wil yells, his voice building with angered impatience.

In a whisper, the old woman responds, "A few miles."

"Let's get out of here," Kyle says, then walks over and rights the table that Wil knocked over. We put a couple sticks back on the table, before we head back toward the dark slanted room.

"Wait. One last thing, mam," Jody says, "As an official sheriff of the woods police department, I'd be remiss if I failed to inform you that we have been getting reports of people being attacked by a shadow in these very woods."

"That shadow wasn't attacking you... it was fleeing who it was attached to," the old woman explains.

This confirms that we need to exit this home immediately, and Kyle, the last one out of the bright room, asks, "Do you want this door shut?"

"Please," the woman responds.

As Kyle completes this request, he hears what sounds like dozens of wooden crucifixes tapping against the back of the door, their protective aura creating a barrier between the old woman in the light and the young kids in the darkness.

In the uneven room, Wil shines his cell light on the pile of camping supplies one last time.

It's perfectly quiet for a moment, then a light flashes in the pile and a sound rings out.

This noise sends our hearts into our throat and our bodies collide as we rush outside.

Jody slams the door to the old woman's house.

Back out in the cold, we listen as, inside the slanted room, the song Rob played earlier in the night repeats once again.

XIV. At Least We Still Have Our Cell Phones.

We catch up to Wil and Kyle as they dust up the sandy trail, their steps creating little puffs, their breath creating little puffs. Wil's pompadour is being pressed down from his interlocking fingers resting on the scab that runs across the crown of his skull. Kyle holds out his phone for a light, as he rants, "That's going to be good karma. Ransack an old blind lady's house? Awesome. Great. Your guitar is going to end up at the bottom of the slant in that room. And remind me again why instead of getting directions to the Parkway, we got directions to R.F. Behringer's house? Not exactly the time for site seeing right now, Wil. I'm not all that interested in checking out some reclusive, old, dead author's house."

Wil, viewing himself as the hero, asks, "Kyle, don't you get it? If this rich author guy was living in the middle of nowhere, his house is probably filled with a bunch of shit that will keep us comfortable until the morning, at which point we can drive his car back to the van. The whole reason we want to get back onto the Parkway is so we can find a place to stay the night. Why not just go to Behringer's house for a couple hours, grab something to eat, get some sleep, then head home in the morning?"

A screech comes from the woods and everyone freezes.

"What the fuck was that?" Wil asks under his breath.

The sound of sticks breaking gets faster, indicating that not only is someone approaching, but they're also gaining speed.

Both Lennard boys assume trained fight poses, while Hummingbird stands behind them. Wil and Mike look for Morgan, but can't find her.

"Someone took Morgan," Mike says.

"How long ago?" Kyle asks, the sound of cracking sticks getting louder.

"About five minutes ago, maybe a little longer?" Mike estimates.

"Why didn't you say anything?"

"She's back," Mike states casually, as Morgan steps out from the darkness.

"Morgan, what the fuck were you doing?" Wil growls.

Hummingbird scuttles over and hugs her best friend.

"I stopped to pee," Morgan admits, then Hummingbird immediately ends the hug and takes a step back.

"Guys. Wait," Morgan says.

"What now?" Wil asks.

"This is where we parked the van," she says.

"That's impossible," Kyle says, shaking his head.

Morgan grabs Kyle's phone, then shines it at the ground. We see a collection of footprints in the sandy soil.

Mike bends down and picks up his phone. He had dropped it when the video revealed to him that the shadow had returned.

"Morgan. When you left the van, did you wake Rob up?" Kyle asks carefully.

"Yeah, of course," Morgan responds, "I didn't want to go into the dark alone, so I asked Rob to go with me. When he said he was going to stay in the van, I split because I didn't want to get butt-fucked by a shadow-man."

For a split second, Jody smiles at this, realizing that Morgan is listening to his every word, then he declares her considerations, "Prudent."

Morgan shakes her head no.

Wil shakes his head no as well, but not in mimicry. He chastises Morgan, "You left Rob with the van? On what planet does that seem like the safe idea?"

"I don't know. Maybe he went to get help. If that's the case, it's an awesome idea," Morgan defends herself.

"You left Rob in the van with the keys?" Kyle asks.

"You just placed Rob behind the wheel to... be Rob?" Wil piles on.

"Maybe if you didn't store me in the back of the van like band equipment, I would have been able to figure out that Rob is persona-non-drive-a," Morgan says, finally comfortable enough to speak to the band like she'd speak to Hummingbird.

Bending down, Morgan picks her phone up off the ground. She enters her lock code, closes her camera roll, then says, "I'm using my phone to find out where we are."

We wait for the GPS information to pop up on Morgan's phone. Finally, the screen changes and the location establishes. "We're in the middle of the Pine Barrens," Morgan announces, once again. This time the information is accompanied by escape routes.

"I'm now Officer Captain Sheriff of the Pine Barrens woods police," Jody says, smiling at this self-appointed position. "The Pine Barrens is where dreams come true. How cool."

"This isn't a dream, Jody. Does this look cool to you?" Hummingbird asks hatefully, gesturing to the black woods.

Mike's eyes turn to slits, then he decides, "It's too dark to judge the coolness of this place right now."

Jody puts his hand on Mike's shoulder, "We're not just gonna stand here and discuss the coolness potential of this place. We all know that Pine Barrens is a super cool name, and this place has provided rich opportunities to us, but I think we need to focus on me, and I want to get my drink on."

"Great," Hummingbird says sarcastically. "That's how people survive in the forest, with the 'I want to get my drink on' mentality."

"You have a point," Jody admits, then adds, "Sounds like a desert mentality now that I review it."

"Everything is under control," Kyle says, maybe only to himself, "I'll call Rob, then I'll give him our exact location based on Morgan's GPS."

As long as Rob hasn't overdosed or crashed the van, this plan will work.

Kyle puts his phone on speaker, then selects Rob from his contacts.

The phone instantly goes to voicemail.

"He didn't pick up," Kyle says to the glowing screen of his phone.

"Because his phone is in the slanted room," Wil says quietly.

Kyle in an attempt to make this unlikely reality the paranoid fantasy he needs it to be, says, "So you're telling me a blind old lady went out, stole our van, with Rob inside, killed Rob, then left Rob's cell in her hoarder pile?"

"She also could have been whittling his bones at that desk," Mike says meekly.

"I don't think the blind lady stole the van, but when we were in that house..." Hummingbird starts to say, then pauses to recall the moment. When she mentally confirms its validity, she finishes her statement, "...I heard someone upstairs."

"Gee, it couldn't be the 47 cats that she was probably hoarding," Wil says.

"I'm just telling you what I heard," Hummingbird growls.

"Rob's phone only works on WiFi," Mike's little voice reminds us, and reality reenters the situation.

"I'll call someone else," Kyle says instantly.

"Who?"

"A tow truck," Kyle decides.

"To tow our missing van?" Jody asks.

"Call the park authority," Morgan suggests, "I'll bring up their website."

"No. Dude. No," Jody cuts in emphatically. We begin to suspect that the Officer Captain Sheriff of the Pine Barrens wood police doesn't want his authority questioned.

"Could you not call me 'dude?'" Morgan requests.

"Fair enough, dudette," Jody concedes, "My point is that one time, my friend, Steve, got this kayak and he kayaked down some river and eventually he realized you can't reverse kayak because this river wasn't like the lazy river at the waterpark he got kicked out of for kayaking at- this was a real river, and he was passing down it fast because he was a kick fucking ass kayaksman. Being so experienced and also having played a buttload of that game Oregon Trail, he knew that you could die or lose pelts in a river easily, and you should ford with caution so he kept his cell phone in a ziploc bag for emergencies. He ended up super far downstream and was lost as fuck, so he took his cellphone out of his baggy and made a call to the park ranger. The woods police came in a chopper and rescued him, and he was like, 'Thank you,' and they were like, 'Three grand or we push you out of this helicopter, *Scarface* style.' So... by a raise of hands, who wants to get murdered out of a helicopter or has three grand?"

Jody surveys a group of people with their hands pinned at their sides like they were Mike walking.

"Oh, zero hands raised, besides mine, my hand is raised, because I do have three grand, and that's pretty awesome of me, but I won't be using it for our rescue."

Kyle walks away from the group, then asks the sky, "Is everyone here incapable of taking a deep breath, looking around and-"

A loud *Pop-Pop-Pop*, like a series of gunshots, interrupts Kyle and sends us all to the ground.

The girls are screaming, and the air fills with the smell of electronic singe.

Jody barks out, "A sniper just shot me. Us. All of us. A sniper just shot all of us in the dicks. We're going to be the band of guys without dicks because snipers shot our dicks off."

After enduring the initial shock of the flash-bang, one by one, everyone reaches down to make sure their parts are still intact. They are.

"Check your phone. I think we just entered some magnetic interference field. My phone, like... exploded?" Morgan says, confused.

Warmed, steaming, ash-blasted front pockets and gloved palms confirm Morgan's theory. Upon review, the phones- all different models and ages-universally have their display screens shattered to pieces, their backs blown off, and their interior melted into one large black piece of coal.

"Kick fucking ass," Jody exclaims as he cups himself. "You'll have to do better than that dick sniper!" he yells, then thinks better of it, and adds, "On other people! Practice on other peoples' dicks, please!"

"Your phone is ruined," Mike says to Morgan, feeling less bad about dropping his phone and scuffing it up earlier.

"Good," Morgan nervously giggles. "My mom said that I couldn't get a new phone because my old phone was fine, but now I can get something better, and she can't bitch about it."

XV. We're Fucked. We Don't Have Our Cell Phones.

We walk in the dark, our eyes darting everywhere, only to reveal nothing. This absence pushes our mind to find form in the formless, and this is not a good thing.

The van is lost.

Rob is lost.

All of our cell phones exploded simultaneously.

We are trapped in the Pine Barrens.

"Guys. Guys!" Hummingbird screeches and everyone looks back to where her squawk originated.

"What now, Hummingbird?" Wil asks.

"Lights," she says quietly.

Two yellow glimmers peak through the trees, watching us. They move. They slither closer, growing in circumference.

No one wants to confirm that they see the lights because it will make the lights real. These are two distinct radiant globes that could be Rob returning in the van, or it could also be a piney.

Everyone steps to the edge of the path, just in case Rob is driving.

When it's clear that the vehicle is not the van- that it's a Jeep with no visible body damage or lengthwise scratches- Kyle starts jogging down the middle of the road, waving his hands and barking out a desperate request for help. His soft voice cracks with uneven edges and it makes both Morgan and Hummingbird look away and open their mouths in a near-gasp at the realization of how unsure everything has become.

"I have a bad feeling about this. That car looks straight out of Atlantis City," Jody says, and unfortunately we know he's not joking because Jody believes in everything. *Everything*. In a place where anything is possible, his openness makes him both a necessity and a nightmare factory.

The woods get brighter as we wait in anticipation to find out if we're saved or doomed. The brakes squeak on the Jeep Grand Cherokee as it slows to a stop for the slight-framed boy who has positioned his body in the middle of the one lane dirt road. Kyle has both gloved palms raised out to the car, as though he could stop the Jeep with some sort of telepathic burst. The screeching strain of the brakes proves that Kyle does not have any such powers.

Straightening his hoodie collar like it's a fine suit, Kyle approaches the vehicle, while we stalk down the path in a group to intimidate whoever is inside the Jeep.

Kyle stands two steps back from the window of a vehicle that shouldn't be suspicious, but in the context of the events of the night, feels threatening.

As the window rolls down, Kyle looks into the dark front seat of the Jeep, then says, "Hey Sir- man. Hey, man," editing his statement to be less formal when his eyes adjust and he sees that he's speaking to the exact type of person his mind assembled when he first heard the term "piney." The man appears to be in his early 40's, but there's also a youthful energy around him. His eyebrows give his face a sinister glee, and Kyle relaxes when they disappear under the brim of the presumably once green, now haphazardly camo, cap. Kyle finds it easier to trust this man when he's not making eye contact.

"You look lost," the man says with a voice that seems too manic for this late night situation. He has a snake-like delivery, that's what Kyle thinks to himself, *This man is like a snake.*

"We got lost," Kyle confirms.

"I'd say so," the stranger responds, then he glances over at us, calculating if we pose a threat. He nods, maybe only to himself, before popping open the car door and getting out to meet us. Instead of joining our shivering cluster, the stranger walks around to the front of the car, and rests his ass on the grill of the Jeep. The headlights bookend him and make it hard to judge the expression he's wearing. When he passed by the left headlight, we saw him wide awake and smiling. He might be on one of those drugs like crystal meth. There's minimal doubt that something is off about him.

"We were wondering if you had a cell phone," Wil says.

"Doesn't your dad?" the stranger asks.

"My dad?" Wil responds.

"Big boy over there," the stranger says, his arm reaching out, breaching a headlight beam to point at Jody.

"No. I don't have a cell phone, sir. For your information, my cell phone exploded near my dick and balls," Jody says, his tone formal and respectful.

"That'll happen here," the man says, then gives a casual shrug.

"So, you have a cell phone?" Wil asks, getting back to the point of this roadblock.

"Sure do," the stranger confirms.

"That we could use?" Wil adds.

"Sure don't."

"I'll let you hold my wallet as collateral," Mike offers, but the stranger returns to what Jody said, "So you're telling me *all* your cell phones exploded at the same time?"

Everyone nods.

"That is quite the tale," the stranger observes, "I know some bizarre things have happened in these woods, but I'm sure you can understand my... trepidation, about approaching a group of young people, very early in the morning, with a very odd story. If you're looking for someone to help you load a sofa into a van, I'm sorry, but you've got the wrong guy."

"We have neither furniture, nor a van," Mike says.

"So you expect me to just hand over my cell phone to a guy whose last phone randomly exploded? I'm sorry, but I've tried really, really hard not to break this phone. Do you know how hard it is to keep a cell phone screen pristine nowadays? One mistake and you'll spider crack the glass," the stranger hisses, and we can't be sure, but we could've sworn he winked at Wil after he said this.

"You can hold the phone. You can even make the call for us. If you could just call 911," Kyle says.

The stranger leaves his illuminated stage and walks toward Kyle. He shakes his head and begins to say, "No offense..."

"Kyle."

"Jack," the stranger says, almost as though he was renaming Kyle instead of providing his own name. "I'm not exactly thrilled with your track record when it comes to cell phones."

"So, there's no way you can help us?" Wil asks, on the brink of becoming rude.

"I didn't say that," Jack growls, turning to Wil. He's still sporting that mischievous smile, "I'm not a heartless bastard. I can assure you of that because I hate it when my ex-wife is right about things." After a pause, Jack tells us, "That was a joke, kids."

Jody lets out an obnoxious laugh, and the stranger looks at him skeptically, then nods, "Of course I'll help you," he says, fixing the brim on his hat, "I wouldn't have stepped out of my heated luxury vehicle if I didn't plan on helping you."

"That is a pretty sweet ride," Jody says, pointing at the idling Jeep.

Jody has bad taste in almost everything.

"You know anything about the Cherokees?" Jack asks us.

"I know that they look sweet as fuck when they drive through a snow pile," Jody instantly responds.

"Sure do. How about the Cherokee Indians?" Jack asks.

Jody makes a displeased face, then shakes his head.

"Yeah. Me neither. Because we slaughtered them all before we could learn anything about them," Jack says, then shoots machine gun laughter out of his mouth. When no one joins in with this amusement, he trails off. Suddenly, he arches an eyebrow and asks, "You kids here because of *The X-Files?*"

"What the fuck is an *X-Files*?" Wil asks.

"It was a very famous show, once upon a time," Jack says, thinking about the years that have flipped by. "When I first saw the show, I was in my early 20's, like you kids. Not you though," Jack says, gesturing to his right.

"Yeah, I'm the most experienced of this ragtag crew," Jody says.

"I was talking to your lady friend here," Jack says, then turns to Hummingbird and purrs, "No way you're a day over 18."

Hummingbird struggles to stay awake while standing.

"So, I got into this show pretty heavily, and I quickly found out that they filmed an episode of the *X-Files* about the Barrens," Jack says, holding out his hands to hug the scenery. The Pine Barrens is the set of this one man play and Jack is the leading man. The audience just wants to get out of the cold and find a place to crash. They want to figure this out in the morning, not discuss pop culture. Aware of these facts, yet not caring, Jack continues his monologue, "I was excited about the episode. I thought they would finally focus on the... the dry peculiarity of this place. This would be when the world would finally hear about Ms. Leeds-"

"-this is interesting and all-" Wil pushes forward, but Jack pushes back with an aggressive snarl, "-you have women tendencies. Why would you interrupt someone telling a story?"

"Because we want to go the fuck home, dude," Wil says, not backing down.

The stranger's body language changes. He nods at Wil's lingering statement, then he says, "Since you want to get home, I guess that means all of you will listen to my fucking story."

No one objects. Going back to his snake-like manic delivery, the stranger says, "So finally this *X-files* episode comes back on TV, and they- a redhead and some guy with the government mandated 90's haircut for men- show up in a place that's clearly not the Barrens, but it's supposed to be the Barrens. And you know what they were chasing? A were-woman."

"Cliff was right," Jody whispers in awe.

The stranger doesn't acknowledge Jody and continues his rant, "Now, I've seen some things in these Barrens, but you know what I haven't seen? A were-woman. We have a devil in these woods and they chose to make an episode about a lady who just needed a Gillette and a bath. I mean, is that why you're all looking into those dark woods with that fearful expression? A girl who needs a bikini wax?" Jack asks, then that rapid-fire laugh returns.

We're not sure if our problem has been solved or exacerbated by Jack's presence. Does this man drive around the Barrens, looking for kids doing drugs? Is this a buzzkill routine that he's grown fond of performing, if for no other reason, than because *The X-files* isn't on and his nights are open now?

Jack keeps looking out into the woods, and Mike asks him, "Sir, have you been drinking?"

"Yup. Sure have."

"Alone in the woods?" Morgan asks, breaking her silence.

"I wouldn't say alone," Jack responds, then he leers at each of us, his grin expanding as his head turns.

Jody desperately wanted to get drunk tonight, but this was not the Jack he imagined he would find.

"Now that you know we're not X-Filers, how about letting us use that phone?" Kyle asks, steering the conversation back on course.

"Of course. No problem," Jack says, and the group immediately begins to loosen up.

There's still time for a celebration. Jody is confident he can salvage this night.

Jack walks back to the idling Jeep, then opens the front passenger side door, and announces "Pocahontas, your Cherokee awaits."

Jody shrugs, then begins his approach.

"Her," Jack growls, pointing at Hummingbird, and Jody stops walking.

Everyone looks around, wondering if we should sacrifice Hummingbird to this manic piney on the off chance she can actually find help. Jody is worried about Hummingbird, but he's also wondering if Pocahontas was even a Cherokee. Jack's statement might be offensive, Jody can't be sure. Jody wants to make sure that Jack is called out for being offensive, just as Jody had been multiple times this week for his ethnically charged, highly questionable statements.

"I've always viewed John Smith as a troublemaking paleface," Jody declares, unwilling to use Hummingbird like a pawn. Even if Hummingbird and her overweight friend allowed the band van to be stolen by shadow-people, she doesn't deserve the scary repercussions that come along with entering a stranger's car for the second time tonight- she barely survived the first time she made that mistake. Jody's goal is now to keep the drunken Hummingbird alive. He's going to make sure that she lives another day, to make another horribly regrettable decision.

When Hummingbird doesn't approach the Cherokee, Wil suggests, "I think we can make the call from outside your heated luxury automobile."

Jack hangs on the open door and looks at Wil, then calmly asks, "So you expect me to drive to my house, get my cell phone, drive all the way back here, then give it to you? There are favors, then there are impositions. I believe what you're looking for just went from category A to category B. I'm a good Samaritan, not a dumb one."

"Not very smart to leave your *mobile* phone at home though, is it?" Wil says, "You're like my Mom, leaving your cell phone in the charger all day long."

"Whoa there. A guy who almost castrated himself with his phone is calling *me* a girl for what I choose to use my phone for. That... takes balls," Jack says, then his gleeful laugh returns again.

"What if I go with you?" Kyle suggests, hopefully bringing this odd game to a close.

"What if you don't," Jack says, dismissing him.

"You aren't getting Hummingbird," Jody says, "But Kyle is my brother and he's effeminate so if you close your eyes-"

"-listen," Jack interrupts, "This isn't some creepy sex thing. This is an image thing. People know me around here. I've lived in the Barrens all my life. People recognize my fine American made sports utility vehicle. Now what's Mrs. Mary Sullivan going to think if she sees me driving around with a strange boy in my car in the middle of the night? It's going to look odd. But with this one," Jack points to Hummingbird, "Nothing odd about that."

Wil shakes his head, "Oh, so it's fine for you to be seen with a teenage girl in the middle of the night?"

Jack holds his arms out again, and proclaims, "Always, my friend. Always."

"Beat it, Jack. We don't need you," Wil says.

"I won't be shown out of my own woods," Jack retorts, slamming the Cherokee door.

"You're right," Kyle says, using his soothing voice, "We're just looking for the exit, then we'll be out of your woods in no time."

Jack considers this, then begins to approach us.

We don't run.

Smiling, Jack puts his hand on Kyle's trembling shoulder. This action is more of a warning than a gesture of camaraderie. Kyle can easily intuit the monologue running in Jack's head, *I can touch you, but you can't touch me. I'm in control. These are my woods and I won't let them get invaded by men in eyeliner. You're all worse than David Duchovny.*

"Know what?" Jack asks, then waits for an answer.

"What?" Mike asks, becoming the only one willing to provide a response.

Jack smiles, then says, "I'll give you an official escort out of these very woods."

"You'll give us a ride?" Kyle asks.

Jack laughs, then removes his hand from Kyle's shoulder and makes his way back to the Cherokee, "No. I won't give you a ride, but I'll drive slow enough that you can run behind my Jeep.'

"Jody, can you carry Hummingbird's drunk ass?" Wil asks.

"There's no ass I'd rather carry in the entire world," Jody responds, then tips his hat at the shivering girl.

Everyone instantly accepts Jack's plan and begins stretching their cold limbs.

Jack returns to the driver's seat of the Cherokee, then puts her in drive.

We begin following this pace car, and things begin to feel not only physically out of the woods, but musically as well. Tonight was about reaching a dream, and that dream begins to come back into focus. On that stage, Kyle looked out and saw bodies crushed up against each other in pure pleasure. He watched the crowd part with Biblical preciseness, at his command. Kyle stepped off that stage and he stood in front of the separated people then, with one unifying movement- his gloved hands locking together- the crowd closed the gap, smashing toward each other with chaotic smiles creasing their faces. During this well-controlled riot, our heart pumped double beats, and not just because of the breakdown chugging along onstage. As Kyle runs alongside his bandmates and new friends, he feels the same way he did on stage. How lucky to be able to experience this type of excitement twice in one long day.

We follow the Lennard brothers, running behind the Cherokee, free from the binds of technology that prevent experiences like this from organically occurring back home. Jody views this moment as man at his most regressed. A very similar run through these woods could have been made hundreds of years ago as a very different Cherokee lead lost white people home. Sometimes that home was an entirely new place.

Jody is wearing Hummingbird like a backpack, her legs locked around his waist. He looks over at his brother and notices that Kyle's smiling. He hopes Kyle finally found faith in these woods, but he's aware that it's more likely that Kyle attributes this moment more to his own two gloved hands, than an invisible palm pushing him to this point.

Wil sprints next to us, his face red from his misused lungs finally being called upon to perform their intended purpose. The red in Wil's face burns even brighter when Jack taps his brakes and the lights on the Cherokee confirm we won't be left behind.

Jody's face begins to redden like Wil's as the run continues. He doesn't smoke cigarettes like Wil does, but Jody is running for two. He had thought that Hummingbird's slight frame would match her light nickname, but she's beginning to weigh him down. Her warm cheek stays pressed against Jody's stubble, even when he starts to sweat, and the fact that she's remained so tightly wrapped around Jody made him push on further. He's helping this girl, he's saving this girl. The girl is hugging him tightly, by choice, because Jody is the only one who can do this for her. Today, tonight, this morning- all of it, even with the van disappearing and his phone exploding- immediately ranks as one of Jody's favorite days. Soon, the sun will rise and Jody will fall asleep, feeling like he's truly lived, and when he wakes up at lunchtime, he will feel reborn.

As Hummingbird holds on tight to Jody, she thinks, *Fuck. I got too drunk tonight. I hope I don't puke on Jody. Don't puke on Jody. Don't do it. He's giving you a piggyback ride. Haha. Piggyback. Get it. Because he's overweight. Speaking of, where's Morgan?*

Morgan's long gasps are only being noticed by a consciously paced Kyle. He knows Morgan won't be able to run much longer. Morgan knows this as well, but she makes a decision that she needs to push herself. She can't have Kyle hold everyone up for her because that would be twice in one night. That's pathetic. Morgan spends every desperate step wishing that she was Hummingbird. She has never been the girl that gets hoisted onto a boy's back. Morgan looks to Mike, but he doesn't look back at her, and he doesn't suggest that Morgan hop on his back. It's almost as though Morgan doesn't exist to Mike right now.

Mike, arms still at his side, performs his awkward ostrich-like run. His black off-brand sneakers clop through the sandy dirt, and we begin to believe that this is a day at the beach for him. The van full of instruments is gone, so Mike is free from music for the first time since high school. The burden of beautiful responsibility has been lifted, and Mike is in the woods, once again. This is a return to the hunt. When Mike would go into the woods with his father, he'd never trap the animals- there's little skill in trapping. There's supreme skill in hunting prey though, and Mike has missed flexing this skill. He didn't ever feel trapped by the music, but now he'll have a chance to focus his attention on everything he put to the side for the band. There's a wobbly vision of the past he's been glancing, and he doesn't know if he wants to capture it, or let it go.

There has always been a purposeful distance between the boys in Lies As Language in an attempt to protect the band. A million metalcore bands came before, only to break up because of a shared lover, an unshared credit, a shared rumor, or a disproportionate share of publishing. Mike is the "treasurer" of the band. Only he and the band's management know that Kyle will get the biggest share of the money made tonight. Kyle's frontman status makes him the revenue magnet. He's the lead singer. He's the cute one. He's the one with the crisp voice. He's the one that the young girls, flush with their father's cash, scream for. Everyone else in Lies As Language gets an equal cut. Now, Lies As Language is a band with no instruments. This is bad for the band, but this may be good for two very different brothers. It doesn't matter that there could be the threat of outside forces disrupting Lies As Language while they make their way home; the precious stasis needed to maintain the band is no longer necessary now. Maybe the boys can finally get closer and become men. Maybe Jody and Kyle will stop trying to beat each other senseless.

Mike chooses to savor this temporary freedom, aware that it will dissolve once the boys are reunited with their instruments. Tonight's performance marked the end of Lies As Language's unnoticed, insignificant, dispensable lives, and now it's just a matter of staying alive to enjoy the change. The group runs together, hoping that their final destination is a modest suburban home filled with bulk quantities of snack foods that could be pillaged from a tall cupboard. The snacks would be brought into a basement where we'll watch *The Shining* on a giant TV, and it will be scary, even though the sun has already risen. We'll wake up at 3 PM and Morgan might have the skills to make us all Taylor ham and cheeses. At worst, we'll have an awkward morning with Hummingbird's disinterested and unconcerned parents, then we'll all go to the Verizon store and get new phones.

In the very same moment this fantasy could become a near-certain future, we watch our future pull away as the Cherokee speeds up, then the tail lights disappear behind the trees.

XVI. Still Fucked.

We pant heavy breaths in the dark. This is not the good type of in-the-dark panting... it's the defeated type.

"This time, the Cherokee has triumphed against the palefaces," Jody says, gasping for air, looking off into the distance, searching for brake lights.

As we wait for Hummingbird to return from her bathroom break, Mike asks, "What now?"

Not letting a silence accumulate, Kyle pants, "We know he's leaving the woods, so we'll continue, as fast as possible, on the path he's driving."

"That's your solution? Power walking?" Wil asks, gasping in smoke from a cigarette.

Hummingbird appears back on the road, cutely suggesting, "Orrr we could go crash at the house I found," then she points into the darkness.

"There's nothing there," Mike says, verbalizing the obvious.

"That's what I thought at first, but while I was peeing behind those spiky bushes, I felt like someone was watching me, but it turns out it was the windows of the house that had a clear view of my cooch."

"Do you think it's the Behringer house that the old blind lady was talking about?" Wil asks.

"I bet it is," Hummingbird says, desperate to find somewhere, anywhere, to end this night that has spilled into the early morning.

"What makes you think it's his house?" Kyle asks.

"The front door is wide open," Hummingbird says, "If someone was in the house, the front door would be locked to keep Pineys out. If some loser Behringer fans were last there, they'd leave the door open for other losers."

"Why would Behringer fans be dedicated enough to travel out into the middle of nowhere?" Kyle asks.

"He's the dude who wrote books about some little douche who does magic. People love that shit," Wil responds.

"How do you know about that?" Morgan asks, through her chomping gasps.

"I wasn't always the crown prince of darkness, I had a childhood too," Wil says, his voice raspy from smoking, then smoking more, then running, then smoking his current cigarette.

"I say we at least check out the place," Mike votes.

"Yes!" Hummingbird declares, "I need to go in a house. I bet they have a sofa. I want my body on a sofa."

We all look back into the darkness, searching for Rob. We turn and look forward into more darkness, searching for Jack. When neither man materializes, we stumble behind Hummingbird, who leads the way toward the house.

"I peed somewhere around here so if you step in wet, then my pee is on you," Hummingbird says plainly.

We cut between tall pines, and almost as though our redirection walks us closer to the light, the sky begins to purple, ever so slightly. Above the tall pines crests the impending dawn, while between the tall pines sits a house that smiles at us. It stands alone, but doesn't a exude loneliness. The interior is dark, but it also seems to burst with an electricity. The house is in perfect condition, seemingly immune to vandals, while simultaneously inviting them inside. It's a simple house, not extravagant yet not a cabin either. A stone lined porch. White, dentless, painted aluminum siding. A green slanted roof. A second floor that doesn't stretch as far as the first floor does. No garage. No car. No satellite dish, just a lightning rod in the exact center of the roof. This house is an island surrounded by the dry broken pines of New Jersey.

"Welcome home," Kyle says in a whisper.

A shiver of fear slides up Hummingbird's spine, then dislodges a lesson that Kyle taught her, "I'm afraid to go in. I think the toughest person should take the lead."

Jody immediately steps forward. Hummingbird's call for help inserted a solid backbone in the solitary man that stands amid a group of slouching kids. Maybe Jack was right? Maybe Jody is a father to these weary children.

We hide behind a tree, as Jody's scuffed black Dr. Martens crunch across an open patch of woods, then climb up three steps onto the stone porch.

We can't see Jody's reaction to what he's reviewing, but he doesn't cut and run, so we make our way toward him.

Our eyes bounce from the house, to the woods, to the ground, to each other.

We climb three steps onto a stone porch that's empty except for a chaise lounge. It doesn't make sense why this home's footprint is so long and

skinny when it could have expanded out for miles without intruding or
aggravating neighbors. The Pine Barrens must be protected by the
government. Bad soil or not, capitalism doesn't allow this much untouched
forest to remain unexploited unless there are excessive federal penalties for
digging and building here. Even in a place where rules seemed to get
thrown away, Uncle Sam likely looms with rigid construction codes.

Jody approaches the cracked entrance to what may or may not be
Behringer's house.

For a moment, we all stare into the dark abyss.

"Hello?" Jody bellows out.

No response.

Once again, designating himself as the leader of the group, Jody looks to
his right and sees that the door was once kicked in with force. He reaches
down and grabs a jagged piece of the door frame, then yanks hard,
separating it from the house. He's now armed.

We watch Jody continue into the house with the piece of frame cocked,
ready to smash whoever, whatever, he can manage to make contact with.
We follow behind him, trying the light switch to our left, but it seems to do
nothing when flicked. It's noticeably colder in the house than it was
outside, like an air conditioner was left pumping, but there's no labored
buzz to indicate that this is the source of the chill. The air is cold, but we
can't see our breath. It feels like we should be able to see our breath. Why
can't we see our breath? Why can't we see anything?

In front of us might be... stairs?

We walk closer, moving to the right so the blooming morning outside
can creep through the door and illuminate what we're trying to identify.

We squint. Three wooden stairs, covered in dark carpeting, face the
door.

If we were to walk up the three stairs, we'd be standing on a square
landing, then we'd have to take a right and climb more stairs on our way to
the second floor. Right now, we aren't comfortable enough with the first
floor to pursue other curiosities, despite the fact that we know that the
second floor is where the bedrooms will be.

Jody yells, "Is anyone in here?" then, without waiting for an answer, he
hangs a right and walks down what appears to be a stubby, wood paneled
hallway. We're at a disadvantage in these close quarters, so we don't follow
Jody. We want confirmation that this hallway doesn't lead to danger before
we begin to explore further.

Stuck in the mouth of the house, all we can do is listen. We can hear
Jody moving somewhere further down the hall, but we can no longer see

him. There are no sounds of a struggle. There are no voices coming from elsewhere in the house.

"Hello?" Mike asks, at a conversational level.

"That last wizard book read like bad fanfic!" Wil yells.

Everyone waits for a response. Nothing.

"Looks like we have the place to ourselves tonight," Kyle says.

Now that the most careful member of the group confirms that we're safe, the situation gains an ease. We don't quite believe we're alone in this house, but it makes us feel a little better that Kyle is not in a cold sweat panic like we are. Despite the low temperature and the suspiciously inviting open door, there are no weird Pineys chasing us away or van stealing shadows looming in this home.

When Jody's actions at the end of the hall go silent, Kyle steps forward to begin the search for his brother.

Frozen fingers become locked together for support as we make our way down the hall. We walk next to Wil, as the human chain in front of us forms a protective wall. Mike holds Morgan's left hand, Morgan holds Hummingbird's right hand, Hummingbird holds Kyle's left hand, and Kyle's right hand makes a light thumping noise as his exposed fingertips skip over the seams in the wooden wall. This is hardly a log cabin, but it's clear that the person who had this house built was very proud that he or she was able to put down roots in such an exclusively protected area. These wooden walls seem to evoke an eerie theory that this house was not constructed, but instead grew out of the ground.

We move quietly, and we have to trust that Jody won't think we're a menace and unleash an attack.

The threat of even a minor injury in this house gains lethal implication because we're stranded here, unable to call for help. If the electricity is out, the phone lines are probably out too, unless a dead man is continuing to pay his phone bills. This isolation becomes a liability. None of us know how to fix anything, treat anything, or heal anything. Before, we'd just google it.

This house in the Barrens feels both infinitely abandoned and recently inhabited. The more our circumstances change, the more they stay the same. The more things stay concealed, the more they stay creepy and undesirable.

The first room we pass on our right is a bathroom. The porcelain throne glints just a hint of a reflection in the lethargic dawn.

A little further down the hall, a second room on the right reveals itself, but this time the door is closed. We don't remember hearing this door creak shut, so Jody must have continued past it, not noticing it in the dark.

"We need to go in here," Mike says, breaking the human chain, then moving toward the door.

Kyle nods to Mike who reaches over and wraps his fingers around the brass knob. After a silent 3 count, Mike sends the door flying open.

The gaping mouth of the room soundlessly yawns at us. There could be people asleep in this dark room and we wonder if we'd prefer to be chased away or invited to stay here. It remains unclear as to which one of those two options provides the safer outcome.

Kyle enters the dark room, and he's able to make out only vague outlines of objects thanks to the subtle illumination provided by a window that looks out to the stone porch. From the hallway, we watch as Kyle passes from one side of the room to the other, until he seems confident no one is in there.

Then, once again, the human chain reestablishes, as we all seek security because at the end of the dark hall, we hear footsteps.

"If you're Jody. Say you're Jody," Wil calls out, facing the noise.

The room at the end of the hall begins to glow, then a candle floats out to illuminate a door frame. The candle moves up and down, and a dreary, "Woooooeooeo," noise accompanies it.

When the candle gets too close to the door frame, Mike warns, "Jody, be careful. You might set the house on fire."

"Whoooo is Jody?" we hear Jody ask, as he hides behind the door frame, raising and lowering the candle.

Kyle walks out into the hallway, and in the dim light we see him smile, then he asks, "Oh, Great Spirit, may we enter your eternal chamber?"

"Only thine with the Hummingbirds above her titties may enter," the ghost responds.

"Ugh," Hummingbird sighs, then begins walking down the hall toward the candle. The unknown possibilities of what was hiding in the dark corners of the rest of the house somehow manage to seem worse than Jody's candlelight creeping to her.

We follow behind Hummingbird, hoping that there are more candles so we can illuminate the far corners of the house, then go to bed before the birds who postponed their flight to Miami start chirping.

The candle moves away from the door when Hummingbird arrives in the door frame, and Hummingbird follows the light like a moth. Relieved that Jody was able to conjure fire and locate supplies, we join him in what we quickly deduce is an office. Along the far wall are bookcases filled with tightly crammed lines of books. To our left is a desk. Jody walks the length of the office, about fifteen feet, until he reaches the window. He looks outside. Morning seems reluctant to arrive, as it hangs in a delayed state.

We rushed into this house, while the sun has kept its distance. We want to shed light on this place, and the sun seems content to spread itself elsewhere.

Wil drifts to the desk that's pressed up against the wall opposite the window. He opens the top drawer to find it's filled with various pens, and thankfully, three long, purple candles. How long has this house in the middle of nowhere been without electricity? No wonder Behringer killed himself.

Wil begins lighting the candles with his green lighter.

As the candles are distributed, Hummingbird celebrates, "Wil, this is perfect! Candles are like cell phones... except if you try to call people on a candle, your hair will set on fire."

We remember how to smile in the house, but we wear this badge of comfort for only a moment.

A jarring thud smacks the front of the house and our open mouth gawk returns. Everyone instinctively backs against the book-lined wall. Wil, Mike, Jody and Kyle all blow out their candles, and we return to darkness. The noise sounded like someone had thrown a basketball against the house.

"What the fuck was that?" Hummingbird ekes in a small whisper, "What. Was. That?"

"There's only one way to find out," Mike says.

Wil lights his lighter and each boy leans their wick into the fire.

"Why don't the girls get candles?" Morgan whispers.

"Because if we're going to be trapped in this house, I don't want the candles running away," Jody says loudly. He looks us over once, then walks out of the room to find the source of the noise. Morgan follows Jody, and we all exchange glances after witnessing the formation of a truly bizarre alliance.

Misreading our confusion, Mike says, "Something is mad we're here," then he holds his candle under his chin like a choirboy on Christmas night. Why couldn't it be Christmas night? Waiting for the Holy Spirit is way nicer than waiting for an unholy spirit to pop out of the dark, explode your eyeballs, then feast on your flesh.

Kyle surveys us in the light of his candle, then explains, "We're going to check the entire house. Once we're sure we're alone, we'll each pick a place to sleep. When everyone wakes up, we'll go home. No. Not home. We'll wake up, eat, then we'll search for Rob."

"I'm sure he already split," Wil says, tired of Rob's ability to disappear.

"I'm not sure of that, okay?" Kyle responds, impassioned. "I'm not so sure he's safe," he adds, then walks out of the small office to find Jody.

Making his way back to the front door, Kyle holds out his candle, trying to distribute its weak light. We move cautiously behind him and listen carefully, waiting for a repeat of the violent noise.

Clearing the short hallway, Kyle steps out onto the porch to make sure Jody isn't still studying the dent in the siding. Finding nothing, and feeling appreciative of this stillness, Kyle returns inside, pulling the front door shut behind him. When there's no objection from the house and no new noises, we progress into the living room.

Hummingbird flies close to Kyle's light. She glances toward the sofa on her right, but she doesn't collapse onto it because a portion of the sofa remains in the shadows- enough that there could be someone sitting there, watching us, and Hummingbird wouldn't know until she was lying next to him.

Jody and Morgan are staring at a piano in a window-walled corner of the living room, and the absence of Rob arrives like an elephant. We stop listening for a moment, because we're afraid we'll hear Rob playing his keyboard. We don't need that reminder of where we were mere hours ago.

To defuse the silence, Jody points at the piano, then leans toward Morgan, and says, "I bet that piano starts playing all by itself tonight and scares your tits off. Hell, it might even scare my tits off. All tits are on the table tonight."

This is why Jody has been essential throughout our detour into the Barrens. His indecorous humor slices the tension that seems to build organically in this house.

We look down, at the green wall to wall carpet, then our eyes run across it, to a brick-lined fireplace. Part of us wants to start a fire, the other part just wants to go to sleep immediately, then get the fuck out of here as soon as possible.

Continuing his sweep of the house, Kyle moves toward what must be the dining room. There's a long set of windows that face the backyard, which we assume looks exactly like the front yard. It's acceptable that the windows run the length of the dining room table because when you're this deep in the woods, you could live in a glass house and still have complete privacy.

We drift in a careful mob, past the dining room table, into the kitchen. In this tight square of a room, cabinets line the walls, and when Kyle pulls one of them open, he finds they're well stocked. In the dim light, it appears that the kitchen is clean and oddly insect-free, which is impressive considering the space it inhabits in the Barrens.

The tension returning to his posture, Kyle moves out of the kitchen and takes a step down into the portion of the house that has no second floor above it, only a roof. We reluctantly follow along, finding ourselves in a long rectangle of a room. The room is open- there are no dividers or walls. The floor is tiled, making the room less naturalistic than the rest of the house.

Two sofas are illuminated by windows that face out to the front yard. Kyle doesn't approach these windows- he's still more concerned about the possible unseen occupants inside the house.

"Alright," Kyle says, "Hummingbird, Morgan, you can crash on the sofas in here and-"

"-what about the upstairs?" Mike interrupts, stepping into the room. We were avoiding this question; it's nicer to assume that things are fine upstairs, instead of going up to the second floor of a strange house, then finding precisely what we feared the most. The only way to escape something that can be sensed, but can't be seen, is to deny its existence.

Jody hands his candle to Morgan, then twirls the piece of door frame in his hand like a sword. "Don't worry, I got this," he declares.

"Damn it," Kyle sighs, then he hands Hummingbird his candle. Staring down Jody, who continues to swing the piece of door frame, Kyle says, "You're not going alone."

The Lennard brothers have always been bonded by the allure of a physical altercation. They both step up the single step to the kitchen and the rest of us double-time it to follow them.

Hummingbird, Wil, Morgan, and Mike shield the flames of their candles so these swift movements through the house don't extinguish our only source of light.

When footprints hammer above us, everything stops.

Our eyes lift toward the ceiling. The frenzied pounding thuds directly over us, then continues moving to the far end of the house.

"What the fuck was that?" Wil asks, his voice suddenly airy.

"Someone's roughhousing upstairs," Mike says plainly.

Slam. A door somewhere in the house shuts with force.

Jody charges toward the staircase, while Wil and Mike follow close behind, doing their best to shed some light on our path. Morgan and Hummingbird follow the boys because they don't want to be alone. Now that the girls have been granted candles, they can see what's going on, but the light only stretches an arm's length away, and once someone gets that close, it's too late.

We follow Jody because... why are we following him? Why are we going upstairs to meet the being who slammed the door? Why was it running? Who was it running from?

Looking left, we see the front door is still shut, but it can't be sealed because of the broken lock. We know this was not the door that slammed shut, but the broken lock also means that if we go upstairs, someone could slip into the house undetected. Unless we have Jody stand guard at the door, no matter how many times we clear these rooms, someone could always slip inside when we're dealing with a distraction upstairs.

Jody leads us up the staircase that runs parallel with the short hallway. We follow him, ready to run back downstairs at the first sign of someone who didn't arrive with us. It's perfectly silent in the house, except for the stairs creaking under our feet.

When we reach the top of the stairs, we survey the second floor. Directly facing the top of the stairs is a door, shut. Running parallel to the stairs are four more doors, and at the opposite end of the hallway, another door. All of these doors are shut, and one of these doors was slammed by whoever or whatever was running upstairs.

Jody steps toward the first door, then motions for his lighting man- Mike, and his designated door opener- Wil, to flank him.

Behind the trio of woods police, we notice that Morgan and Hummingbird have locked hands with Kyle, and the intimacy of his bare fingertips seems to comfort them.

When Kyle was performing onstage, he skimmed his hand across the audience, but he didn't touch Hummingbird or Morgan. Their first contact with him came later, as they gleefully struggled to keep him afloat on a sea of hands. Those same fans are here now, in the hallway, and they're still desperate for Kyle's touch. At the venue, Kyle relied on this contact to keep him safe, now the girls are asking the same from him.

In a house that greeted us with an open front door, the upstairs feels like a contradiction. The closed doors create a sinister game show where all will be revealed, but there will be no cheering. The anticipation will be at a screaming pitch, but when the door is flung open there's a throbbing need to see nothing at all.

The plan is in place: Mike controls the lighting, Wil controls the opening, and Jody controls the swinging of the weapon. It's logical in theory, but the system quickly falters when Wil's fingers wrap around the brass knob of the first door, then he pushes hard, but makes no progress. He decides to pull on the knob, only to feel the door press tight against the lip of the frame.

"It's locked," Wil whispers.

"Break it down," Mike says in his normal voice, and for the first time since he's been on stage, Mike sounds too loud.

"I can easily break it down," Jody says, then adds, "But it will make too much noise and the spirits will be disturbed."

"Then hit them with your door frame weapon," Hummingbird whispers.

"If they can go through these locked rooms, this jagged piece of wood isn't going to stop them. They'll pass through it and bite my neck or face," Jody says.

"Why are you so sure they can go through walls?" Morgan asks.

"The floors out here are carpeted, but we heard running on hardwoods so maybe the rooms have hardwood floors, and they're all connected? It's possible that the door we heard slam isn't even in this hallway," Kyle realizes. He feels a shiver creep up his spine. Heat rises. Why is it so cold on the second floor? Kyle can't dwell on these questions. He needs to deal in facts, "The ghost- not that there is a ghost-" he whispers, turning to the girls to clarify, "-slammed the door so he obviously can't move through your piece of door frame, plus, Jody, no offense, but I'm not going to take paranormal expertise from a guy whose only research material about the paranormal is our VHS tape about a dead boy who's hanging out with a prepubescent Christina Ricci."

Kyle once again flaunts the simplicity of rational thought trumping our fear.

Jody nods, reminded that there are some friendly ghosts, then he makes his way to the next door that must be checked. The escape from whatever is behind door number two will be more difficult. A straight line escape requires a jump over the banister, then a redirected thundering trip down the stairs, or it will require passing by that locked door, again.

Wil reaches for the knob of the second door, turns it, and it's not locked. The door creaks open, and we stare into the near dark of the strange room. Everyone stands back, including Jody. The distance from the other doors seems to indicate that this is a bedroom. If someone was in this house, this room is most likely where they would be. With an open front door offering the lost some complimentary lodging, a drunken hiker or hunter could easily walk into this house and curl up in Behringer's bed for a rural Robert Downey Jr. moment.

"Hello?" Jody bellows into the room.

No one wakes in a panic. No one responds.

We slide inside.

This is *Miami Vice* in the Barrens. This is *Ghost Hunters* with rock stars, instead of charlatan douchebags.

Orbs of light circle the room like the fireflies that are curiously missing from these woods.

The walls are coated in faded tan wallpaper depicting blue vines climbing from the floor to the ceiling. Or are they hanging down from the ceiling toward the floor? In the center of the room is a bed- that's the good news. The bad news is that above the bed is a window. No one in this house trusts the windows.

Kyle checks the rooms for any doors that may lead to the other rooms, but his search comes up empty. Mike gets on his knees and checks under the bed, but finds nothing. Wil moves his candlelight across the closet, making sure that no one is hiding amongst the clothes.

"All clear in here," Jody declares, finishing his sweep with a flourish, then returning to the door.

A fat candle on the dresser is lit by Mike so the girls won't be left in the darkness. This bedroom feels safer than the other rooms, and not just because it's been carefully searched.

"I'll stay in here with the girls," Kyle says, establishing himself as a barrier to danger, like a locked door. The bedroom door will remain unlocked and open only the tiniest of cracks because if Jody does unearth something or someone in this next room, it will be Kyle's responsibility to make sure the girls get out of the house safely.

Morgan considers asking the other boys to stay in the room. She just wants everyone to go to sleep, together, and when we wake up, we can see everything for what it truly is in the light.

This is girl logic, not boy logic. Girls make homes. Boys protect them.

With this girl/boy behavior standard set, Jody, Wil, and Mike go back into the hall, while Morgan and Hummingbird move toward the bedroom closet. The space has already been checked for people or ghosts, but it hasn't been checked for women's clothes. It's time to do a little in-house shopping. Shopping makes Morgan feel better. Shopping takes Hummingbird's mind off all the ugly thoughts that send her to a bathroom in search of a blade to extract her stress. In the dim light from the single candle, the girls are surprised at the array of clothes they find in the closet.

XVII. Looking.

Outside of the bedroom, Jody, Wil, and Mike continue down the hall because there are more doors to check. One comfortable second floor room doesn't mean the house is secure. Whoever is playing this game of hide-and-seek obviously *enjoys* games. This game feels nothing like the amusing childhood competitions held across endless summer dusks where everyone picked a bush in the front yard, then peeked around to see if someone was coming. This is the childlike survival technique of keeping all feet and hands under the blankets, because something may be waiting in the darkness... something that might reach out and hurt us.

Wil throws open the next door, and just like the girls in the bedroom, we find ourselves looking in a closet.

Jody runs his hand across the line of coats that are neatly hanging from a horizontal bar, and he mocks Behringer's work by asking, "Do you see any wizard cloaks?"

As the coats are parted, Wil spots something on the floor of the closet. Squatting down, legs pressed tight against his chest, is a small boy with gray skin. The boy looks up at Wil, his red eyes pulsing to the beat of Wil's heart.

Jody casually lets the coats fall back into place, as Wil springs away from the closet, hitting his spine on the banister, then falling on his ass. His candle lies on the carpet, but instead of stomping out the flame, Wil immediately kicks the closet door shut, then presses both his boots against the door. *Whatever* is inside the closet must remain there. Wil picks up the still-burning candle and holds it out toward his boots so he can watch the door.

"What happened? Are you okay?" Mike asks, taking a knee.

Wil flips the question in his head, as sweat bubbles from his pores, and he concludes, "We need to get out of here."

"What was it?" Jody asks, his anxiety heightened after watching someone normally so apathetic become reduced to a human doorstop in a matter of seconds.

"Don't open it. Do not," Wil says, at full volume, pointing at the door, "Get everyone out of the house. Then I'll stand up."

"We're not going anywhere until you tell me what you saw in that closet," Jody says, captain of this ship docked in a sandy port.

Wil stares past the flame, his eyes wide and unblinking.

Jody pulls Wil up by his white, sweat soaked collar. Wil's feet wobble under him, then he begins to push Mike toward the stairs. Mike pushes back, swiftly pinning Wil to the closet door with a forearm across the throat. Wil's candle falls to the ground again.

"I'm going to look in this closet," Mike says, without inflection.

This entire turn of events is an unusually bold gesture from a quiet man. When quiet men make loud statements, the world listens.

Is Mike possessed?

No.

Are we intrigued?

Yes.

Is Mike enjoying this uncertain chaos?

Maybe.

Could it be that this broken night is a gift from some shadowy force permitting Mike to go back and fulfill an opportunity he previously mismanaged? High school is over; an itch went unscratched. Wil and Jody hadn't seen this side of Mike since before they were a band. Before the instruments... Mike had this idea...

The instruments are gone, and now the idea could be resurrected.

"There's no one in there. It's okay. It's okay," Jody says, breaking the two men apart, then picking up Wil's still-burning candle.

"We're opening that door," Mike announces.

Wil backs into the dark, lighting a cigarette, feeling for the cracked bedroom door. When he spots the dim glow of the dresser candle, Wil yells, "Kyle, I'm coming in," then slips inside. Wil shuts the bedroom door behind him, then locks it. No more open doors. Initially, the open front door to Behringer's house was odd, but not scary. Everyone here grew up in the suburbs. We've all woken up in the morning to find that the front door was left open all night. The scariest thing that resulted from that indiscretion was increased levels of hostility on the ride to school, featuring a curt speech about "individual responsibility" that was largely ignored and snarled at. Wil knows that a locked door is a physical barrier secured to block unwanted contact. It's a conscious way of saying, *You're not welcome*, or *I don't want you to see me... yet.*

Wil's fear is now obvious, he wears it like a mask of dripping terror. Seeing this, Kyle volunteers himself to return to the unknown. He says nothing to the girls or Wil before leaving. The moment he steps into the hallway, he hears Wil dash to the door and click the lock to secure the room. Jody hears it as well, quickly turning, then giving an appreciative nod when he realizes that his brother has returned to help.

Kyle takes his place next to Mike, at the second to last door. Jody hands Kyle the candle Wil abandoned, then turns to Mike, and says, "You're the doorman now."

Mike accepts this responsibility. After the disappointment he experienced when they reopened the closet and found nothing, Mike is ready to see what Wil saw. He burns to sweat out that fragrant fear Wil has become drenched in.

Mike grabs the doorknob, first slowly turning it, then violently throwing the door open. Kyle rushes into the room- fast enough to catch whoever might be hiding, but steady enough that his candle doesn't go out.

Mike and Jody don't follow. They snigger in the dark.

Kyle's eyes dart around, and that's when he spots the toilet.

We're standing in the bathroom.

Out of curiosity, Kyle walks over to the marble sink, then flicks on the water. The sink nozzle spits a pressurized sneeze, then water begins flowing out smoothly. He puts a gloved hand in the sink, but instantly pulls it away when he feels the near-boiling water hit his skin. He holds his fingers, afraid to look down and find his fingerprints burnt off.

"How is there hot water but not electricity?" Mike asks.

"It must be well water," Kyle realizes aloud.

"From the Jersey hot springs?" Mike responds.

Kyle looks at the tops of his fingers. The skin isn't peeling on them. He's okay.

"Regardless of whatever well it's coming from, the question remains, how am I supposed to wash my dick with that fire water?" Jody points out.

No one wants to provide alternatives to Jody, and we make our way to the last door.

Jody, fixated, continues to complain, "I'm going to get johnson abrasions- it'll be a flashback to when I found the password to take the parental controls off the family computer."

Kyle chooses to ignore this disturbing moment of misplaced nostalgia. One more room, then we can go to sleep. Tonight, Kyle won't sleep in a bed; he'll sleep with his back to the locked bedroom door.

Mike approaches the final door with a noticeable impatience.

Once we're set in position, the door is thrown open. Jody bursts in the room aggressively, while Kyle tails him with the candle to provide some much-needed light.

We find ourselves in what appears to be Behringer's writing room.

"We know you're in here! We checked the other rooms. You can't hide from us!" our fearless leader yells, and he hopes it strikes fear in whoever is striking fear in us, because, the fact is, whoever or whatever slammed the door *can* hide from us. So far, other than the closet mishap, they've done a damn good job of hiding from us.

Behringer's writing room is spacious, and it feels as though the source of the cold on the second floor originates in this room. Vaulted ceilings arch above us, so high that the candlelight can't reach the peak. The other rooms we've entered didn't have vaulted ceilings, yet the roof is pitched, and that would leave room for a crawl space or an attic. If someone was trying to hide in this house, the attic would be a perfect place. Faintly, we see that running across the ceiling are wooden rafters. This running holds things steady, while the running that led us up here left everything disjointed. It would have been easy to put in a ceiling and extend the attic, but whoever built this house chose the more creative route. Why not have high ceilings in a forest that's filled with tall trees as a canopy?

The windows on the exterior wall allow the hesitant morning light to outline a desk. Kyle moves toward the outline, searching for answers. Instead of a laptop, sitting on the desk is a typewriter. Behringer using a typewriter to write a bunch of boy wizard books is like Kyle using an orchestra to compose a Lies As Language song. He would do it for the experience, but it's something that the fans neither demand nor respect. The windows would provide a beautiful view in the morning light, but Behringer's desk faces *into* the room. This seems intentional. Maybe Behringer was a man who found himself so easily distracted that his habits demanded that he shut himself off in this remote house, then take even further precautions to maintain concentration once he arrived here. It adds to the eeriness of this house to think that Behringer moved out to these woods, not because he looked to nature for inspiration, but because he needed a hideout. Supervillains never build their lairs in condo complexes-it's always the perch built into the side of a mountain, the multiple cabins of an abandoned summer camp, or, if they have the funds, sometimes even the moon is an option. America went there once, then never went back. It would be a good place to go to remain completely undisturbed.

Bored by the desk, Mike searches around Behringer's office, his candle flickering light onto posters for books that were so successful they could never be escaped. These books brought about movies and the movies brought about hordes of overly obsessed fans. Maybe that's why Behringer took his own life? Maybe he needed to darken that legacy? He was an author forever bound to wizard books, but Behringer must have had other novels in him. It must have hurt to keep those fresh ideas buried so he could collect another check by extending an adventure he no longer desired to trek.

Mike feels a small amount of sympathy for Behringer. To have an escape become a prison is a fear that every creative person has. Lies As Language has always matched exactly what Mike was looking for creatively and the fact that the recording process hadn't become a similar trap to what Behringer's writing process might have been was comforting. The moment Lies As Language turns their desk toward the door, the rest of the band will have a perfect vantage point to see Mike leave. None of this room's scenery satisfies the hunger for a thrill that Mike has been developing a taste for tonight, so he finds himself like the desk, turned to the door, waiting.

Mike was able to play his first real concert, and it felt good, but now his training and instincts are battling his best attempts at repression, enticing him to accomplish something he longed to do in high school.

Mike has always been drawn to the darker moments. In school, he never cared about the parties, or the road trips, or the Friday night football games, yet on more than one occasion, he overheard his classmates talk about how they broke into an abandoned orphanage, and *this* was what aroused his jealousy and made him regret his alienation from his peers. Now, he finally has this romanticized moment, and he wants our dimly lit search to stretch forever. As a bizarre side effect, the frustration and the anger Mike harbored in high school has also come bubbling back up, and oddly, it feels good to him.

"I guess we'll have to check the basement next," Mike says, with no enthusiasm, but in his head, he demands the presence of a basement. He *needs* this house to have a basement.

"No," Jody says, pointing at Mike, "We are not going down in some creepy-as-fuck basement. That's where I say no. *That* is where I draw the line. The fuckin' family room in this place gives me the willies, so no way am I going in the basement. I can't even go into my own basement and I've lived in my house for over 30 years. Fuck that. No thanks. If we go into the basement, I will shit. Literally, I will shit. Then I will have no pants because I didn't bring any spare pairs. Without pants, I'll have to walk around all the time, forever, with no pants, and the girls definitely won't stay. Plus, you can forget about being saved. No pants-less man has ever been saved from anything... besides chafing. So no basement, ever. Do you know how Charlie Manson kept his Manson Family together? With love, acceptance and not letting anyone go in the fucking basement," Jody rants.

"You don't know that," Mike says, offended that Jody would make an assumption about Charlie Manson.

Mike walks out of the room, with his candle carefully protected, and Jody follows swiftly through the dark. Jody is scared of the dark, but at least it's a second-floor-dark. No one ever says, "...then they found a pile of bodies in the second floor hallway." It's always the crawl space or the attic. It's always the basement. It's always the places Jody has said, "Fuck no," to tonight.

Kyle stays in Behringer's writing room... listening.

He hears a door open.

He hears Jody ask, "What the fuck are you doing? Are you in on Cliff's basement expedition? I have bad news for you, if you couldn't handle the closet-"

"-I'm leaving," Kyle hears Wil say. Kyle stays motionless, his reflection looking back at him in one of the tall windows that line the writing room. He wants to feel like a stranger listening to this group of annoyed travelers. He wants to know how Lies As Language comes off to their second audience of the night.

"You're not leaving," Mike's voice joins in, "We're going to the-"

"-no," Kyle barks, breaking his silence. He doesn't walk out into the hall; he stays staring out the window, as though the pane was a teleprompter with his words on it. Eyes peering out the window at the Barrens, Kyle lets out a brutally true assessment of the current situation, "We've checked the upstairs, there's no one here, unless they've locked themselves in the room at the top of the staircase. We have no van, we have no phones, we have a house. Let's weigh our options. We could sleep in the house. Or we could freak ourselves out and... I mean... God." Frustrated, Kyle is about to turn away from the window, but before he can, he sees *it*, for a second.

A face.

We might have seen *it* too.

It wasn't a human face. There were a multitude of variants that kept the face from belonging to a person. It was the red eyes, the pitch black skin, the lack of lips, and the curling horns. Before we were able to get a better look, Kyle dropped his candle.

On the wood floor, armed with nothing to protect himself with, Kyle rights the still-burning flame of his candle, then closes his eyes. Heavy breaths gasp deep into Kyle's lungs and he uses this increased oxygen flow to amp himself up. He can't stay hidden; he must stand and face the window. Slowly, and carefully, Kyle gets back on his feet, then rises to perfect posture. He stares into a window that, for a moment, felt like a mirror.

Wil dashes into the room, responding to Kyle's yelp. He needs to know if Kyle saw what he saw. He needs to be close to Kyle, because after Kyle was confronted with this chilling image, he didn't kick the door shut- he left it open and had the strength to look again.

Kyle can see Wil in the window pane's reflection. Wil's candle is radiating a circle of light; his bloodshot eyes are searching Kyle's face. "You saw it too," Wil says.

Wil saw *something* and he had forced himself to regard it as a mistake. It was fear and sleeplessness causing his mind to play tricks.

Then Kyle saw *it*. That makes *it* real.

What Wil saw was inside the house.

What Kyle saw was outside the house.

That's good for the people inside the house.

That's bad for the person outside the house.

XVIII. A Reluctant Morning.

We wake in the sun-drenched living rcom.

For a house that was so dark last night, everything seems to be beaming with light this morning. The sinister vibe that this house perpetually omits still hangs, but it has decidedly softened. The sunlight is too bright; the surrounding trees should filter these beams, but somehow don't.

When people die, they walk into the light.

Are we dead?

We look to our right and see Jody, in blue checkered boxer shorts, semi-covered in a purple blanket, passed out or. a flower printed sofa. He opens one eye, then looks around the room and displays a range of emotions that whirl from excitement to worry; from responsibility to "I want to go the fuck back to sleep."

The air is thick with flecks of dust that hang motionless; they don't drop, they don't float- they remain- like static. Jody stands up, then shuffles through a patch of the dust that's illuminated by the sunlight entering the window next to the fireplace. He arches his neck to look outside, hoping to see something in the distance beyond just pines and clouds. No landmarks are visible through the trees that surround the house.

Jody looks back at his path and sees the dust still hanging as though he had never stood up. He expected to see an outline of his body. The dust is not alone, also hanging in the air is a smell. It's a familiar smell. There's nothing foreboding or musty about this aroma, it's more... nostalgic. With every foot-dragging step, Jody's sense memory improves. This smell takes him back 20 years. The memory forms- a woman chose to wake up earlier than everyone else, just to make everyone else's wake up a little sweeter. With this invisible helping hand, the rest of the house won't just pull themselves out of bed, they will rise.

Jody snatches the purple blanket off the sofa, then drapes it around his shoulders. His pants are crumpled on the carpet, and he makes no effort to pick them up. Last night, Jody was worried that no one would save him if he wasn't wearing pants. Today, he's not that worried about being saved. In the light of day, solutions, and options, and the simplicity of being lost in modern day New Jersey fills Jody with confidence.

Before entering the kitchen, Jody grabs his piece of door frame, then hides it under the purple blanket. There's a chance that the mystery chef in the kitchen didn't arrive with Lies As Language last night. Jody makes a careful approach, and his socks slide across the carpet, but he feels no sparks or static. For such an electric house, things seem very grounded.

Pausing next to the dining room table, Jody watches Morgan, on her tiptoes, reaching toward a high shelf in the kitchen. She's wearing a pair of short shorts and an almost too small blue t-shirt with a raptor on it. With this amount of arch and stretching, Morgan's stubby body elongates, and maybe it's because morning erections come standard with the being-a-man plan, Jody finds Morgan sexy for the first time ever.

"Allow me," Jody says, entering the kitchen, his blanket-cape flowing behind him, his erection at half-mast. "We all know cooking is a woman's work, but it doesn't mean that kitchens were built for their stocky body types," he tells Morgan, pretty much negating what could have been construed as a gentlemanly gesture.

Jody feels a warmth in the kitchen. "It's nice in here," he says, as Morgan backs away from the shelf, and returns to the stove to tend to the pancakes. "The rest of the house is so claustrophobic it's like being buried alive," Jody adds, negating what could have originally been construed as an appreciative observation about their new vacation home.

Morgan flips a pancake, it sizzles, and she says, "It's the oven, and the sun," then she pauses, considering if she should share more. She notices that Jody is paying attention to her, so she adds, "You know what's dumb? I half expected the sun to not even come out this morning."

"That *is* dumb," Jody says, then laughs at Morgan as he places an unopened bottle of Aunt Jemima syrup on the counter. Noticing Morgan shake her head in a twitchy punishment for her comment, Jody adds, "Or maybe it just seems dumb to me because I'm so well versed in the Astronomies and I often take my supreme knowledge for granted."

"Speaking of science," Morgan remarks, equally dividing her attention between cooking, and the man in the purple cape.

Jody finds this endearing, since he assumes it's hard for a fat girl to concentrate on another person when there is food around. Before Jody can ruin the mood further with this observation, Morgan asks a question. "How is it that Lies As Language is self-classified as a space-metal Christian metalcore band? Do space-metal and Christian metalcore really overlap?"

"Good question," Jody says. He quickly opens the maple syrup bottle, casually takes a sip from it, then responds, "And the answer is... hell no."

"So doesn't that leave your fans feeling a little... conflicted?" Morgan asks, as a fan, conflicted.

"Oh, you mean because most space-metal bands are atheists? We're not interested in that. You know what we're interested in?" Jody asks.

"Monochrome clothing?" Morgan jokes.

"Absolutely, but besides that," Jody says.

"God?"

"Correct. How come God and space have to be separate? Space seems like a pretty good place to see evidence of God. What if I told you, Heaven is on Jupiter?"

"I'd tell you the atmosphere would murder everyone in Heaven."

"I'm not telling you that I know the location of Heaven," Jody says, discouraged.

"You don't know where God is keeping Heaven?" Morgan asks with faux shock.

"No. Only God has that GPS," Jody says.

"Well if he has a spare, we could really use it," Morgan responds, flopping more finished pancakes onto a tan plate that's ringed with blue floral etchings.

Jody unhelpfully lingers, the blanket flowing as he moves. Morgan smiles at him, then asks, "So you're the ghost that has been haunting us, huh?"

Jody looks at Morgan, confused, so she tugs on the blanket he's wrapped in.

"This? This is not a ghost sheet, it's a cape. Obviously. All seductresses... all male seductresses, like the vampire Dracula, wore capes."

"Oh, I'm sorry, I didn't realize that you're a male seductress," Morgan says, playing along.

"That's part of the male seductress code," Jody explains very seriously.

"Ah, a veil of secrecy to go with the cape of seduction."

"Speaking of clothes, why are you dressed like me at age 10?" Jody asks.

Morgan looks down at her raptor shirt, "There's a bunch of kids clothes upstairs. I think Rachel and I slept in Behringer's son's room last night."

"Who the fuck is Rachel?" Jody asks.

"Hummingbird," Morgan says, a little offended that we're all living under the same roof, yet Jody didn't even know Hummingbird's real name.

"Hummingbird is dressed like a child as well?" Jody asks, perking up.

"Ugh," Morgan snorts, once again coming in second to her pretty friend.

There's an awkward silence that's punctuated with Morgan shutting down emotionally.

"I think Wil saw him," Jody says, sort of spacing out, looking out the window above the stainless steel kitchen sink.

"What?" Morgan asks, an edge in her voice.

"I think Wil saw Behringer's son. That kid was probably the one messing with us last night. Apparently, he's also dead and a Casper," Jody says.

"Eek!" Morgan shrieks, like the oatmeal on the back burner spit at her, "I'm wearing some dead baby's clothes!"

"Yeah," Jody confirms casually, "You should probably take them off before he comes back for his stegosaurus shirt."

Morgan looks at Jody from the tops of her eyes, then turns the heat off on the burner. "Raptor," she says in a little voice.

"Pardon?"

"It's a raptor," Morgan says, then pouts while looking down at her big boobs.

"Lucky raptor," Jody says.

Morgan smiles at this comment, then at the meal she's prepared. She's been good with her diet so she'll allow herself to enjoy this somewhat unhealthy food without the usual guilt. She ran last night. She worked up a sweat last night. She fasted last night. Now, it's time to eat. The full menu is going to be pancakes, oatmeal, iced tea, and potato chips because... well, why not? There's more than enough food in the house. There's no produce or meat, but we clearly have enough resources to survive on for a while. Canned goods, and pastas, and jarred sauces are lined up neatly in the cabinets. It seems bizarre that a guy who was going to leave by his own hand would choose to leave with such full hands. Behringer must have received shipments of this stuff, like he was a shut-in. Morgan imagines that he must have first lost his son, then lost his will to continue on.

In the same house where a man isolated himself, a girl finds a family.

Walking out into the dining room, a plate in each hand, Morgan feels at home for the first time in years.

XIX. A Bunch Of People Ignoring Rob's Absence.

We admire the red, yellow, and black plaid tablecloth that has been spread on the table by Hummingbird.

Hummingbird's outfit- a tiny Spider-man T-shirt, and a pair of equally small shorts- is at odds with the temperature of the house and we can see the hair on her arm standing on end as she arranges the plates Morgan has brought out.

Once we all take our seats, Jody says, "Please join hands for grace."

"Is 'Grace' your real name, Hummingbird?" Kyle asks, and Hummingbird smiles then shakes her head.

Kyle is still wearing his black hoodie, but the makeup has been washed off his face and his blue piercing eyes seem almost naked now.

There's no protest of Jody's pre-meal ritual because he makes the band say grace before every show, and the girls go along with it because they're both well aware that they're seated with a space-metal Christian metalcore band. Plus, praying to God certainly can't hurt at this point.

Jody, still wearing his purple cape, reaches out to lock hands with Hummingbird and Morgan. Next to Morgan, to Jody's right, is Mike. Next to Hummingbird, to Jody's left, is Wil. We sit across from Jody, at the opposite side of the table, without a plate.

Everyone closes their eyes, then Jody begins, "Dear, Jesus-" but a loud, shaking thud from somewhere in the house causes Morgan to echo, "Dear, Jesus!"

Jody opens one eye, but keeps the two clammy hands locked in his own, and he quickly continues, "Okay, Jesus. Please make the demon entity who lives with us, um, not die because we would not pray for you to cause death, but maybe you could just make whatever it is lose its kneecaps or you could revoke its ghost superpowers. The power of Christ compels... Christ... to... help us. That sounded pushy. I apologize, Lord. I am your humble servant. Please protect us from the demons living in the basement."

Mike lets out a rapid-fire laugh, then says, "Amen?"

"Amen," we all respond.

It's silent for a moment, then Jody grabs the syrup to show us that it's okay to eat, but Hummingbird has to ask, "Have you gone down into the basement?"

Jody keeps pouring more and more syrup on his pancakes as he looks at Hummingbird. He tries to put together some sort of answer, but can only assemble, "The basement? Uh. We... are... already in the basement?"

"The syrup," Mike says, and Jody stops pouring at the point where half the bottle of Aunt Jemima coats his meal.

"The basement is somewhere you don't want to go. It's filled with stuff that girls hate. Like... what do girls hate?" Jody asks Wil.

Wil shrugs, then says, "Humidity, overcrowded movie theaters, the Republican National Convention."

"Yes," Jody responds appreciatively, "The basement is filled with hats and buttons from the Republican National Convention. You probably don't want to go down there. I think I saw a mural of George W. Bush painted on one of the walls."

Everyone starts eating, but Jody continues, "On a quiet night, some say, you can still hear Ronald Reagan uttering, 'I am paying for this microphone, Mr. Green.'" Jody segues into laughter as he ends his fabricated story. Looking around at the mildly confused, uninterested diners, Jody asks, "What? That is a famous quote that... ah, fuck it, let's go look in the basement," Jody relents. He really doesn't want to go into the basement, but he also doesn't want to sit and explain his joke. Fears are weird like that. Sometimes words can be scarier than fucked up basements.

"No. We're going to finish our food," Kyle says, suddenly sharing the dad role with his brother. Noticing the shift in the house, Kyle softens. He chooses positivity instead, "We're going to enjoy this beautiful meal that the lovely Morgan has prepared for us."

"Yes, it's not very often I get to dine on gruel in a haunted house. What a luxury," Wil says, then rolls his eyes.

"That's oatmeal you a-hole," Morgan says, then she reaches over and takes Jody's cape off his shoulders. Now that she's out of the kitchen, the room feels cold again, so she wraps the purple blanket around her shoulders like a shawl.

Mike bends his pancake in the middle like it's a taco, then says, "I'm waiting for maggots to come out of this food."

Everyone stops chewing, then swallows hard before gulping down their entire glass of iced tea.

Morgan, pouty, says, "You're such a glass half empty boy, Mike."

"No," Mike says, shaking his head, holding his pancake taco an inch from his mouth, "I'm a, 'The mere existence of this glass is a burden on me,' type guy."

"Since we're all here," Hummingbird says, pepping up, trying to shake off the negative energy, "I think you should tell us how you guys formed the band."

Everyone at the table is quiet.

Wil finally speaks up, quickly, without nostalgia, "Kyle drove around the east coast going to basement shows and stole us from other bands."

"You were like an emo Robin Hood," Morgan marvels.

Kyle shrugs, "I just wanted the best band. I wanted to do it right the first time."

"Is that why you wrote, 'Killing Floor?' Hummingbird asks.

"What?" Kyle responds, then nods his head, "Oh, yeah. That's why."

Hummingbird sings, *"I saw you there/ On the cold floor/ Abandoned/ In my care..."* then she tells Kyle, "That song always gives me chills."

"If you can quote our lyrics, how come you asked us how we met?" Wil asks, displaying an unusual curiosity.

"Because I wanted to see if you would tell me the same lie you tell everyone else. And you did," Hummingbird says.

There's a quiet moment at the table.

"Camping is nice," Morgan says, attempting to redirect the topic of conversation again.

"Morgan, this isn't camping. You just made food on a stove," Mike points out.

"It's like in-house camping. The old lady had all that gear because she's in-house camping too," Morgan says.

A pile we tried to forget; a melody we can no longer remember.

"She probably sacrificed those campers. She's probably a Wiccan," Wil says.

"Like the Wiccan Man?" Hummingbird asks.

Kyle shakes his head, and says, "That's *The Wicker Man*."

"I went to Wicker Man once, it was terrible. White girls with dreads and hippies everywhere," Jody says, then shakes his head.

"That's Burning Man," Kyle issues another correction.

"What is?" Jody asks as he wipes off his shirt, "Did I drop candle fire on myself? Sheiiit."

"No. What you went to is called 'Burning Man,'" Kyle states correctly.

"You little kids can keep speculating, but as your elder, I know things about old people. I know exactly why that old ass lady lives in these woods," Jody announces to the table, raising his chin so everyone is below him.

"Tell us the reason, oh old one," Morgan jokes.

"The old lady lives in the woods... because she's an old lady," Jody says.

"Wow, what insight," Wil responds.

"I'm not done yet. That old lady is an old ass lady and nobody wants some old ass pussy."

"Okayyy, Jody," Hummingbird says, not willing to have this conversation with brunch still on the table.

"Probably smells like a truck of baby powder flew off an embankment into a fish hatchery," Wil says, letting himself laugh in the house for the first time.

Morgan throws her napkin down, then says, "Wow. Didn't-"

"-but old ladies have needs too, they go through metal paws and they start-"

"-Jody, please tell me you did not just say 'metal paws,'" Kyle balks.

Morgan, in a high voice, squeals, "Of all the things he's just said-"

"-yes, someday you girls will go through metal paws," Jody says, proclaiming this as though he's dishing out hard truths, "It's part of getting older. So the paws part-"

"-Jody, if this is about an elderly woman moving into the woods so she can get oral from a brown bear, please stop telling your story," Kyle warns.

"If it was up to the Wiccans, weird old people will be able to marry black bears for interracial inter-species breeding and then you will have a bunch of half bear kids running around like the fuckin' Berenstain Bears," Jody informs us.

"Are you done?" Morgan asks, wanting to get everyone back to appreciating the meal she worked hard on.

Jody begins counting on his fingers, "Let's see? Metal paws, a beaver eating old person pussy, Wiccans monopolizing the in-house camping scene... yeah. I think I smashed that one out of the fuckin' park."

XX. How Did People Travel Before GPS?

We watch six nomads make this house of horrors a *home* of horrors.

The dishes are washed with the scolding hot tap water, then dried with a towel branded with a Behringer character. Everything is put back in its rightful place- maybe to keep the beings in the house at bay, maybe to place a little order in a house that seems to pulse with unpredictable chaos.

"So what do we do now?" Jody asks.

"We find the phone," Kyle says.

"I, um, looked, already," Morgan makes a clipped admission.

"You went walking around this house without a tough guy with rugged looks to protect you?" Jody asks, undoing the apron he had put on to do the dishes.

"You were asleep on the sofa, so you were sort of there," Morgan says.

"That's a risky move. We need to stay together," Kyle says.

"Did you go into the basement?" Mike asks.

Morgan shakes her head, and admits, "No, I was too scared for that."

"Good," Jody says, stamping out this possibility. It was finally light out, but this place is still creepy, and cold, and weird. All of those descriptors are also stereotypical basement attributes, so Jody shudders to imagine what horrors lurk below our feet.

"I think we have to open that door and walk down those stairs," Hummingbird says, grabbing onto Jody's shoulder, whispering in his ear.

"Why?" Jody mumbles, appreciating the touch, but not the suggestion.

"Because, we heard something down there during your prayer. Something fell down there... or something was thrown," Hummingbird whispers.

Jody, voice booming so the entire house can hear him, responds, "This is true, Hummingbird, but after we finished our prayer, our Lord and savior destroyed the beast and sent him back to the hell from whence he came."

"That means it's safe, Jody," Morgan says, putting her hand on Jody's other shoulder. Jody instantly drums up vintage fantasies plagiarized from issues of *Penthouse* he kept in a rusted oil drum in the woods near his house when he was 12. It was the businessman with the maid and his wife. It was the camper with his girlfriend and her best friend. It was that one really bizarre story about the two female aliens who needed to harvest human DNA with their soft mouths.

Primed to get the girls alone, Jody springs into action, and points at Kyle, then says, "You, Mike, Wil- you're hashtag *TeamInferior,* you'll search the upstairs for demons, treasures, and phones. I'll go in the basement with my team, hashtag *TeamAllTheGirlsNotCallingMyselfAGirl JustSayingIHaveAllTheGirlsAndYourTeamHasZeroGirls.* The teams will split up and look for cool shit, then the first person to find a phone is considered the hero who will save us all and receive all of our well wishes and admirations."

"Sounds fair," Mike says. He wants to go into the basement, but he also wants to get into that locked room at the top of the stairs. Teamed with the two men who have seen *something,* Mike is optimistic that he will be next to experience what Behringer is trying to show us.

"If you find the phone, here's what I need you to do," Kyle instructs the girls, "Dial 911 because they will know exactly where we are and people are probably worried about us. I bet they're searching already."

"Who's worried? Who would search for us?" Mike asks.

"Your mom... our other fans... besides Hummingbird and Morgan," Kyle lists, and hopes he won't be asked for more examples.

We stand awkwardly in the kitchen and try not to provoke or encourage Jody. He seems ready to pounce on the "other fans" comment, but he nods once to confirm the plan.

Jody and the girls go downstairs into the basement.

Kyle and the boys go upstairs to get into the locked room.

Which part of the house are we more curious about?

If we're more curious about the basement, we should continue on to the next page.

If we're more curious about the locked room, we should skip ahead to page 86.

It's our choice.

XXI. Jody And The Basement Babes.

We hear a *Plink, Plink, Plink* and we try not to think about it. We try not to focus on that repetitive drip. We focus on the wooden stairs under our feet. We feel them bow in the center so we move to the edge and grip the railing tight.

Despite making this exploratory trip into the basement in the middle of the day, Jody has to carry a candle, in addition to his piece of door frame, because the basement has no windows. This basement is dark, always.

"I swear if a bat flies near my face, I will barf," Hummingbird announces.

We reach the bottom of the rickety stairs. No bats are rustled. Hummingbird doesn't barf.

Jody's candlelight isn't nearly powerful enough to illuminate the length of this concrete foundation, and for the first time we realize that, sure, this house might not stretch for acres, but the basement might.

From what we can see, carefully crafted pieces of wooden furniture have been stacked and left to gather dust in this basement. Coat racks, and bookshelves, and deck chairs, and rocking chairs are stored in a haphazard way that creates an obstacle course. All it would take is a scared man and a fallen candle to turn this place into a concrete oven- there are no windows to escape out of and the stairs are made of wood. Perhaps we've been baited to enter this basement? Jody runs his hand along the back of a tall dresser. Nothing in the basement feels dry. It may not even burn. Jody thinks about how, last night, when Wil dropped his candle- it didn't go out, it didn't singe the carpet- it kept burning, but never left a destructive mark.

"This place is long enough to store my penis," Jody whispers, trying to will a *Penthouse* moment into reality.

Both girls display a disgusted snarl that's obvious even in the candlelight.

"My penis isn't really this big, that was an exaggeration to get you thinking about my penis. It's a comfortable size. Think of your favorite dick you've ever seen and you're probably not that far off," Jody says, looking back and forth between the girls on either side of him. The mood Jody is creating is distinctly "creepy basement" and not *Penthouse*. "My penis... is whatever size you prefer, it's like one of those adjustable baseball caps," Jody adds, trying to fix things.

"I bet your penis is as dusty as this place," Morgan responds, looking at the walls, a faded book-page yellow that stretches far beyond the range of the light.

"Psh. No. That is... you wish," Jody responds, lacking a comeback.

Confused and creeped out by pretty much everything in the basement, both tangible and intangible, Hummingbird asks, "Why would she wish that?"

"I don't know, why does the caged bird sing?" Jody asks, and the basement responds with a grainy squawk.

Both girls go rigid, and Morgan whispers, "Please tell me that the singing bird is inside a very secure cage."

"Please tell me that it's a very tiny one- like the type of bird that helps Disney girls get dressed," Hummingbird adds.

"Wait. Very tiny one?" Jody asks, but before he can get too offended, he's jolted by another squawk, which redirects his attention, and the girls become his tail as he moves between the furniture, toward the noise. They trust him, so they follow him. We're interested in the basement, otherwise we'd be upstairs, so we follow Jody as well.

As we approach the corner, a red glowing eye pierces through the darkness and becomes the focus of Jody's attack.

Without looking, Jody reaches to his right and grabs a three-pronged pitchfork that's hanging on the wall, then he motions with his candle for the girls to take two steps back. When the girls are a safe distance away, Jody hands Hummingbird his candle, then, aiming for the glowing eye, Jody quickly javelins the tool across the basement. This is the type of thing Morgan and Hummingbird were taught a man should do. Jody is taking charge and throwing pointy stuff at the scary weird thing. The noise that led us to this corner of the basement may not have come from a helpful little cartoon bird, but Jody's actions are some princely Disney shit. A plastic clatter occurs when a prong of the pitchfork finds the red glowing eye. It was a good shot and Jody excessively celebrates this fact.

The eye now faces the ceiling, unblinking, a red laser slicing through the dark. Whatever the eye is attached to is gurgling out a noise that's distinctly identifiable as an alarmed warning.

Jody takes his candle back, then we move in a stoplight formation toward the red light.

Red means stop. That's pretty universal. Yet we approach.

Jody's drifting candlelight continues to reveal a circle of insight into the portion of the basement we've found ourselves in- it passes across the furniture, across the toys, toward the glow.

One hand extended out to illuminate our way, one hand reaching back to "accidentally" paw one of the girls, Jody approaches the red eye. His stance relaxes when the candlelight reveals that the eye belongs to a plastic box, not a villainous bat creature.

"Pretty sure we were being victimized by a CB radio," Jody says, picking up the off-white hunk of plastic.

"Have you ever seen a CB radio before?" Morgan asks, studying the source of the squawks.

"Yeah. It... looks... like this?" Jody says, losing confidence.

"You're holding a baby monitor," Morgan says.

"But there are no babies here," Hummingbird says.

Jody begins turning down the volume on the monitor, then says, "At least we don't hear a baby on this motherfucker. I mean, imagine if it's not a ghost inhabiting this house, but instead a real human baby. *Horrifying*."

"I know right. That's how I feel every time I go to the doctor's office and he uses the stethoscope. I'm like 'Fuck, please don't hear a baby heartbeat in me again,'" Morgan says.

Jody and Hummingbird stare at Morgan.

"I'll be like, 'You can find a heart abnormality inside me, just don't find a normal baby's heartbeat.'"

"Dude, how many times has that situation arisen? Morgan, how old are you?" Jody asks.

"How old are you, dude?" she retorts.

"Okay. Point, Morgan. You just fenced me in the fuckin' eyeball," Jody says, admitting defeat.

"What's that weird drainpipe for?" Hummingbird asks, pointing to the edge of the sphere of light coming from the candle.

"It probably floods down here when it rains," Morgan says.

"Give me something to drop down the pipe," Hummingbird demands, moving closer to the six-inch wide hole.

Jody bends down and picks up an action figure of some shitty Behringer character off the ground, then hands it to Hummingbird. The girl in the child-size Spider-man shirt reviews the figure. Maybe she had a figure like this at home. Maybe she was a fan of Behringer, but felt too old to still enjoy the books.

Illuminating the concrete floor of the basement, we look down at the six inch circular pipe that extends up from the floor about a foot. Just how much does it rain in the Barrens? The surrounding soil is sandy and it hasn't rained at all since we've arrived here.

"I'm going to drop the boy wizard down the pipe," Hummingbird announces.

"We're a go for kid wizard in the pipe," Jody says into the baby monitor like it's a walkie talkie.

We giggle. Maybe the basement isn't so bad.

Hummingbird releases the action figure, then we hear it clink and clank as it hits the sides of the pipe on the way down.

Our ears lower to the concrete floor to listen for a splash or a thud.

The clanking noise seems to continue until it simply fades away.

We never hear the figure hit the ground.

A silence hangs in the basement, until the baby monitor crackles louder and plays the sound of the boy wizard continuing to clatter down the pipe.

XXII. Kyle And "The Boys."

We stand next to Mike as he gives up trying to open the locked door at the top of the stairs.

Wil and Kyle make eye contact, each one waiting for the other to try to break down the door. We miss our "leader" Jody, and this acknowledgment of a pronounced absence prompts Kyle to ask, "Do you think that Rob is okay?"

Neither Mike nor Wil look at Kyle, so he begins to ramble, "I mean, he disappears all the time. That's what Rob does- he disappears. But he always comes back. He comes back. Rob comes back," Kyle repeats, almost as a mantra, "He's going to come back and things will be okay."

As Kyle obsesses over Rob's safe return, the rest of our team silently remains distracted. Mike smoothes out his eyebrows with his fingers. Wil lights a cigarette, then stares down at his nearly empty pack of Pall Malls.

"He took the van home. He's safe at home right now. I swear, if he's at her apartment. If he sells any of our- no. You know what? Let him sell it. I want him to sell our stuff. It means he's still around, and that's all I want, for him to still be..."

Unwilling to remain a bystander to Kyle's panic spiral, Wil hands his cigarette to Mike, then turns toward the stairs. After moving Kyle to the left a couple of inches, Wil lifts his right leg, then sends a thundering donkey kick into the old wooden door. Wil's black boot leaves a footprint- a dust jacket for the story of how yet another locked door was splintered.

Surveying the brute force entry he just orchestrated, Wil says, "I didn't think I could do that," then takes his cigarette back from Mike, who, in his bizarre, staple-armed walk, scoots inside the room.

Mike turns right and looks at the wall, then says, "What. The. Fuck."

"What is it?" Kyle asks, walking into the room.

Wil waits just outside. He doesn't want another "what the fuck" moment. He wants to enjoy the rest of his cigarette.

Kyle and Mike stand frozen, staring at a wall, and we stand behind them, looking at the rows of Polaroids of little boys that cover the wall. The photographs were taken inside this house. Some of them were taken in this room.

"Behringer liked his grandkids," Kyle says, again hoping for the best.

"That's a lot of grandkids," Mike says.

This is why Behringer bought this house.

This is why Behringer wrote books for children.

This is why the desk is facing the door.

Hopefully, this is why the sick fuck killed himself.

Kyle's blood feels like it's crackling.

They were just little kids.

Innocent little kids.

"Let's burn this place down," Wil says, in the door frame, having only glanced at the photos before turning away.

"It's the only place we have. We'll probably die in South Jersey if we get revenge on this house. I'm not sure burning a dead perv's secret hideout is worth dying in Jersey for," Mike says. It's a compelling argument.

The house growls and pops. No. It's not the house. The noise is coming from *outside* the house. Wil walks to the window, fully focused on the noise. He pulls away discolored drapes, then peers outside.

After only a moment of surveillance, as quick as he kicked in the door, Wil rushes past his bootprint, then directly down the stairs.

Kyle looks at Mike, and we hear Wil screaming, "Rob! We're here."

XXIII. So... Apparently Rob Is Alive.

We rush out onto the porch and see Rob behind the wheel of the black band van. As Rob tries to put the van in park, everyone takes a collective step back. While it's triumphant that Rob is alive, the fact remains that he's behind the wheel so we're still worried not only for his life, but also for our own.

"He's not dead," Jody says, dashing out onto the porch.

Morgan bursts outside, and feels both relieved and afraid. She looks at the boy that she didn't know- then did know- then didn't know again.

Rob hops out of the driver's seat, and announces, "I found you, you sneaky fuck-faces!" This feat of successful driving is celebrated by Rob doing air guitar in front of us. Rob is the keyboardist of Lies As Language. He doesn't know how to play the guitar. Everyone shakes their head. It's good to see this big nosed Charlie Manson, even if he is already making the group wonder why his absence felt so significant. Despite Rob's uncouth nature, it's refreshing to encounter someone this happy in the Barrens.

Rob seems... not high, and that's good.

Kyle smiles and walks out to his old friend. We follow.

"Group hug," Rob says, opening his arms, his jean jacket accepting us in an embrace that makes it clear that yeah, he is high. He reeks of pot.

"Are you guys impressed that I didn't crash the van?" Rob asks, as we hold him.

"Where were you?" Mike asks.

"Passed out, then I woke up, then I took a huge shit in the woods, then-" everyone lets go of Rob at this point, "-I waited for you guys before I left, but, like, you guys didn't seem to be around anywhere. I looked around the van for a while, then I found our GPS so I turned that on and started driving. It got me pretty lost, no wonder we never use it."

"We don't have a GPS," Kyle says, "We just use our phones."

"You've clearly never looked in the glove box," Rob says.

"There's nothing in the glove box. I cleaned out the glove box so I could use it to store my cowboy hat," Jody says.

"There's a GPS in the glove box," Rob maintains, "Want me to go get it?"

"No, Rob, wait. Just explain this to me... you plugged this GPS in the cigarette lighter and it took you here?" Kyle asks.

"Yeah, I hit 'Home,' then started following the British robot's directions. She told me I arrived at my destination at the same time I saw your new home. I assumed this was the place you stole the GPS from, but then, bam, you all started rushing out onto the porch!"

"Well, come on in," Wil calls out, standing in the door frame.

At ease, in the daylight, reunited with our once-missing friend and the once-missing van, we begin to walk back to the house, and that's when we see Wil's eyes go wide. With those valuable instincts again coming to his rescue, Wil dashes into the house just as a blast thunders across the

Barrens, blowing everyone's hair forward from the sheer force. We all whip around to where the van is... was....

We stare at a pile of twisted steel and smoking black ashes.

"No," Kyle mouths.

Jody charges forward to inspect the scene.

Rob, crumbling to the ground, repeats, "No. No. No. No!"

We keep a distance, letting Jody once again become the leader we've silently elected him to be.

"My shit was in there- I mean, equipment. My equipment was in there," Rob says, twitching, attempting to cover his secret. Rob's manic demeanor slides off him like shower water and what's revealed is a hopeless and fragile frame.

"Our entire band was in that vehicle," Kyle says.

"Our way out of the Barrens was in that vehicle," Morgan says.

"I need that stuff. I need that stuff. I'm pretending like this never happened. I'm hallucinating. The van is fine. This is all in my head," Rob mumbles.

"For once I wish this was just one of your drug induced delusions," Kyle says to Rob.

"Is this another sniper situation?" Wil asks, reappearing in the doorway, fixing his Elvis coif then lighting a cigarette.

"The engine exploded," Kyle responds.

Wil exhales a cloud of smoke, then asks, "So, what, either we ignored the 'Check Engine' light for about 100,000 miles too long, or Rob picked up a hitchhiking bomb?"

Mike walks over and touches the ashes, then marvels aloud, "Everything is already cool."

"No, Cliff. There is nothing cool about this," Jody says.

"Do you know how long it takes for a van to burn to ashes? A while. Trust me," Wil states, then stares off into the woods.

"Whatever burnt this van, it wasn't fire. Look, the ground is perfect, none of the leaves are singed at all," Jody says, poking the area with a stick, careful not to get any of the possibly toxic char on him. "It's like someone torched the van, then brought it back here."

"I saw what happened," Wil says.

"What happened?" Mike asks.

Wil shrugs, "That shit blew up."

"Maybe Jody is right. Maybe they didn't burn the van," Morgan says, "...maybe the van was microwaved."

Jody smiles a pleased smile at Morgan, then the smile fades and he declares, "If whoever is toying with us has the power of microwaves, then we're super fucked."

"Let's think critically here... what could cause the van to explode?" Kyle asks the group.

"Recalls that were too expensive to fix, so the company covered them up?" Mike suggests.

"Fireball asteroids from space?" Morgan suggests.

"Atlantis City aqua-people with some military surplus rocket launchers?" Jody presumes.

It has to be something natural. There has to be a natural explanation.

Kyle reviews the options, but none click. He walks over to the black frame, touches it, then walks away quickly. "Give me your phone," he demands from Rob.

"I lost it, and I don't know the WiFi password for the woods anyway," Rob says.

"Fuck!" Wil yells.

"It's okay, dude. I'm sure my phone will turn up," Rob says.

"None of us have phones," Mike tells Rob.

"None of you?"

"Our phones exploded just like the van," Mike explains.

"That's awesome for you, Morgan," Rob says.

Morgan blushes and nods her head.

"How is that awesome?" Wil asks, trying to remain calm.

"Because Morgan's phone fucking sucked. We took pictures with it and they came out so muddy that we looked like shadow people. It was like a Jobs era iPhone."

"But I bet it made calls. And, right now, that's really all we fucking need," Wil says.

"This house is the problem. The GPS brought Rob here for a reason. This is part of some sick plan. We're leaving this house," Kyle says, more to himself than anyone else.

"We're in Jersey, so..." Hummingbird says.

"We're in *South* Jersey," Wil says.

"Shit. You're right. We're fucked," Hummingbird easily concedes.

"This is what happens when you trust a 609 girl. You *never* trust a 609 girl. They are all damaged and fucking insane," Wil says.

"You just watched your van spontaneously combust, and your beloved guitar is gone. You're officially damaged and seeing insane shit. Guess you're a 609 girl now too," Morgan says.

Kyle, forever trying to keep things rational, says, "We'll pick a direction, then we'll walk for an hour. If we don't find anything in that hour, we'll return to the house. The next day, we'll set out in another direction."

"How are we going to know when it's been an hour?" Hummingbird asks.

"We'll walk until the sun is there in the sky," Mike says, raising his finger toward the tops of the trees.

"This is some prehistoric shit," Jody says.

"We're better off separating, each walking for an hour, then all returning back to report what we found," Hummingbird says. "That's four directions in one day. It will get us out of here quicker."

"'Let's split up,' is a *Scream* rule, I think."

"'Crop top sweaters are in,' was also a *Scream* rule. Maybe it's time to update the rule book," Morgan says.

"Crop top sweaters were 'in' in *Clueless,* and *Clueless'* fashion is iconic," Hummingbird responds.

"I'm pretty sure that Dee wore a top hat in *Clueless,*" Morgan counters.

"But Cher wore chic workout clothes in a post-Jane Fonda, pre-Lululemon world," Hummingbird asserts.

"We're going to do this together, we're not splitting up," Kyle says, attempting to redirect the tangent that the conversation has taken.

"So we're 'Rollin' With The Homies' which is still very *Clueless,*" Hummingbird says.

"All of us seem very clueless," Wil says, as puffs of his guitar blow in the wind.

"We're going, now," Kyle says, walking in a straight path from the door of Behringer's house, out into the woods.

We follow.

As Wil passes the ash pile, he glances at a piece of rectangular plastic sticking out from the carbon, and only makes it two more steps before he doubles back to pick up the familiar item. It's the Punchcunt Love EP. Far in the woods, tortured screams echo. Wil looks back to study everyone's reaction, and when he's sure no one is looking, in a single fluid motion, he slides the warped CD case into the back pocket of his pants, then untucks his white shirt, leaving fingerprints of black char that illustrate his actions.

We walk in a line, each of us only diverting from the straight path if there's a tree or picker bush in our way and after we pass it, we instantly correct our course. We're trudging through a post-blast moment that makes no sense, and Jody construes our silence as an open door for a story. He doesn't ask us if we'd like to hear something interesting, he just starts talking, and we listen because we need a distraction.

"It's terrifying how dangerous automobiles can be," is how it starts, then Jody continues, "One time, I read this story about a truck holding 20 Mexicans. It was an F250... you know what one of those look like? It's a big bastard. It would put a Grand Cherokee to shame. So these Mexicans, they were sneaking into our country because, oh, I don't know, maybe America is the shit. I presume the back story was that a Mexican got the truck and other Mexicans kept being like, 'I don't want to be stereotypical, but can I get a ride with you too?' Apparently, the driver was like, 'Yeah, hop in,' so eventually they got 20 people in this truck. Mr. Math tells me that's at least four Mexicans in the front- I feel sorry for the guy who got the gear shift, but desperate times... So let's see, that's four Mexicans, then there is probably eight Mexicans on the bench seat because you have four across, then Mexicans sitting on other Mexican's laps, then you just gotta fit, eight, plus, four, twelve, like, shit, I don't know, eight in the bed of the truck- it actually seems similar to how we used to travel to gigs."

"Jody. What the fuck is the point of this?" Wil asks.

"All I'm saying is the truck lost control and rammed into a tree and most of those Mexicans died, so I think that the lesson here is we should not be overloading vehicles or they will explode and this is Hummingbird's fault because she fucked up the numbers by letting Morgan come with us."

Morgan lets out an extended sigh.

"We don't think the van exploding is her fault," Mike tells Jody.

"Know what?" Jody says, "The more I think about it, the more the numbers simply do not make sense. If I make some additional calc- yup. Figured it out."

"I know I'm going to regret this, but what did you figure out, Jody?" Wil asks.

"I know how they got 20 people in there."

"You just expl-"

"-the crash was a massacre of 20 Mexican *midgets*. Incredible," Jody says, shaking his head in disbelief at this scene.

"Did you just sit in awe about a complete lie you created in your head?" Wil asks.

"It's not a lie. That's the work of Mr. Math," Jody says.

"Well can we ask Mr. Math how, in New Jersey, we can walk for long stretches of time without hitting any sign of civilization? No roads, no paths, no buildings, no signs, no trail markings. How the fuck did we not pass a mall like six times just walking to the mailbox?" Wil asks.

"What?" Kyle responds, quickly turning around.

Wil brushes shoulders with Kyle, then stops to have the conversation. "Relax. It was a joke about the consumer culture that pervades-"

"-no. It's good. It's genius," Kyle says, retracing his steps back toward the house.

"I thought it was a little funny, but..." Wil responds modestly.

"Come on," Kyle says, gesturing for us to follow him.

"Where are we going?" Morgan asks.

"There are no malls close to us," Mike responds, "This isn't the good idea that Kyle thinks it is."

"Are we turning the house into a Forever 21 because we'd have no competition?" Hummingbird asks.

"If you build it, they will come," Mike says.

Kyle moves faster and faster through the monotonous surroundings, and we have no choice but to keep pace with him. He's still infected with an optimistic hope that we want to catch like a cold.

Eventually, the pines part to reveal the house, just as we left it, front door wide open. Of course the house is still there- it wants us to return. Despite this predictable certainty, we weren't totally sure the house would be where we left it. There's this weird sensation we have that the house is a prop- it feels like a movie set- something that could be pulled apart and wheeled away.

We trust Kyle has figured out a solution because this is a boy who, after viewing the Polaroids upstairs, is now aware that this house was the site of habitual and perpetual evil. He stepped back inside Behringer's house without a second thought. We choose to follow him, because the other option is to make another trek into those woods that repeat such regularity, they could lull us to sleep.

Kyle immediately begins his search, but we still don't trust this house and the thought of moving through it recklessly scares us. We wait at the bottom of the stairs, staring down the wood paneled hallway, until Kyle appears and announces, "Mail. Look for mail."

Normally, this would be a simple request, but in Behringer's house, being asked to "look around" is the last thing we want to do.

We make our way into the living room as a group, then gravitate toward a wooden cabinet in the dining room. Jody begins opening the drawers. Inside, there are all the components you'd need to write a letter- pens, envelopes, stamps, even stationary with "R.F. Behringer" embossed on it- but nothing with an address stamped on it.

We check the kitchen to see if the boxes of food have any shipping labels. They don't.

We check the living room for a receipt to see if we can find a store Behringer seemed to frequent. An address would either give us a location, or a destination to set out toward.

A voice from deep in the house is ranting, "There's no mail in this entire house. No mail. How is there not a single letter? He was a writer. How is there not a bill? How is there not a fucking Bed Bath and Beyond coupon?"

"Here's a bill," Jody says, removing a makeshift bookmark from one of Behringer's own works. On the cover of the book is a screenshot from the film adaptation of the novel. Grant Anders, at age thirteen, grits his teeth as he points a wand at an ugly ogre-like creature. Grant stopped working after the boy wizard movies were over. This absence now chills us like Rob's did.

We all crowd around Jody to read... the P.O. Box number on the bill.

Behringer was even hiding from his mail. He wanted to create his own little world in this house, and he succeeded. He bought his food in bulk. He got a P.O. box so no one would show up here, even the mailman. There would be no reason for someone to stop at this house, unless they were trapped in the Barrens. Behringer could, and most likely did, create a little society that he ruled over with impunity in his house. In the end, Behringer was overthrown because of his own actions, as all rulers who abuse their power eventually are. This home ended up claiming Behringer and the world he left behind seems to have an insatiable hunger.

"So, how the hell did you guys get invited to R.F. Behringer's house?" Rob asks, looking out a window that faces the thousand acre backyard.

"Behringer killed himself here," Wil says.

"The door was open," Mike says.

Rob turns to us, then his eyes go wide, and he asks, "Are you telling me we have this entire house to ourselves?"

Kyle storms back into the room, then says, "There's no electricity. It's not ideal to-" but Rob puts his hand on Kyle's shoulder, then interrupts, "-dude, why are you being so uptight? Weed doesn't need electricity."

"You don't want to be high in this house," Kyle warns, as Rob starts rummaging through the pockets of his jean jacket.

"So what, there's no TV or something? We'll go look at shit in the basement then. Problem solved."

"We're walking to go get help," Kyle says, not willing to spend another night in this house.

Still fiddling in his pocket, Rob says, "You need a way to relax. You know... maybe..."

"I'm not exactly in the partying mood," Kyle says, then Rob pulls out a big bag of weed from the interior pocket of his jacket, "This!"

"Brandishing a bag of weed isn't going to instantly put me in a party mood. I'm not a Neanderthal," Kyle says, but Jody immediately pushes past his brother, saying, "Oh shit, look at those nugs. This is KB. Let's go into the mini-office. There's some-"

"-no. Guys. No," Kyle says, protesting.

"Why are you so scared of fun?" Rob asks.

"I'm scared because we're trapped! I'm scared because our phones are gone! I'm scared because our van blew up! I'm scared because we are in serious trouble!" Kyle yells. Quietly, he adds, "I'm scared of what I saw in that window."

"Dude, that's the beauty of it, we're so deep in the woods that no one can narc on us," Rob responds, "If we see people peeping in the windows, we can be sure it's just a hallucination."

"And if it's not, we'll have been saved," Mike points out.

Inspired, Jody declares, "The plan for tonight is to have a party so dope that people from miles around show up. Once all the weed is smoked, we'll bum a ride, borrow a cell, then we'll make a call on speaker so it doesn't blow off our face muscles."

Rob lays it out for Kyle, "Dude, think about this. It's Friday... maybe. No. It's Sunday? Well. The day isn't important, what *is* important is that you ain't got no van, you ain't got no job, and you ain't got shit to do. None of us have jobs. Well, maybe the girls do."

"No one is hiring someone with those tattoos," Jody says, then points to Morgan and adds, "This one probably has a job though."

"I do. I work for Michaels," Morgan responds.

"Michael's? She works for you, Mike? What's she do, stuff all those dead animals in your living room?" Rob asks earnestly.

"Michaels is a craft store," Morgan clarifies.

"Do you get a store discount on top of the already marked down Halloween merchandise?" Mike asks.

"I do indeed. My room is decorated for Halloween year round."

"I hope to see that someday," Mike responds, and hearing this makes us feel hopeful. Maybe this house isn't cursed.

Jody steps in, "Listen, it's clear there are attractions and common interests abound, and I think these are the building blocks to a night of weed smoking and maybe petting. It could evolve into that. Who knows? We'll never find out if you keep standing around looking like y'all just found out 2Pac died. We have to stay in tonight. We can't go outside. We might explode."

"Is that really a possibility?" Hummingbird asks, her voice metering up.

"No one is going to explode," Kyle says.

Jody begins to count on his fingers, "Let's see. Van explodes- outside. Phones explode- outside. Things that have exploded inside? Maybe my incredible speed when I was running away from various scarinesses, but other than that, nothing. I lost my van today, I lost my cell phone yesterday, I lost my instruments today, apparently I had a GPS I didn't know about and I lost that too, which blows. The GPS on my phone was fu-"

"-fine. Fine," Kyle says, giving up on today's hunt.

Jody, deadly serious, says, "I think we can all agree that we were sort of being pussies before. Rob always goes missing and does dumb shit, then once again, he went missing and did some dumb shit and we lost our minds and assumed that the boy wizard hermit curse befell him, then a Wiccan made crafts from his bones. That's pretty fucked so I think we need to be a little more mature in regards to our conduct. Now let's go get high while looking at weird shit in the basement."

XXIV. American Folklore - The Art Scene.

We stand in the basement and wiggle out a chill that reminds us of waiting in the merch line in Connecticut. The show at Scott Trunkett's was supposed to be the end of Lies As Language appearing together in a basement of doom. It was the end of worrying about their guitars clipping exposed piping or piercing through weak ceiling tiles. It was supposed to be high ceilinged plazas and theaters and ballrooms forever now. If Lies As Language ever showed up in a dive again, it was supposed to be their choice. Yet, here we are, in a basement not of our choosing- again.

"If that door at the top of the stairs doesn't open, we'll be trapped down here forever," Mike says, looking around the candlelit windowless basement.

"Cliff, your preoccupation with this house murdering us and rats eating our flesh off is becoming a distraction," Jody says loudly.

Hummingbird, now on the lookout for flesh eating rats, notices a folded green blanket atop a wooden toy chest. She picks up the blanket, then snaps it in the cold, frozen air. After she walks through the static of the dust, Hummingbird finds a bare part of the concrete floor, then lays the blanket down and smoothes it out. This large green blanket is perfect to share with friends. It's the type of blanket that would be ideal to build a fort with. It's the type of blanket that would've been ideal to build a fort with when we were kids, but we're no longer kids- which is a positive in this house.

Morgan walks over and sits down on the indoor picnic blanket, then looks over at the boys loitering in a dingy basement, each of them adopting a different pose like they're shooting an album cover.

Jody, raising from his bent pose, proclaims, "Let there be light," then a lighter is flicked and an oil lamp is lit. "Let's get puritanical up in this motherfucker," Jody celebrates.

Rob's eyes go wide, as he marvels, "Whoa, that's a crazy looking bong. Where did you find that?!"

"It's an oil lamp," Hummingbird points out.

"It was sitting on the basement floor here the entire time," Jody says. "This is a sign that we need to find light in the darkness."

Wil coughs a phlegmy noise of disapproval, then sits down next to Kyle on the green blanket.

"Kyle, what did you see upstairs?" Mike asks, and the timing of this question feels bizarre. This silent man never initiates a conversation, but now that things are mellow, he did. This question wasn't to add to the atmosphere, it was to bastardize it. For a moment, we consider that Mike wants to see the worst that this house has to offer.

Kyle doesn't answer Mike, he merely stares into Jody's lamp.

Since it's quiet, Mike continues, "Girls and Jody, did you know that inside that once-locked, now very open room on the second floor, there's a picture-wall of Behringer's victims. The pictures are of children. The children are-"

"-why would you tell me that shit, Cliff?" Jody barks, setting down the lamp, then sitting down Indian style on the blanket. "Now I have to celebrate in a house that I've just been told has a second floor creepy sex pedo museum. Who knows what type of butt-hurt spirits are floating up there."

"Suddenly the basement doesn't seem so bad," Morgan says.

Jody points at Morgan, then says, "Exactly. A very minimal number of buttholes have been violated down here, I suspect. It's just a feeling I have. I don't have hard evidence to back it up. Some people can sense danger, like Spider-man or 50 Cent; my instincts are sort of like that," he explains, then apologizes for his shortcomings, "I'm going to warn you in advance that there's a very good chance that this lamp I've found which is currently illuminating our smoking sesh will mostly likely explode hot oil everywhere and turn us into burn victims. I'll take full responsibility for it, should the event happen."

"Could that happen?" Hummingbird asks.

"I'm not going to lie to you. It's almost certainly going to happen," Jody responds, then he begins to twist a key-like nob on the lamp brightening the basement further.

"Could you just stop fiddling with that bomb and get high with us?" Kyle asks.

"I wish someone said that to Ted Kaczynski, then a lot of people would still have hands," Mike says.

"I hear ya. Angry people need to put down the bomb and pick up the bomb ass weed," Jody agrees, then says, "I'm going to lead us in a prayer so that if I explode us while smoking pot, God will forgive our THC dusted souls."

"Is this really the time?" Wil asks, taking possession of the freshly rolled joint from Rob, then lighting it with his lighter.

"Yes. We might all be dead soon," Jody says.

Rob, mad that the party atmosphere keeps being redirected, says, "Dude, don't ruin this for me. I will time out your ass like the-"

"-don't," Kyle says, putting his hand over the barrel of a verbal weapon that was about to be shot directly into Jody's fear receptors.

"Dear Lord," Jody says loudly, "Bless us, filthy pot smokers, as we sit next to this lamp that not only illuminates this creepy basement, but also serves as an acknowledgment that no matter how cold this house is, your flame burns inside, warming us to our very core. We have your love, so we don't need luxurious giant green blankets- they are mere extravagances you have bestowed upon us. Please allow this lamp to safely burn for as long as you see fit. Please also protect our skin, which you have so generously chosen to be whi-"

"-amen!" Morgan yips out to slam the breaks on the prayer.

"Amen," the group repeats.

"Look behind you," Wil says, breathlessly to Kyle.

"Stop it," Hummingbird demands, raising a finger to Wil.

Kyle realizes that Wil isn't playing a Jody-like joke, so he turns to see what has made Wil go an even starker shade of pale.

In black ash, on the basement wall, is a message in a child's handwriting.

Jody looks at the scrawled warning, but then notices the joint is being passed to him and this redirects his focus instantly.

Mike takes the lighter out of Jody's hand, then with his left arm pinned to his side and his right hand holding the lighter up, he moves the flame toward the message.

"It's wrong," Jody says.

"What's it mean?" Hummingbird asks, paranoid.

"That's Lies As Language up there," Jody says. "We have a fan."

"Those aren't our lyrics," Kyle responds.

"They're the lyrics to 'Reflection,'" Mike reminds the lead singer. "Misquoted, but they're ours."

"He was probably rushing through it and messed up," Morgan says. "You know how when someone texts you something and you have the perfect joke as a response, so you start typing super frantically to get your joke out before they say something else that would ruin the setup, but AutoCorrect chooses the wrong word and now there's this misplaced word which ruins your joke momentum? That's probably what happened with the ghost boy, but he was just like, 'Ah, fuck it. They'll get the drift.'"

"But people who constantly correct grammar and spelling are of the devil so a demon spirit would have perfect grammar," Hummingbird points out.

"This is like the time we let Rob print the fliers and half the information was missing because he got distracted mid-statement," Jody says, laughing at the moment, trying to recruit others.

"Dude, fuck you. I apologized for that and I learned from my mistake," Rob says, a wound opened.

Hummingbird continues to study the unfamiliar words scrawled on the wall. "You don't have a song named 'Reflection,'" she says, sure of this fact.

"It's unreleased," Wil growls.

"It was supposed to go on the album," Jody says.

"But..." Hummingbird responds, looking to the boys who universally seem unwilling to have this discussion. Jumping in to save Hummingbird, and giving her a reprieve so she can take her turn in the rotation, Morgan asks, "How did a guy in the middle of the woods get your lyrics?"

"I was wrong. We don't have a fan here..." Jody remarks, as he walks toward the writing, then he points at the wall, and finishes his statement, "...we have a fucking super-fan!" He looks back at everyone with an open-mouthed smile, then lists, "This guy must have the album cuts, the demos, the B-sides, the remixes, the acoustic shit, and the unreleased shit. Incredible."

"But, *how* would he get something we didn't release?" Wil asks.

"How did the song go?" Hummingbird asks, now feeling like an un-super-fan with only iTunes cuts.

"*You see you and you don't see,*" Mike says, quietly reading the wall, fixing the words, then adding the additional lyrics, "*The ground beneath you trembling.*"

"What's it mean?" Hummingbird asks the lead singer.

Kyle's eyes go everywhere except on us, and that's when he sees another sign. "Look," he says, then points the orange tip of the joint at the wall.

"You mean that weird crack?" Hummingbird asks.

On the wall, slowly expanding, are two rust colored semicircles pressed together.

"Yeah," Kyle says, then takes the lighter.

"It sort of looks like ass cleavage," Rob says, as his red eyes study the crack.

"Sure does," Jody agrees gleefully, then he walks over and pretends to lick the ass-crack that has appeared.

"Guys, don't you think whatever is fucking with us is going to get mad if we keep turning his messages into penis jokes?" Hummingbird asks.

"This is a butt joke. I haven't even drawn a penis going into the butt yet," Jody says.

"Right, but you were going to," Morgan says.

Not denying it, Jody merely responds, with a *Braveheart*-like delivery, "To take away our penis jokes, is to take away our souls."

"But- but- I," Hummingbird stammers, until Rob hops in and demands, "Give the joint back to Hummingbird," like he's a doctor issuing a prescription.

Hummingbird shakes her head no, but Rob says, "I think you need it. We're all just unwinding and you're..."

"I'm not unwinding," Hummingbird says, filling in his sentence.

"Kinda," Rob says carefully, then adds, "I mean, you smoked, but you still seem... not sad, but..."

"Guarded," Hummingbird says.

"I think it's healthy to be guarded- just not all the time. You'll have to let your guard down to get through this," Rob offers, stoking the pot-talk.

"Tonight or in general?" Hummingbird asks.

"I think in general," Rob says, looking up at the lyrics on the wall, "You should."

"Unwind?" Hummingbird asks.

"Yes."

"I don't know if that's such a good idea," Hummingbird says.

"You have to or you'll go crazy," Rob offers.

Jody watches Rob and Hummingbird in their exchange. He sits down next to Wil, then says, "If Rob fucks Hummingbird, I will Behringer myself."

"You'll switch to little boys?" Wil asks.

"I was trying to imply that I'd commit suicide, Behringer style, then I'd probably come back and haunt this house way better than Behringer or these fanboy ghosts are doing right now. Dead Jody would be creating totally original scares, not shit we've seen on Netflix before. I mean, Dead Jody would also spend a significant amount of time watching Hummingbird in the shower, but then he'd knock over books and shit. Everyone would see the classics *and* the new stuff. Dead Jody would be like the Tarantino of the specter world."

"Jody, can you stop talking? Can you just stop? There are messages being written to us on the wall," Morgan says, finally refocusing our attention on the words that were initially considered a fan letter.

"I can't stop, Morgan. It's who I am and... And..." Jody pauses, then incorrectly reads the situation, and says, "I'd also watch you in the shower. Don't worry. You keep my ghost updated on your shower schedule and I'll be there, writing shit in the fogged mirror and watching you lather up."

"Don't pity-perv on me, Jody," Morgan snips, "Do it because your ghost boner demands it, not just as a prerequisite to complete so you can move on and see Hummingbird nude."

Jody, somewhat bashful, admits to Morgan, "I'd be lying if I said I wasn't strangely attracted to your untoned body & lame ass tits."

Before Morgan can process this backhanded compliment, Mike starts yet another conversation, "I was just thinking... when we were talking with Cherokee Jack, he mentioned a devil living in these woods."

"Oh shit. Here we go," Hummingbird says, lying down on the blanket, then pulling an edge piece over her body like she was about to go to sleep.

Mike frowns, then adds, "Doesn't it seem weird for him to mention it, then all of the sudden..."

"Morgan, tell them the creepy ass story," Hummingbird sighs.

"Don't say it like that," Morgan responds, "It sounds like I used to date the Jersey Devil or something. Which I didn't, FYI."

"So is he the devil-devil or is he just the Jersey Devil?" Kyle asks, wanting to know whose fire fueled eyes he looked into last night.

Wil wants to light one of his final Pall Malls, but he resists. Time frames are beginning to expand and suddenly his pack of cigarettes becomes an endangered resource until things resolve themselves.

Jody looks up at the unreleased words on the wall, then says, "I think people want a polar opposite of God so they made the devil singular, but those people underestimate God's power. If the devil was as strong as God, the world would be a lot scarier place. I think, due to being overpowered, the devil made sure he existed in massive numbers. I mean, I once rented a car to these blonde twins who were convinced that there were demons in Maryland."

Everyone is quiet as Jody's discourse veers from the vulgar to a profound statement regarding the battle between good and evil, then back to what surely will end up being a story about how he made sweet love to twins to cleanse the state of Maryland of demons.

"Wait, but who the fuck is the New Jersey Devil?" Rob asks.

This is dangerous. Usually, when you repeat an evil villain's name three times, said being appears. This knowledge sends the group close to each other on the blanket. We wait for the Jersey Devil to show himself. Rob studies the wall for additional etchings.

The baby monitor begins to crackle static in the far corner of the basement. Maybe, if this was an episode of *Ghost Hunters*, the static could be recorded and processed and pitched up and "voices" could be heard. Lies As Language lost all their audio equipment in the van so this analysis is not an option.

"Ugh, well, ugh, okay, this is a dumb story," Morgan says.

"Stop right there," Jody says, as though he's afraid of discussing the New Jersey Devil in this house.

We all pause, and fill with fear.

When he doesn't elaborate further and our anticipatory gaze becomes too much, Jody barks, "What? I'm doing you guys a favor. If a woman has the presence of mind to say that her story has no point, then you know the story will be extra shitty because most of their stories simultaneously go nowhere and everywhere, yet they think they're Willa Shakespeare or something."

We're all silent. Even the house seems minorly appalled by this statement.

"Please continue," Mike says, giving Morgan permission to tell her story.

Jody stands up and waits for someone to tell him to sit down. No one does.

"Jody, you can go if you don't want to hear Morgan's story," Mike says, and a hate burns behind his eyes as he refuses to let Jody prevent Morgan from speaking.

"Psh. Okay. I'm outtie. Enjoy hearing about puppy dogs and babysitting and shit," Jody says, then stomps into the darkness like a surly ghost failing to scare a second tier metalcore band with his writing on the wall.

"Sorry about that, he likes to be the one with the stories," Kyle explains.

Morgan looks into the darkness, searching for Jody, which makes Wil beg, "Just tell the story, if for nothing else than to get a break from whatever you're afraid might be looming near Jody." This inadvertently serves as a reminder that we aren't hanging out in Morgan's living room-we're hanging out in the basement of a house so remote that it could imply guilt merely by placement alone. We're in a house so cold that it feels unwelcoming, even when benign. We're in a house so bizarre it remains distinctly South Jersey.

"Okay," Morgan whispers, her voice quietly excited as she exhales the four letters. We scoot our butts closer to conserve our body heat in a room that's getting more frigid as each minute passes. The lantern flickers and this truly feels like indoor camping. No one here has ever been camping, but it's always been on the to-do list. When pictures pop up on Facebook of friends sleeping in a truck bed or looking out at a stretch of preserved woods, we wanted to be there. Morgan for the intimacy; Wil for the privacy; Kyle for the freedom; Hummingbird for the distance; Mike for the early morning hunt.

"There's this story about... okay, just hear me out on this before you start making fun of me... every place has its own spooky legend, ours just happens to be super fucking stupid because people from South Jersey thought it up. Anyway, this is the story... of the Jersey Devil."

We wait a full ten-count for a noise, a message, a voice.

When nothing happens, Morgan feels secure enough to begin her story, "There was this lady who lived in the middle of the Pine Barrens with a bunch of Pineys and she was a huge skank or something. You know how huge skanks just keep making more babies? Well, this one had like 12 kids and I guess after that her vagina looked super tragic and she couldn't take any more babies shooting out of there so she said that she'd give the 13th baby to the devil, maybe, like, in exchange for some supernatural vaginoplasty after she popped out lucky number 13. So, the devil took the deal, because, I'm told, there's a lady hormone that makes you really love your kid no matter how busted it looks so most ladies don't give up their babies, which makes the kid a prize for the devil. Ms. Leeds was not like most ladies, and it's a good thing most ladies aren't like Ms. Leeds. I mean, she had 12 kids. That's like 2.5 boy bands- no one should be able to release that much evil into the world. So, she has this 13th kid, and I guess he had the face of a horse, and some horns, but he also had wings and stuff, so he flew away."

Slowly, something emerges from the shadows.

Everyone huddles together on the green blanket.

Jody moves into the light, casually re-entering the safety of the lantern's glow because the story has scared him.

Rob, high, confused, asks, "So, he still lives in a house in the Barrens?"

Morgan shakes her head, then says, "No, he escaped out the chimney."

Kyle is silent because the mental sketch Morgan created happens to match what he saw in the window on the second floor.

"But he could come back," Rob points out.

"If you looked like something that should be painted on the side of a pedovan, would you start showing up at random places?" Morgan asks.

"Could I breathe fire?" Jody asks, from the edge of the lantern light.

"No," Rob says, but follows that up with, "Can the Jersey Devil breathe fire?"

Morgan shakes her head no.

"Okay, then I'd just probably stay at home and play Xbox," Jody decides.

""Maybe Behringer was using the legend for his next book, and that's why he ended up in Jersey," Mike theorizes.

"This dude wrote about wizards and shit. He didn't care about vengeful demon corpse babies with large extended families," Jody points out. He sits back down on the blanket, then buries his hands in a bag of chips that Morgan had brought down to pacify the impending munchies, knowing that no one would want to run up the stairs for a snack. Morgan had also brought down a "pee bucket" because no amount of pee pain is worth a solo trip away from the presumed safety of staying in a group.

"He probably just wanted to finish the last book in the series using some of this lore, then move onto something different. Something a little more sinister," Mike says, "Maybe he's still writing... on the wall?"

"Enough about the fucking wall. All of them- basement walls, Polaroid walls- if they weren't protecting us from bears and dragons, I'd say tear every wall in this place to the ground" Wil says.

"Maybe Behringer went into the woods when he knew he was gonna die. Just like my dog, Scrambles," Hummingbird says, then pouts.

"I don't think many guys have that instinct," Mike responds.

"Who knows. I mean, he spent a decade of his life pretending to be a boy wizard. At some point, you have to grow up," Wil says.

"What's your point, Wil?" Jody responds, and a heavy moment waivers between the two men. Jody's dream is to be like his rock star idols, but the only way he's like them is the fact that they're getting old, fast. The dream is getting further out of sight and Jody's vision is worsening, further complicating things. He wants to be a famous drummer, but it's almost as though his arms are shortening with age.

"How do you retire from your art? What do you do to get your mind off of it? Do you go on vacation and do stuff you hate if your job is something you love?" Kyle asks. It's unclear if this is a question for the boys, or *about* the boys. To stop the ugly silence, Kyle answers his own question, "Going off into the woods seems like what you do."

"Apparently it is," Mike says.

"I don't get why men don't go on a rampant sex spree before they die. Why go into the woods when you could be pleasing your wood?" Morgan asks, then adds, "Serious question."

This sends Hummingbird further under the cover of the green blanket. This is her cue to go to sleep. There's a 50/50 chance that these boys think their days are numbered. Morgan's "what if" might be planting a seed regarding planting seeds that Hummingbird would want to spray weed killer on.

Jody answers the question, "You find your faith before you're about to die and you want your paperwork to be in order as you reach those gates."

"Please," Wil says. "The reason why guys don't do it is because by the time you're dying of an old man disease, you're pretty weak, and sex sprees are just too much work, unless you're a very careful planner. And imagine the eulogy: 'Wilem died doing what he loved...'"

The group giggles, then a wave of static washes over the basement, matching the laughter, then eventually overpowering it.

"It's just the intercom," Jody says.

Is it? a crackle over the intercom responds.

Jody turns off the lantern, then we all get under the big green blanket. It's totally dark, as the static fills the basement.

Rob lights a candle and angles it sideways so it doesn't burn the blanket. The light is just bright enough that we can see that more than a couple of people are smiling wide at this nervous fun.

Under the blanket, we start to feel like kids again.

Then we remember the wall of kids upstairs.

The worst thing you can be in this house is a kid.

XXV. Hunter-Gatherers.

We didn't want to sleep in the basement. It was too closed off, too dangerous, too much like a concrete coffin.

Kyle opens his eyes. He's lying with us on the floor of Behringer's living room. *Ms. Leed's living room?* Hummingbird is on the flower-patterned sofa. Jody is sleeping, sitting upright in a dining room chair, his doorframe weapon resting in his lap. Mike is missing. Rob is sleeping on the table, wrapped in the flannel tablecloth. Morgan is missing too.

Kyle stands up, squinting as the light pours into the dusty living room. Doing everything he can to avoid dwelling on the deficient roll call, Kyle walks over to the fireplace. Bending down, he sees that there are brutal grooves in the solid brick. These "claw marks" are not from something entering the house, but instead from something making a frantic escape.

"What did you see that night when you were alone in Behringer's office?" a voice asks.

Kyle's head whips around, and in a flash-bang clatter it all comes blasting back for a second and he *feels* the moment again.

Fighting the psychic assault, regaining control of himself, Kyle swivels his head, limbering up, then makes his way toward the door, bellowing, "Let's leave. We need to leave. It's morning. Let's go."

Hummingbird squeaks, "I didn't mean to..." then her mouth forms the rest of the sentence but no sound follows.

Kyle is a man transformed. He's snapping his fingers at us, and saying, "Party's over. Get up. Come on," like he was a cop that walked in and found us squatting this house.

Everyone slowly begins their day, fearing what caused this freakout, but also too groggy to properly panic. A chorus of husky-voiced, "Wait, I need to get my..." excuses begin, as Kyle moves frantically through the kitchen, packing food in a child-size backpack featuring a picture of Behringer's boy wizard.

Joining Kyle in the kitchen, Rob turns on the water and gulps from it, taking breaks to say, "Ow." When he turns the water off, we hear the stairs that lead to the second floor creaking like a ship in a storm.

Kyle and Rob race down the wood paneled hall, toward the noise.

Everyone holds their breath as... Morgan appears. She looks like shit. Her Mia Wallace hair is now knotted in a bun on the top of her head. She's wearing a too big black T-shirt and a towel as a skirt.

"Are you okay?" Rob asks, walking into the living room.

"Yeah. Are you?" Morgan asks.

Rob nods his head to confirm he's fine.

"Okay, good. We're all okay. Let's keep it that way," Kyle says, pumping with renewed purpose. "Morgan- put on pants. Everyone else- pee. We aren't going to rot in this house."

"You heard the man," Jody says, standing up, undoing his pants.

"In the bathroom," Kyle says, backing up in horror, "Individually. That is how everyone should pee. I mean, come on, Jody."

Jody nods at this, then zips himself back up.

"I was thinking... if this Behringer guy killed himself, then why isn't there any crime scene tape or any other sign that the police have been here at all?" Rob asks, as we march to the first floor bathroom to take turns peeing.

"Well, the body's gone," Morgan says, then adds, "At least I hope it is. I mean, they probably had someone come to clean up the mess, then when their work was done the crime scene transformed. The dude killed himself- the investigation pretty much ends where it begins. We had to chase a Piney's car here, so the chances of people stumbling across this house don't seem very good. You'd have to be really lost to end up here."

"Or be born here," Wil says, and this sends Morgan back up the stairs.

Hummingbird slides into the bathroom, then shuts the door.

"But the front door was open. Don't you think the cleaning crew would have at least locked it behind them?" Rob asks.

Everyone is silent, waiting for the house to respond.

"Are you listening to me pee?" Hummingbird yells through the bathroom door.

"No, we were being creeped out, not being creeps," Rob clarifies, then pushes forward, "There's something fucked up about this house just because it's empty. What's a house in Jersey cost now, Hummingbird? Not a good one, just a shitty one in South Jersey?"

"I dunno, three hundred, four hundred thousand maybe," Hummingbird yells through the door, ballparking real estate prices while pissing.

Rob marvels, unable to even picture that amount of money, "Three hundred thousand dollars for a house, so here we are, sitting in hundreds of thousands of dollars going unclaimed. It leaves you with one thought. Why? Why on earth would someone not claim this house? Why would they not move in here, sell the place... at least shut the front door? America is too greedy for this to happen. I say we've been given a gift and until a dead author, or the dead author's relatives, or the demolition crew, or the pigs, or the devil evicts us... this is our fucking house. I say we stay." Rob seems to lose his point in the middle of making it and no one is persuaded.

"This isn't our house. We need to leave. Let's go, let's walk," Kyle demands.

Hummingbird opens the bathroom door a crack, then peeks out at us, and says, "The Pine Barrens go on forever and if we pick the wrong direction, we'll be trapped in the woods- which is a situation that may or may not be worse than being trapped in this house. I don't know. I just don't know anymore."

"We have no way to protect ourselves out there," Rob points out.

"We have no way to protect ourselves out there," Rob points out.

"I'm on it. I'll build us a way to protect ourselves. If you need me, I'll be in the basement," Jody says, stone-faced, but no one is particularly supportive of this idea. He waits with his hand out, until Wil reluctantly provides his lighter, then a very determined Jody storms toward the basement, ready to go to work.

We listen as the basement door creaks open. We listen for Jody's scream. Nothing. It's totally silent, until a mechanical click from behind us makes us jump. We turn toward the noise, and face the stairs. We face Mike. We want to run.

"We'll protect ourselves with this," Mike says, holding a cocked shotgun, his posture bolt straight, but also casual.

Hummingbird screams and slams the bathroom door.

"When I was looking for mail, I saw shells in the desk downstairs and I figured, 'Hm, there must be a gun,'" Mike tells us, walking downstairs, cradling his weapon.

"No, Mike. No guns. We're gonna be okay. We're gonna walk, and we'll be fine," the once frantic, now exceedingly careful Kyle says. "For all we know we're in the backyard of some middle school. We'll walk to find help today. There's probably a Quik Stop 100 yards from here."

Mike doesn't respond to Kyle. He walks into the living room with his gun.

Rob gets excited about this scenario. "The camera pulls out from Leeds house, and we're only like a half a mile from civilization, but you guys have already killed each other. While I'm walking away from the bloody scene, I hear the sound of a tractor trailer truck horn, and I run to it, then I realize that civilization was so close all this time, but it's too late; I'm the only survivor. I get a book deal and exploit all of your deaths for minimal profit and hopefully sell the movie rights to some vulture who rationalizes picking your bones by telling me he'll 'do your story justice.'"

"What the fuck is he talking about?" Morgan asks, appearing on the stairs. She's wearing jeans and a T-shirt that features a picture of a dolphin jumping out of the pure blue of the rest of the shirt.

Hummingbird cracks the bathroom door open when she hears her friend's voice. Staring at Morgan, Hummingbird asks, "Are you wearing eye makeup? Have you been holding out on me?"

"You'll judge me if I tell you," Morgan says in a little voice.

"Morgan! I feel ugly," Hummingbird yells.

"When Wil was picking through the van remains, I was too. I put some of the ash in my pocket," Morgan says, carefully descending toward us one stair at a time.

"You're wearing our van on your eyes?" Wil asks, then smiles.

Morgan nods.

"Looks good," Wil says, a rare compliment made possible by the fact it sets up this joke, "Kyle, if you want to go out there and get some too, no judgment."

We laugh at this, but the laugh is short, then a silence hangs when we realize Mike has gone missing, and he's armed.

We look to Kyle to see if we should go into the living room, or if we should just start walking to go find help. Kyle glances at Morgan's black-rimmed eyes, and he's about to say something when we're jolted by the sound of footsteps hammering upstairs.

Raised eyes and a desperate mouth-agape expression becomes the uniform we all wear as our minds race a million miles an hour trying to form a rational explanation for the noise. A visual recount of everyone is made. We now must habitually pay close attention to where everyone is in the house. Before this, people could drift in and out of our lives and it wouldn't matter because their exact location wasn't essential to our security. Before, a moment away from the group was coveted; privacy was a valued commodity- something we actively fought for. Now everyone in Leeds house finds themselves getting angry when someone has the audacity to step outside of the room without issuing a verbally geo-tagged route plan. It's the, "I'm going to use the ladies room, downstairs. I won't be reading, just in case you're wondering about the duration of the trip," or, "I'm going to go grab a sweater from Behringer's closet in the master bedroom- the door will be left open behind me," or, "I'm going to go do some weird loud shit upstairs so when you hear weird loud shit, there's no need to stare at the ceiling like it's screening your favorite movie that's been mysteriously re-cut with never before seen footage."

"Who's still up there?" Wil asks.

"I was the last one up there. I'm sure of it," Morgan whispers.

We know that Jody's in the basement, and Mike is... not on the second floor. We listen to make sure that Mike is still in the house and we hear a chair move in the dining room. We don't check to see if this noise was made by Mike. We trust that whatever he's up to, he will protect his friends, new and old.

"Get everyone out of the house," Kyle barks, and this desperate command makes Morgan's heart hop in her chest.

Wil, Rob, and Hummingbird don't need to be convinced, they immediately make their way out to the front yard.

Morgan, almost on autopilot, passes the open front door, then walks into the living room. Kyle is trailing close behind- for Morgan's safety and for his own curiosity.

We stare at Mike's back as he peers out the living room windows. One of the windows has been opened. Morgan leans toward Kyle, then whispers, "You go get Jody, I'll get Mike to put down the gun."

Kyle nods once, confirming that he'll follow Morgan's plan.

Once in the kitchen, Kyle opens up the door to the basement then yells, "Get your ass up here, we're leaving, with or without you."

"I'm building something to protect us!" Jody responds, annoyed at the interruption.

"You better be building a friend because you're going to be awfully lonely when we're gone," Kyle tells his brother.

The sound of hammering, distinctly different from the sound of the footsteps on the second floor, echoes through the basement.

"Jody," Kyle yells down the stairs, "I know I owe you already, but I'm asking for another favor. Please, leave."

The hammering stops. Kyle peers down into the dark and an orb begins to move toward the stairs. Jody appears, his forehead shining, then he climbs the stairs holding only a candle. Whatever Jody was building to protect us with has been left in the basement, hopefully not to be used against us in the future.

When Jody reaches the top of the stairs, he makes it very clear to his brother, "You don't owe me."

Nodding to confirm he understands, Kyle makes his way to the wood paneled hallway and Jody follows him toward the front door.

Kyle looks to his left and sees the bathroom door is shut. He walks past the bathroom, past the front door, then he enters the living room. Mike is still standing at the window, staring out at the trees that line the backyard.

Morgan is nowhere to be found.

Jody casually walks out the front door, his eyes squinting as they adjust to the bright light.

Kyle doesn't join Jody outside. He returns back to the bathroom door and tries the knob. The door isn't locked. "Morgan," Kyle whispers loudly, and while he doesn't receive a response, he can hear her making noise. "Morgan!" he growls through gritted white teeth.

Meekly, Morgan responds, "Kyle, don't come in. I-"

"-you're leaving," Kyle says, swinging the door open.

We see Morgan standing in front of the mirror, the van ash sliding down her face, riding heavy tears.

"Aw. Listen. Shh. Shh," Kyle says, but his shhh's are to calm her, not to silence her. "It's gonna be okay," Kyle tells her, us, himself. Kyle lightly embraces Morgan and her hand limply hangs over Kyle's shoulder. "I'm just very stupid and confused," Morgan says, in little huffs.

"You're great. Listen. You are great. You've won over more than one heart in this house, I can tell you that much," Kyle says in a soothing voice.

Morgan pulls away from Kyle, then her drenched eyes, smeared with the aftermath of an explosion, search Kyle's face, looking for the truth in what he said.

"I'm really scared," Morgan admits. "There's something different about Mike this morning. He has all this anger that he's holding onto now that he's not screaming in your band."

"Mike has a more detailed eye and a more attentive ear than most people," Kyle says, "He sees and hears a lot of things that he feels are wrong, and I do think that he's holding onto some anger right now. You're right, in a way, that the band pacified a lot of his transgressive instincts, but he still has us."

Morgan nods at this, then begins fixing her makeup. She feels better. She forces herself to feel better. She reminds herself that she would've killed to be in a remote house alone with Kyle mere days ago.

A couple long days have changed everything, and now Morgan wants to either get infinitely closer or infinitely further from Kyle. To search for a direction, Morgan uses her charred eyes to review an eye makeupless Kyle until she finds confidence in his unfamiliar face.

Kyle looks back toward the hall, then asks, "What did he say to you?"

Morgan shakes her head, unable to repeat what she was told, and Kyle winces. In order to rationalize Mike's behavior, Kyle tells Morgan, "Jody's really helped Mike channel his rage, but now Jody is distracted with keeping all of us safe, and Mike doesn't have his full attention."

"I'm not sure that Jody's friendship with Cliff is keeping either of them sane," Morgan mentions.

"They're best friends, you can't try to dissect it."

"You have to admit that Mike lets Jody get away with a lot though," Morgan says, acknowledging that Jody's lack of maturity was probably due to the fact that no one has ever forced him to grow up.

"Jody is like the nicest douchebag you will ever meet," Kyle says, with the warmth of a brother, "It's his personality. He was just vulgar enough at his job that when they wanted to fire him, they couldn't, because he de-escalates every situation with humor, and when angry customers were transformed into mildly disgusted, semi-entertained customers, it made him worth keeping around."

"Well, I'm not sure he thinks I'm good enough to keep around," Morgan says, folding her arms across the dolphin on her shirt, "You heard him last night."

"You're wrong," Kyle says.

"How do you figure?"

"He loves to make fun of you," Kyle says, then smiles.

"Wow, you know how to make a girl feel special. Maybe I can borrow that gun from-"

"-that's a sign you've made it with Jody," Kyle says, canceling the pity party, "The fact that he argues with you, or makes fun of you, means that you matter to him. When you should be scared is when Jody doesn't talk to you or jump in on your conversations. That's when you know you've messed things up with him- when you're at the dinner table and he's not making fun of your hair. From the moment he saw you, he took notice."

"Because it's hard to see around me," Morgan says.

"See, that's a Jody-joke you just made," Kyle says, then lets out a quiet laugh. "You get it."

"So... you think he likes me?" Morgan asks.

"If he doesn't, I'll have Mike scream for you at the next show," Kyle says, putting himself back in power by reminding Morgan of her fan status.

This momentary return to normalcy is shattered when an eardrum-rattling boom hammers through the house. A single gunshot reverberates, then leaves a pinging noise that hangs in the air like the dust and makes us hold our ears and close our eyes.

Kyle turns to the door and Morgan grabs onto him, begging, "Don't go. We don't know if Mike shot at something, or if someone is shooting from the outside, in."

"Come with me," Kyle says, grabbing Morgan's hand, pulling her out of the house.

We search for the gunman. There's no one in the front yard. There's yelling coming from the backyard.

As we carefully creep around the house, our backs to the white siding, we see Rob, Hummingbird, and Jody standing in a stunned group.

Hummingbird has her hand over her mouth. She shrieks through her fingers, "You killed Black Beauty!"

We stare at a dead horse, as it leaks a dark pool of red into the ground.

Mike appears behind us, and we dart to the side, almost falling over.

The man with the shotgun silently walks over to his kill, then drops to his knees. Mike sets his weapon on the ground. For a moment, we mistake his awe for regret-soaked disbelief.

Observing his prize with complete concentration, Mike speaks to himself, "One shot and I did it. My dad would..." he looks up and makes eye contact with a disapproving Kyle, who asks, "Why, Mike?"

"I'm not sorry," Mike says in his quiet voice.

Jody bursts out of his shock, yelling, "What the hell! Come on, guys! Who let Mike have a gun?"

"He found it upstairs," Morgan says.

"Of course he found it," Jody sighs, "Weird ass white males always find firearms- the point I'm making is that no one thought to take it away from him? Mike is a 'nice guy who keeps to himself.' Does that sound familiar? It should, because it describes every white dude who has put a bullet in someone in a non-combat situation this year."

We're silent as Jody walks over and claims the weapon.

Kyle attempts to calm everyone, "Jody's right, guys. We have to keep it together here. I think we all need to be mature about this. We need to be extremely, extremely, careful with our... what are you looking at?" Kyle asks, turning around to find Jody pointing the gun at imaginary intruders, pretending to blow their heads off, complete with mouth-made sound effects.

"Who let Jody have the gun?" Kyle asks, marching over to his brother who continues to mime his rampage.

"He told us it was dangerous to have a weird white dude control the shotgun," Hummingbird mumbles.

"Then why didn't you listen to him?" Kyle asks, as he becomes the third man to take possession of the firearm. Turning to his brother, Kyle says, "Jody, it's really hard for me to side with you on your gun safety speech if you're pretending to shoot off my arms," Kyle says.

"Not to worry," Jody responds, "I was shooting *beyond* you."

"I'm going to be totally honest with you, that doesn't make me feel one bit better about the situation," Kyle says, then he points to Mike, "And you. This-" he growls, redirecting his finger to the horse, "-shouldn't have happened. You know better."

"I do know better, and I applied common logic to our problem," Mike defends himself.

"This is not what common logic looks like," Kyle says, again pointing at the animal on the ground.

"Do horses generally live in the Pine Barrens, Kyle?" Mike asks, then turns to Hummingbird and Morgan, and inquires, "Girls, you live in South Jersey, do you see a lot of wild horses? I'm going to go out on a limb here and say no. Does anyone have information that proves me wrong?" No one raises a hand or offers an opinion. "That's what I thought," Mike says.

"Someone led this horse here, or the horse escaped its stable and made its way through the Barrens. I could be spilling a sad truth here, but someone is going to miss this horse and they're going to go looking for him- which is a lot more than I can say for us. Not a great thought, I know, but it's probably pretty accurate. So I did it. I took the shot. And I won."

"Fine. You won. Let's just get out of here," Kyle says, crunching through the leaves, away from the horse. Mike's actions have a certain logic to them, but a live horse would've achieved the same end.

"I'm not going. I just fired off a rescue flare into this horse," Mike protests calmly.

"You fired a flare alright, but I don't know if it's going to bring help, or danger," Kyle responds, pausing, waiting for us to join him.

Mike steps forward and stares at Kyle. We watch this scene- Mike filled with adrenaline, Kyle filled with... fear?

A loud rhythmic slapping breaks the tension of the moment and refocuses our eyes.

Mike turns around, and Jody asks him, "Get it?" hoping someone else would display an emotion other than sadness and bewildered fear.

"Oh, you're beating a dead horse. Creative," Mike says, as Jody continues to hit the horse's corpse with a stick in rhythm with his chant, "We're all fucked. Let's go walk for help. No, let's stay inside. Let's go walk for help..."

Jody eventually gives up on the stick when his arm starts to get tired.

"This is wrong," Kyle says, thrown for a loop by the violent moment. "And you're right, Mike. That the horse was out of place and that's why we should be worried. He knew what you were capable of, and that's why he let this happen."

"Who's *he*?" Morgan asks.

"How would *he* know that Mike is capable of this violence?" Hummingbird asks.

Lies As Language exchange concerned glances. There's a story that a devil would know about Mike's thirst for armed vengeance.

Mike is now fixated on a new story- one not about birthing evil, but instead extinguishing it. Gone is the confused blood lust of high school. Finally, Mike has gained an adversary that is undoubtedly worthy of his wrath. It's now his singular goal to kill and stuff the New Jersey Devil. Mike's father will have no choice but to return so he can view the ultimate hunting trophy.

As Mike begins to walk away from the house, we follow him, at a distance.

XXV. American Folklore - Six Flags.

We walk nowhere, together.

"We're going to need to pass the time on Kyle's nature walk, so tell your story, Cliff," Jody demands.

"About the guns?" Mike asks.

"Why does Mike have a story about guns?" Hummingbird asks, concerned.

"Maybe because he's a fuckin' psychopath," Jody says, but not as though it's a bad thing.

"Yeah... maybe," Mike says, "Do you want me to tell the one about Six Flags?"

"How many gun stories do you have, Mike?" Morgan asks, as a dread she had left in the bathroom catches up with her.

"Bunches, but, okay," Mike says, then lifts his arms and flattens his eyebrows. In his little voice, Mike begins his story with a common sentiment, "High school... I didn't like it. I didn't like the people there. Do I need to elaborate? I think we've all been there... Hummingbird?"

"Yes, I went to high school, you ass. Just because I have tattoos doesn't mean I was raised by bikers from Southern California."

Mike, emotionless, says, "I guess we've both learned something about each other today. This is good," then he hops back into his story, "When I was in middle school, my dad was still around and we would go hunting. On my favorite trip, we flew to Texas to hunt javelinas. We spent a lot of time hunting them. My dad took some shots and missed. One morning, I had a clear shot, so I took it, and it was incredible when I saw it hit. It was something that my dad couldn't do, and I did it. I went to Texas to shoot a javelina and I shot one. It was probably the only time my dad was proud of me."

"That's disgusting, those javelinas are just trying to get over the border into America and you're picking them off for sport? Is it because our corrupt government turns a blind eye to this 'cleansing?'" Jody asks.

"Jody, you've heard this story before; you're the one who asked him to tell it. You must know a javelina is a pig," Kyle says.

"They're still people, just because they haven't been born on the 4th of July with a-"

"-they are literally pigs, Jody. They have snouts and hooves," Wil says.

"Oh. Oh. Okay. Yeah. Fuck pigs," Jody decides, happy that Mike was exterminating them for sport.

"Jody, if you make a joke I will strangle you-" Morgan says, knowing the setup is too good.

"-then my dad left," Mike interrupts, going back to his story, "And I had to go to school, where I found a new pig- Dave Callahan. Dave was fat and mean. When Dave punched my only friend in the locker room, an idea that had seemed merely like a daydream gained focus. My fantasy became like an answer. If Dad was thrilled in Texas, he'd definitely take note of what happened at school." As Mike explains all of this, his tone never edges with malice. He continues walking, like a robotic program that had been executed and was merely working toward the logical end. "So I started planning. It was a lot of planning. Planning something like that was like planning a wedding. I had to figure out where everyone would be sitting, what I would wear, and what time it would begin and end. There was extra stuff too. I had to draw maps. I had to follow people and memorize their schedules. I had to order equipment off the internet. I had to keep my mom out of my room. All of it was so much work that it ended up taking a lot longer than I thought it would. When you're a kid, summer seems too short and the school year seems to crawl. I was relying on that fact, but before I knew it, I was a senior and finals were a week away. I learned that a supremely important part of planning a wedding is the date. Couples send out those little "Save the Date" cards so there's a deadline. No matter what happens, on a certain day, ready or not, the entire deal has to happen. With my plan, I never really picked a specific date because there was always more work to do. Finally, I decided that I just had to do it. I teased my hair, I put on the outfit I bought. I loaded up my mother's car, and I drove it to school without asking her. What was the worst she was going to do? Ground me? Force me to stay inside my room, just like I already did every day anyway? That was the joke," Mike says, then laughs at himself, "So I get to the school and there are all these travel buses lined up. They weren't the usual school buses. This was different; it was unexpected. I got out of the car and Mrs. Roberts quickly walked over to me, saying, 'Michael, you made it,' and I was pretty confused because Mrs. Roberts didn't help me in the planning stages of my big day. She pointed to a bus and told me to hurry. I asked her where we were going and she said, 'It's your senior trip. You're going to be very hot in all black, but maybe you'll get a little color.'"

We crunch deeper into the woods, no sign of civilization, and we're happy that Kyle didn't take the gun; we're happy that the weapon is hidden in the house. Unarmed, Mike continues, "After all that planning, I had scheduled my big event on the one day none of my targets would be there. I couldn't leave school because a teacher had found me and people were waiting, so I got on the bus and went to Six Flags. Since I was so late, I had to sit next to Mrs. Roberts. I thought about getting off the bus, then tailing the convoy in my mom's car. I wanted to move my plan, but no one would let me borrow their map of Six Flags so it would've been a poorly executed mission. Once we got there, I stayed on the bus because I didn't want to get the outfit sweaty and I didn't have a change of clothes. The only other person on the bus was Rob, who had done a lot of ketamine and was trapped in a k-hole on a bench seat in the back of the bus by the bathroom. I told Mrs. Roberts that Rob had food poisoning, and I promised I would take care of him, then I sat on the bus and thought about how stupid I was for procrastinating. How high school of me to procrastinate a massacre. I started thinking that maybe everyone plans the things I wanted to do, but because high school kids are so lazy, only .1% of them ever follow through with it. It made me realize that if you don't off yourself or go to jail for life after your rampage, then colleges should be interested in you because you were able to plan this massive undertaking, then make it happen. That's more impressive than being on the debate team; it shows you're an implementer, not just a brainstormer. Despite all this, what it came down to was that I had shitty grades, so college wasn't the future I would be offered. While I babysitting Rob on that bus, I began thinking about what type of future I might want... and... it was just... blank. Besides my botched plan, I had no plan. On my phone, I listened to a song by some actor turned singer who claimed that music was his 'real passion' and I wondered if anyone ever really knows what they want their future to be. There was that question about if I would ever feel content or if I would just keep naming new passions, then declare them my 'real passion.' As the actor's song continued, I confronted myself with more questions. If I didn't carry out my plan the next day, would I have to wait yet another year? Would I have to come back to the high school and pick off random kids? I didn't want to be the guy who graduated, but couldn't let go of high school. That's no way to live. I thought about maybe doing the plan at the local community college, but I figured I'd probably end up with some medal of honor for taking out a bunch of people who would eventually just be a drain on society. While I was thinking about all this stuff, I remember looking out the window and seeing Mrs. Roberts walking back to the bus with Wil. I hated Wil because he seemed to have co-opted a lot of my look, but he was still popular with most people. He had the wallet chain, but he didn't have the chains of virginity like I did."

"Like you *do*, you no pussy-gettin' motherfucker," Jody says, and this is surprisingly one of his few outbursts during Mike's entire story. Maybe, for once, he's listening.

Morgan is listening too and she snips at Jody, "Yeah, good idea, make fun of the kid telling the story about an intricately planned rampage."

"Psh," Jody scoffs, "Wait till you hear how this shit ends. Walt Disney would jack off to this ending it's so fuckin' syrupy."

We continue to walk, time passing quickly because we're not focusing on anything besides the ground and Mike's timid voice.

"So, I take it you didn't shoot Wil?" Hummingbird says, getting Mike back on track.

"I didn't have my guns," Mike says casually, then pushes forward, "So, Wil got quarantined on the bus, and I started listening to the conversation that he was having with Mrs. Roberts. From what I gathered, Wil was caught smoking cigarettes, which wasn't illegal, nor did it occur on school grounds, but Wil was on a school trip, so it put Mrs. Roberts in a tough place as far as what the appropriate punishment would be."

"She had just gotten off the Batman ride, and I think she was inspired by Batman's vigilante work," Wil adds, clarifying the situation.

"She did refer to you as The Joker at least once," Mike says.

"I was *a* joker, not *The* Joker," Wil responds.

"In the end, she decided that Wil would have to sit on the bus for an hour as a 'scholastic penalty,' ensuring that he had received a quantifiable punishment, but then after he did his time, he could still ride some cool rides before the day was out," Mike explains.

"Wait, is this the story about how you guys all met? What about that whole explanation Kyle gave about riding around in a van picking out people from other bands who 'understood your vision?'" Hummingbird asks. She's very well versed in Lies As Language's Wikipedia page and even made some edits on it that weren't taken down.

Jody, now out of breath, gasps out, "Listen, Mike's little yarn would be a great band formation story... if we were trying to form some sort of brutal bloodbath death metal band, which we weren't, and we all agreed that space-metal Christian metalcore bloodbath bands are generally unattractive to audiences. It's too many hard sells in one super-genre."

"So you guys met when you were seniors?" Morgan asks, finding the cuteness in this story, "How old are you now, Mike?"

"I'm 20. This was two years ago."

"You don't know that for sure," Jody says, looking up at the treetops, "Not in these woods."

"Two years was approximately two years ago," Mike says, "I'm confident in this fact."

"The Barrens and Behringer's house both manipulate time," Jody responds, without providing any evidence.

"You think we've been here for years?" Morgan asks, then adds, "Once Mike is done with this story can anyone explain to me why Jack Torrance sees himself in the picture at the end of *The Shining*?"

"It certainly feels like it's taken two years to tell this story," Mike says quietly, then answers the original question, "And, yes, this is how we met. Wil was on the bus, Rob was coming out of his k-hole, then we got our last visitor. Out of nowhere, Kyle appeared on the bus with his phone in his hand. He asked if we knew how to save a wet phone, but beyond just leaving it on the hot bus, we didn't. From there, it turned into this weird *Breakfast Club* moment. We never revived Kyle's phone, but they asked me to put on a song, and I chose a playlist of metalcore songs, which began a discussion, and from the discussion we formed the idea for the band. None of us had instruments of our own, but we all decided we'd learn, then we'd try to get booked for local shows. Since Kyle mentioned that his brother had a lot of equipment, we asked Jody to join the band too," Mike says. The entire story- from the dark plan, to the bus conversation, to the band formation- was given the same amount of intensity and inflection by Mike.

"Crazy fuckin' story, right? Imagine if we were a white power band, we would be so famous and doing county fairs everywhere." Jody says.

Morgan furrows her brow, then searches for the meaning, "So the lesson is that no matter how shitty things are..."

Mike looks back at Morgan, and quietly says, "One of these days you'll be forced to visit Six Flags and your future will change. Change isn't always something to fear."

XXVI. American Traditions.

We've been walking for hours. It doesn't matter if we turn around now or not. Twigs cracking, stones being kicked, leaves crunching- the soundtrack of our slogging has become a static that we've learned to tune out.

The rhythm that we've reflexively adopted is suddenly broken by a visual monument that makes our heartbeat speed up and our hair stand on end.

"What. The. Fuck," Hummingbird says, in a little voice.

We stare at a tree. We've been staring at trees for hours, but this tree is very different. This tree is not unlike a Christmas tree, but at the same time this crude trail marker is very different from a Christmas tree.

In the middle of the Pine Barrens, we've found a Christmas tree decorated with dead animals that hang like ornaments.

Rob leans over and pukes. Jody steps in front of the girls. Kyle turns away. Mike begins slowly walking up to the tree. We want to yell at Mike to stay away, but that act would only serve as an obvious way to announce our presence.

All eyes eventually focus on Mike, as he walks up to a dead horse that hangs from the tree by a thick rope, slowly rotating about five feet off the ground. He puts up his hand to stop the horse's slight swing, and he finds himself standing face to face with the bullet wound he inflicted. "Impossible," Mike says, then he looks back at us, and confirms, "This is impossible."

"That's not the horse," Kyle says, pointing with two fingers at the beast barely being supported by the old rope.

"Yes, it is," Mike says, "The horse I shot at Leeds house is now hanging from this tree." He refers to the house in the Barrens as Leeds house instead of Behringer's house. There wasn't a possessive to his pronunciation. The house doesn't belong to Ms. Leeds, but it does stand as a monument to her mistakes.

The horse is just one of the many ornaments on the tree- dogs, cats, raccoons, deer, and foxes all hang from branches as well. Do we see a wolf at the top of the tree? Is that a black bear cub in the middle of the tree, next to those ducks? Each of the freshly killed animals wears a rope necklace that's attached to a specific branch capable of supporting their weight. Their bodies are perfectly preserved, and only the horse has a visible wound.

As Wil stares at this brutal trail marker, a photograph he had once seen flashes in his mind- a girl who was engaged to be married, but couldn't accept her new life, had gone to the top of a tall building, and jumped off. According to the note she left, she wanted to be forgotten, but the way she landed prevented this final wish from being honored. A photographer at the scene took a picture of the tragedy, and in this photograph, it appeared that the girl was merely sleeping, and the crumpled metal of the car under the girl almost resembled bed sheets. A girl who had been subsumed by panic looked so peaceful, and her final image is one where beauty and tragedy wrestle to be the commanding emotion for the viewer. Wil is glad there will not be a picture of this tree because he never wants to revisit it.

Through tears, Hummingbird asks, "Is this why we haven't seen any animals besides the horse in the woods?"

"These aren't just animals from the woods," Rob says, "Some of them are pets." He points to a collar on a hanged German Shepard to support this theory. Since there's a pet in the tree, where's the owner who was walking it? We don't scan the tree for a human body because we know that if Wil locates one, he'll check its pockets for a cell phone, and that desperate act will bind him to the tree like he was Mike.

Everyone is very silent as we try to figure out who created this display, the implications of the display's existence, and finally, what the chances are that one of us will end up in the tree.

"Losing a pet is hard," Morgan says, "I had three hamsters when I was a kid and every time one of them would die, I'd cry my eyes out... except when the last one died because I had my bunny by then and I didn't care about my hamsters anymore."

Jody begins to look at Morgan in a new and different way. Here's this girl, in an ugly moment, with a statement that's funny. Jody lets out a laugh. Rather unexpectedly, Morgan copied Jody's de-escalation tactic, and being on the other side of it for the first time, Jody becomes less embarrassed about his immature approach to the terror between these pines.

Jody turns away from the tree. His laughs come out easier when his view simplifies. "I bet to get all these animals, all he had to do was go to the old blind lady's house," he suggests.

Wil turns to Jody and Morgan with a disapproving look, then asks, "Are you saying that the blind cat lady was... robbed blind of her cats?"

Morgan and Jody laugh. Wil laughs. Rob laughs even though he didn't meet the blind lady. Hummingbird flutters toward the turned group, staggering, sputtering, "Did-" she bursts a laugh, "Did-" another laugh.

"Is Hummingbird crying?" Rob asks.

"No, she's laughing," Morgan assures us.

Finally, Hummingbird finds her center, and asks, "Did all these animals commit suicide because they were embarrassed about being forced to eat a Wiccan's pussy?"

We let out the type of laugh that echoes across a church service when someone farts.

"Do you guys not comprehend how screwed we are?" Kyle growls, walking in front of the crowd that's refusing to take this brutal message seriously. The shock tolerance in this group is so high that as long as their feet remain on the ground, they'll try to joke away the fear.

"I'm not in jeopardy. I'm not even like one fifteenth animal," Jody says, "Other than my horse c-"

"-Jody. Don't make jokes. Even though this does look like Mike's family's Christmas tree," Rob says, then starts laughing at his own joke.

"That's it, laugh this off," Kyle says, turning away from us. With his voice sitting in the back of his throat, he says, "I'm sorry if I don't find humor in victimized animals hanging from a tree. This is not an accident. We didn't stumble onto this. He built this for us. This is to send us a message and if he put this much work into a massive shocking display, he's going to stay around to see the reaction. This is a surprise party that he's throwing for himself. Actually, it's a reverse surprise party where the guests are the ones who get surprised. Do you think that your laughing is going to make him stop?"

"So, what do we do?" Hummingbird asks, and this question comes out like a challenge.

Kyle addresses the group, minus Mike, who remains transfixed by the tree, "This is a message- we can't run away from him and we're going to lose the daylight. We have to go back to the house."

"Then what?" Jody asks, another challenge.

"At least we'll have shelter," Kyle says.

Once bitchy, now just afraid, Hummingbird nods in agreement with Kyle, then begins to trot back the way we came. This is her coping mechanism. Hummingbird never tries to fix her own problems, she always runs from them instead.

Morgan looks back to the tree, then yells, "Mike, come on!" through cupped hands.

Mike puts his hand up to indicate that he just needs a moment, then he'll join her, and that's good enough for Morgan. She begins to follow the fluttering Hummingbird.

As Morgan gets closer to Hummingbird- as she runs faster- she feels more alive. Suddenly, Morgan realizes that standing still is not only lazy- it could also be deadly. This acidic pill, this pill that's impossible to swallow, is the best diet pill Morgan has ever taken. Inactivity is poison now. Morgan finally finds the passion for exercising. This is a bizarre gift that she snatched out from under that evil Christmas tree.

With the group breaking apart, Wil decides to join those heading away from the stench of the merciless trail marker.

Jody is frozen, but only for a moment. He needs to protect his friends, and most of them are now running through the woods. Jody is not given a choice, he must return to Leeds House. He starts running at the exact moment his brother does. When Kyle picks up speed, so does Jody, and this renewed competition allows them to catch up to the group quickly.

"Where's Mike?" Morgan asks, looking back, desperate for breath, but concerned enough to waste gasps on the odd boy with the scary story. No one responds to Morgan's question, everyone keeps stride. This lack of an answer, and the presumed answer, creates a moral imperative that begins to weigh not only on Morgan, but also on one of the Lennard brothers.

Kyle stops running, his sneakers disappearing under the dead leaves. He takes only a split second to consider his actions, then he turns to run back to the tree, even though every fiber of his being is afraid of what he will find. "I'm going back for him," Kyle yells.

Making a curling redirection, Wil tails Kyle until he can reach out and grab Kyle's hoodie.

Wil plants his feet, while Kyle keeps moving- his hoodie stretching from the tension.

Through gritted teeth, Wil says, "You're not going back for him," and Kyle is anchored, so he's forced to rotate his shoulder aggressively to break the unwanted bind.

In the same deep breaths that would accompany a cry, Wil demands, "Kyle, listen to me, if you know what's good for you, you'll go home. Go home, Kyle."

"We don't know how to get home, so I might as well be out here," Kyle huffs.

"Don't do this, Kyle. I swear, if you run any further, I'm writing you off like I wrote off that sick fuck under the tree."

"That sick fuck is our friend," Kyle says, his blue eyes trained on Wil.

"He has no friends, did you not hear him yammering about high school? He has nothing. He shot that horse to see how we'd react- he has no way to meter his problems anymore and he's going out of his mind."

"Go home and get the gun from inside the piano bench. The seat lifts up and there are music books inside. That's where I hid it- under the music books. Make sure it's still there. If it isn't, *he* brought it out to the tree with the horse, to return it to Mike, which means don't come looking for me," Kyle tells Wil, then he resumes his run.

Kyle is going to have to head back alone- at least to the tree, but hopefully not to the house. As he sprints away from Wil, Kyle begins to feel his bruised ribs throb. The fight with Punchcunt is such a distant memory that this pain comes as a surprise. The time warp Jody mentioned, that was largely regarded as a joke, begins to seem like a plausible reality now.

Kyle runs through the pain, and when the gauntlet of trees breaks, we see that the transfixed boy hasn't moved from where we left him.

Mike is standing bolt straight, eye to eye with the hanged horse. It's almost as though he's watching a film in the horse's black iris.

"Mike," Kyle calls out, then makes a gesture like he's helping a friend back their car out of a tight driveway.

Mike turns his head like an owl toward Kyle, but his body doesn't move.

The questions now pile up- was Mike not moving because he doesn't want to? Was Mike not moving because he can't? Or was Mike not moving because he's the bait in this hunter's trap?

Kyle approaches his friend slowly, but keeps his sight-line raised to the surrounding trees. He searches for a face he never wants to see again.

"Please. Come with us. I was wrong to freak out on you in the yard," Kyle says.

"You weren't. You needed to do it to deliver me here," Mike responds, his small voice calm and steady.

"I was wrong to treat you like that, make no mistake about it, but I want to walk out of here with you. It's time to leave, Mike... Leave, Mike.... Leave, Mike!" Kyle continues to escalate the moment, chanting his demand.

"Leave Mike," Mike responds, changing the command, and throwing it back at Kyle. "You were right about the house and you are right about this place. This tree is a sign for me. He made this for me."

"No, Mike, don't turn this into something about your father. This is not your living room."

"I understand now, Kyle. You were right when you said we have no home," Mike responds.

"If you're looking for home, this is the farthest thing from it," Kyle tells him.

"You have no idea how deep these woods stretch," Mike says, then he begins to climb the tree.

XXVII. The Girl In A Ball Needs Help.

We follow Kyle back to the house. He left Mike under the tree. Kyle had backed away, hands raised. He backed away from his friend. He backed away from the idea of Lies As Language. He backed away from the idea of any escape from Leeds House. Kyle allowed Mike to stay under the tree because the house might be just as dangerous.

As Kyle runs, he feels a layered helplessness. Jody would have been able to help Mike, but he was forced to help the desperate majority. Kyle doesn't have the way with words that Jody does. In the same way Jody can construct an inappropriate joke, he can locate the appropriate reaction to unexpected behavior. Nothing is too strange for Jody because Jody is strange himself. Kyle left Mike because he didn't want to make things worse. The self-destruct button inside Mike is still there, and the tree of death has lifted off the protective cover. Now the button is waiting for someone to reach over and apply pressure. Kyle remains unwilling to be that force.

Keeping his eyes on the ground, Kyle follows the footprints in the sandy soil. He doesn't have to look up- it's tree after tree, all of them a relief because none of them have animals hanging from their branches nor do they have devils perched on their limbs.

When he's hit with a wind tunnel of cold air belching from the front door of Leeds house, Kyle raises his head and sees that Mike's shotgun is planted barrel down in the dusty dirt of the front yard like a tiny tree.

Kyle approaches the gun carefully, then places his finger on the trigger. He wants to fire down into the ground, wounding the devil, but he doesn't pull the trigger, because there's a very real possibility that Mike might be buried in the ground, under the gun.

Pulling the shotgun from the ground like it was Excalibur unsheathed from the stone, Kyle accepts the burden of this weapon. Wil was given one task when he was sent back to the house- he was supposed to control the gun. The gun is here, and Wil is... hopefully inside.

The cool air whooshing from the house is a relief after such a long trek back. Once the group of runners returned to the house, the front door should've been slammed shut by someone in tired frustration, but Kyle knows that Jody left it open for him. No. Jody left the door open for both Kyle *and Mike.*

Kyle approaches the door slowly, alone. He wants to aim the gun at the door, but he suspects that's precisely what's expected of him. He fears that as soon as he steps onto the porch, the devil will kick Jody down the stairs and the flopping figure will be met with a shell from a nervous gunman. Kyle rests the gun on his shoulder, its barrel pointing backward so no one can sneak up on him. When he reaches the splintered door frame, he can hear something inside being dragged, but what's being dragged, where it's being dragged to, and where it's being dragged from, for the moment, remains a mystery.

Stepping inside Leeds house to search for the source of the *Shhpt, Shhpt* noise, Kyle finds nothing but the lingering dust that fills the house and clouds his desperate lungs. Looking down the wood paneled hallway, he sees that the bathroom door, the door to the small room, and the door to the office are all shut. Another *Shhpt* gasps a hiss, and Kyle approaches the bathroom door- the first door that must be cleared. He places his hand on the knob, then slowly turns, and since Mike is gone, Kyle has to fling the door open himself.

In a grand reveal, we see that on the tile, next to the toilet, is Hummingbird, and she's holding a steak knife. Kyle instantly puts down his own weapon and rushes inside the bathroom.

Hummingbird doesn't drop her weapon. She keeps the knife clutched in a two handed grip, tears streaming down her face, snot dropping into her mouth. She's sitting in her underwear and bleeding from her right leg which is covered in surgical slices.

"What happened? Where's everyone else?" Kyle asks, rushing to the injured girl.

Hummingbird tries to stop crying. Her gritting sob reveals itself as the *Shhpt* Kyle was searching for. A frothy mixture of spit and snot spurts from between Hummingbird's teeth and lands on Kyle's face as he searches Hummingbird's eyes as though they could play back her attack in their reflection.

"You saw him," Kyle says quietly, then he slowly reaches his gloved hand over and takes the knife by the blade. He trusts Hummingbird, and she trusts him back.

Kyle gasps out an apology, "Fuck. Fuck. I'm sorry. Listen. I'm sorry." He wipes a tear off Hummingbird's face. "We are going to fix you up-"

"-you can't," Hummingbird says, her face shining with tears. Everything about her gleams like the blade of the knife.

"Who did this to you?" Kyle asks, looking down at Hummingbird's leg.

"I did," she responds.

XXVIII. We Need To Talk.

I need to ask you something...

Damn. Scariest part of the book, right?

Okay, so here's the deal. We've silently watched this story about a home in the woods unfold, from a distance that is oh-so-close, yet oh-so-safe.

We've been on this journey together. It's not over. Maybe. Maybe. Maybe.

Listen. Do you really want to continue on with this adventure?

If the answer is no, goodbye.

If the answer is yes, good. Just... good.

Do you think all the "no-ers" are gone?

Okay. Now we can talk shit about them.

Did you see how slow the "no-ers" read along with us? It's like, you do know that you don't have to be shitting to read a book, right? You can read books in places other than the bathroom.

Any more "no-ers?"

We'll wait for you to leave.

So... you're still here.

I question your decision making abilities.

Why are you still here?

Kyle? Morgan? Jody? Hummingbird? Rob? Mike? It can't be Wil.

If you decide to stay- to continue on- I understand.

I've always found myself pulled back to this story, and I think you feel it too.

What a pair we make.

So, come on, let's go back, together, into Leeds House.

You could have escaped.

You didn't.

I think I'm going to start killing.

If you leave now, if you don't return to Leeds house, I won't kill anyone.

If you continue past this page, people will die.

You can either put this book down now and rejoin the real world with a clear conscience, or you can turn the page and cause terrible things to happen.

It's your choice.
These deaths will be your fault if you continue reading.

I follow you to the dinner table and we sit down.

A very motherly looking Morgan walks out with two steaming pots. An apron covers the dolphin logo on her T-shirt. "I made pasta with the garlic and green pepper tomato sauce," she tells her adopted family.

"Does garlic protect you from the devil?" Rob asks.

"No, only vampires," Wil says, but he still immediately grabs one of the pots and begins piling pasta onto his plate.

"It didn't work on them in the River White movie," Kyle says.

"Okay, then garlic only works on repelling dates," Wil says.

"How about dates with the devil?" Rob asks.

"Nope," Jody responds.

"The devil seems like a divorcee. He'll go on a date with anyone," Hummingbird says.

With a full meal on the table, Jody asks, "Would anyone like to say grace?"

"You're good at it," Morgan responds, "You say it."

Jody nods, then offers his hands to the sky. Tonight, people reach for each other to form a chain at the table. Participation in Jody's prayer circle has increased. Eyes that once rolled, are now closed in concentration, meditation, prayer.

"Dear Lord, we thank you for this bountiful feast which we are about to enjoy. We also thank you for protecting this feast from having weird maggots and other insects explode out of the pasta after we've already eaten some of it, otherwise we'd all be like, 'Ew, did I already chew some maggots and not notice? This has been a pretty good dinner, despite being made of bugs. Am I into maggots? Is that going to be my new thing?'" Jody's goatee bordered smile drops as he continues, "We, uh. Wow. Uh, we also lost one of our friends today. We ask that you protect him, Lord. Please shepherd Mike away from danger, as you have in the past. Amen."

This time, the "amen" is fully echoed, not with a rushed delivery, but with sincere intent. Talking to someone you can't see and have never met seemed silly and desperate, until we cried out into the Barrens at what could be a cursed-dragon-devil-child of a whore. If we granted this monster a dialog, surely a boy born to a virgin mother was deserving of a couple quick words.

The Leeds devil was born in this house, turned away by his community.

Jesus was born in a stable, turned away by his community.

The Leeds devil fired himself like a cannonball out of the chimney, alone.

Jesus stayed where He was born, amongst family.

After he was born, society rejected where the devil called home and ceased to travel there.

After He was born, society ascended upon Jesus' makeshift home, their long journey born out of odd revelations and blind faith.

One birthed in sin; one birthed without.

The devil claimed this stretch of sandy soil filled land, while Jesus was born in the desert.

The Pine Barrens' pristine forested acres are abounding in beauty, so much so that even the devil himself ensures these woods remain untouched. It's certainly not a surprise that New Jersey would be chosen to host this sinister birth. Forever the foster mother for the imperfect and undesirable, New Jersey sustains this unholy landscape in an industry-free stasis.

Jesus' birthplace is one of the most well-traveled and tumultuous places in the world- and it always has been- and it appears that it will continue to be that way.

Why do we stay in this cursed home when even the devil fled this trap?

Why do we stay in this corrupt place instead of walking on the path of faith?

Maybe our homes are decided not by where we belong, but instead by where we're most needed.

"I have an announcement to make," Rob says, scooting out his chair, then standing up. Rob's conversation starters are almost always unsolicited and provided without fanfare, almost as though he was directing the observations to himself, not others, but tonight he's chosen to pause our meal to tell us something, so we pay attention. Rob, looking out from under the bangs of his shaggy hair, says, "Last night, after the rest of you moved upstairs, I was walking around the basement because I heard... these... radio transmissions. I was having trouble sleeping because I felt like there was a pervasive... din? Is a 'din' a thing? That's what I thought the sound was, a din. I followed the din, purely out of misguided curiosity, and I found a transmitter."

"It's just a baby monitor," Morgan says.

"True indeed, so I was walking around with the monitor, rapping into it," Rob says, framing it as though this was the most logical of progressions.

"You were rapping into the fuckin' baby monitor?" Jody asks.

"Yeah, do you have a problem with that?"

"Of course I do. You should have invited me down there. We could've rap battled. You would have gotten your ass roasted," Jody says, then surveys his fork to make sure it's not covered in maggots. When he verifies that his prayer worked, Jody shovels the pasta into his mouth.

"Okay, we can battle later, but you can't get weirded out about what I'm going to tell you because this story has a happy ending," Rob says.

"Not another one of these. I can't handle another one of-" Hummingbird starts to say, but is interrupted.

"-you look stressed," Rob says, like he was an Indian guy approaching a lone girl in the mall who looked like an easy mark for purchasing the soothing hand cream he sells from a kiosk outside of MasterCuts.

"How can you not be stressed in this house?" Hummingbird asks, reaching for more comfort food.

"I'm getting to that," Rob says, happy with the way this is going, even though, to us, it appears that this conversation is going nowhere. "So I was rapping," Rob continues, "when suddenly, I forgot some of the second verse to 'Niggaz My Height Don't Fight' by Eazy-E."

Everyone shakes their head in disapproval.

"And a voice came over the monitor," Rob says, then those same heads that were shaking over a trivial social taboo now seek direct eye contact.

"There was a voice on the baby monitor?" Hummingbird asks, a lump in her throat.

A baby born in this house was cursed before birth.

"He started giving me directions," Rob says.

"What do you mean *directions*?" Kyle asks quietly, like he was Mike. *Poor Mike.*

"He told me to walk over to the bookshelf where all these *National Geographic* magazines were lined up in neat rows."

"You followed the voice's directions?" Wil asks, intrigued.

"Of course. I love *National Geographic*," Rob responds simply.

"Every now and then you get lucky and find Afro-American pancake titties," Jody says, in another Eazy-E moment.

"Those are regular Africans. America's prudent 'No Shirt, No shoes, No service' rule prevents us from enjoying the same freedoms those Africans most likely take for granted," Rob points out, then moves on, "So the voice on the monitor was like, 'Pick up the third issue on the top row,' so of course I did it. As I'm flipping through the issue, a key falls out from inside the pages. It was an old looking key- it's not the type of key that has a bunch of teeth like an alligator. It had a long neck like... those birds with long necks, or whatever, I don't know, their name was probably in the *National Geographic*, but I was concerned with the key at that point and I didn't know I would use that comparison later on so I apologize for the mental lapse."

"What was the key for?" Wil asks.

"A closet."

"There are no closets in the basement," Jody says, confident that his scoping of this house was thorough.

"That's what I thought too, but have you seen a boiler in the basement?" Rob asks, and everyone runs through the basement in their minds.

"No," Jody says, knowing that all this hot water must be coming from somewhere.

"The boiler room is hidden," Rob reveals, "It's behind this tall metal door that has no handle. The only way you can get into it is by using a key, then you pull the key toward you, which is what the voice told me to do, which is what I did, and after that the door opened."

"You go inside?" Wil asks.

"The voice told me to. So I did."

"What was in there?" Morgan asks, letting her food get cold.

"The boiler. Haven't you even been paying attention to this rambling and only occasionally creepy story?" Jody responds.

"Yeah, there was a boiler in there," Rob says, then his eyes light up and he continues, "but there was also a barrel that was turned sideways and elevated off the ground. At the end of the barrel was a spout. The voice over the monitor said to me, 'Drink.'"

Everyone is silent, waiting for Rob to admit if he willingly made an *Alice in Wonderland* magnitude mistake.

"So, I drank from it," Rob says, not amping up the suspense, "I turned my head to the side, then I twisted a little copper handle, and I tasted the wine. Not gonna lie, it was by far the best red I've ever had in my life. The bouquet had hints of roasted almonds and smoke."

Just as Mike's story forever changed our perception of the meek boy and his motives, our image of Rob has become fogged.

"Please tell me you're joking," Kyle says.

"I know what you're thinking," Rob responds, "I'm aware it's important to let the wine breathe, so obviously I got a cup with a wide mouth instead of just drinking straight from the tap. It's an outstanding vintage."

"Of course it was outstanding," Kyle sighs, "Do you even understand what you've done?"

"Got the party started?" Rob asks, his eyes darting around the room for clues on what he's set in motion.

"We need to destroy that barrel. Tonight," Kyle tells the table.

"I don't get what the big deal is," Hummingbird says, burning for a drink.

"In church, we drink wine. It's the blood of Christ," Jody explains, "And last night, you drank the wine in the basement of the house that birthed the devil."

XXX. ■ Scars As Montage — Performing For The Band.

We sit on the piano bench in the living room with Morgan. The key cover on the piano is still down, which was Jody's idea to "decrease the general scariness potential of the living room."

Morgan had somehow been left alone with us, while everyone else fled to separate parts of the house after the dishes had been washed.

All Morgan wants right now is someone to speak with. She wants Mike back. She wants confirmation that he's okay. She wants the noises from the basement- the rhythmic smashing- to stop.

Taking inventory, Morgan figures that Kyle and Hummingbird are upstairs. Rob is... where *is* Rob? Jody and Wil both went down into the basement, and now the noises are coming from the basement. Are they being hurt? Are they hurting each other? Are they destroying the barrel of wine?

The violent hammering in the basement shakes the house, and knocks a name out of Morgan's mouth, "Jody?"

The force of the smashing rattles everything around Morgan, bringing once still objects to life.

"Jody?" Morgan asks searchingly, amid another series of hammering thuds.

"Jody!" she shrieks loudly.

Morgan remains frozen at the piano bench, as the noises in the basement stop, then they're replaced by the faint sound of footsteps.

"Jody?" Morgan says again, quietly.

Please be Jody.

The door to the basement creaks open.

Please be Jody.

Except for the heavy breathing of a man approaching the living room, the rest of the house is silent.

Please be Jody.

"Fear not, young lady," Jody says, walking past the dinner table and into the living room.

Morgan looks relieved, until she spots the weapon Jody is holding- a wooden 2X4 with various sharp objects crudely hammered into it.

"Jody?" Morgan asks, but this isn't a call for help, it's a request for mercy. "Where's Wil?" she wants to ask, but her vocal chords are frozen.

"Jody?" Morgan asks, but this isn't a call for help, it's a request for mercy. "Where's Wil?" she wants to ask, but her vocal chords are frozen.

Jody lowers his weapon, studying it, and he says, "Fear not, I've created this instrument of revenge to destroy evil relics and demons, not people. In fact, I'm probably gonna fuck that wine barrel up with this baby, Donkey Kong style."

"What... is it?" Morgan asks.

"It's a 2X4 with a bunch of sharp shit nailed into it," Jody says. He raises an eyebrow, then asks, "You go blind or something?"

"Is that a Barbie leg stuck in there?" Morgan questions, reviewing the impossibly long, unachievably proportioned piece of plastic stuck in the board.

"Certainly is," Jody confirms. "I ran out of nails. Do you know how hard it was to get a Barbie leg in there? Those legs are certainly not made to be affixed to a weapon that will be used to destroy a satanic wine cellar."

"You made a mace to protect us?" Morgan asks, hoping for the best.

"Yes, I did," Jody says with conviction.

The fact that Jody seems focused on protecting his friends is enough to lift Morgan's spirits and restore her confidence.

"Put that down, then come here," Morgan says, patting the open space on the piano bench.

After doing a visual sweep of the room, Jody places the mace on the floor, then carefully approaches the piano. Unarmed in a house with an open front door, with a girl who sometimes doesn't laugh at his jokes, Jody feels vulnerable. By leaving his weapon on the ground and the door wide open, Jody is sacrificing his friends' security for another friend's safe return. Mike will not be locked out of the house; Jody wants to leave the Barrens with *all* of his friends.

Jody sits down on the piano bench, and instead of giving him room, Morgan scoots closer to him.

"So can you play this motherfucker or what?" Jody asks.

"I can't play like Rob can," Morgan says, nervous.

"Oh. Okay. Let's get Rob here then," Jody says, misinterpreting the comment.

When Morgan doesn't start playing, and Jody doesn't pick up his weapon, there's a beat of silence, but we can tell that both people on the bench are happy to not be so alone.

"I miss music," Jody admits.

"It's sad that your instruments are gone," Morgan agrees.

"Cliff is gone," Jody says, widening the scope.

Morgan flips the key cover up on the piano and it makes a reverberating bong. She looks to Jody, noticing a small smile that appears at the corner of his lips.

Morgan's fingers immediately begin playing, unable to fix so much, but confident in the favor they are about to return.

Jody exhales, then closes his eyes as music returns to his life. The notes being played aren't exactly haunting, but they're distinctly minor key. Morgan lets her sounds hang; she lets her melody mix with the dust.

"Michael will find us," Jody comments.

"That's the first time I've heard you call him something besides Cliff," Morgan says, continuing to play.

"I meant Myers. Michael Myers is going to stab our flesh and bodies with one of those knives from the kitchen. We now live in a supernatural dimension where his powers reign supreme and our bones are the only valid currency," Jody says, his eyes going from closed to wide as he makes this definitive statement.

"Michael Myers, one- is fictional, and two- is in Haddonfield, not New Jersey," Morgan says.

"There's a Haddonfield in Jersey," Jody responds, "I wanted to book a small venue there, but we decided we were too big for the gig and didn't want to take the risk of being murdered to death."

"Yeah, well, Michael Myers was in Haddonfield, Illinois, and there's a ton of land between here and Illinois. That's a shitload of walking.

"Michael Myers would never walk here, he'd drive. Don't you remember the movies? Michael Myers lived all of his teen years in a mental institution, somehow broke out, then got behind the wheel of a car for the first time ever, and he was immediately a better driver than Rob," Jody says.

"Yeah, I do resent Rob for stealing the van. We had to run. I hate running," Morgan says.

"Me too. Obviously," Jody says.

"I always have to run. No one will ever carry me. That's depressing," Morgan says, her eyes staring straight ahead at the window as her fingers glide over the keys.

"Carry you?"

"You said that there was no ass you'd rather carry in the whole world than Hummingbird's," Morgan says, wiping hair out of her face as she plays the piano with one hand.

"I wanted to carry your ass. I promise I did. I just didn't know how long we'd be running, and honestly I probably only had about 50 yards worth of strength to carry you."

"You really are an asshole, Jody Lennard," Morgan, says, shooting a glance at him, her fingers never stopping, never stumbling. If only Morgan's social grace was as measured and sure as her playing.

"Thank you for noticing, Morgan... whatever your last name is. You're a good person to talk to about life stuff," Jody says, in a moment of sincerity.

"I consider myself an expert when it comes to life stuff," Morgan says, finding her reflection in the window and momentarily not recognizing the blushing girl she sees looking back at her.

Jody nervously looks away from the window, over to the fireplace. He feels a sudden urge to brick up the birth canal that delivered the devil to New Jersey.

"We're moved in," Morgan says, pulling his attention back, "We're pineys now."

"Like the old bitch?" Jody asks, then makes a disapproving face.

"Yes. The old bitch is a piney. So is Jack. So was Ms. Leeds. We have to stay good."

"I'll be good," Jody responds, then begins to lean over toward his weapon.

"You said that you'd be good, then immediately scooched over to grab a giant mace covered in nails," Morgan points out.

"I never said I wasn't going to be prepared."

The song continues to play itself without Morgan focusing on the notes. She's still pressing down the keys, but it's almost as though a second set of hands- an invisible set of hands- is teaching her this song, guiding her fingers, helping her to continue on without pause.

Everything begins to fall away, as Jody's presence on the bench acquires a stretching distance. Morgan is enveloped by the familiar loneliness that she will never feel comfortable in. She's tried to battle this discomfort by devoting herself to making Leeds house, our house.

Morgan has devoted herself to making Leeds house, our house.

To make things feel like home, she's made sure that everyone in the house has a meal, not only for their well-being, but also for her own. If people gravitated toward her when dinner approached, it would show how essential she is. It's not lost on her that she's only in this house because of Hummingbird. Blame and appreciation, shame and the pointlessness of it all- these emotions continue to swirl inside Morgan, even after so many meals she's put on the table.

To make things feel like home, she's tried to move closer to the boys in the band. She took care of their needs. She made sure that what she lacked in looks, she made up for in exposure. But this didn't keep them close- Mike could be miles away right now.

To make things feel like home, she works to create music for the boys whose instruments were destroyed. These notes were supposed to bring everyone into the living room, but everyone remains distant.

As the music continues to climb through the house, Morgan arrives at the realization that she feels so connected to this house because, in many ways, she *is* Leeds house.

Leeds house is a suburban staple transplanted where it doesn't belong.

Leeds house is alone in the woods, and the only visitors it receives now are the lost.

Leeds house is walled in with history, making it a cage of mistakes, wrapped in an unassuming exterior.

Leeds house is without electricity, and any attempt at illuminating the darker corners fails the moment the boy with the light departs.

Leeds house was polluted by the actions of a woman who tried desperately to build a big family within these walls.

Leeds house is forever open, its gaping mouth accepting anyone indiscriminately.

Morgan is a haunted house and anyone who's dumb enough to enter her is doomed.

XXXI. Scars As Montage — Duets.

We lie on the wood floor of Behringer's writing room, next to a splayed out Hummingbird and Kyle. We had originally entered the office to search Behringer's bookshelves. We wanted to see if there were any journals describing Behringer's experience here. We weren't looking for a suicide note, or at least that's what we told ourselves. We don't care why Behringer killed himself, just that his own hands carried out the awful deed.

When the piano started playing, just as Jody predicted it would, we weren't afraid. Morgan had told us that she knows how to play. The fact that she was comfortable enough to sit at that bench and indulge her talent was proof that the night had calmed itself. As Morgan's beautiful gesture filled the room, Hummingbird and Kyle stopped looking for Behringer's notes, and they began to appreciate Morgan's. They got down on the wood floor, then listened to the music seeping through the cracks of the old house.

Now we watch as Hummingbird's hand begins to creep toward the beautiful boy to her right. This is how moments happen. This is a fully scored scene from Hummingbird's before-bed fantasies.

Searching for the resting place of Kyle's gloved palm, Hummingbird's hand slips too low, and her scar brushes across Kyle's fingertips.

"What happened to your wrist?" Kyle asks, his hand moving away, his body contracting into a sitting position.

"Nothing," Hummingbird says, but before she can pull her sleeves back down, Kyle grabs Hummingbird's wrist and, in the light of the oil lamp, we see a jagged scar.

Body tense, eyes blurring unfocused on the ceiling, Hummingbird lies on the floor and lets her wrist be inspected. "It was a mistake. I fell on a champagne glass at prom," Hummingbird says- mechanical, distant- as Kyle reaches over her and grabs her other arm, regretfully finding the same sealed slice- only the jagged details differing.

"Another champagne glass?" Hummingbird says, almost in a way that it makes it a question. "I really like champagne," she adds with a small laugh.

Kyle wonders why Hummingbird is still giving him excuses, especially after the scene he witnessed in the bathroom.

"Let go of me," Hummingbird whispers, pulling herself away from the boy she wanted to pull herself close to moments ago.

Kyle can't lie back down next to this girl. There's a pulse that pumps in him that makes relaxation impossible now. "Listen, I know how confusing things can be. I know that people do stupid things to cope," Kyle says quietly.

"Fuck you, you know nothing."

"I do know what it's like, Hummingbird," Kyle says, looking at the worried girl who just had her hands caught in a razor edged cookie jar.

"You know nothing. You're the lead singer. The lead singer never knows what it's like," Hummingbird says, dismissing Kyle, closing her eyes, fleeing to the music.

"Rachel."

"Stop. This conversation is done."

"No," Kyle responds, shaking his head, "It's not."

"Trust me, you want this conversation to be done, Kyle."

Energy flowing through his body, music taunting him, adrenaline and fear fueling him, Kyle demands, "Look at me."

The growled mandate is so severe that, when paired with the quiet music, it forces Hummingbird to push herself up on her ugly wrists. She looks at Kyle, who, kneeling like he's about to pray, lifts his left hand, then pulls his glove off. After tossing the compression glove onto the floor, Kyle holds his hand out to Hummingbird, near the light of the oil lamp, and says, "Tell me I know nothing about scars, Hummingbird. Look at my hand and tell me."

Hummingbird gasps. She looks down at the melted, grafted, rough skin that stretches across Kyle's palms.

"How?" she questions, her eyes flickering in a phantom pain.

"Burning metal," Kyle says quietly.

"Metal from what?"

"A motorcycle engine," Kyle says, the flames flickering in his eyes.

"You crashed your motorcycle?"

"No. I just walked out of the house. And. Uh. You know... how they say... that most accidents happen within ten miles of your home?"

Hummingbird is too fixed on Kyle's eyes to nod.

"Well. This one... happened closer. And. I didn't hear it happen for some reason, but, uh, I heard his screams."

"Whose?" Hummingbird asks like a little owl.

"Jody's," Kyle exhales, then looking up at the rafters with the same unfixed vision, he says, "I guess. It was a little dark or... something... and Jody was riding his motorcycle down our street. There were always cars parked on both sides of the road, and I don't know, maybe his lights weren't on, but this van- a lady was sending a text- and-" Kyle snaps his fingers, "-BAM. Jody was pinned between a parked car, and the van, and the motorcycle was burning his legs so, uh. I ran. To him. And the lady couldn't open the door, because she'd press on him harder. So I had to pull the motorcycle out, to unwedge it. And, well," Kyle holds up his hand.

Hummingbird grabs Kyle's ungloved hand and she kisses it. Once. Twice. A tear slides across the surface of Kyle's graft, and for a moment he feels healed.

Kyle had saved Jody and ruined a bit of himself. This is the cancer of caring. Kyle wants people to grasp him. As a rock star, one of the things he always does is hold out a hand to the crowd. When the crowd is drifting, the frontman demands, "Put your hands together."

Kyle decides to do this with Hummingbird. He puts his hand to her's and their fingers lock.

Now, Kyle can relax; now, Hummingbird once again believes that the lyrics she relates to so completely were written by this beautiful boy.

Hands still locked, Kyle and Hummingbird once again return to the floor as the sound of the piano continues to score their moment.

Kyle looks up at the rafters, then says, "I wanted to be able to hold my hand out and have people reach toward me, not away. Those gloves aren't a fashion statement, they're therapeutic compression gloves. I need to wear them, I don't choose to wear them. So Hummingbird, I do know about hiding scars, just as much, if not more, than you."

Hummingbird wipes her wet face on her shoulder, and in a muffled comment, says, "You got yours in a beautiful way, and you're still ashamed. I got mine in an ugly way, so…"

"Why can't you stop scarring yourself?" Kyle asks.

"No one loves me," Hummingbird says in a tiny sob.

"I find that very hard to believe."

"Me too," Hummingbird responds.

XXXII. Scars As Montage – Phantasmagoria.

We watch Wil put his back to the boiler and take a sip from his red plastic tumbler.

We don't like being alone with Wil, but damn does he like being alone with himself. Jody had followed Wil downstairs, but in a house where sound travels, a call for help will always be answered. The sound continues to carry down the stairs, through the basement, and the faint music from the piano creates an illusion of tranquility. Wil welcomes the music, and relaxes against the warm boiler, enjoying his cup of wine. His body is still; his mind is drifting. This is not Rob's playing- Wil is sure of it. This is one of the girls. The fans are now performing for the band boys.

The artist and the fan have a complicated relationship. Since the artist we're trapped with has a complicated relationship with every person in his life, the fan issue, in his mind, is even more pressing and tension filled.

Wil hates making small talk with the fans. He hates answering questions about why he plays the way he does. He hates posing for cell phone pictures, knowing that he looks sweaty and tired. He hates trying to sell merch, begging people to buy a T-shirt bundle for "the best deal."

To Wil, the fans are a tapeworm, feeding off of him.

Performing is a jolt, but during the creative process is when Wil feels truly alive. Once the music is released, he often loses attachment to it. He has to distance himself from it. The only time Wil was quoted in the Lies As Language interview with *Kerrang!* was when he said, "If you dig a grave, then the grave is dug. Throw a body in there and cover that shit up. Let's not keep re-digging this grave with the same sadness we felt after the first shovel full of dirt."

There's a new freedom brought about by the van disasters Wil has been a part of recently. Metalcore, declining in popularity, has been dying in vans across the east coast. If Mike doesn't come back, Lies As Language will be over, forever, before the band truly started what could have been an amazing journey.

Metalcore is about palatable extremes and jarring transitions. Unlike the ease of a casual rock song featuring a single singer performing catchy lyrics, metalcore is a true collaboration in which every member must display complete commitment or the song crumbles.

There was a time when metalcore provided a predictable comfort that was otherwise absent from Wil's life. He had felt very safe working inside the rigid structure of the genre. Classic mainstays that appear on all metalcore records were used to ensure that no song Lies As Language worked on could be considered an out-and-out failure. When people complained the songs were too hard, Kyle's clean vocals could bail out the band. Adding cleans would set off a chain reaction though- Kyle's crisp, clear presence could be seen as "betraying" the raw assault that Mike inflicts on the fans with his screams and growls. The cleans act as the sonic equivalent of the magic wand in the Behringer book. Remove the wand, and you're just left with the story of an angry, fucked up boy.

Creating music that the audience can take an active role in performing is crucial to the live experience for a metalcore band. Lies As Language, a band that thrived on the stage, used gang vocals on many of the songs that made their debut album. During the live show, the gang vocals are a way to get people involved, and to gauge how well the audience knows the material. This technique has always been a cheap ploy for audience interaction, yet it also provides Wil a chance to participate in the singing so he doesn't resent the gang vocals as much as one would expect him to. Being "part of it all" is now an audience need. The modern metalcore fan has endless demands: they want to follow your posts on the internet, they want to look at your pictures, they want to hunt down who you're dating, they want to submit questions to you, they want to get acknowledgment because they actually bought your work instead of stealing it, which makes them feel like they are part of the band's success. For established fans, the gang vocals feel like the band is saying, we built this part for you and it will only work if you join us. It introduces an interdependence. The fan thinks, *I need to help these guys, I'll sing with them- I need to help these guys, I'll buy a t-shirt- I need to help these guys, I'll let them sleep at my house and I won't fuck up and blackout in the middle of giving them directions.* That's when the breakdown happened in the fan interaction this time.

A very different breakdown is also a mainstay of the metalcore genre. When Lies As Language shifts the time scale they're playing in and Jody becomes the focus, the breakdown is born. Mike's screams are transformed into guttural woofs. Wil's guitar playing chugs through a single note repeatedly, while Jody's double bass drum technique hammers the audience and stirs them into a frenzy, setting off a mosh pit filled with crashing bodies and hardcore dancing. It could be assumed that slowing the tempo of the song would zap the energy, but the opposite happens with a metalcore breakdown. The breakdown is for the kids in front, the kids in the pit. This is the shit that the teen girls hate- it sends them to the wall, which sends Kyle forward after the breakdown, to extend his fingertips out and heal the damage. Space is made when the breakdown begins, and it's sealed when the breakdown ends.

The "space" element of Lies As Language's excessive genre clarification was introduced by Rob. He wanted to create a "simultaneous undercurrent of dread and calm" that would run under every song. Rob's keyboard and MPC became crucial in crafting this atmosphere. He pre-programmed samples on the pads of the MPC that he would tap out while his other hand played the keyboard. When he would stab those pads and slam those keys, he created an otherworldly, transporting effect. It was piano lessons gone mad. It was "Mary Had a Little Lamb" meets *The Silence of the Lambs*. Rob's playing sometimes sounded like the music leaking down from upstairs and other times sounded like a return to the womb.

This house has taught Wil that life lacks structure, and since metalcore relies on it, the music now feels disingenuous. Wil must depart from the metalcore genre entirely if he wants to create an emotionally true record.

Searching for a way to escape everything he's built this year, Wil sits facing the wine barrel, and he stares at a crack in the wall. He wonders what would happen if he applied some force to the fractured foundation. There's a chance he'd only find the sandy soil of the Barrens beyond this thick wall, but there's also the equally likely outcome that he'd discover that this basement contains more rooms, hidden rooms.

Wil takes a sip from his cup and the bitter red causes him to wince. When he opens his eyes, he sees a tiny flame begin to slide up the crack in the foundation. When the flame reaches the ceiling, the entire room becomes instantly walled with flames like the wine cellar was wallpapered with gasoline. The fire licks at Wil's neck and singes the hair on his arms. In a panic, he tries to scream, but almost as though Mike took his trademark sound with him, Wil's vocal cords make no noise. Around his waist is a tight seat belt that he immediately attempts to free himself from. The moment Wil grips the restraint, it thickens and rounds- it becomes a black snake, and the sizzling flames hiss in conversation with the beast. As the room becomes an unbearable tomb of flames, Wil splashes the wine from his cup on the wall across from him, and this instantly puts out the fire, suffocating it across every wall, leaving an ashed tranquility. The snake slides off Wil's lap and slithers behind the wine barrel. Assessing the damage, Wil rolls up his sleeves and finds he has suffered no burns. He feels the back of his neck, then looks at his hand. A mix of sweat and ash greases his palm.

This was a warning. Wil could've ended up like those fucking losers in Punchcunt Love, but he didn't. He escaped because he followed his instincts. The wine that his "friends" deemed poison was actually the solvent that saved him. This wine has led Wil to the answer. His new goal becomes to never feel like Punchcunt Love again. He can escape the van by switching genres. By going solo, those snakes that restrained him cannot hold him back anymore.

After refilling his cup, Wil begins his plan for a new independence that will allow him to flourish. He'll switch genres; never again will he return to the breakdowns, or the gang vocals, or the band of boys who put him in danger. At first, the transition will be hard, but Wil is used to being left all alone. The first song will be the most difficult sell. A genre switch always sends the fans fleeing, and when they disappear, they'll take the glamor and excitement with them. If the old fans are stuck on the old genre, then Wil is ready to find new fans. It's easier than ever to put out music, but it's harder than ever to find people who'll view your work as something more than a seven-megabyte file. Wil has the task of convincing strangers to drink his bitter wine. Integration is essential now. Cross platform agreements and alliances are the shining hope for Wil's rebirth. A lonely girl will be watching a movie, a TV show- hell, even FM radio might end up playing one of Wil's songs, and the girl will think, "Yes. This is where I'm at right now. Someone understands me completely." She'll go hunting for the song, maybe holding her phone up to the speaker so an App can listen along for a couple seconds, then reveal Wil's name on the screen. There will be no moniker for this project- Wil can finally present himself, unrestrained. Or maybe this girl will find the song while caught in a YouTube click spiral where she's hopping from video to video. Suddenly, she isn't looking for a TV episode, she's looking for an album. She might illegally download this mysterious album- just for the song. She'll get the song and she'll fix the tags on it so that it looks right with the rest of her collection, then she'll listen to the song- again, and again, and again. She'll need more. She'll start listening to the other songs, once padding, now the focal point of her hungry search. This is a solitary task. She's grasping for a sustained connection. Her friends don't get her. Her parents are just trying to keep her alive. She feels all alone- no matter how big or small her group of friends is, no matter how empty or packed her house is. When those texts go unanswered, when the night doesn't turn out the way she planned, when 11 PM becomes 4 AM and everyone else is fast asleep... Wil's music will be there, and that's where it ends.

Wil is now free to show his true self to the world, and if they don't like what they find, they can go to hell.

XXXIII. Scars As Montage — Echo.

We stand in the office at the end of the wood paneled hallway, and we watch Rob, because someone needs to. He sets a lit stubby candle on the desk, then hangs his jean jacket on a brass hook affixed to the back of the door. He's sweating, and in this house, it's a new feeling, but not a warm feeling. To be hot in the devil's home is a bad omen. Rob is reminded of the horror films that he and his friends would torrent five-at-a-time. When the characters could see their own breath, they knew that some sort of spectral vision was going to appear. It was that idea that if you can see the normally invisible air, what else might be able to materialize in the vapor? Rob is fighting his own demons in the small office, and seeing his breath would actually be a relief at this point. It would remind him that he's still breathing, that the demons haven't won yet.

So much has changed since that night that Rob was dropped off at Cari Simmons' house. Arriving at Cari's, creating an unexpected stop for the van, Rob had raised the suspicions of his bandmates. He used the merch money he pocketed to make a purchase that night. Rob still refuses to admit to his friends what Hummingbird's shoelace was used for, why he fell "asleep" in the van, or what happened after everyone else ran and the band boy was left with a fan.

Tonight, at dinner, Rob was punished for telling the truth. When he mentioned the wine, he thought that it would renew the summer camp-like feelings that his arrival caused. The wine was supposed to provide an escape, not set everyone on edge. Sitting at the dinner table, being scolded for his discovery, Rob was reminded that he is an addict, and an addict doesn't view things in the same way "normal" people do. A beverage or a syringe isn't the answer for people who have managed to cope with life's challenges in sober days, and responsible nights. Rob lost his friends' trust by sharing his discovery with them, so no more. Instead of seeing the wine as the perfect way to enjoy this odd situation, everyone viewed it as the bottled blood of the Leeds devil's victims, that was consumed by a careless and self-destructive boy.

Rob knows that this is how rock and roll works as well. The new prince of darkness drinking the blood of the former king. Ozzy was the worst, until Alice was the worst, until Marilyn was the worst. These men wrote songs and inherited blame for the actions of madmen. It felt weird to Rob that rock could be used as a scapegoat for a mistake an individual chose to make on their own. Rock saved Mike from carrying out an act that people would have considered rock an accomplice to. It's bizarre that we all remain so ignorant regarding the causes of violence. The way Rob views the changes born in this house, Mike lost his instrument, then his instrument became violence.

Rob wants to step out of this room, to follow the music. It didn't occur to him, until Morgan started playing, that he hasn't lost his ability to make music just because his keyboard and MPC are gone. Morgan's soft, sad notes remind Rob of his talent.

Despite this, Rob doesn't leave the room- he doesn't approach the piano- because if he starts playing, he'll start drinking. Creating keeps the selfish from taking, and most great geniuses needed the relaxation of a vice to allow them to flourish as God intended. Rob relates to this. He wants to get high as much as he wants to play that piano, and he can do one, then do the other, to great results.

A year ago, in an amateur video interview conducted by the YouTube user RoxxsKidRoxxSht, Rob, in exchange for four lines of coke, said, "I have to get fucked up to play, to feel the music. It's like, there's this zone that I create in. Some people have booze- some writers can't write without it. Drugs are my booze. I need them if I'm going to be creative. When I'm not doing drugs, I can't focus on anything because I'm just thinking about how much I'd rather be doing drugs. You know those license plate covers that say, like, 'I'd Rather Be Playing Pool?' well if it wouldn't lead to me getting busted, I'd buy one that says, 'I'd Rather Be Doing Drugs.'"

This was Rob's creative process. Do the uppers, or the downers, depending on what he was able to afford, or what generous charity he could find. When the band took the floor, or that rare time there was a stage, Rob would lean on the keys, blasting out a wave of droning atmosphere. He'd sway, not just at his keyboard, but *on* his keyboard- the keys crashing like turbulent waves, eroding the jagged edges. The stand he kept his equipment on was cross-reinforced three times so that the keyboard and synthesizer were almost impossible to tip. Playing or not, Rob's hands would remain on the keyboard and his belt buckle stayed pressed against the table's sturdy bars so he didn't topple over. In the end, the van explosion destroyed this entire indestructible setup.

Tonight, Rob's need for something beyond wine isn't just about creating, it's also about satisfying a need, finding an escape. The apathy Rob finds in Wil is something he now desires. It's the way Wil can become annoyed, but never worried... frightened, but never afraid. There's a detachment there- the way he left Mike was so simple. Rob knows that when Wil circled back on that run it wasn't for Mike. Wil either didn't care what would happen to Mike at that tree, or he wanted it to happen. No. It can't be the second one. Things should be easier now that the boys aren't officially a band anymore. No one needs to be in perfect time with each other now and that should ease the tension.

As Rob acknowledges that Lies As Language has died, the piano goes silent. Almost as though this absence of music removed the oxygen from the room, the stubby candle on the desk flickers. The wick is almost completely submerged in a pool of liquid wax, and the light may disappear soon.

Making use of the light, Rob begins to search the desk drawers. The first drawer contains nothing of value. The second drawer in that aged desk contains such familiar objects that it practically glows. Impossible. All of this stuff was in the van, yet now it's sitting neatly in the drawer. *No, No, No,* Rob repeats in his head. This has to be one of those mirages- a hallucination- a test. Was it the Leeds devil who organized these items in the drawer?

Rob touches the familiar items. They're real.

A decision flickers.

Rob walks to the door. His right hand moves to the doorknob, his left hand moves to the lock.

XXXIV. When The Music Stops.

We wake up under the comforter from the bedroom, but we're in Behringer's upstairs writing room. A purple dawn peaks through the trees and spills in through the tall windows. We know what time it is. This is the broken clock existence we must now accept.

We're next to Kyle. Kyle is next to Hummingbird. Hummingbird is next to Morgan. Morgan is next to Jody.

Last night was quiet, and musical, and reflective- it brought the people in this room closer together, while pushing the missing further away.

Under that warm blanket in the cold house, the menace is absent, until the alarm clock of reality hammers on the door of the writing room.

We all spring up, on guard, broken apart by the angry slams against a locked gate to the unknown. With rhythmic, repeating thuds, someone or something attempts to force the office door open.

In the hallway, behind the door, doing an imitation of Mike on stage, Wil screams, "You fucking assholes. I know you're in there."

Jody moves toward the door, then Kyle gives him an approving nod to slide the horizontal lock back. These angry, drunken rants are familiar to the Lennard boys. Back in Connecticut, Wil had left Kyle's apartment like this hundreds of nights. All too often Wil's internal pain regarding his mother became external outbursts that ended with violence against defenseless objects. Jody knew that Wil had found the wine. When Rob and Wil didn't make it to Behringer's office by bedtime, he suspected they were in the basement indulging in Rob's discovery. The warnings given at the dinner table should have stopped them. Then again, maybe all the warnings we've received should have sent us out of the house, yet here we are, still.

The door bursts open, and we're presented with a very different version of Wil. His hair is limp and his eyes are bloodshot. His dirty shirt is stained with what we hope is just red wine. "How fucking cute, you sad little shits," Wil slurs, looking at the makeshift bed on the ground.

"Wil, you're drunk," Jody states the obvious, "Kyle told you..."

"Ah yes," Wil responds, gliding across the room, "The gloved one had issued a decree. Those who do not comply will be cast out. Is it time to send me out to die, like you did to Mike?"

Kyle steps toward Wil, and in his soothing voice says, "I did everything I could to bring him back here and-"

"-and you failed," Wil hisses, "Twice."

"Why twice?" Jody asks.

"I don't see Rob in here..." Wil says, then he lets the moment hang.

Morgan joins in on the fight, "Rob became your responsibility the second you started drinking with him, you-"

"-no. No. No," Wil says, "I thought he was sleeping in the mini-office downstairs, but when I went looking around this morning, No Robby. Checked the living room. No Robby. Checked that weird part of the house that doesn't have a second floor, and... well, I'm sure you get the point by now."

Rob has a history of disappearing and coming back fine, so everyone relies on this happening again.

"So, Kyle," Wil says, his bitter feelings of betrayal now being colorized with pleasure, "Looks like you've done everything you can to bring people back and they keep leaving. I have to ask, sage leader, what's the next step? How do we further alienate our friends under this roof?"

"This is not you," Kyle says to Wil, who immediately hisses back, "Oh, it most assuredly is."

"You shouldn't have reopened that barrel," Kyle scolds Wil.

Wil laughs. Wil Laughs. Wil keeps laughing. "You fucking assholes," he manages to say between gasps. "We're all going to die here, and Kyle, if you walk away from this alive, I hope you carry a supreme guilt. You'll never wash your hands of our blood."

"Okay, looks like you volunteered," Jody says.

"Pardon?" Wil asks.

"You're the next member of this house to get the fuck out," Jody says, grabbing Wil by the yellowed dress shirt, ripping the collar as he pulls him toward the door.

"Wait," Wil calls out, but when his demand is ignored, his tattooed hand delivers a crisp slap across Jody's face.

His eyes remaining closed, Jody pauses his retaliation. He doesn't want to react to behavior fueled by the contents of the barrel in the basement. That would be Jody following Leeds' plan to the letter.

"What's wrong with you, Wil?" Morgan spits, the words being expelled like they taste bad.

"Go back to sleep, Morgan. You have no idea how doomed we are. I'm the only one who's witnessed that we're not alone here, besides Kyle." Wil shoots a pained look in Kyle's direction, then he continues, "He saw it too, but damn it, Kyle, you've gotten so good at pretending you don't see the obvious," Wil says, pointing a crooked finger at the other Lennard he plans on hurting this morning. "Once I'm gone, buddy boy, you're going to be the only one who knows what *he* looks like, so, Kyle, please describe what you saw so no one mistakenly shoots any other woodland creature, or worse, one of us."

"No one is shooting the gun. I have it," Kyle says.

"That worries me," Wil responds, eyes wide.

"It shouldn't. I'll use it to protect my friends," Kyle says.

At least one person in the tall-ceilinged office finds comfort in this statement. Let's hope that the nice guy is a good shot. Maybe the rest of us have secrets that can help keep everyone alive. Our individual talents can be revealed, one by one, eventually leading to a communal force field that will sustain us until help comes.

"So, there's evil outside and evil in the barrels downstairs, and evil hanging from the trees. What should we be looking for Kyle?" Wil prods.

"We have to figure out what's going on, then address it with our full attention," Jody says, in a tone usually reserved for car trouble.

"No, we don't," Wil says matter-of-factly, then when the statement sits on his stomach, it pushes out his fury, "We don't have to figure out what's going on here. That's not our responsibility."

Hummingbird tries to defend Wil, "He's just shaken up from-"

"-from the fucking tree decorated with dead animals? I'm not 'shaken up' from that. Being shaken up means that things will be rocky for a moment, then everything will settle. This will not settle. I. Will. Not. Settle," Will says, his teeth gnashing, his fists clenched.

The drunk boy in the torn shirt moves toward the bookcase at the edge of the room and starts taking out books. "It's the dead author," he says, throwing a hardcover at us. He turns back to the shelf to reload, "It's the devil," he says, launching another book. Now that there's a divot in the careful line of books, Wil uses his arm to slice the hardcovers off the shelf. If there is an angry spirit in the house, the books slapping to the floor like little gunshots will absolutely get its attention.

Suddenly, the wine in Wil's body gets its revenge by evolving into a truth serum.

"It's us. It's me. It's you," Wil says, staggering toward Kyle. "It's you, Kyle. You did this. You know that... you know that... I love you. You fucking know it, Kyle," Wil sighs, instantly melting, his anger gone, his sadness soaking everything. Tears cut down Wil's dirty face, washing away the scowl of an angry drunk, initiating a transformation. "You. Know. How. I. Feel," Wil chokes, as Kyle backs up. "You were always with *him*, but where is he now? Is he looking for us like you're about to go looking for Rob and Mike? I fucking doubt-"

"-okay, time's up," Jody says, grabbing Wil by the arm. Wil resists a little, but he has no adrenaline left and he allows himself to be pulled out of the room by a Lennard because a Lennard didn't pull him close when he admitted how he truly feels... about everything.

"If you disappear, I'll look for you, but you never even looked *at* me, Kyle," Wil yells from the hallway, then Jody slams the door shut.

XXXV. Demo(n).

We listen as Jody plays club bouncer in the hallway, "Stay in the fucking bedroom or I'll put you in the closet." There's a pause, then a little softer, a clarification is made, "And that wasn't a bit of homophobia there. I have no problem with your proclivities. I was referring to the fact that you were scared by what was in the closet before, and I'll put you back there to face that fear. I'm fine with you being gay... but.. sometimes I have to ask myself if I'm the only one in this house who doesn't love cocks!"

On the other side of the door, Morgan has burrowed under the comforter, seeking a couple more hours of sleep, but Hummingbird and Kyle are pumping with confused emotion. Kyle stands in front of the window, looking out at the purple dawn, and Hummingbird walks behind him, then asks, "Why didn't you recognize those lyrics on the wall in the basement?"

"What?" Kyle asks, his face contorting, "I'm not doing some fan interview for you," he scoffs. The house is silent as Kyle stares out the window, and it's almost as though he's not in the same room as us, choosing instead to remain distant after discovering the feelings of a man he thought was straight, up until this morning.

"Downstairs. The lyrics on the wall," Hummingbird says, as her eyes remained fixed on the spot where Kyle saw the devil.

Kyle glances at the windowpane and sees Hummingbird's face, precisely where he saw the devil's face and he realizes that the devil had been standing behind him. The devil had been over his shoulder in the room, and there's no evidence to indicate he's not here now.

"You've been lying to us," Hummingbird says, then looks toward the lump under the comforter that is her best friend.

Kyle suddenly gets the chilling feeling that Hummingbird is now reading from the devil's teleprompter. This topic of conversation had never been brought up to Kyle or the band, and it had only been casually discussed among "The Liars." That was the irony. Since Lies As Language's fan base was growing, the hardcore fans wanted to brand themselves, and they chose "The Liars" as their moniker. As these like-minded people discussed anything and everything about Lies As Language, Kyle's honesty, or lack thereof, came into question. Up until recently, Hummingbird had never considered herself one of The Liars who had reservations about what

Kyle was misrepresenting- what Kyle was suppressing- who the real Kyle was. If Hummingbird ever gets back to a computer, she doesn't know what she'll tell the other Liars. Maybe, now that she finally knows the people behind the instruments, she'll confirm that The Liars were right, Kyle is a fraud.

"Why didn't you recognize those words from the demo on the wall? *You see you and you don't see. The ground beneath you, trembling,*" Hummingbird says.

Kyle thinks about how to tactfully answer Hummingbird's straightforward question, then he decides on his response, "I don't know why I didn't recognize the lyrics. I guess they just weren't that meaningful to me." Kyle makes sure to say this quietly, so he doesn't wake Morgan. Morgan is another Liar, and this conversation is already filled with them.

"Why do you sing 'she' in all your songs, Kyle?" Hummingbird asks. This interrogation will not end until another confession is made in this room.

"Ahhh," Kyle groans, bouncing away from Hummingbird's image in the window, even though she wasn't attempting eye contact.

"That's not an answer."

"Yeahhh," Kyle creeks quietly, as he rubs the back of his neck, while wiping the hair out of his eyes with his other hand. His hair is getting long. How long have we been here? How long has Hummingbird known Kyle? A week? A day? A minute?

"Everyone knows," Hummingbird says, boldly turning around, then she kneels down and picks up a book off the ground to restore a little order to the room. When she scoops a second book off the ground, she's careful not to look at the page it's opened to. She doesn't want to receive any messages. The pages of these books are flopped open, craving to be read.

"Everyone knows what?" Kyle asks very deliberately.

"Everyone saw those pictures of you with *him* at his gallery opening. The kiss..."

There's a moment of eye contact between Kyle and Hummingbird that's lost when Kyle's eyes drop toward the floor, to the mess of books. He responds, in a low tone, "I've never made my life a secret. We're just not a big band so..."

"You've made it a secret in your music," Hummingbird responds, walking back to the bookcase.

"Where's this going?" Kyle asks, walking toward the door, but he pauses, "I can't give some *Tiger Beat* interview with... with... all that's happening around us."

"It's Jody isn't it?"

"Isn't what? Yes. Yes," Kyle says, initially ready to continue his posturing, but instantly too tired to continue a futile fight. "It's Jody," Kyle responds.

"I knew he wrote those songs," Hummingbird says.

"And he doesn't get any of the credit," Kyle caps off the implication, then provides the excuse, "I'll have you know that he- the guy who produced the record- was doing us a favor, so we couldn't question him. He said that... I guess... it's better to have the lyrics come from the heart and mind of..."

"An attractive boy instead of an ugly man?" Hummingbird asks, and when Kyle doesn't respond, she admits, "He's right... in a way. But it's weird to find out that the oft-quoted words you attributed to a boy you liked were actually from a man you're disgusted by."

Those lyrics were why Hummingbird and Kyle ended up in each other's lives. This realization makes Kyle hate his actions for reasons beyond betraying his brother.

"You took the credit, then you let Jody be the punchline," Hummingbird says.

"He offered," Kyle says, in a way that feels like a "he hit me first" defense.

"Honestly," Hummingbird says, rolling up her sleeves, physically and verbally, "That doesn't surprise me. But you've surprised me, Kyle."

Kyle wants to tell Hummingbird that she has surprised him too. He could remind Hummingbird that she's not a perfect little princess, but he doesn't say these things because he doesn't have to. Hummingbird already knows her own failings, and that's why her body looks the way it does. Kyle seeks the path of least resistance, "It makes more sense. We'll get a bigger fan base if people think-"

"-I'm already a fan. Morgan is already a fan. And you still lied about everything down there," Hummingbird says, pointing to the wooden floorboards. When she sees her finger gesturing below, she immediately balls it into a fist. How deep does the foundation of this house go?

"I did lie. I guess... I was just going along with the plan," Kyle mumbles.

"What happens the next time someone brings up how brilliant of a writer you are?" Hummingbird asks Kyle, and he responds in a way that he knows will hurt her, "We won't have to cross that bridge the way things are going now."

Startling both Kyle and Hummingbird, Morgan pops up from under the covers, and looking at the liar, she says, "I love your songs."

"They aren't mine," Kyle responds.

XXXVI. It'll Last Longer.

We follow Morgan down the hall to the door of Behringer's room, which is now a makeshift drunk tank.

"Can you just listen to what I'm saying to you!" Morgan demands as she stomps toward Jody.

These two seem like our parents. Both of them are trying to do the right thing; both of them are trying to protect a mistake-afflicted boy locked in the bedroom. "All I'm saying is that it couldn't have been easy for him to say those things," Morgan argues.

"It was incredibly easy. Follow these steps. One- get fucked up. Two- be a fuck up," Jody says, counting out a game plan that Wil seemed to be carefully following today.

"What we witnessed was a cry for help," Morgan whispers.

"And no one's listening," Jody responds back.

"I'm listening," Morgan hisses, then almost on cue, an electric hum bursts across the hall.

Jody and Morgan both stop arguing and search for a logical reason as to why a distinctly digital sound exists in a house with no electricity.

A wave of static roars, hissing a demand for attention.

Morgan slowly moves toward Jody as the static continues, uniform in its volume, unmistakably not from the baby monitor. This is an analog TV stuck between channels.

"It's coming from the room at the end of the stairs," Morgan says.

"Fuck," Jody says. "Fuck," Jody says. "Fuck," Jody says.

Morgan nods in agreement with Jody's repeated reaction.

"Some creepy shit is going to be in there," he verbally acknowledges, pointing down the hall.

"Fuck," Morgan says.

"We should probably go in there and get it out of the way," Jody suggests, like the investigation was a trip to the dentist after too many nights of passing out in mid-Cheeto-chew.

Jody leads the way down the hall, fist cocked, as though he could punch away any beast that's riding the static. Morgan follows behind, ready to confront this creepy shit because it's easier than dealing with someone harboring secret feelings for another member of the house.

Jody slides into the room at the end of the stairs. The sick photographs still line the wall to his right. To his left, is a box glowing under a white blanket.

"The TV is on," Morgan marvels, unsure of what to make of this discovery.

"Under that sheet could be a fuckin' Casper," Jody says, not trusting anything about this creepy pedo room.

"Jody. I don't think you understand. The TV is turned on, but there's no plug," Morgan says, circling the sheet.

"Holy shit," Jody says, then he smiles, "We have a TV up in this motherfucker! What time is it in real world time? What if the Devil's game is on?" Jody asks, grasping the edge of the sheet and pulling it off dramatically like the reveal on a magic trick. This sweeping gesture exposes a faux wood frame TV on four stubby legs. Morgan was right- there are no cords hanging down from the TV.

"I think the Devils are playing the Bruins," Jody gleefully tells Morgan.

"Seriously? The Devils' game?"

"You're right. That was in bad taste. We'll root for the cocksucking Bruins," Jody says, playing with the knobs on the TV.

The New Jersey Devils had become Jody's favorite team after the 1997 relocation of the Connecticut Whalers to North Carolina. Jody held "the devil" responsible for this move and began closely following the Devils while planning an "inside attack" that would bring "the Devils to their knees and the Whalers back to Connecticut." Jody's Devils theory was loudly underscored by his observation, "They play in Newark. Read the papers. The devil must live there."

Sitting down in front of the box, twisting the knob on the front of the TV, surfing through channel after channel, Jody finds nothing but static.

"This sucksss," Jody exhales, "No wonder this thing was under a sheet."

"This TV being on without any power is meant to scare us," Morgan says, trying to make sure the reaction that was anticipated by Leeds was received in full. If the devil's reveals are met with shrugged shoulders, the next reveal will certainly be bigger, more shocking, and more dangerous.

Jody stands up, admitting defeat, growing bored with the new oddity. "When you're done in here, turn the TV off. we don't want to waste magical demon fairy-dust," he tells Morgan.

As Jody turns to leave, he comes face to face with a familiar face in one of the pictures on the wall. Inside the white border of the photograph is a black boy with his shirt off, standing in the Polaroid room of Leeds house. This is the young Afro-American boy that Jody saw the night before he left for New Jersey.

XXXVII. Divined A Torch.

We watch Morgan collect the syrup-covered plates from the dining room table.

We have no choice but to give up on the silent hope that Rob would smell the pancakes and return to the house, or come out of hiding. He's just hiding, right? We have to be sure he's not in the house. Before the dishes are started, we begin to search for our lost friend.

Following behind a well-armed Jody, we begin at the far end of the first floor and scan the house in the comfortable safety of the afternoon light.

We check the kitchen. Nothing. We check the living room and the dining room. Nothing.

Jody lights a candle on the oven burner, then passes it to Kyle.

Hummingbird carries the oil lamp and we make our way down the creaking stairs into the basement. Morgan is at Jody's side- their disagreement, forgotten. Kyle and Hummingbird are shoulder-to-shoulder even though they look like they want to elbow each other. Wil is upstairs in Behringer's bedroom, sleeping off his brutal morning.

"Rob?" Jody calls out. Nothing.

We move in a tight square around the basement.

Still buzzing from the admission that he made to Hummingbird, Kyle moves away from the group, toward the wall. He wants to look at the lyrics, but someone has turned the page already. There's no trace of the the graffitied lyrics that were a topic of conversation this morning. They had accomplished their purpose, then were wiped away, and now a new topic has been provided to us. Kyle reaches up and touches the fresh markings, desperate to know what medium was used to deface the wall.

"So, what, we have some sort of malevolent Banksy in this house?" Hummingbird asks, handing Morgan the lamp, confident enough to face the darkness until she reaches Kyle.

"That's kind of redundant- Banksy *is* malevolent," Kyle responds, then he hesitantly reviews the residue on his fingers from the markings.

Morgan follows behind Hummingbird, and this causes Jody to redirect his course since he's bound to the circle of light. When they reach the wall, Jody points at the new message and says, "I bet we could sell this to some fuckin' yuppie."

"How do we remove it, though?" Morgan asks. "If we can't even get ourselves out of the woods, how do we get the basement wall out?"

"We'd probably have to recreate it. Maybe make an underground donation to the Red Cross in exchange for bags of non-HIV-non-hep blood and we could mass produce this stuff," Jody says.

Still studying his fingers, Kyle says, "It's not blood," but this doesn't sound as reassuring as it should have been.

We watch the worried group pontificate about the art in front of them. They stand in a mix of postures that range from casual to disinterested. If someone had photographed this moment, it could be confused as a low-rent-chic gallery opening. Brutal surroundings and tame conversations.

Everything is a song title.

Everything is a movie scene.

Everything is an amateur YouTube clip, because if it wasn't, it would be real life.

We know how those gothic songs end, with people dead.

We know how those horror movies end, with people dead.

We don't know how those amateur YouTube clips end because we stop watching them when we realize it's some amateur garbage and no one cares about normal peoples' lives.

There's an active need to not dwell on the message, but we also feel compelled to keep looking. On the wall, in rusty lettering, is the message, *You saw and I did too.*

These are not lyrics from a Lies As Language song.

The temperature drops further in the basement.

"Guys," Jody says, breaking everyone out of their trance.

We whirl around to find Jody proudly holding up a Pokémon flashlight.

"Very nice, Jody," Kyle says like a mother whose patience is wearing thin.

"You don't understand," Jody maintains.

"Kyle can't comprehend a flashlight that's molded in Pikachu's image?" Morgan asks, confused.

"This is a sign."

"I don't think we need any more signs that Behringer was a kid mongering creepy balls," Hummingbird says, shivering in the basement.

"In the Bible, God sent people signs," Jody reminds us.

"Oh no," Kyle says.

"Some of those signs, like the Star in the East, helped guide people to where they needed to be. Others, like setting someone's landscaping on fire, was to convince Moses to get the Israelites out of Egypt."

"Because they broke the sphinx?" Hummingbird asks.

"I don't think he wanted them out of Egypt because the Israelites were vicious vandals, but I mean, recently..." Jody ponders, then shrugs. "Basically, what I'm telling you is that God was like, 'Moses, sup? Go to Egypt. Help me out. Here's a cool bow staff. Yes, it's lacquered. You probably haven't even seen lacquer ever, but it rules and really gives bow staffs a beautiful shine and a durable hard shell.'"

"So what's this sign supposed to mean? I don't get it," Hummingbird says.

"Who knows," Jody responds. "I think that we must leave this basement, my dear Hummingbird. I have been given my bow staff, now I must lead us on a journey to get our friends back... or find help."

"And this flashlight is your bow staff?" Hummingbird asks, teeth chattering from the cold of the basement.

"It's my torch," Jody declares proudly, "I am the keeper of the torch."

"That's not a torch. That's a yellow Pokémon flashlight," Kyle says, unwilling to accept Jody's delusions of grandeur.

The flashlight clicks on and a beam of light moves directly into Kyle's eyes.

Kyle raises his gloved left hand to block the light.

"I don't see you dismissing my torch right now," Jody says.

"We'll go out, tonight," Morgan says, accepting the sign.

"I never thought I'd say this, but I'd really just prefer to stay in on the couch instead of going out tonight," Hummingbird whines.

After a momentary pause, something clicks inside Kyle, and he says, "Exactly." He points at Hummingbird, "That's exactly what he wants. He knows that we're already afraid of the dark. He thinks that we're too scared to step outside so he plans everything around us being in the house after nightfall. Let's reverse his plans."

"He can hear this," Morgan says, looking into the dark.

"How do you even know?" Hummingbird squeaks, then reminds everyone, "Going outside at night is an incredibly stupid idea. We handicap ourselves by choosing to head into the darkness"

"It handicaps him too. You know that it's all about presentation with these messages, and if we can't see whatever he's trying to creep us out with, we'll be fine," Kyle says, becoming increasingly convinced this plan is legitimate.

"We can still see at night. Candles, flashlights..." Morgan says.

"And?" Jody says.

"And?" Morgan responds, looking at Jody.

"He wants you to say 'torches,'" Kyle sighs, annoyed.

"What if we all make torches? What if we start a fire? Someone will have to come to put it out. A helicopter or something," Morgan says, excited at this idea.

"We aren't burning anything. Do you really think the devil's plan could be thrown off by fire?" Hummingbird responds.

"I appreciate what you're saying, Hummingbird," Jody comments, "And as long as I can call the flashlight a torch, and I retain full control of it, you can discuss fire safety bullshit like a boring mom and I won't interrupt you."

"What? Sure. Sure. Fine," Hummingbird says, flustered, "You're the torch-master."

"So it has been christened," Jody says, proudly holding up his Pokémon flashlight like it was a mighty sword.

XXXVIII. The Hits Keep On Coming.

We stare out at the orange hue of the disappearing sun peeking through the gaps in the pines that surround us.

Rob is gone, Mike is gone, Kyle is nowhere to be found, Wil is still passed out in Behringer's room, and we're here, on the porch.

We watch Jody peer out from under the brim of his cowboy hat as he stares down a tree. The tree doesn't make the first move, so it's up to Jody to strike. The girls join us in the audience, as Jody begins practicing the spontaneous art of hitting tree trunks with a long stick he found on the ground.

"This is sad," Hummingbird says quietly, as she watches a man in his 30's act like he's 7.

"I think it's... cool?" Morgan says, attempting to be supportive of Jody's "training." The once inactive girl walks out toward the overactive boy. "How will you hit the devil with that? I mean, how's that flimsy-ass stick going to stop the devil himself?" Morgan flirts, approaching the man as he slashes away at a tree.

Jody winks at her, and says, "This is how," then he puts all of his weight into a spinning strike against the tree. The force of the connection causes the stick to splinter, and the largest piece of the debris smacks the confused look off of Morgan's face.

Instantly letting out a piercing yelp, Morgan falls to her knees, holding her face and making noises that sound like an injured aquatic animal who's accidentally washed up on shore and can't make it back to the water.

Morgan begins rolling on the ground to the soundtrack of Hummingbird's unrestrained cackles.

Jody drops his broken weapon and charges over to his unwitting opponent.

"Fuck. Please have both eyes. Please have both eyes-" Jody begs, rolling Morgan over. "Let me see," Jody says, then slowly removes Morgan's hands from her face. "Yesss," he celebrates, "You still have both your eyes. Oh man, I was not looking forward to my eyes getting plucked out in retribution for my carelessness."

"I hope you know that fucking hurt really bad," Morgan says.

"I'm sorry," Jody says in a high voice, and this causes Hummingbird to laugh more.

"Make it better," Morgan demands, pouting, sporting a red mark that climbs up her cheek, toward her eye.

"I'd kiss it to make it feel better, but I don't want to kiss your eyeball. That would exacerbate things," Jody says, showing care and consideration- the two things Morgan needs at this very moment.

Her lower lip protruding as she milks an injury that stopped hurting once the shock and embarrassment melted away, Morgan suggests, "How about kissing my eyebrow to make it better?"

"Will I kiss it off? Don't you draw your eyebrows on using the ashes of my incinerated dreams?" Jody asks.

"Closed mouth. No tongue," Morgan demands, her pointer finger raised to Jody's face as though she was about to slice his cheek with her nail in swift revenge.

"Okay," Jody agrees.

"I'm glad you smashed me in the face with your stick," Morgan says.

"Why?" Jody begins to ask, then Morgan kisses him on the lips.

A single person applauds, but it quickly becomes clear that the muffled claps are not a celebration of approval or amusement- they're a call to action.

Kyle walks out the house and makes a beeline across the front yard. "Come on," he demands, his gloves clapping, rallying the troops, "We're getting out of here."

Hummingbird hops off the porch and catches up to Kyle. She has to go on this trip because her best friend is all loved up in a hateful place. The type of spontaneous tenderness she just witnessed should be cradled, not destroyed, and if we stay in Behringer's house, this garden will not grow.

Whatever Morgan and Jody have started will be crushed if we stay in Leeds house and this type of jarring destruction would make *him* stronger.

Jody stands up, then he offers Morgan his hand. He makes sure not to grunt a straining noise when he pulls her up. This is progress.

Morgan and Jody's hands remain locked as they walk into the unknown together.

Kyle's goal for this evening's journey is murky. Either he's trying to leave the house for good, or he's trying to find his friends. Dual goals increase the odds of the trip becoming a success, and right now, Kyle desperately needs a victory. We have to ignore the fact that we're also leaving a friend behind. Wil is asleep in the house. No one has been visited in their dreams by the devil so this likely means that Wil is in the safest possible place he can be, unlike the two men we search for now. Finding Rob is important- he simply isn't equipped to survive on his own. Finding Mike is important- Mike's mother has already lost a husband, she shouldn't have to lose her son too. Kyle knows that Ms. Connor is uptight, but she allowed the band thing to happen because she saw how it saved her son. This is also why she let Mike hang out with Rob, despite his reputation. In one of the possible scenarios regarding the disappearance of these two boys, Rob has gone out into the woods to look for Mike. Rob is a good friend, behind his undependable nature; Mike is an aggressive man, behind his docile persona. None of the members of Lies As Language are without their defects, and this seems to feed the malice of the house.

With his free hand, Jody takes his Pokémon flashlight out of his back pocket. This is the only item he's armed himself with on this journey into the unknown. The mace stayed at home, hidden from Wil. The shotgun stayed at home, hidden from Wil. Jody is happy with his torch- it gives him a focus, a responsibility, a sign that God is with him. He's careful to never exclusively rely on it though. He has seen too many horror movies to trust this flashlight to stay on for an extended period of time, so he has a candle and a lighter in his pocket for when the inevitable happens. He's purchased too many vanity products from China to believe that this flashlight won't fail when most needed. He's also aware that there is potential that this torch was provided by the devil and at any moment it will burst into flames in his hand.

Jody assumes these risks because, deep down, he believes he deserves to be burned. He's the reason why his brother has to wear those gloves.

XXXIX. Through The Dusklight.

We watch Wil vomit into the kitchen sink.

Between the blood-vessel-popping retches, there's a creaky squeak that slowly rises in pitch. Wil recognizes the noise- it's a door slowly being closed, the old hinges whining. In this house, the front door is always open, but what if it's finally closing? What if it's closing for good?

Wil dashes into the wood paneled hall, then puts his back to the wall. He wipes his vomit glistening mouth on the sleeve of his disintegrating shirt.

He waits. We wait. No one seems to travel in or out of the house.

"Just shut the door," Wil says out loud.

"It's cold," Wil says out loud.

"It's Rob," Wil says out loud, then he drifts down the hall.

Sure enough, the front door is closed, defying its broken frame. Without Mike to open the door, or Jody to provide the muscle, Wil has to deal with this situation all by himself. This is what he wanted. This is what he asked for.

Wil wraps his fingers around the doorknob, then yanks the door open. Cold air rushes out of the house, into the yard, as Wil surveys the black uncertainty. There's no one at the door. There's no one on the porch. There's no one in the yard.

Standing in the open mouth of Leeds house, Wil's eyes adjust, and a familiar shape separates from the darkness.

Wil looks left, then right. When he feels it's somewhat safe, he moves toward the object.

The closer he gets, the more the fear, the resentment, and the excitement swirl inside his stomach.

When he's a foot away, Wil becomes certain that he's looking at his old acoustic, planted in the ground like a tree.

After Punchcunt's van tipped, Wil carried this ruined guitar back to his lonely house.

This guitar was left on the dining room table in Connecticut.

It *was* left there.

Now it's here.

This is the moment where Wil was supposed to fear for the safety of his loved ones at home, but it's far too late for that.

Knowing that this could be a trap, but desperate for the comfort of music, Wil carefully leans over and pulls the acoustic from the ground. Nothing happens. He turns the guitar over, then runs his hand across its smooth back. For the first time, the Barrens healed something, instead of causing further destruction.

Wil can begin his solo album now.

He has no choice but to play alone, because we left him that way.

XL. Through The Torchlight.

As we walk by a shallow stream lit by the moon, Jody observes, "All the water here looks like Mother Nature perioded in it, so how is there fresh water in our house? Who ran those pipes? Can we just follow those pipes to the water main, then follow the main to the road?"

"The color of this water is a mix of stuff leaking out of the cedar trees and the iron content in the soil," Morgan says, unwilling to think about the logistics behind the scalding tap water.

"We have well water," Kyle says, keeping Jody from returning back to the house to dig up pipes.

In an effort to make sure everyone continues on the intended path, Kyle repeats the plan, "We're doing one thing tonight- we're walking to the old woman's house. We went from her house to Behringer's house, and it's a common trip from what she said, so this is the best course of action."

"So you really think the old lady is going to help us after the way Wil acted that night?" Hummingbird asks.

"She has no choice but to help us. She pointed us in the direction of Behringer's, so she has to point us in the direction of civilization to fix things," Kyle reasons.

"We have no idea where her house is," Hummingbird says, planting her feet.

"Keep it movin'," Jody says, waving his flashlight, again tapping into his inner security guard.

We continue on, through the looking glass of Jody's "torch."

"We should have brought real torches," Hummingbird says, "It's getting increasingly dark and creepy, and cold, and dumb out here."

"Luckily, the one member of Lies As Language who isn't a giant gaylord will keep you girls safe," Jody declares.

"Jody!" Hummingbird tweets, "You can't say that!"

"I certainly can. The proof that the rest of the band are a bunch of gaylords seems to be multiplying exponentially. Think about it- they all wear makeup, only Kyle can fight, and he utilizes Greco-Roman tactics. Then there's Wil- he just asked for Kyle's hand in holy matrimony wedded marriage."

"So you don't mean gaylord in a derogatory way. In this band, you're actually the queer one because you're different," Morgan says, trying to salvage Jody's argument.

"When you put it like that, yes, I'm queer as fuck," Jody says with pride.

"Help!" Hummingbird screams.

Jody swings his torch so the scream queen is in the center of his light. "What is it, what's on you?" Jody asks, taking control.

"Nothing," Hummingbird says casually, then turns and screams, "Help! Help me! Help! Help! Help! Help! Help!" Howling desperate cries into the woods, Hummingbird shows just how panicked and fed up she's become. After another round of screams, she trips over her own feet and falls on her butt. She moans, "This is insane. This is some kind of purgatory."

"No. It would be way fuller if this is purgatory," Jody says, moving his torchlight a bit to show that we are very much alone.

"This is some *Lost* type shit," Morgan says.

"This isn't some stupid show," Kyle growls, but when he sees everyone wince, he softens his statement, "It's more like a movie. Like *The Blair Witch*."

Jody's light moves off Hummingbird as he crosses his arms, causing his flashlight beam to point out toward the pines. "That's fucked up, Kyle. That is. Fucked. Up," Jody's dark figure lectures.

"Oh, shit," Kyle says, realizing his careless mistake, "I didn't mean to mention the B.W."

"Well, you did," Jody responds, "I didn't even think about the possibility that we're being tormented by the Blair Witch, but now I'm totally sure it's her. This is just great. How could we have been so stupid? Of course she's involved in all of this. I bet she ate all those children when Behringer was done with them," Jody says, then Morgan immediately gravitates toward him asking, "What do you mean she's here?"

"Kyle willed the Blair Witch here," Jody says, "So you should both thank him for his great work while you still have your tongue and teeth."

"We'd be better off if it *was* her," Hummingbird mumbles.

"What do you mean?" Morgan asks.

"What we're up against is totally different and far worse than the Blair Witch," Hummingbird says, still seated on the ground.

"Like *Book of Shadows: Blair Witch 2*?" Morgan asks.

The younger members of our search party aren't able to muster the fear that Jody is displaying toward the Blair Witch. Morgan, Kyle, and Hummingbird all saw the film on their laptops and recognized the guy who plays Josh from other more recent movies and TV shows. They knew he wasn't dead, even if he died on screen, and a quick read through of the film's IMDB page revealed that all of the backstory was merely a plot device. Jody saw the movie in a theater, before the internet was a full blown research tool. He watched a group of people he had never seen before, and didn't anticipate seeing after, because the movie felt that authentic. Even after learning it was a setup, that initial fear Jody felt, his new mistrust of the woods, all of it had an effect that simply is not achievable now that everyone can find the answer to anything with a couple taps on a screen. Or at least they could until their phones exploded.

"What was that?" Hummingbird asks.

We didn't hear anything, but Jody, being the protector, scans the torchlight across the trees, searching for the cause of the noise. Throughout the entire sweep of the surrounding woods, nothing that would cause alarm appears framed in Jody's steadied beam, but this only makes us look deeper into the darkness. We're presented with no images to provoke fear so we begin to search for them. Kyle was right when he said that if we made this walk during the day, it would widen the spotlight on the stage, increasing the chances of bigger, uglier displays. For now, whatever is tormenting us is relegated to the beam of Jody's torch.

"Do we go forward or backward?" Morgan asks.

"Which way is home?" Hummingbird asks, still on the ground, her head between her legs.

"We're going forward. We'll walk for 30 more minutes," Jody says.

"Why?" Hummingbird asks him, not following physically or mentally.

"Because I'm the dude with the torch," Jody says, then he teams with his brother to push forward into the unknown.

Jody's answer becomes immediately valid when Hummingbird finds herself in the dark, with the only light source moving away from her. She quickly catches up to us and remains silent, her ears perked for the return of the noise.

When the familiar yellow windows of the old lady's cottage fail to appear, and the repeating scenery sends us into a trudging trance of tedium, a familiar scream bursts from the trees and we all stop moving instantly.

We've heard this scream before. Mike. "Where does that scream come from?" Hummingbird remembers thinking while looking at the placid boy after the show. She's thinking this exact thought again. Before, it was about mood. Now, it's about location.

There's no second scream. A second scream would freeze us again, but it would be a confirmation. It would be proof that there's a reason to continue on and not turn back. It would be the fuel that would power us toward where we need to be to save our friend. The scream never arrives. The devil does not drop breadcrumbs in his Barrens.

We keep moving, we keep walking, maybe for 15 minutes, maybe for a half hour. Jody becomes loose armed, and his flashlight bobs up and down, the pendulous motion providing glimpses of the woods- a dark, monotonous path leading toward an uncertain future.

The flashlight swings up- trees, rocks, leaves.

The flashlight swings down- a moment of total darkness.

The flashlight swings up- leaves, rocks, trees.

The flashlight swings down- a calm tranquil black.

The flashlight swings up- a man turned, standing completely still, dressed in all black.

The flashlight swings down- Hummingbird and Morgan both shriek and reach for each other, forming a single terrified being. Jody cups his hand over the torch. "What the fuck was that? Who the fuck was that?" is said by at least two members of our party in hushed panic.

Jody doesn't speak, he merely uncups his hand from his torch, then gradually scans the beam of light across the trees and a static stretch of leaves, eventually returning the spotlight to the hooded figure.

Jody fixes his light on the back of a person who's still frozen in place. The person does not move, but his image seems to flicker because Jody's hand is trembling.

The figure is either dressed in all black clothes to facilitate moving through these woods undetected, or he's in a metalcore band.

What was Mike wearing when we left him?

What was Rob wearing when he disappeared?

Everyone in this fucking band wears black hoodies, it's impossible to tell who this is.

"Hey! Sir? Are you lost?" Kyle calls out, and the echo of his voice skips through the Barrens.

Jody flinches, anticipating a response that never arrives.

This stalemate cannot continue, and Jody understands that it's his responsibility to take action.

With his torch trained on the frozen body, Jody approaches with extreme caution. Careful steps over crackling leaves bring him a foot away from the mysterious, possibly immobile being.

Jody's left hand points the torch at the person's hood, then his right hand reaches out to issue a careful, non-threatening tap. The precise moment before Jody makes contact, the man turns and looks directly into Jody's eyes, and a screeching, almost digital noise accompanies this action.

Jody falls to the ground, screaming in desperate panic.

The beam of the torch dances haphazardly, as Jody flees in the direction we came.

"Jody! Jody!" is the desperate chorus we chant, as we stumble toward a trembling beam that searches to identify obstacles in the way.

For the first time, Jody's protective, father-like instincts have disappeared. He becomes every father who left his son on that Everest trip when an ankle fracture became a death warrant. He becomes just like every dad who ran from fired shots in a dark theater and left his child in the seats. He joins every man who failed at the precise moment he was truly needed.

This is proof that the instinct to survive trumps the instinct to preserve.

When the pumping light finally dances off the demonic house, we feel a tiny tinge of relief, like waking up from a dream, but the closer we get to the house the more we realize we were dreaming about certain realities that we can't escape.

We heave heavy breaths as we reach the stone porch, then we watch Jody sit on the stairs and cry.

"He's coming. I saw him behind us the whole time we were running. He's coming," Hummingbird is blubbering.

We wait, sick with a hopeless fear, and we stare into the dark wilderness.

A branch snaps. Then another. Then another.

These ominous brutal breaks cause something inside Jody to click back into place.

Standing up, Jody wipes his eyes, then walks toward the unseen threat. The snapping branches reminded him of the first scary moment of the night that ended in a kiss. "Who goes there?" he calls into the dark abyss, inviting the danger as an investment toward future reward.

Suddenly the noise changes direction and we hear it to Jody's left. It's no longer just the sound of branches breaking- now it could also be the clatter of two rocks being struck against each other? Trees snapping at their trunks? Bones br- now it's to Jody's right. It's moving too fast for him to track with the beam. This can't be one person, there's no way he could run around the house that fast. If this is a single being, then it would have to travel over the roof to change directions this fast. The noise never comes from two places at once, but it changes sides when the torch is redirected.

When the noise gets louder, we suspect it's also closer, and this edges us back to the open door of the house.

Jody lets out a whisper of, "Hello?" then clears his throat, but the words don't come, even when unobstructed.

Suddenly, a figure appears behind us, and sings, *"Wel-come to the Devil's house,"* then this statement ends with a "stinger" noise, and our entire body jolts into a shoulder-arched rigidity. Why are sound effects being played to facilitate the jump scares?

Jody's torch swings to the doorway, and it instantly becomes a spotlight.

We whip around to find Wil standing like a zombie Johnny Cash, and he's holding an acoustic guitar. The guitar must be what made the stinger noise. The woods go quiet, almost as though what we just heard was the applause a musician would receive when he steps on stage, and now the audience has settled, ready to be entertained.

Wil sings, *"Wel-come to the devil's house. In New Jersey or Hades' mouth? Our friends are dead, our hopes are fucked, and all these assholes still pray for luck."*

We can't tell if Wil is possessed or just hungover because he looks to be both.

Kyle steps forward, and Wil smiles wide, then continues with the rest of the song, *"And-"* is all he gets out, before the music ends abruptly with a screech. Kyle snatches away the guitar from Wil and storms inside Leeds house.

Running his hand across the body of the guitar, Kyle confirms what he feared to be true. He remembers that the night before the Jersey gig, Wil refused to leave this guitar in the van. When we left for Jersey, Wil didn't take this guitar, and even if it did end up in the van, the van is now ash. Wil has received this guitar as a gift, and a gift given in this house always doubles as a bribe, or a prop, or a piece of an ugly puzzle that's better left unassembled in the box.

Hummingbird blasts past Wil and catches Kyle's arm as he walks onto the green carpet of the living room. This grasp is distinctly different from what they shared on stage because Hummingbird and Kyle are on the same level now.

"Give it to me," they say to each other at the same time, while jockeying for a solid grip on the guitar's neck. Kyle feels the pulsing instinct to yank the instrument away, then smash it on the brick fireplace, but he's also aware that the last time he almost destroyed a guitar, Jody fought him. The house must possess a sense of history beyond what has happened inside these cursed walls. This guitar isn't here because of Wil; it's here because of

Kyle. If history repeats itself, Kyle and Jody will fight each other tonight, and the house will decide the conclusion.

Kyle hands over the instrument to Hummingbird, but he makes sure it comes with a warning, "You do realize that's a bribe in your hands. Not from me, but from *him*. I tried to eliminate it from the equation, but it's clear you're happy to put us all in jeopardy. That guitar-"

"-do you hear yourself?" Hummingbird responds in a shrill voice. Aggressively pointing, her face bunched up with disgust, Hummingbird yells, "You... are the voice of reason. You... are the one who's supposed to keep a level head while living wall to wall with damaged people. You... don't care about us- you only care about getting out of here," Hummingbird chastises Kyle, reminding him of how a leader acts, and how a coward acts. "Yet here you are, freaking the fuck out. I'm sorry, but sometimes a guitar is just a guitar. Sometimes-"

"-you return that guitar to any member of Lies As Language, and you're aiding the puppeteer," Kyle warns Hummingbird.

"Well, I'm sure the Jersey Devil will keep you around the longest so you both can bond over your passion for behind the scenes manipulation."

XLI. The Soundhouse.

We follow the glow of Morgan's candlelight up the basement stairs, then into the kitchen, where she continues to pile her supplies. It could be 10 PM, it could be 3 AM. Time stretches to the point that it no longer becomes relevant. It's taken her a while to bring her materials up from the basement because she had to hold a candle as well.

After she reviews her pile of repurposed junk, Morgan begins to look for her friends. They've scattered themselves again. It was something they knew they shouldn't do, but that knowledge has little effect on their actions now that the tension has risen to record levels and any option of mental escape has the potential to become a breeding ground for psychological programming. If we search for an escape, we may find it on the unplugged TV, as it begins its first broadcast directly from hell. The books that remain on the shelf could be Behringer's key to take this house back. In a home that feels watched and studied, time alone becomes more important, but less safe.

To cope with this harsh reality, Morgan has resumed her maternal rituals. She drifts up to the second floor, cooing, "House meeting in five minutes." Acting like a dorm RA- not poking into the business of the residents yet still watching over them- Morgan sets out to collect everyone for a mandatory meeting in the green carpeted common space. The, "I'm not in the mood," or the, "How do I know you're the real Morgan?" or the, "I'm shitting!" responses are ignored.

We wait within the light of Morgan's candle at the bottom of the stairs.

Suddenly, this house becomes the venue for Morgan's party, and if no one attends this party, she will cry, she will want revenge, and she will do something that the house will smile at.

We exhale relief when we hear footsteps upstairs. A noise that once sent a chill up our spine now warms our heart.

One by one, our housemates reappear and descend the stairs.

Like a flight attendant wearing a T-shirt she found in a child's carry-on, Morgan directs us to where the meeting will take place.

With everyone collected in the living room, Morgan walks in front of the fireplace and uses the little brick hearth as a stage. She fixes her hair and licks her lips. She seems worried, but it's not a, "Fuck, this food is going to turn into maggots soon, I'm sure of it," worry. It's more the, "I'm introducing my favorite band," type of worry.

"I feel really bad about what's happened... to us," Morgan says. She takes a deep breath, then crinkles her toes on the brick floor. The fact that she has her shoes and socks off proves that she doesn't plan on running anywhere tonight. She stands on the cold brick, as if her feet were planted in the hot sand of the Jersey Shore on a summer afternoon.

Morgan continues, "I like you guys, all of you, so much. And, you've lost your friends. And I know how that is. I've lost my friends, too- at the exact same time you lost yours. I want them back. I would do anything to get our friends back. I think you would too. I know, this is- actually, never mind." Morgan suddenly shuts down, displaying another personality change reminiscent of Wil going from angry drunk to loving drunk in a matter of seconds upstairs.

"Morgan," Hummingbird says, unsure of how to approach her question. "When you had your free time tonight, did you, drink, any, wine?" Hummingbird asks, as though each word was a careful step on a tightrope.

"Were you about to give us a surprise?" Jody asks, buying into the idea of a house meeting being established with the goal of changing the mood of everyone still present here. If Morgan intends to create a Christmas morning moment in the living room, Jody will go get that stick he broke on her face, then he'll decorate the bastard like it was a Christmas tree.

"Okay, this seems so dumb now," Morgan says. She smiles and twitches her nose, waiting for Jody to organize an exodus, but it never happens.

It's silent in the living room; Jody simply bought her some time, then he gave her back the stage.

Morgan has worked for this moment, planning it from her heart, which means the only way Leeds will be pleased by what Morgan has created is if she buries it out of shame. After taking a deep breath, she admits, "I really liked going to your concert, and I wish I wasn't as drunk as I was when I went. I mean, I wasn't as drunk as Rachel was, but I still had a good buzz."

Wil rolls his eyes, and Morgan ignores him, "I wish I knew all your lyrics like Rachel does. I wish I knew those lyrics on the wall downstairs. I want to be as big of a fan as Rachel is."

Jody doesn't make a fat joke or ask who Rachel is.

Morgan exhales, then tells the remaining members of Lies As Language, "I kept thinking about how I wanted to go back and see you guys again, even while I was standing in the crowd at your concert. I couldn't accept that the feeling that you gave me would be surging through me only once. I needed to know that I'd see you again."

"Morgan, are you behind what's been happening recently?" Kyle asks.

"Do you honestly think I'm doing some sort of quintuple *Misery* thing here? I mean, I have a plan for tonight, but I don't have a plan like *he* has a plan," Morgan says, and she points back to the fireplace. The gesture, almost instinctual, reminds her of the history behind the structure she's in front of. She steps onto the green carpet, then continues, "I really wanted to feel the happiness I felt in that crowd again, but then the van exploded with all the equipment inside and it seemed like an end to the band. Then something incredible happened... when we got back to the house tonight, I saw Wil, on the porch, playing a song- playing us home in a way- and it reminded me of how I felt when our trip began."

Wil huffs at this misinterpretation, then clarifies, "I was trying to insult-"

"-Wil, shut up," Morgan says, holding up a finger that was meant to stretch across the room to press his lips closed, "Your intention doesn't matter. You played us inside. And now were here. It might be fucking weird in here, but out there..." Morgan's voice cracks, then she shakes off her weakness. "Wil, trust me. You don't want to be out there. You want to be in here. I need you in here. You are essential."

Wil nods at this, agreeing instead of fighting her.

Morgan smiles, finally ready, and she asks, "Do you want to let go of the selfishness and cagey self-preservation we've all been guilty of in this house, so that- it's my hope- we can bring back our friends?"

Everyone nods in agreement, which sends Morgan rushing to the kitchen.

The uneasy silence becomes tolerable thanks to the odd amount of hope that lingers in Morgan's wake like the dust in the air.

The girl with the plan returns carrying two large plastic buckets and two bare sticks that look like they were stolen from the old blind lady's house.

Morgan places these items in front of the fireless fireplace, then runs back into the kitchen.

We notice that we hold our breath when Morgan disappears.

When Morgan reappears with a hair brush, we exhale. She hands the brush to Kyle. "Don't worry, I cleaned it off. It's okay to put it near your mouth," she informs him. Kyle sends Morgan a smile. He understands now. This understanding keeps him seated and quiet, even when Morgan returns with Wil's guitar.

Morgan hands the guitar to Wil, and we notice Hummingbird smile at this gesture.

Morgan runs back into the kitchen, and we don't hold our breath this time.

The excited girl returns holding a wooden frame with rubber bands stretched across it, creating a harp-like structure. "This was a stretch," she says, handing Hummingbird the harp. "Get it?" she asks her best friend.

Understanding what this arts and crafts project is supposed to accomplish, Hummingbird commands her best friend to, "Get to the fucking piano, bitch. I want you to play so shitty that Rob has to come back and kick you out of the band."

Morgan giggles, then skips over to the bench and sits down.

The band waits for Jody's count in, but before he begins, he moves his drums so his back isn't to the fireplace.

Everyone accepts their role, right where they belong, in hopes that it will force the rest of the band to return to their rightful places as well.

"Let's play our boys home," Jody says, clacking his makeshift drumsticks together to lead a new band into their first song. Sticks that seemed like a waste of time in the old woman's house suddenly make sense to Jody. He begins a song that no one has named and no one has ever played before.

Kyle holds the hair brush, listening to the music that Jody plays, that Morgan joins in on, that Wil arrives atop, that Hummingbird struggles to match.

Kyle freezes, and he feels the house smile.

Waiting for the lead singer to finally write his own lyrics, Hummingbird places her rubber band banjo on her lap. Kyle looks to her and his mouth forms a word, but no noise comes out. She has to look away, blink hard once, then she begins to sing, *"They blew up our minivan in the front yard one night."*

"Now we're stuck in this house, too."

Bruce. We're in Jersey. Of course it would be The Boss.

Hummingbird continues, *"Down in the Barrens, they're gettin' ready for a fight, gonna see what those emo boys can do."*

And when the chorus hits, we all sing together, *"Everything dies, band boys that's a fact, but maybe everything that dies, one day comes back?"*

XLII. Deep Cuts.

We're back in the bathroom with Hummingbird. She's holding the knife again. She tries to return to the concert in her mind- not the one we just had in the living room- the one back at the venue. The cloudy recollection Hummingbird has of Lies As Language's set is still special enough that it might evolve into a coping mechanism. The blur of the night, the heat of the show, the crispness of the fall... all of it mixed in her body when she was capable of feeling something besides only just the cold. It was a sensory memory. It was a smell- sweat, mixed with autumn, and vodka. These are the smells that Hummingbird loves, that make her curious, that announce to her that something important is happening. That pleasant combination of scents swirling in the air brought a much-needed break for a girl who habitually writes her story on her body to warn people, to keep them away, to isolate and destroy herself so all of the damage can be her fault, and she won't pull anyone else down with her.

To Hummingbird, the concert was a pure release from the pressures she felt at home. Her boyfriend had moved across the country- voluntarily- and that hurt. Her mom got a new husband, with new kids- kids that didn't have tattoos and did land on the honor roll- and that hurt. Hummingbird's dad is finishing his jail term in a jail nicer than Hummingbird's house- for the money he "invested" that actually belonged to the parents of Hummingbird's friends- and that hurt.

Music was supposed to fix it all, but it didn't make Hummingbird whole. It fixed Mike for a while, until he lost the music and ended up like a wrapped present under that tree of gore. It didn't bring Rob back. It didn't bolster Morgan's sense of self.

Tonight, Hummingbird played alongside her favorite band, helping Kyle find his voice, but the emptiness that remains sucks the magic out of it all.

As soon as everyone finished the finale and blew out their candles, Hummingbird felt the darkness return.

Rachel sits on the bathroom floor and organizes everything with care and satisfaction.

The steak knife was sharp enough to be an adequate substitute for her usual setup. It had a different slice to it, but no tug, which was good.

Picking up the knife, Hummingbird tries to find her reflection in the blade, but she's unable to locate anything beyond an abstraction.

The candle flickers- and wax slides down the stick.

The blade drags across the skin- and red slides down her wrist.

This is the only type of hurt that Rachel can control in this house, so she cherishes it fully.

XLIII. The Calm.

We wake up on the floor of Behringer's bedroom.

It's the only bedroom in the whole house.

Maybe the room between the office and the bathroom downstairs is a tiny bedroom?

Maybe the Polaroid room was once a bedroom?

This is a house in the middle of the woods and there's only one actual bed inside it. The message is clear. Visitors are not welcome.

Too many beds to choose from got Ms. Leeds in trouble.

Jody and Morgan loudly claimed the bed last night, sending Kyle out into the hallway. Jody remains in the bed, wrapped around Morgan like a protective half shell.

Morgan opens her eyes. She kisses Jody's hand that lies at rest by her lips. She presses her body tight to him. Becoming a graduated alarm clock, equal parts warm, sexual, and nagging, Morgan wakes Jody. He turns in the bed to share his smile with Morgan. She returns the smile.

"I'm so glad I finally have you," Morgan coos.

"You didn't want one of the other guys more?" Jody asks, in a moment of vulnerability.

"Never. Even when you were making fun of me, I was only interested in you."

"My jokes were dope as fuck," Jody says, returning to his normal personality.

It's silent for a moment, then Morgan says, "I had a weird dream last night."

"Oh really," Jody responds.

"Yeah I-"

"-that wasn't a 'keep going' *oh really*," Jody clarifies.

Morgan can't help but ask, "What type was it? It sounded encouraging."

Jody sits up, breaking the romantic gaze. He's deadly serious as he explains, complete with hand chop motions, "Anytime someone monologues about a shit ass dream, it always has some profound importance later on. And, besides... want to know what my dream was last night?"

"Sure," Morgan squeaks.

"Okay, yeah you do because you're obsessed with me, but imagine I was, like, a person driving a purple minivan, would you want to hear my dream then?" Jody asks.

"I'm not sure, can you tell me more about the people in the van?" Morgan asks, reserving judgment. She's taught herself to do this. At first, she thought Jody was an asshole, now she thinks he's a charming asshole. "The van doesn't blow up because of me, does it?" she asks in a playful way, backing Jody into a defensive mode, asserting her power.

"It's a minivan. That is purple. Do you really need to get a look at those people to know who they are?" Jody asks, semi-outraged, semi-hard.

"No. I guess not," Morgan responds.

"Would you want to hear purpyvan's cream?" Jody asks, struggling to reach a point he seems to be distancing himself from with every additional word.

"No. Probably- wait. Are you saying I'm purpyvan?" Morgan asks in a shrill voice.

"No. I'm just saying that your dream is going to be something where you're like, 'There was a snake and he wrapped himself around me, but he wasn't getting tighter, it's like he was hugging me, protecting me by coiling around my body. I couldn't tell if he was killing me or saving me.'"

"That's a pretty interesting dream, was that yours?" Morgan asks.

"No! It's just the type of dream that will come back later to haunt us and everyone will be like, 'Oh no, the snake is Jody's arms and he's protecting Morgan,' but that's bullshit because my pipes are way thicker than any anaconda," Jody says, slightly losing his point.

"So, you think that dreams predict the future?" Morgan asks.

"I'm saying that dream recaps prefaced by the phrase, 'I had this weird dream last night,' always predict the future. If you keep your dream in your head, fine. If you give it significance, a snake will wrap around you and pop your tits off. It's a law of the universe. Read some science."

"Who writes the laws of the universe?" Morgan asks.

"God. Jesus Christ, our savior," Jody proclaims.

"Is there a branch for checks and balances?" Morgan inquires.

"Checks and balances? You want to check and balance God?"

"No. I guess not. He *is* infallible," Morgan acknowledges.

"Exactly."

"I wonder why he made that dream law?"

"I don't know... maybe he did it so He wouldn't feel like He was wasting time generating all these dreams," Jody suggests, then looks at the ceiling- it doesn't cave in. He didn't cross any lines. "He was probably like, 'Boring! These guys are just dreaming for a third of their life! I thought about making them gain their power from the sun like Superman, but I had second thoughts, and now I have a bunch of dreamy dreamers. I need to fix this.'"

"Yeah, we would just shut off without dreams," Morgan says, then thinks about it for a moment, and decides, "I might almost prefer that."

"No. Then we'd be dead," Jody points out.

"No. We'd be alive, just not thinking about anything... what did you see last night?" Morgan asks, unable to resist the question.

"Last night," Jody begins, serious, "I saw you on the ride of your life as I laid the cock like an Adonis."

"I wasn't talking about your skills as a cocksmith," Morgan says, "I meant what did you see when that digital man turned around?"

"Digital man," Jody laughs.

Morgan doesn't laugh, "Listen, I was there. I heard..." she twitches as it replays somewhere in her neck, "...a noise a person doesn't make. Tell me who or what you saw."

A piercing scream from outside of Leeds House ends this discussion immediately.

XLIV. Black Clouds.

We stand in the yard, unwillingly becoming the audience for a Lies As Language reunion show.

Morgan throws up.

Rob staggers forward, wearing Mike. Mike's skinned flesh is draped over the shoulders of a man we wouldn't have been able to identify as Rob if it wasn't for that beak of a nose. Mike's face has been sliced down the middle, all the way to his Robert Smith hair. His scalp now sits atop Rob's head, as though Mike's face was a hood. Every visible vein in Rob's body is black. Tree branches of tar stretch across his biceps, up his neck, across his forehead. His arms drip black at the elbow, because that is where they now end.

"Help," Rob screams, and more black bursts from him with this noise. The pudding-like mixture slides down his chin, and we can smell this midnight muck from 20 feet away- the stench is like a lock of hair left on a curling iron for far too long. Rob is cooking from the inside out, and the hell in his stomach is breaking through the crust, rising to the surface.

Rob limps toward us, without hands to wipe the black vomit off his face, but his shortened limbs still make attempts, twirling in futility.

"Who are you?" Wil asks, maybe because it's easier to believe this is a stranger or a creature, instead of a person.

"What happened to you?" Kyle calmly asks, despite knowing that these questions will remain unanswered.

Jody makes his way closer to the returning victim. We aren't sure if Rob's affliction is bite-related, and only Jody is brave enough to reach out and offer help.

After another purge of the burning goo, the handless being begs, "Stop..."

"Stop what? What do we have to stop?" Wil yells at Rob.

"You... know," Rob says, then vomits black all down his neck again, and this time the liquid starts to corrode through Rob's neck just under his Adam's apple. Jody, working from instinct, puts his right hand over the expanding wound. For this act of kindness, Jody gets burned.

Pulling away like he had placed his palm on a hot stove, Jody screams, "My fucking hand. My fucking hand!"

Morgan races over to Jody, then yanks him inside by his good hand. The urgency of the situation is made unmistakably apparent by the fact she can smell Jody's flesh melting. "Not you too. Not you," she begs, as she drags a pale Jody toward the kitchen sink. The knowledge that this goo will keep eating until the muscle is burned clean through and the bone is visible makes Morgan crank both sink handles and the steaming water shoots out with force. Jody slides his hand under the faucet, but it's as though the water is repulsed by the burn, and it redirects itself away from the festering black flesh. There's a solid half inch between where Jody's hand is, and where the water flows at a ninety-degree angle.

Jody trembles as the black continues to feast.

Aware of the recklessness of her actions, Morgan does the only thing she can think to do- she puts her mouth over the black wound on Jody's palm and sucks. When she gets a mouthful of the black, she spits it into the sink. Like she was resuscitating Jody's hand, Morgan repeats this gesture until she sucks every last bit of that flaming hellfire off the man who has tried to save everyone, yet has only received injuries and eye rolls in return.

When she's sure that Jody is safe, Morgan sticks her finger down her throat and gags more black gook into the sink. She spits. She spits into the sink again. She spits into the sink again. Jody stands, butt to the counter and he holds out his hand. It no longer hurts. His palm already feels like it's healing itself. The human body has the amazing ability to regenerate when it has a reason to do so.

Jody hugs a crying Morgan, and says, "You're the best girlfriend a man could ever get lost with."

"Girlfriend," Morgan repeats, and the word fixes her burnt tongue.

"Are you okay?" Jody asks.

Morgan shakes her head yes.

Jody kisses Morgan. He kisses her again. He kisses her deeply. Then he spits in the sink.

"That last part wasn't because I'm grossed out. It's just so I could be sure I didn't have any Rob in me," Jody clarifies.

Morgan nods, then wipes her mouth. Her throat stings.

"He's still inside that monster. What do we do?" Jody asks, knowing today's fight is not over.

"Rob is missing limbs. He can't be healed, and he's in pain," Morgan acknowledges.

Jody nods at this, and closes his eyes for a long moment. "Stay here," he instructs Morgan, then he walks with purpose into the living room.

After opening the piano bench, Jody reaches under a stack of marked sheet music for simple songs like "Twinkle, Twinkle, Little Star" and he grabs the shotgun. It doesn't need to be cocked. It's ready.

Bursting out onto the porch, Jody sees that Rob has continued to erode to the point that he's lost the ability to make a noise.

Stumbling toward Kyle, the shell that used to be Rob steps onto his own jaw, which sits on the ground covered in sandy soil.

Jody takes aim, then we watch as the Lennard brothers begin yet another fight.

"Jody. No," Kyle says, inserting his body between the barrel and the broken boy.

"We need to," Jody claims.

"No. We don't."

"He needs us to!"

"No! We are not shooting our friends! You don't shoot your friends!" Kyle yells.

"We can't do it. The last guy who shot that gun is Rob's hoodie now," Wil says.

"That's not Mike on him. That's not Mike," Kyle begins screaming, and Hummingbird dashes to his side, putting one hand on his shoulder, then holding the other out to him. She begs with her eyes, *Hold my hand and I will help you with your pain.*

"I know what has to be done," Jody responds.

Rob is gnarling, writhing, being eaten by his own burnt and blackened blood. Being held by Hummingbird, watching his friend disintegrate with no foreseeable release from the pain, changes Kyle's plan from *save Rob*, to *save Rob from the pain.*

"Maybe we should pay our respects and say a prayer?" Morgan suggests, "I'll go first... Rob, in the short time I met you-"

"-you might want to wrap that speech up, dear. I'm about to explode corrosive blood all over the yard," Jody says.

"-and I'm sorry we did this. We love you so much, Rob. Bye!" Morgan rushes her prayer to an end, and everyone shouts, "Amen," as they make their way into the house so they aren't contaminated.

"Alright," Jody says, standing 15 feet from his friend who's wearing his best friend like outerwear. Jody's voice wavers as he says, "Rob, I hope you understand that I had to do this, and I want to hug you, but I'm not going to let shit get *Cabin Fever*ish up in this motherfucker. So this is goodbye, Rob. You were a beautiful human, but now you're melting. You were the best drug addict keyboard player a band could ever have, but your toxic blood burnt my towel throwing hand, and I'm pretty sure you're already gone, so I'm going to have to shoot you. Give me a sign if you don't want me to do this."

We watch Rob's heart spit black ooze- it still beats despite the fact it should have given up long ago.

This is how it ends. Rob's body fights to survive, just as it did when it was pumped with poison back in Connecticut. Luckily, Jody is here, just far enough away from Rob that he won't be infected by Rob's toxicity when it blasts into a midnight splatter.

We take multiple steps back.

This moment doesn't cripple Jody because it pales in comparison to what he saw last night. He realizes that he must follow the light when the only other option is to be alone in the dark.

The trigger clicks and the gun's blast bursts through the Barrens.

Rob is dead.

Mike is dead.

Black is everywhere.

Laughter falls from the trees like leaves.

XLV. Behind The Clouds.

We watch Morgan cry in the small office on the first floor.

Kyle lingers outside the door, and when there's a break in the sobs, he says, just loud enough that Morgan can hear, "I hate knowing that someone is watching us."

"You're not alone," Morgan says, and the statement, in its vaguery, lures Kyle into the room.

When Kyle steps inside the office, Morgan looks up, and she smiles. She smiles a smile that Kyle did not expect and it scares him, in a good way.

"This is what happens when you aren't worth a guardian angel," Morgan says, and it scares Kyle, in a bad way. It causes him to shut the door and approach Morgan. This girl needs a friend, so Kyle wedges his skinny ass in the soft crimson chair next to Morgan's big ass.

Morgan puts her arm around Kyle's bony shoulder, just so they can both exist comfortably in the chair.

"We lost them," Kyle says, looking to his right, his face close to Morgan's.

Morgan opens her mouth to provide comfort, but Kyle turns away.

"Before, this. I don't know. It was like a game," Kyle says, reflecting on his time at Leeds House with a new distance and perspective, even though we all still inhabit the house. "Part of me hoped that all of this was in our minds; that we were making up these demons. It's felt like Halloween night for so many timeless days in a row. When Rob and Mike were-" Kyle exhales the word, "-alive-" then continues, "-it honestly seemed like I was 12 again and it was the 31st of October. I've always loved Halloween, but each year after I became a teen, I found myself more excited by the nostalgia than the actual day."

"It's November though," Morgan says, wiping her eyes, the ash blackening her palms.

"That's your issue with my delusion? The incorrect date?" Kyle asks, then he switches topics to the reason why he sought out Morgan, "How did you heal my brother?"

"With my mouth," Morgan says, then giggles.

"Oh," Kyle gasps, then looks away, "I didn't-"

"-no, like I put my mouth to his palm, then sucked," Morgan pauses, then mentions, "It's weird, Jody predicted I would have to do that, even when he was consciously making an effort to not predict it."

"Like he had information about what would happen today?" Kyle asks, about to get up, but Morgan puts her hand on Kyle's skinny leg to keep him seated.

"Has he ever purpyvaned you?" Morgan asks, then quickly reviews Kyle's confusion and bursts forward with her explanation, "Basically he told me we can't discuss dreams because if we dream about a giant snake, then we'll have to battle a giant snake later because that's how things work in every movie or TV show about some creepo place. I agreed not to share my dream, but when Jody couldn't wash off Rob's brutal mark, I remembered the snake thing and I realized I had to suck the poison out of him, like you'd do with a snake bite. So, in a way, his example dream became an almost reality."

Kyle smiles at this and lets his hair hang over his eyes, "Thank you for doing that for my brother," he says.

"He's not just your brother. He's also my boyfriend."

Kyle wipes the hair out of his eyes and he looks at Morgan.

Feeling scared, and appreciative, and vulnerable, and intimate in the wake of a devastating evening, Kyle squishes his lips together, pops them, then says, "I have a boyfriend at home. Or, I did."

This was finally an acknowledgment. For Morgan, it wasn't surprising to hear- it was just a relief. Understanding the transition, she says, "You never wrote him a song because you couldn't ask your brother to write a song about a man."

"Do you girls tell each other everything?" Kyle asks, angry with Hummingbird.

"*You* tell me everything. I wasn't asleep in the room when you were speaking with Rachel," Morgan says, a little too strong. "I knew that Jody was responsible for the lyrics. The way he acts around me told me."

"Awesome," Kyle responds dismissively.

"Where is he?" Morgan asks.

"Outside digging graves for our friends," Kyle says.

"No. Where's your boyfriend?" Morgan asks.

"Home," Kyle says.

"Home?" Morgan asks, like the concept was foreign.

"Yeah."

"He didn't go to the show?" Morgan asks.

Kyle shakes his head no.

"Why?"

"Really?" Kyle asks, snarling.

"Yeah, really. Maybe it's about time you answered some questions instead of just trying to escape constantly," Morgan says, pushing forward with a demanding passion, which in turn causes Kyle to react in the same tone, when he says, "Okay, that's unfair," then he tries to move away from Morgan even though they're crammed intimately close.

"What?" Morgan asks, a little offended.

"Just because I turned Wil down, doesn't mean you can start questioning if I'm-"

"-if you're so gay, then prove it," Morgan says, like a child.

Kyle shakes his long hair, "This is-"

"-you turned Wil down."

"Because, I have a boyfriend."

"Whom you won't talk about," Morgan snips.

"He hates it, he hates this. He hates the band. He said that it would destroy me," Kyle exhales all of this information in a pitched voice, all of it still hurting. Maybe it hurts more now that Kyle's boyfriend was proven right. Lies As Language became a bad thing.

"Oh. Oh... oh," Morgan says, evolving in the chair as she processes each statement. This was a nightmare coming true again.

"So, that's why I don't want to talk about it. He's going to think I left or... I changed because I didn't come back."

"Have you changed?" Morgan asks.

"We've all changed," Kyle says, almost as though he's trying to convince both himself and Morgan of this, but he gets stuck on the question, and ends up answering it again, "Of course I've changed. Of course..."

"So, that's why he didn't support you? He thought he would lose you because of the music?" Morgan asks, reining him in.

"Because of how I went about it, Morgan. He didn't like the lie I was parading around. I mean, he's right. Look how we got into this situation- I literally pulled you girls out of the audience. He didn't like my act because I would do things like that and he felt it was disrespectful to him, to you... who knows if he picked up on the Wil thing."

"It's part of your act," Morgan rationalizes.

"My stage act. It's not an act-act. Not that it matters now. The next time, that stage is going to be half empty. What am I left with?"

Morgan stands up and she points at the wood floor, then with impassioned fire on her tongue, she lists, "Me. Jody. Hummingbird. Wil. Us."

Kyle gives Morgan a look that signifies he doesn't believe in the permanency of this list. In a way, he's already buried Wil, even as Wil is out helping Jody bury their two other bandmates.

XLVI. Rob Martin.

"A shotgun blast completes the rock cliché bingo card. Sorry to the people who had 'Turns Satanist' left for the win. I managed to dodge that one. I guess it didn't do me any favors in the end though.

Maybe, if Jody is right about all this garbage, I'll be seen as some sort of martyr. I mean, I'm not trying to eat at the martyr table. Imagine that. I sit down at the martyr table and a guy leans over and says, 'They crucified me for five days, how did they get you?' and I'll be like, 'You'll never believe what happened, I thought I was just doing some heroin, but it turned out to be a demon sludge that melted my physical form!'

I'm so stupid. Everyone warned me that I was on the path to becoming rock cliché.

Jody would always talk to me about the Forever 27 club. Cobain and Joplin. Morrison and... Amy Winehouse? Who knows with her. Sometimes she looked 18, other times she looked 40. Her habit of dressing like a slutty old Jewish lady always made it difficult to judge Amy's age. 27 feels right though.

Jody seemed to use the Forever 27 club as a meter stick of where our band's success should be. Jim Morrison was 24 when 'Light My Fire' came out. In Jody's mind, we needed a 'Light My Fire' by the time we were 24. Kurt was 24 when *Nevermind* came out. That meant, to Jody, that we needed not only a 'Light My Fire' single, but also a *Nevermind* album by the time we were 24.

For Jody, those milestones were already in his rear view, but they were my future, and because of this, I looked at the Forever 27 club as a different type of marker.

I knew that if I saw myself rolling up on 27, still rolling up joints with high school kids, then I'd be a fool. I looked at those bands, those old guys- like Punchcunt Love- playing in teenagers' basements, rebelling against a system that they've lived in long enough to know is impossible to change.

The only reason it was okay for those 27+ year old men to be in that scene is because of a sound. They could make a great sound, so Scott Trunkett's mother let them enter her house to play for those kids.

There were so many young bands at the basement shows and it made me feel excited that metalcore wasn't being crushed by music that's easier to dance to. The fans were great, and always growing. I liked the free drinks the kids would give me. I liked the drugs they shared with me. 'I smoked a joint with the keyboardist from Lies As Language,' could be their story and it was always worth letting me take a couple tokes.

When I saw those guys teetering on 27 doing the same things I was doing at 20, it made me sad. I know that men have a hard time leaving high school. We lost Mike because he returned to his high school mindset. That swinging body count in the tree was what could have been- what would have been- without Lies As Language in Mike's life. He couldn't let it go. Maybe the guilt got to him. When he saw the horse that he shot strung up, it either made him feel like the man his father wanted him to be or it reminded him of who he really was. Maybe he still saw himself as that guy showing up, ready to wreak havoc with a careful plan. Without the band, all Mike had was a long-delayed project that needed a grand finale. He was still that kid from high school who searched for answers and seeing himself as *that kid* kept him working at the mall for two years after high school. Seeing himself as *that kid* with the weird walk made him want to stay in one place. Other kids beat it into Mike's head, *Do not move or it will be your ass*. It could be that Mike thought the safest option was to stand still under that tree.

I guess I should talk about me though, right? I felt I needed to explain things for Mike since he doesn't want to speak with you. I could tell you still wanted the dirty details from him, so I had to give you something. You demand easy answers. Even the guy being led to the electric chair gets a 'last word' because we're curious. There's the feeling of, 'Yeah, this guy is a sick fuck... but when else will we have a chance to safely hear what a crazy motherfucker like this has to say?' I'm sure you relate.

I was telling you about the Forever 27 club, because I knew that, at 27, it would be pathetic to still be doing drugs. I used to get high and watch old cartoons and once I saw this weird government sponsored PSA at the end of a show that used the cartoon characters to teach a moral lesson. We learned that we shouldn't eat candy or something. There was a tagline at the end of the PSA that was like, 'And knowing is half the battle,' and that always stuck with me. Knowing *is* half the battle. In my high mind, I was like, 'Well, what's the other half of the battle?' Although incomplete, the statement stood out as less of a celebration of awareness and more of a warning. 'Knowing is half the battle!' and the other half of the battle is, 'It feels good. It feels so fucking good you will not believe it.' I fought a battle with addiction. There was no logic to it. People will call what I did a suicide because I found that needle and I knew what was inside of it would probably hurt me, but I still did it anyway. Maybe it's self-hate. Maybe I wanted a way out. Maybe I wanted to find a place where I understood what was happening. Maybe I was searching for a familiar feeling.

Those talented bastards who ended up in the Forever 27 club all knew better, but still did what they wanted to. So did I.

Jody, Kyle, Wil, Morgan, and Hummingbird are over halfway through the battle and learning more every slow second.

A lot of people get lost halfway, so my friends aren't doing half bad."

XLVII. At The Edge, Afraid of Heights.

We watch a filthy Jody fall to his knees in the front yard, next to a sealed grave. He wipes his wet forehead with the rag he's tied around his injured hand. The rag leaves a red smear across his forehead, and Wil has to look away.

"You're definitely the best grave digger out of all of us," Hummingbird had said, knowing it would send Jody out to do the digging immediately. Now, with the work done, the compliment makes Jody feel better about the fact that he spent the last two hours digging a grave for his best friend, Cliff, whom he abandoned, and his good friend Rob, whom he killed.

It's just Jody, Wil, and the cloaked inhabitants of the Barrens in the front yard, as the sun runs away from this difficult moment. Everyone else is inside, and their absence buzzes with a static discomfort.

It becomes important to assemble everyone in the front yard.

When someone dies, it's turned into an event because the ritual provides closure, or at least it's intended to provide a monument beyond just the headstone... but the search will always continue. If a person is murdered we've been conditioned by TV and films to wrap up the loose ends, and only then can we find closure. Once the box is buried and the funeral is over, then we need to figure out who killed the victim. Once we figure out who did it, then we need the person to be sentenced. Once the person is sentenced, then we need to understand why the person did it. On the off chance we find out why the person did it, we'll be haunted by the trivial reason that our loved one was taken away from us. The closure never comes, so those of us remaining in Leeds house will just learn to protect what hasn't been taken from us yet.

The stars begin to appear in the purple sky. We look up at them, as they sit in a new silence. So much of the "space-metal" genre classification Lies As Language embraced was brought to the table by the sound Rob created. Without Rob, the band loses the "space." We're encountering the empty space. There's a void. Everything will feel and sound different from here on out.

Jody puts his head between his knees, but a tap on his shoulder sends his neck craning.

"I'm finished," Morgan says, sitting down next to Jody.

"Me too," Jody says, then he eyes Wil who gives him an understanding nod, before slinking away.

"Sit Indian style," Morgan demands, her own legs following her command.

"No. I'm not going to sit here and drink that devil's wine," Jody says, with a scowl.

"Just cross your legs," Morgan requests, "I want to show you what I was working on inside."

Next to the graves, Morgan and Jody sit Indian style, facing each other so their knees touch. Morgan reaches into her purse and carefully pulls out a rolled piece of green fabric. She holds it out to Jody and he takes it.

Jody unrolls the fabric and sees that in cut out and sewn on white letters, it declares, "Here Doesn't Live Michael Clifford Connor."

Jody believes in eternal life. He believes that Cliff was saved from that unforgivable sin. This triangular tribute to his friend declares that Cliff won't have to stay at Leeds House forever, and this knowledge becomes a comfort. Cliff will be invited to another house, one that is warmer and bigger, calmer and brighter, freer and most importantly, peaceful.

"It's a piece of the blanket from the basement," Morgan says, running her hand across the flag.

Jody remembers that night under the blanket- it felt like camping- at least the way camping should be, not how camping really is. It was a sleepover. It made Jody feel young again. When he was a kid, there was something electric about staying up with friends. It was being in someone else's house, at night, with nothing to do besides laugh, or scare each other, or just enjoy a couple B-movies. It was both similar and different to the feeling we had in Scott's basement.

Morgan, looking at the slice of the blanket, says, "That night, we all felt really good. And really excited. And it was really fun. I want the boys to remember that. I want them to feel like that now. I made one for Rob too," Morgan mentions, pulling a second flag out of her purse.

"This is nice," Jody says, admiring his girlfriend's work. These flags are not headstones. Headstones are permanent. These flags could get blown away, they could get unraveled and used for the construction of a bird's nest, they could sop up rain and organisms could live inside them. The flags are a perfect way to mark where Rob and Mike were freed from the Barrens.

"I got the idea for these flags from a project I saw back when I was working at Michaels," Morgan explains, "I picked up a lot of stuff about making things look cute for my house. Our customers were a bunch of bored ladies who would come in and tell us about their crafts," Morgan says. "I was always like, 'Get a fucking blog,' but every now and then, I'd get shown something cool."

Jody nods along with this, and says, "Because their pussies don't get wet anymore so they need to work on other stuff, like arts and crafts, to keep their mind off it."

"Yes, Jody. I'm sure that's the logic behind it," Morgan says, knowing better than to battle this assessment.

In quiet reflection, Jody says, "Seems crazy that Michaels can have an entire business model based on some Sierra Desert-ass pussies."

"I'm sure the board of directors has marveled about this on more than one occasion," Morgan says, then she looks to Leeds house and spots Wil on the porch, smoking a cigarette.

"Where did you get that?" Morgan gasps, realizing that Wil hasn't had cigarettes for days, and now he's smoking again.

"What are those?" Wil yells, pointing at the flags, his uncommon interest vaguely troubling. It's almost as though he wants to see if his name is already on a flag. Wil squints, takes a drag of his cigarette, then saunters off the porch toward the mourning couple.

Standing over the grave markers, Wil says, "You made those from the blanket," then his smile drops, "Don't make one of those for me," he requests.

Morgan's upper lip snarls at Wil.

Pleased that he redirected the smoking intervention, Wil takes a long drag on his cigarette, then does a half spin in his boots so that he's looking back toward Leeds house.

"Yes," Morgan says.

"Yes, what?" Jody asks.

"Wil has started a now-necessary conversation. It's time to talk about what we'd want to happen if we die. We each need to create a living will."

"Or a dying Wil," Wil says.

Ignoring the joke, Morgan yells, "Hummingbird! Kyle! Get out here."

Almost instantly, the tattooed girl and the beautiful boy appear on the porch, looking frantic.

"We're all alive," Wil says, waving off their panic.

"And we need to talk about what we want to happen if we end up not alive," Morgan adds.

Hummingbird looks at Kyle, then they nod at each other simultaneously and walk over to the flags.

"I think that the flags are inspired by my signature towels," Jody says, temporarily redirecting the grim moment back to the stage.

"Jody, you had no signature towel. You used Martha Stewart towels. There was $50 budgeted for towels every gig, but if we had forgone that expense maybe we'd have had money for a GPS," Kyle says, not in the mood to discuss the past because it seems so far gone. This was to be a conversation about the future, about the end.

"One," Jody says, getting worked up, "Martha Stewart is a saint. B, her Halloween magazine this year was the best yet, and B2, those towels are part of the Lies As Language experience. They're souvenirs for the people who are too impoverished to buy a T-shirt. Maybe a gal will sew the sides of the towel up, cut a head hole, then leave some room for little arm holes, thus making a tank top out of the towel. I'm not going to take a makeshift shirt off a girl's back... unless she asks me to."

"It doesn't matter. The towels don't matter," Kyle says, exhausted.

"You underestimated the importance of the towels. If you see Aerosmith, you want Steven Tyler to have those rags on his mic stand. I mean, you also want to see his daughter's butthole, but you know that's not going to happen, so at least you have the rags. It reminds you of why you love Aerosmith, and honestly, you can just go home and jerk off to photoshopped speculations on what Liv Tyler's butthole might look like," Jody says.

"And statements like that are precisely why I didn't stop you from getting the towels," Kyle says.

"Another argument won by the all-time great," Jody celebrates.

"Neither of us is winning right now," Kyle says, mulling over how he wants to be buried.

"I'm pretty sure I just won an argument," Jody says, "And a *W* is a *W* no matter how you score it. You can put asterisks on my shit, I don't care. They took those wins from Paterno for a little while when they found out he was protecting a Behringer, but that doesn't mean he didn't win all those games."

"I have no idea what you're saying. The towels are a good idea because they bring people closer to the stage. I'll admit that." Kyle says.

"What?" Jody asks.

"The rags. It brings people very close to the stage. If people think we'll throw them something, they'll come closer. That's why we look popular. That's why the other bands got jealous. I understood what you were doing. The towels had a manipulative purpose."

Jody quietly considers this because Kyle was able to observe everything that was happening in the most intimate of distances. Throughout the chaos, Kyle has been making careful observations and interpreting behavior, while leaning on Jody's words.

The drummer is always at the back of the stage performing at a distance from the crowd. To reach across the gap Jody added theatrics. When his eyes met with an enthusiastic girl in the crowd, Jody would smile, wipe his face with a black towel that he kept on his drumstick bucket, and send the wet rag flying into the crowd, toward the girl. His throw accuracy was perfected over years of toilet papering houses on Halloween. Jody has always loved the ghastly beauty of a house that blew in the wind, but after he became a drummer he realized that his entire toilet papering experience was just practice for throwing these towels. Even if one of the fans didn't end up with the sweaty rag as a souvenir, she would have the memory of reaching for it, and memories have always had worth to Jody.

"When we make it out of here, we *will* have a concert," Morgan says, "But, if we don't make it out of here, then it's important for each of us to give verbal instructions to the group on how we want to be taken care of if... Jody, you start," Morgan reaches for the help of her boyfriend.

Jody scrunches his nose, like he's imagining his future, but it's more a past image he's tapping into. Breaking through the flashback, Jody decides, "I want something that will remind you of me. I want something simple. Like fireworks that spell out 'Jody Lennard' in the sky, then a fucking prop plane flies through the fireworks, but the guy flying the plane is wearing goggles because I don't want to share my funeral with some shitty pilot who can't anticipate the hazards of his job. After the pilot does a fly over and everyone is losing their fucking mind, you'll all watch as the Jersey Devil pisses out of his ass because he's so mad that he helped me get such an awesome funeral. The devil will be pulling at his horns and he'll heavily second guess himself, like, 'Damn, this dude just started the party of the year, and everyone is screaming *Jody! Jody!* instead of *Jersey! Jersey!* and I'm feeling like a pretty big failure right now.' That means, while the Jersey Devil is distracted, you'll all steal a van from the aqua-peoples and drive to safety. I don't want to make myself a posthumous hero, but when the coffin fits, wear it."

We're all silent for three long seconds.

"Jody, I don't think we have any of the resources here for that," Hummingbird says.

"Yeah, if we had a plane, we could fly the fuck out of here," Wil says, bitter that this ludicrous plane doesn't exist.

"Actually, we'd probably explode on a tree," Kyle points out, ever the realist in a band of fanatical maniacs. "We simply don't have a long enough stretch for a clear takeoff."

"I think we need to scale your living will down," Morgan suggests delicately to Jody.

"Yeah. I suppose," Jody huffs, "I'm a humble man. So... I guess... just fabricate a bottle rocket in the basement, then shove that up my ass."

"What?" everyone asks.

"You'll build the first human corpse launched into space, and its name will be the UASS Jody Lennard. Fucked up pineys will be like, 'Momma, what's that? Is that a shooting star?' and Momma will be all like, 'No honey, that's Jody Lennard. His friends put a bottle rocket up his dead ass and he became the first human corpse rocket ship. Now he rotates the earth like a satellite, protecting America from the South Korean missile system.'"

"First, what was that little fantasy play you just performed? Second, I think you mean the North Koreans," Kyle edits the will.

"See, this is why I need a bottle rocket in my dead ass- because of Americans like you who don't realize we're being targeted," Jody says.

"Maybe we should come back to Jody," Hummingbird suggests, not confident in her ability to build any type of rocket ship.

"Okay, what do you want, Rachel?" Morgan asks.

Hummingbird, not expecting to be next, buys some time, "I... want..." she closes her eyes, then says, "...flowers."

"We don't have those either," Kyle points out.

"Exactly," Hummingbird says, then smiles.

XLVIII. Evil Read.

We all sit at the dinner table, as Morgan cleans up our mess, and no one offers to help because we get the feeling Morgan wants to be the one who takes care of us.

When the last plate is cleared, Morgan sits back down, then turns to Jody, and says, "We need to talk."

Jody shuffles his feet while still sitting, then announces loudly, "I found a book!" Something pushed this information out of his mouth, and he keeps yammering, "It's got fucking spells, incantations, potions... limericks. All sorts of magical shit."

"What are you talking about?" Morgan asks.

"Take your asses to the basement, and I'll show you," Jody says, standing up, almost like he's trying to reset the night.

"You expect us to believe you're all into black magic, Christ-boy?" Wil asks. Everything seems to be exhausting to Wil after this physically and emotionally taxing day.

"Well, he did dabble in Ouija," Kyle says, standing up, lighting his candle.

We get up, mimicking the rest of the people at the table, other than Wil.

We don't wait for Wil. He is a fallen leaf on the floor of the Barrens and everyone has chosen to step over him, even though we possess the knowledge that, at some point, a careless act will crush him.

"Don't listen to Wil. Jody believes in everything," Kyle says, walking through the kitchen.

"Except dieting," Morgan says, then when she doesn't get a laugh, she sheepishly acknowledges, "I'm fat as well."

"And most of what he believes in is horseshit. Let's just establish that," Wil calls out, and a second later he's behind us, candleless.

"There have always been doubters and there always will be," Jody says, lighting the oil lamp, then leading us downstairs. "Shit, I bet there were even doubters when that guy uploaded the first cat video to the internet. Now look at him, he's a billionaire."

"The guy who uploaded the first cat video to the internet is definitely not a billionaire," Kyle says.

"Check that shit out, people are still doubting him," Jody says, shaking his head at his brother's foolishness.

Jody's belief has always carried him, but it needs to be strong enough to carry *everyone* tonight. The man who digs graves has been called upon to make us forget about our ever quickening approach toward a home located under the sandy soil of the Barrens. It's Jody's responsibility because Kyle can't take another night of planning an escape- where would we go? What other option do we have besides studying why the walls seem to slowly be closing in on us while whispering cryptic messages?

We stand at the edge of the green blanket. It's stretched out on the floor of the basement, and now it's two triangles smaller. The lamp goes in the center of the blanket illuminating the vertex of the geometric figure we create- a figure that's now two sides smaller.

"So when's your Ouija board mysticism presentation going to begin?" Kyle asks, teasing his older brother.

"I don't fuck with the Ouija anymore," Jody says, his chest puffed out.

"Wait, I feel like there's a story here," Morgan says, anxious to learn more about her boyfriend.

"Oh. There is," Kyle assures her."When we were kids, or, when I was a kid and Jody was in his early 20's, our neighbor girl next door was this weird, lonely, fat goth."

"Hey, she had friends," Jody says, taking offense to the wrong part, but in his mind, it was the part that needed clarification.

Kyle nods sympathetically to Jody's correction, then continues his story, "I remember one day I walked downstairs in the middle of the summer to get a popsicle, and the girl was sitting on our kitchen floor. It was a really weird moment. I looked at the goth on the ground, with a lumpy backpack by her side, and I thought to myself, 'This is how I die. A goth girl is going to sacrifice me to the Beelzebub.'"

"What did she do when she saw you?" Hummingbird asks, worried that this girl had found Mike's weapons cache after the Six Flags field trip.

"Nothing. She did nothing, then Jody walked into the kitchen and introduced me to her. I got us popsicles, then we ate them while sitting on the kitchen floor. I remember there was black lipstick melting down this girl's red white and blue bomb pop. It felt like a weird moment of Americana. While we're sitting there, the goth- Audrey was her name- goes, 'Want to see something?'"

"I thought it was going to be her pussy," Jody says, then punctuates the statement with a frown that indicates it wasn't her pussy.

"Right. I didn't think that though, so I said, 'Sure,'" Kyle continues, "Audrey opened up her backpack, which of course matched her outfit, because that's what goths do- they love accessorizing- and she took out what I thought was a board game. I presumed it was something like Monopoly or Trouble or Life or another game created by adults with a name that warns us about our bleak future. I was like, why does this queen of darkness carry around Candy Land in her book bag?"

"To be fair, she was overweight so Kyle was not incorrect to expect we were about to play Candy Land," Jody defends his brother's past presumptions.

"Right, it's believable that she would want to live in a land where all building tools were edible, so I guess it shouldn't have struck me as odd, but it turns out that what she had brought over was a Ouija board. She asked me to turn out the lights, so I walked over and flicked the switch. It was still pretty bright out because it was maybe 6:30 at night, in the summer, but she still insisted we light a candle that she brought. Audrey said that the flame was important, not for a light source, but for an energy source. I was like, okay, fair enough, and I diverted to the expert. Once everything was finally in place, it was time to Ouija, so we all put our hands on the-"

"-oh my gosh, you contacted a demon?" Hummingbird gasps, now unsure if the house is cursed because of Ms. Leeds actions or because the boys on this blanket engaged in reckless Ouijaing.

"Maybe we communicated with a demon in Jody's pants," Kyle says, "The 'spirit' we spoke with said his name was 'Mortimer' and after announcing his presence, Mortimer immediately requested to 'see titties.'"

Morgan giggles.

"And Audrey knew that it was one of us messing around, so Jody pins it on me."

"I wasn't going to let Mortimer cockblock me when Kyle was obviously a juvenile gaylord so he wouldn't mind taking the fall for this miscalculation."

"That's the other fucked up part. I was 9, Jody was in his 20's and this neighbor girl was like 17."

"Hey, she was a fat 17, which is like a normal 22," Wil says, siding with Jody.

"I'll accept that," Morgan says, "We do get titties earlier."

"You sound like Mortimer now," Kyle says. "So I leave and... Jody, what happened? I never asked."

"We contacted spirits," Jody says, his chin high.

"Okay, so apparently Jody spoke with a spirit, then like a week later I'm bringing my laundry down to the basement, and I see that he's building something. I ask him what he's doing and he just shoos me away. Jody has always been pretty handy, you've seen his mace crafting skills, so I didn't think anything of it."

"You build more than just tools of destruction, Jody?" Morgan asks, intrigued. Jody builds, Morgan decorates- it could make for a nice little life.

"Of course I fabricate various things," Jody says, as though his craftsman abilities should be implied, "Christ chose the profession of carpenter, and I chose it for the same reason."

"Your 'profession' was assistant manager of a car rental place," Wil snarls.

"Yes, slash contractor. Jesus managed people too if you think about it. He just didn't collect any money for services rendered. It was like 'Hey, blind guy, you got blinded... by.... desert wind or whatever, come here. Okay, now that I've touched your head you're made whole again with eyesight. Hey leper, you... probably had relations with a corpse or something. I'll cure you anyway, because that's the type of guy I am, but please stop doing that. It's super weird and probably a sign of some other issues you really need to work out.'"

"What have you built?" Hummingbird asks, not sure if the point of Kyle's story was that Jody has always built things, or that Jody has always loved fat chicks, or that Jody has been using the devil to seduce younger girls for years now. The point of this story better not be that the Lennard brothers raised a demon which has now returned to bury them.

Luckily, Jody is willing to elaborate on his building history, "I fabricated Kyle a tree fort that was so fuckin' good we had to start charging cover. Not for chicks of course- they got in free. Did we start a little business? You could say that. People would ask, 'Nine dollars for a bologna sandwich?' but they paid those prices because of the atmosphere."

"Let's fast forward again," Kyle says, returning the story to the reason why it was told, "Two weeks after our first interaction with Mortimer, I'm in the backyard, mowing the lawn, despite being only 9 and having a physically capable older brother who should have been doing it, and if you stood on the hill in our backyard, you could see over the fence into Audrey's yard. She had a hot tub- one of those deals that's built into a cedar deck, and out of boredom while mowing, I looked over into the yard, and I saw Jody in the hot tub, with Audrey, and they're both looking down. I immediately start panicking, thinking, 'Am I watching my brother get a hand job from a fat 17 year old goth?' Since I obviously had to find out the answer to this question, I kept watching, but I was already at the edge of the hill, and the mower was making so much noise that there was no way I could just stay there so I had to mow across the yard to keep things sounding like normal suburban background noise. I didn't want to let them know I was watching because Jody does eventually reach a point where the shame of his actions becomes too apparent to ignore. As I made the return toward Audrey's yard again, the scene was slowly revealed to me. She wasn't looking at Jody's penis- she was looking at his wood. On this piece of wood that Jody had fashioned in the basement, was a crudely Sharpied version of a Ouija board. These two were surrounded by candles, Ouijaing on a plank, in a hot tub, at 5 PM on a Wednesday, in the summer daylight."

Everyone sitting on the blanket giggles at this, even Wil.

"Let Jody explain himself," Kyle says, holding up his gloved hands, as though he could block the laughter.

Jody nods appreciatively at his brother. No longer did a fist fight erupt between these two men at the first sign of disrespect. Leeds house has changed them- and this is a positive change.

"Well," Jody says, stroking his goatee, "I can't defend myself regarding these allegations because I did do all that shit Kyle just said, but you have to understand... chicks love Ouijas and hot tubs, so when you combine the two, you have a girl with basically no clothes on, who's scared and wants to be comforted."

"I'm smart enough to know which fifty percent of that compliment to take," Jody says, pointing two fingers at Hummingbird.

"So do we get to see the notebook?" Wil asks.

"Kyle tells one romantic story and suddenly Wil wants to watch *The Notebook*?" Jody lets out a rapid-fire laugh. "I don't even think the demon TV has a DVD player and if it did the devil would never let something as pure as the love and loss of Ryan Gosling and Rachel McAdams play in his home."

"You said you found a notebook. A physical notebook," Wil reminds him.

"Oh. Correct. Yes, I am in error on this one," Jody says.

Wil returns to his skeptical self, and asks, "So... what? You're going to do some magic spell and bring our dead friends back? Things will seem normal with them, but something will be. . off, then Hummingbird will remember a part in Behringer's book where the wiz kid brings someone back to life. Morgan will go, 'What happened in the book when the boy wizard brought his friend back to life?' and Hummingbird will whisper, 'The replacement began eating peoples' throats,' then after this revelation, you'll run through the house only to find me with no throat. No fucking thanks."

"Hey! No! No discussion of horror tropes," Morgan says, wagging a finger at Wil, "It just gives the devil ideas. It's like he doesn't have Netflix so he's never seen any B-movies and when he hears us discussing clichés, he's probably like, 'Yes, genius. This is the way I'll finally scare them.'"

"My friend, wearing my other friend, while vomiting corrosive gunk down his melting body was something that definitely scared me. I think you're belittling his work," Wil points out Then, feeling in control, he requests, "Before Jody starts reading fucked up incantations, can you at least humor my probably very accurate theory-"

"-I'd rather not," Morgan says quickly.

Wil looks at Morgan from under his black eyebrows, then says, "But you've accepted you're done for. That's why you two acknowledged *The*

Notebook. Ryan and Rachel die at the end, I presume, and not only do we have a Rachel, but you and Jody..."

"Yeah, maybe we might feel like we're going to die, but there are other people on this blanket who are still optimistic- don't doom them too," Morgan says, pointing at Kyle. This is a reminder that someone might actually walk out of these woods, and it's sad this reminder is necessary.

"God will battle alongside us," Jody declares.

"If He's all-powerful, why doesn't He just save us?" Wil asks.

"Because we have free will that can mess up His plans," Jody explains. "If we follow His plans and continue to follow Him, we will get out of these woods, or we will help someone else walk out of here."

"You believe in all these things as an escape, not because they will help us escape," Wil says, remaining seated.

"You know what?" Jody asks, marching away from the light to get the book. "I believe in all that shit because it's awesome. God sacrificing himself for me. A Ouija hot tub sesh. A mer-fish-woman destroying my van. A magical notebook that will give me time traveling abilities so I can go back and warn pre-New Jersey me to never let Hummingbird give us directions. All that stuff might be made up, but it's beautiful in a way too."

Jody moves into the darkness, then tells Wil, "If you live in a world composed of only things you can see and touch, then there are a lot of things you'll never feel."

XLIX. Leeding Us On.

We flinch when Jody drops the notebook onto the green blanket.

The cover is leather and bears no imprint except for the wear and tear of a difficult history.

Jody claims he found this book when he was looking for parts for his mace.

"Hummingbird, step into the circle and take possession of the book," Jody says, organizing his reading event.

"Oh shit, you guys aren't going to sacrifice me are you?" Hummingbird asks, scooting back, slowly turning the circle into an ice cream cone. No one has ever been sacrificed in an ice cream cone. "I'm totally not a virgin, won't be worth it," Hummingbird states.

The rounded top of the ice cream cone laughs.

"What? Is it funny that I said I'm not a virgin? Fuck you guys. Not literally. Never fucking you guys. I'm not a whore. I'm practically a virgin. I'm virginish."

"Hummingbird, please complete the circle," Kyle's soothing voice requests.

"I've seen this movie before. I'm not-" Hummingbird backs away further.

"-Hummingbird, I guarantee that you will not have to enter the middle of the circle," Kyle says, soothing the paranoid girl.

Jody, to bail out Hummingbird, gets into the center of the circle, turning this into a theater in the round style reading.

Hummingbird begrudgingly completes the very un-satanic form.

Jody holds up the book and proclaims, "The words in my hands are filled with treasures and other general mysticalities."

Finally, someone is going to give us some answers.

"What does it say?" Hummingbird asks.

"Good question," Jody responds, his posture rigid.

"It won't bring answers. It will bring more black blood," Wil maintains.

"This is how the death started. He told me everything, he brought me here to carve this story out-" Jody starts to read.

"Is that from the book?" Wil asks.

"Yes, dude. Do I ever sound like that much of a gaylord? It's Behringer."

"Why does the book look so old and dusty if it's Behringer writing this stuff?" Hummingbird asks.

"I don't know, he was older than me so he was... probably... immortal?" Jody says, only a sentence and a half in, and already struggling to explain what he's started.

With a misplaced confidence in his answer, Jody looks back down at the book, and reads, "Every word of this work is true. Despite my need to embellish, due in large part to my classical training as a fiction writer, my hand is unable to pen any lies. I've seen the way *he* feeds off untruths and for my own well-being I cannot and will not stray from his words- truths as I know them."

"This is the answer," Kyle says, riveted.

"This is worse than his other books," Wil says, put off.

"Jody can read," Morgan whispers, proud of him.

The book is cracked open wider and it makes a snapping noise.

Jody's voice booms across the basement, "And he spoke, 'This is the trial that you are arraigned for. This is Arem truth is dinectu penubra,'" Jody's jaw opens wide and he gasps out, "Atola vidictu,"

"Jody?" Kyle asks.

Jody's eyes roll back, as he drools, "Extanom gothar-"

"-Jody, stop. This is freaking me out," Morgan pleads

"Ventu-"

"-Jody," Kyle calls, springing forward, shaking his brother.

"An-an-aaaa," Jody says, making a clicking noise, and choking on his own tongue, he begins to vibrate. "A-a-a-anddd, I'm totally fucking with you, I'm fine," Jody says, immediately returning to normalcy with a wide smile and an immediate laugh. "Your face, and your face, and your face," Jody says, as he points at each person in the circle, until he reaches Wil, and says, "Not so much your face. But, oh man. I got you all good."

"You're a dick," Morgan says.

"This is just an old copy of the boy wizard book that was in a bucket full of rust and shit," Jody says, flopping the book into the corner.

"Usually when someone calls you a dick, you should feel bad," Morgan says, hoping that Jody takes the hint.

"I was saying a bunch of stupid ass bullshit. You guys are so gullible. Hey. Hey. Gullible is written on the ceiling," Jody points up, then immediately reveals, "It's really not. I'm fuckin' with you again."

Wil looks up.

"You're an ass, you planned all this just for a joke that lasted a couple seconds?" Morgan questions her boyfriend.

"Sure did. While I was grave digging, I had the idea so I just took the dust jacket off of the book, and was like, 'Oh ancient words. How special.' The book is just filled with normal words, all of them English, most of them boring, except for when the baby wizard is thrown in the water, and he's fuckin' drowning, and to make matters worse the reptilators are swimming toward him-"

"-Jody, did you read Behringer's book?"

"What? Me? Reading a book? What? No. I was making a joke. Okay, so he's drowning, right? He's like gasping-"

"- you're a loser," Morgan says.

"So what? I read a little of that old looking book. In fact... Uh. Let's collect all of Behringer's books, then I can burn them. I mean, you could burn them, but if I'm having a book fire, you could just give the books to me, preferably with dust jackets, and that would be cool. I have a pile of things to burn."

"What do you mean, 'a pile of things to burn?'" Kyle asks.

"It's just a collection of various demonic idols that must be destroyed by the fire from whence they came," Jody says.

"Show me your burning pile," Kyle demands.

Jody picks up the oil lamp, then walks over to a portion of the basement that was previously unused and unlit.

"Here's the shit that will be cool to burn," Jody says, pointing at a pile of items he's collected.

We don't leave the blanket, we merely crane our necks and strain our eyes to review a pile that, at first glance, looks very similar to what the old Wiccan lady had collected- Behringer's books, some posters of the boy wizard played by Grant Anders, and Rob's hoodie (the cloth one, not the friendskin one).

"Jody, this stuff is important. This stuff is part of the puzzle. We need to return these books to the shelves in Behringer's room. We need to keep Rob's hoodie because we don't know how long we'll be here or how cold we'll get as we slip into winter. We need to keep... the girls' underwear because... I don't even know how you got those and that's not an invitation to tell me," Kyle informs his brother.

Jody looks down at the pile of shit, then asks, "So, you want me to burn it, right?"

"No, I want you to-"

"-did you do this?" Wil calls out, his neck craned.

"Most likely," Jody responds, lantern raised.

"On the ceiling, it..." Wil trails off, tilting his head back further, straining to see.

"Oh, I get it," Kyle responds, looking back to Jody.

"I'm not fucking around," Wil says.

"Sorry, not falling for it," Hummingbird says, but there's a dash of fear in her voice.

Jody raises his lantern as he walks toward Wil.

"On the ceiling, it says... Stay. Over and over," Wil tells us.

We look up.

Stay. *Stay.*   *Stay.*   *Stay.* *Stay.*

Stay. Stay.   *Stay.*   *Stay.*   *Stay.*   *Stay.*

    Stay.   *Stay.*   *Stay.*   *Stay.*

      Stay.   *Stay.*   *Stay.* *Stay.*

Stay.   *Stay.*   *Stay. Stay.* *Stay.*   *Stay.*

Stay.   *Stay.* *Stay.*   *Stay.*   Stay.

Normally, when a haunted house has been entered, it wants to spit the intruders out. The ghost of the previous owner will want things to stay exactly the same, but the visitors always keep moving things- changing things- erasing his past to make room for their present.

This hasn't happened in Leeds house.

There are no ghosts in this house; there are devils. Devils like company. Devils want you to stay. Devils will convince you they're your biggest fan because they know you can't resist the attention.

Stay- a word that normally tugs at our heart- is now being used to distract us, so our heart can be pulled clean out of our chest.

L. Personal Conversations En Masse.

We lie wrapped in the green blanket, Morgan accepting the cut-up end. Next to Morgan is Jody. "If we're trapped here," Jody says, quietly, "I could see us... having a good-ish life. Other than the almost certain starvation and losing all our friends' parts."

"Forget living the good-ish life, we just need to concentrate on continuing to live *a* life," Morgan whispers, "But, yeah, I'm happy when I'm with you. So, not to sound like a ceiling devil, but, please *stay* with me."

"Of course I'll stay with you. God has a plan for me so I can't die," Jody says.

"I hope God's plan for you is foolproof."

"I'll be okay. I may not be the most perfect person in the world, but think about it, who is? I mean, look at Kyle, doesn't it say in the Bible, a man shalt not do it with another man from behind?"

"It does, sort of," Morgan mumbles.

"You've read the Bible?"

"Parts, you know, the major stuff. Baby in the basket, three wise men, flipping the tables in the temple, parting the Red Sea, walking on water, and the scary ending stuff."

"So, that means, you believe in God?" Jody whispers.

"Hand to God... I believe in God," Morgan declares. How could she not after this? She catches herself in a gray area and says, "God, I'm sorry if I'm not supposed to say, 'Hand to God.' I mean it like a high five. Hi five, to God." She caps off her apology by high fiving the air.

"I think he left you hangin'," Wil jokes, looking over Jody's shoulder.

Morgan scowls, then snips, "You seem convinced that there's an invisible force in this house, how come you have such a problem with believing I just high fived our creator?"

"Because you've been brainwashed," Wil says, across Jody, to Morgan.

"Or, I've just changed?"

"You're just playing along because you can't keep yourself off Jody- among other people- so you need someone out there who will forgive you."

"You're right. A bit," Morgan admits, "But Jody has taught me a lot. This house has taught me a lot."

"Among other people...?" Jody repeats.

Wil, satisfied, lies on his back and looks up at the message on the ceiling. He takes out his cigarettes and lights one with his green lighter.

"Really?" Morgan asks.

"Where do you keep getting those from?" Kyle asks, rolling over to face Wil. Kyle has made it a priority to ensure that nothing has changed between himself and Wil after the drunken rant. That moment in Behringer's office might have been the first time Wil came out to anyone and immediately after Wil exposed his heart, he was thrown out of the room. Kyle carries guilt about this. At the time, he was too overwhelmed to properly deal with the situation, but now that he's learned how much each of his friends mean to him, and how deep the void is when they're no longer in his life, he's not only comfortable with getting closer, he demands it. Wil admitted he loves Kyle. To push someone away because they love you is suicide in this house. Wil is becoming exponentially more bitter since his moment of honesty, so it's essential to prove to him that expressing his true feelings will not be met with hostility, but instead warm acceptance.

Wil exhales a climbing rope of smoke, then says, "Behringer was a smoker and he hid packs from the kids. Smoking wasn't his worst vice, when you think about it."

He can say this because he continues to find half-filled packs of stale cigarettes everywhere- in drawers, on top shelves, inside coats.

Wil needs cigarettes to survive.

Stupid habit.

Stupid dated habit.

Stupid dated legend.

Stupid *Teen Mom* reject, Ms. Leeds.

Kyle turns to face Hummingbird so he's not breathing in the questionable smoke from the cigarette. "Are you doing better?" he whispers to the shivering Hummingbird.

She nods her head yes. "A little better," she says.

"Hummingbird," Kyle purrs lightly, not allowing her to escape.

The yes nods into a no.

"Why?" Kyle asks, his voice still airless, non-aggressive, a tickle.

"I always do it. I did this after we sang together," Hummingbird says, moving her hoodie sleeve up to show a fresh cut.

"Why?"

"It feels like getting a tattoo, it's just not as pretty. I love that feeling... ya know?" Hummingbird whispers.

"You'll have to talk to that guy about it," Kyle says, pointing his thumb behind him. "I'm tattoo-less."

"Why?" Hummingbird asks, as two familiar strangers huddle closer together to understand each other better.

"Because it would prove my boyfriend right- that I'm being consumed by... the scene. Tattoos are a huge metalcore cliché," Kyle reminds Hummingbird.

"I want to take you to get one when we get home," Hummingbird decides aloud. At first Kyle is hurt that Hummingbird would disregard his boyfriend by dismissing his fears without a care, but as Kyle flips the statement over in his mind, he realizes that Hummingbird is thinking about the future rather than losing hope. What Hummingbird proposed could only happen after we're all back on the road. He can't betray the boy who may no longer be waiting, but if the boy is no longer waiting, Kyle may take Hummingbird up on her offer.

"When you visit my house, I can take you to a good place," Hummingbird says, "And we'll take your special guy too. It will be something we'll all share."

"Okay," Kyle says, then smiles, "You and I will go and get tattoos together when we're out of the woods."

"This is my newest one..." Hummingbird brags, repositioning, then pointing at a tattoo of a skull near her right shoulder. "This one is my favorite though..." she says, then slides out from under the blanket, and pulls up her children's shorts. As she angles her left leg toward Kyle, he admires her tattoo of a rose. "It was my first," Hummingbird recalls, "I was so scared. The girl at the tattoo place, Ashleigh- she's my friend now- she kept trying to talk me into something smaller before getting the big rose, but I didn't want something smaller, I wanted the rose."

"Roses are red... Bruises are blue... Cuts are... also red.... and I see them on you," Wil muses, as a clump of ash from his cigarette falls onto his once-white shirt. He notices the clump of ash is too big to have come from the stubby white cylinder in his hand, so he looks at the cherry of the cigarette, and that's when he sees his fingertips are glowing orange.

Letting out a gasping howl, Wil flicks the cigarette into the darkness, ashing his glowing fingertips in the process. Kicking the blanket off of himself, Wil grips his wrist and watches as his disappearing fingertips smolder.

The boy with the glowing hand flees into the darkness, colliding with the random shit that's stacked in formless piles, obstructing his escape.

We scatter, afraid that whatever got on Wil could get on us.

"Did something take Wil? Did something bite him?" Morgan asks, as we hear Wil storm up the stairs.

"He was just lying there one moment, then it's like something… dropped from the ceiling," Jody says. He picks up the lantern, then slowly raises it to the ceiling, only to find the repeated command and nothing else.

Stay.

Was it a warning or was it a demand?

Wil did not stay.

All eyes stay stuck on the ceiling until Hummingbird interrupts the tension with a demand of her own, "Jody, give me your torch."

Jody looks over at Hummingbird and shakes his head in refusal.

"Jody, give me the fucking torch," she growls, eyes burning.

"Why?" Jody bellows back, trying to intimidate Hummingbird into adventureless safety.

"Why?" Hummingbird asks, annoyed, "Because, Jody…" she says, getting close to a shrinking man, "…we buried two of our friends tonight, and I don't want to bury a third. I know that Wil is next, but I'm not going to sit down here and let it happen."

"What makes you think he's next?" Morgan asks.

Hummingbird grabs the flashlight, then whispers loudly to Morgan, "Because he's a fucking asshole, and that means he's next."

Jody raises his hand, then says, "Hola chica, I'm an asshole too, and I'm fine."

"Don't say 'hola chica,'" Morgan demands, "It makes you sound like…"

"Exactly," Jody responds.

"Hummingbird, listen," Kyle says, a soft voice amongst the yelling.

"No. Kyle," Hummingbird says, whipping around, blasting the torchlight into makeupless eyes, "You don't get a say in this. You aren't in the same situation as we are."

Kyle moves toward the light, and this sends Hummingbird dashing through the basement to get to Wil as quickly as possible- to interrupt whatever Leeds has planned for tonight. As she runs, Hummingbird's shoulder strikes a chair and it clatters to the ground, creating an obstacle and slowing Kyle's attempt at pursuing her.

Undeterred, Kyle continues stalking through the dark toward the quickly moving torchlight, calling out, "Hummingbird, get back here, you're freaking out. How can you say that I'm not in this as deep as you-"

"-you're the lead singer," Hummingbird yells back.

"Not anymore," Kyle says.

"Yes, you are. You're still the lead singer and, guess what?" Hummingbird says, climbing the stairs, "The lead singer is essential, while everyone else can be replaced."

The torchlight disappears, then footsteps hammer across the ceiling, our eyes following them, and no matter where we look, we're reminded to *Stay.*

LI. The Room We've Avoided.

We stand in the extension of the house that has no second floor. This is a room we've rarely found reason to enter, and that's probably why Wil fled here, for privacy.

Wil is peering out the window into the totally dark front yard, waiting to see those red eyes, but only finding his reflection. He holds up his black, scarred, slightly shorter fingertips, then presses them to the window, expecting the glass to shatter on contact, but only receiving a casual cold tingling on his wounded fingers.

When a bright swift movement is reflected in the window, Wil's hand recoils from the glass in the same way it would have if his touch did bring its expected destruction. Hummingbird, holding the flashlight, bleeding from her shoulder, stares at Wil's reflection, and asks, "What happened?"

Wil begins to turn around, but his movement hits an invisible wall halfway through his rotation. He sees Hummingbird's injury in his periphery, and asks, "Was that because of your habit or are you just made of tissue paper?"

Quietly Hummingbird huffs, "You think I'm that 2D? Well, you-"

"-the cuts Hummingbird," Wil says, as though he's exhausted, "I was right there when you were whispering about them. I was a single person away and you still talked about it like it was funny or something. Have you run out of room on your body so you have to whisper out your secrets in the most public way possible?"

Rather predictably, the person who rushed to Wil's side is pushed away, and a pouting Hummingbird says, "I was coming here to make-"

"-you're next, Hummingbird," Wil says, and he's finally able to fully turn around because eye contact becomes crucial. "You. Are. Next."

"You're an asshole," Hummingbird says, finally in agreement with the others downstairs.

"Yeah. I am," Wil confirms, his menace getting dimmer as Hummingbird sets the flashlight on a long table to her left. She doesn't want to be able to see the look on Wil's face anymore, but she makes sure that the light is still focused on where he's standing. She can still hear the smile in Wil's voice as he hisses, "I am an asshole, but you're next."

"You're insane," Hummingbird says, grabbing a napkin off the long table, then wiping away her blood.

"Yes. I am," Wil says, "But you're still next."

"And how are you so sure, Mr. Know-It-All?"

"Because, I've seen it happen before," Wil says.

"I'm not like Rob, and I'm sure as fuck not like Mike," Hummingbird says, her voice trembling. She immediately feels a heavy guilt about speaking of her friends so harshly.

"You're not a bad person, so you're totally different from them, right?" Wil asks, and he pauses long enough to give the moment importance, before adding, "Is that what you're saying, Hummingbird?"

"No. No. I loved them both. They were good people. Cliff- Mike- whoever that boy was, he was good. He was good, but they had convinced him he was bad. We abandoned him, just like his father."

"Are you saying that you're not a good person?" Wil inquires devilishly.

"Wil, you're scaring me," Hummingbird says in a paper thin voice. She looks down at the red napkin, only seeing a faint discoloration in the dark.

"And you, dear Hummingbird, hurt me," Wil says, dramatically performing for an audience of two.

"I- uh- never, touched you?" Hummingbird says, taking an inventory of days that seem too long and too circular, yet also pointed, like when she refused to conform to the circle downstairs.

"You are aware that your actions have an impact on others, right?" Wil asks, physically backing off, but still pressing Hummingbird verbally. He returns to the window, the light from the flashlight on the table creating a spotlight on his back. When he doesn't receive an answer to his question, Wil growls, "Well. Are you?"

In a baby sized voice, Hummingbird says, "Yes?"

"Let me put it to you like this. When I smoke those cigarettes..." Wil pauses and lets the thought sit in his head for a moment, then returns to his contemplation "...there's secondhand smoke. The cigarette smoke I inhale is for my pleasure, and it's also to my detriment. When I exhale, there you are, inhaling my corrosive breath."

"What's your point, Wil?" Hummingbird asks.

"I'm talking about actions that defy self-preservation," Wil responds.

"We all have the self-preservation instinct, but... it doesn't have to conflict with your heart. Let's preserve each other together," Hummingbird begs.

"It'll conflict with your heart, just watch," Wil says, turning back to the bright light of the torch that's trained on him.

"Watch what, Wil?" Hummingbird snips, tired of being forced to parse through indirect clipped messages.

Wil lurches toward Hummingbird, and the closer he gets, the less of his face Hummingbird can see. He moves so close that his spit lands on her nose when he barks out, "I watch you mock me with your- your- your- wounds," he says, then turns away and grabs his hair like he's about to rip the follicles out by the handful.

"I have no idea what you're saying," Hummingbird whimpers. It's obvious that she shouldn't cut those notches, but this is not a normal reaction to someone else's pain. This is something different- something far more personal.

"I watched him kick her ass," Wil bursts out, like the words were a demon exiting his body, then he instantly returns to the window.

"Who, Wil?" Hummingbird asks, then picks up the flashlight so his reaction will be illuminated.

"I watched him throw her onto the brick pavers in our backyard because she was 'embarrassing him,' with her 'stupid stories' at their Christmas party."

"Wil, is this about your mom?" Hummingbird asks, approaching the confused boy.

"I didn't do anything," Wil says, wild-eyed, looking at Hummingbird's glowing reflection in the window. "He brought her a pair of pants and an ugly sweater to wear, then sent her back into the party. I didn't tell anyone why she changed from her red dress to such an ugly outfit. I sat there... when all of it happened. I did nothing to stop it. Then... one night... when I was getting high at Rob's house, she finally got revenge- on him, on herself. And you.... you won't let me..."

Hummingbird moves close to Wil and her arm creeps around his stale shirt like a snake. She doesn't have the proper words to ease him at this moment because she doesn't have the entire story.

Wil grits his teeth at Hummingbird's serpentine action, and through his clenched jaw, he explains, "I crept into the house that night, so that I wouldn't get caught for being high. I went to sleep. It was just another night. In the middle of that night, I woke up. There was this tension inside the house. There was an unease. I thought that Rob had bought some shit cut with something nasty. I needed a cigarette. I couldn't get caught smoking because I was only 18 at the time and my parents would have killed me. My grandpa died from it. Lung cancer," Wil says, then he laughs a little laugh. He looks down at the floor, or maybe to Hummingbird's wrist on his stomach.

"I walked into the bathroom with my cigarettes... and... wooh..." Wil exhales, almost as though he was pushed by an unseen force. His hand rests on Hummingbird's wrist, as he says, "I... I... uh... snuck in there... for a little release via self-destruction... and it turns out my mom one-upped me. I was so glad I had that cigarette. I lit it, and I sat down, and I held her cold hand while she took a crimson bath."

Wil won't stop smoking, even though he knows how it will end for him.

Hummingbird won't stop notching cuts, even though she knows how it will end for her.

Why are we even following these two anymore?

We already know how everything will end for them.

LII. Crunching Numbers.

We stand in the front yard, under the gray sky, between the graves and the ash pile.

"We're all here," Kyle says, rubbing his slight beard with a gloved hand. A smile creases across his face as he finds his friends in good spirits despite the grim reality of it all. "We're getting better. We're not getting closer, but we're getting better," Kyle reminds the group.

"We've buried two friends," Wil says, revealing the flip side.

Everyone is silent as we look down at the two flags in the ground. Between us and the flags, we watch a single, small snowflake drift down through the gray sheet of morning.

"You're right," Kyle finally responds, and something inside him breaks, "Those losses were retribution for perceived sins. Mike looked at killing as a sport and collected pelts as trophies. He was killed for sport and turned into clothing. Rob looked at drugs as an escape, ignoring the toll they were taking both on his body and on the emotions of those around him. His body went toxic, and he couldn't escape it. Mike and Rob finally felt the pendulum of their actions swoop back and strike them." The feel good moment of a drifting snowflake is crushed with a verbal sledgehammer that Kyle brings down with such force that it shakes all of us to our very core.

"This makes no sense. Why would the devil punish people for sinning?" Hummingbird asks.

"Listen," Jody echoes through the woods, "It's probably like 9 AM or some shit. We have no clock so it could be even earlier than that, but it's safe to assume it's too fuckin' early to discuss this." Jody's nails are still caked with dirt from yesterday. He had to replace the bandage on his palm this morning. He can't pick up another shovel today.

"I'll make us a special lunch. Anything you guys want," Morgan says warmly, attempting to redirect the conversation. Her cheeks are flush from the November cold, but she likes being out in the crisp fall air... when her friends aren't fighting.

"We're being punished for our demons," Kyle says, not letting us escape this reality. He wants us to be trapped in this knowledge like it was Leeds house.

"Okay. Great, Kyle," Hummingbird says, not exactly blown away by this revelation, "How do you suggest we get rid of our demons?" she asks, hoping that he can provide some sort of answer. Wil and Hummingbird are in a race and Hummingbird knows that she will slice her own finish line.

Kyle shakes his head and in a small voice, says, "I'm not totally sure we can get rid of our demons."

"That's the bitch about having demons, they come with claws," Wil says, remembering the moment last night when his demons and Hummingbird's demons merged.

"Yeah, demons are worse than bed bugs," Hummingbird says.

"I used to know how to get rid of demons," Jody admits casually.

"Used to?" Hummingbird asks.

"Yeah. Then my way blew up," he responds.

"Like, you had an App?" Hummingbird pries.

"A band."

"Oh," Hummingbird says in a small voice.

Jody muses, "I hope that, somewhere in heaven, our van is driving alongside my motorcycle."

"I'm sure it is," Hummingbird tells him.

"I hope Jesus doesn't let Rob drive," Wil says, and it's such a rare joke from him that we don't start laughing until ten seconds after the comment is made.

We arrived with a band, a van, and some groupies. The band is gone, the van is gone, and the groupies are now close friends.

Lies As Language only had the band van because of Jody. He put all of this together, which is probably why he feels such an urgent responsibility to keep it together.

Before the founding of Lies As Language, Jody was an assistant manager at a rent-a-car place. He was an extremely dedicated and hardworking employee, but at the end of the day, he was still Jody. There were the obvious run-ins with HR, due to "inappropriate" and "un-business-like" conduct, but Jody was never formally written up. His charm and naiveté made even the most abrasive statements seem innocuous. Reliably on-time and grossly underpaid, Jody found himself promoted to assistant manager of this large corporate rent-a-car branch merely because his manager was afraid he would leave like so many of the other employees. The promotion was supposed to be a motivator for the other underlings. Stay here long enough and someday you can be a middle management assistant. Embracing the extra responsibility and second tier title, Jody worked the assistant manager job diligently for a decade, with only one vacation- that time he went to Burning Man. On Jody's 32nd birthday, he didn't come to work. This was the first non-hash smoking related vacation day that Jody Lennard had taken. He didn't schedule the day, nor did he announce his absence. "Either the assistant manager's desk will be empty and they'll be able to piece together what happened, or another motherfucker is going to sit down at that desk and there won't be an issue. I won't see why I'd have to call in," Jody told Art Greenblat, an attorney whose law firm he visited that day. In a manila folder, Jody had collected computer timestamps, phone records, and e-mail requests- everything that would prove that he hadn't taken a lunch break or vacation day since starting with the company. The evidence was half an inch thick. It was an impressive collection that Jody put together by leveraging favors, friendships, and self-described "Asian-escue computer hacking skills."

The plan to sue the rent-a-car company was a long-con. Raised on punk rock, Jody realized that the only way to fuck the system was to do it from the inside. This was a technique of acting punk rock to make punk rock. Jody wanted a band, but couldn't afford to devote his life to music as he watched the music industry come crashing down. The suit would pay for the first record, and from there, it was up to the audience to respond.

The rent-a-car company was blindsided by the allegations. Jody's manager was supposed to enforce the missed breaks, but he never did. Why would you stop someone from doing extra? It seemed un-American.

A trial defense of, "Does this look like the body of a man who skips meals?" was feared to be ineffective in front of a group of New Haven county jurors that were very hungry to award a large settlement. There was a high likelihood this case would be seen by the type of jury that wished the "jurors' box" was a sample crave case from a fast food joint that contained numerous different types of hamburgers, and existed as part of a campaign that "lets you be the jury," on which burger should be a permanent addition to the menu. New Haven jurors need that type of power at their diabetic fingertips.

This case was not an instant win for Jody's attorney though. Art Greenblat's case files read, in part, "Mr. Lennard does appear to have been abused by his current employer. He also appears to lack any social grace whatsoever, and placing him on the stand would be a massive liability, especially in front of a jury he could potentially ridicule. Earlier today, when I asked my African American secretary to bring Mr. Lennard a coffee, he responded, 'Whoa there motherfucker, didn't anyone fax you a copy of the emancipation proclamation? Get me the coffee yourself, Art.'"

After making the rent-a-car company's corporate office aware of his lawsuit, Jody eventually received an out of court settlement in the form of his salary, paid in full, with benefits, for a decade- the exact amount of time he was "chained to the desk." When Art Greenblat took his 30% fee, Jody put a stipulation on this payment. One-half of the one-third Mr. Greenblat received was required to go to Art's son, Steve, Jody's unemployed best friend. In the end, Jody felt like he walked away with most of the money. Art had a stipulation of his own though, instead of Jody receiving this money in a lump sum, the settlement money was placed in a trust fund, because, as Art's case notes stated, "Lennard's demeanor lends itself toward 'lottery winner' style money management skills."

The settlement began to arrive at the same time that Kyle graduated from high school, and instead of sending Kyle off to the state school that accepted him, Jody bought all the equipment for Lies As Language, then the Lennard brothers formed Lies As Language. Since the money is still being distributed monthly through the trust, and all of the equipment is fully insured, a new band will be easy to fund, if Jody gets out of the woods. Other than Wil, no one has paid Jody back for their instruments, but this isn't the debt that concerns him. Everyone told him that he had it made when they heard about the settlement, but looking at his life now, it's doubtful they'd feel the same way. Jody chooses to still consider himself lucky, but he can't shake the fact that what was once his proudest achievement- bringing these boys together- is now his biggest regret. He's beginning to realize that if he had just continued to do exactly what he was expected to as an adult- if he quietly accepted his lunchless days at work- then all of his friends would still be alive.

In an attempt to keep the people he still has in his life happy, Jody helps Morgan make lunch. She's cooking for fewer people so she's able to prepare everything much faster, even with Jody in the way. The fact that the number of people she's serving hasn't changed from last night is supremely soothing to her.

Once Jody sheds his apron and announces that lunch is served, everyone migrates to the dinner table.

Forks scrape on plates as everyone downs their food, quietly enjoying the peaceful atmosphere, until an invisible clock ticks too loud in Kyle's head, and he says, "I'm sorry, but we have to talk about what's happening here. We all know what's happening, but no one is saying anything."

"Pancakes are slowly becoming an unlikely diet staple?" Hummingbird asks, desperate to avoid a conversation like the one she had with Wil at the window last night.

"We're being punished," Kyle says bluntly and a chorus of forks being dropped is the only response.

Kyle waits for someone to challenge him. Desperate, he looks to Jody.

"You know what? Sometimes you just gotta smite the philistines," Jody says, then shrugs casually.

"Yeah. I've always said that," Morgan responds.

"What are you even talking about?" Kyle asks, frustrated.

"The philistines were sea people," Jody tells his brother.

"Is that the same as aqua-peoples?" Hummingbird asks, eager to learn.

"Good question," Jody says, pressing his fingers together in a little pyramid, then pointing at Hummingbird, "There are subtle differences."

"Do you still blame the aqua-peoples for this?" Wil asks, enjoying this tangent because it will likely lead to Kyle and Jody beating each other's ass' in the living room

Jody exhales, then admits, "I may have been a little hasty with my accusations towards the aqua-peoples. I will meet with their chief and request forgiveness."

"The aqua-peoples don't sound very merciful based on your description," Morgan notes.

"We need to acknowledge our faults," Kyle says, his voice now booming instead of soothing.

"You're being too loud at the lunch table," Morgan quickly says back to Kyle.

"I don't know how you can joke about this. I don't know why you refuse to take what's going on here seriously when we've already buried two of our friends," Kyle gasps desperately.

"This again?" Hummingbird asks.

"Kyle," Jody addresses his brother calmly, "Normally, I would whip your scrawny ass from here to the cat lady's house, but you make a valid point and beating the shit out of you at the first sign of disagreement is one of my faults, so I'm going to excuse myself from the table and politely ask you to do my dishes, because you are my bitch." Jody stands up, bows respectively to the table, then walks out of the dining room.

"Where's he going?" Hummingbird asks.

"He's probably just going to stand in the kitchen and listen to what we say, while hoping we talk about how brave he is," Kyle responds, "But we need to ignore him and focus on what matters. We're imperfect. We all have something that we need to change. So let's put pride aside and ackno-"

"-this is what he wants," Morgan interrupts, "He wants us to start naming each other's faults so we become judgmental enemies, then we'll end up killing each other before he can get to us."

"I think we're all adults here," Kyle says.

"No. The only adult here just walked out of the room. He knows better than to start pointing fingers," Hummingbird says, adamant.

"This is-"

"-he's targeting you guys," Morgan says. "I'm sorry. They were your lyrics, he's your fan. He's only killed your band members. This is personal when it comes to Lies As Language. Rachel and I are here merely by circumstance."

"That's dangerous thinking," Kyle warns both girls, "Wil, you do-"

"-I'm not making this two on two, Kyle," Wil says.

There's a long silence at the table, then Wil says, "I'm a shitbag, Hummingbird is a cutter, Morgan is a whorebag, and you're a homo. There. Feels great, doesn't it, Kyle?" Wil says, holding his arms out wide like he was holding a million pound weight on the table.

Kyle's gloved hands clasp together, and he says, "We need to fix-"

"-and, yeah, the Jersey Devil is a fan of our music," Wil butts in, getting to the second matter of business on the invisible docket that had been rolled out across the table this morning. "Not like it matters," he adds casually. "You know that he torrents everything. We aren't getting any cash out of this deal. Dude created Kazaa, Napster, hell even Bearshare is probably his."

"Bearshare sounds cute," Morgan says warmly.

"It's not, Jody said it was filled with hardcore porn," Wil responds.

"Oh," Morgan squeaks. She wants to move away from this topic, given her "fatal flaw," so she asks, "If this was all about the band, once he destroyed your instruments, don't you think, like, it would be over?" she asks hopefully.

"He knows we're musicians so we'll just form side projects with new instruments," Wil says. "Rock and roll and the devil always go together. I remember hearing that in the early 90's they said Metallica and *The Simpsons* were corrupting America- like the devil was doing work through doughy looking idiots."

Hummingbird giggles at this, "Makes sense. I want to commit murder when I hear Metallica, but that's only because it's the easiest way to get rid of the person playing Metallica…"

"Great, now we're discussing murder," Kyle mumbles to himself, his face finding his gloved palms.

"What do you want us to do?" Hummingbird yells.

The room is silent.

Kyle lifts his face from his hands, then says, "I want all of you to identify any areas of weakness you may have, then I want you to eliminate them. It's not going to be easy, but at the same time, it will never be this easy ever again. You have one focus as you continue your lives in this house and that is to do everything in your power to continue your lives in this house. That means changing. You can't change who you are in your deepest being, but that doesn't mean you're locked into being the broken person I see before me at this very moment."

LIII. Connected.

We follow Morgan around the house. She's behaving bizarrely, moving in a stutter of a walking pattern. This isn't the focused RA we saw that night the second band was created. This is a woman both searching and hiding.

Morgan is very aware of what this house is capable of, so she takes careful steps, never making snap judgments, and always curving wide detours around items that could pose a threat. She's looking for Jody, the boy who walked away from dinner tonight. He walked away for a good reason so Morgan knows he's safe- she thinks he's safe- she wants him to be safe. She listens for his screams because he might not be safe. The house creaks from places where no one should be. *If these walls could talk,* Morgan thinks to herself, then she remembers they can. The walls have been singing Jody's lyrics; the walls have begged us to *Stay.*

Morgan is about to step out of the kitchen when footsteps hammer across the ceiling. Whoever is upstairs is running hard. The path of the steps is from the edge of the kitchen, to the far wall of the living room, and this redirects Morgan. She returns to the open front door, then looks outside for Jody. Something moves in the darkness, but a lack of reflection, a lack of color, a lack of noise, makes Morgan believe that she's staring at the shadow man that Mike captured on video. *If only we uploaded that video to YouTube before the phone exploded. We could have monetized the thing and made boatloads of cash,* Morgan thinks to herself, hearing Jody in her head.

As she continues her search, Morgan feels proud that she's putting in this effort and staring people in the eyes when important discussions happen. Before, she had a phone that did all the searching for her, and any complicated discussions could happen behind a wall of emoticons.

The girl who arrived in the van is someone completely different from the one that walks out of the open door tonight. There have been some good changes, some not so good changes, and some old habits that Morgan still can't seem to shake. It all seems to mush into a cold stew that's sitting on the dining room table, ready for an unseen houseguest to devour the unpleasantness with pleasure. This unplanned vacation has become a mix of everything Morgan's ever wanted, combined with moments that were born directly from her nightmares. Again, we're reminded of the legend of Ms. Leeds. An imperfect woman had a child that reminded her of a good moment, yet the boy-demon was a physical manifestation of the worst part of an unrepentant whore. Morgan wonders if Ms. Leeds' punishment fit the crime. Was she truly the worst woman in the Pine Barrens, or just the freest? Were the other women just jealous of this freedom? Ms. Leeds wasn't happy, Morgan knows that for sure. The freedom that should arrive after breaking the bonds of a societal contract isn't as liberating as Morgan had imagined. Based on the looming doom, there's now pressure on everyone in Leeds house to transform into the person they have procrastinated in becoming.

Morgan is not self-sacrificing. The meals she prepares aren't just about fueling bodies so they can face the day. It's clear that Morgan always invests herself in people and that's why she needs to please everyone- to make sure they stay. Seeing others experience pleasure has become an obsession of Morgan's. The emptiness that she feels so often can be temporarily replaced with the wonder she finds in a friend's happiness. The sensation of this pleasure is complicated, but it arrives in relaxing rolls like the tide.

Morgan finds the immediacy, the intimacy, the closeness of a band van or Leeds house so comfortable after living so long in a digital web of pinging check-ins. The distance that a phone bridges is something that Morgan never liked because she can't observe the pleasure she may be providing someone. A smile in return for a comment was the only reason for speech. A wide-eyed look of appreciation was the only reason to perform for someone. A warm accepting kiss was the only reason to get close to someone.

When the van was attacked, Morgan watched as her best friend started bragging over text, instead of calling for help. This is just one of the many odd shifts that the obsession with our phones has brought about. Everyone is struggling to acquire and sustain relevancy, so when a possibly troubling event happens, it's a mad dash to update five different social network platforms so that people can write, "OMG ru okay????" It's that extended need for not only the sweet sympathy of those present, but also the combined attention of everyone we've met in the past five years. This image curation has always been difficult for Morgan. She hated the feeling those consistently updating devices radiated- the sensation of toxic waves being shot into her brain and thighs. There were so many moments that she felt haunted by her connectedness. The lonely girl was made lonelier by the fact that a piece of plastic and metal wasn't moved by her existence.

When the texts that Morgan carefully worded would go unanswered, she'd have to go out alone. She could get into the bars that the popular girls would go to, and she'd never get ID'd because everyone under 21 has at least one friend on their arm when they go out. When she walked inside the bar, Morgan immediately felt the looks fall on her, but no one chose to prolong their glance or combine it with a smile. When Morgan would spot a group of girls she went to high school with, she knew what comments were being exchanged. An expectation was fulfilled- Morgan arrived alone, looking desperate, and there was the scary possibility that people were happy she still hadn't figured things out even without her high school reputation holding her back. Anytime she was within an earshot of these girls, she'd watch as they looked down into their glowing phones, sporting self-satisfied smiles, and she always assumed they wrote messages about her to each other. *Lonely. Pathetic. Whore.* The curses placed upon her eventually worked- those words somehow became her identity.

The closeness that Morgan had established with Mike was built on a foundation of very few words, and it now makes sense why. Both Mike and Morgan were weighed down by the persona that was forced upon them by their peers, and even in the absence of these outside forces, both young adults constantly reverted back to being perpetually confused kids who lived in fear of the wordless defectiveness they were emanating.

The house held more promise for Morgan than it did for Mike, and this is why she didn't stay with him at that tree. Morgan had so frequently experienced the palpable feeling of not being wanted, that when she arrived at Leeds house, she hoped if she made enough meals and satisfied enough urges, she would become necessary, even if it was only temporarily. Now, Morgan is bound so tightly to her housemates that she can only find herself in their reactions. In an author's house, with words on the wall- on the girl- in the books- all Morgan had was kind gestures to offer.

Rachel is smarter than Morgan. Those tattoos are there for a reason- they give people information the moment Hummingbird comes fluttering into their life. Only later do these new friends notice the other permanent marks on Hummingbird's body.

Morgan has been allowed to flourish in a house where images from the outside world are absent. Take away the instruments and there's no difference between fan and band. Take away the image on the TV screen and there's no ideal female body type. Take away the running commentary on social media and there's no court of public opinion. Morgan was able to form bonds and create relationships with the boys in the band because they forgot about the alternatives. Bring them back into a world of Kate Moss and pop princesses and Morgan doesn't stand a chance.

These are the parts of this isolated unsigned deal with the devil that Morgan likes. She wants to leave this house, but still carry pieces of the home she created with her. She wants to take pictures because there are moments that occurred in Leeds house that she needs to preserve in vivid detail, undisturbed by time. Behringer obviously has a camera. He would need it to create the perv wall. Why has no one found a camera yet?

Morgan steps out of her thoughts when she hears a stick break. She takes another step and her bare foot crunches down on pine nettles.

Morgan has been walking... by herself... through the woods.

Slowly turning, Morgan looks through the dark, and the house is not behind her. Has she been walking in a straight line? Should she go back? Wherever her body was leading her must be the wrong place. She doesn't want to follow her body anymore. She doesn't trust her body anymore.

Morgan begins her walk back, carefully choosing her steps, but only ten paces into the journey, she looks up and freezes. She sees that she's not alone in these woods. Without making any noise, she studies a looming figure. Squinting her eyes, she recognizes the goateed scowl she's presented with, and she smiles. It's Jody.

Jody doesn't return the smile because he isn't looking at Morgan. It's almost as though he didn't follow her out here, and they're both on independent missions through the dark. Jody's intense focus on the floor of the Barrens makes Morgan slightly uneasy. She keeps her distance, but calls out, "Jody, can you help me with something?"

Jody's eyes twitch when he hears this, then he breaks out of his trance. He says only one word, "No," then he reviews Morgan's face.

Morgan slides one of her bare feet into the oddly warm sand. She had taken her shoes off inside the house which signified an unconscious comfort level. She wants to return to the house, to that comfort level. This moment in the woods is uncomfortable.

Jody turns away, then clumsily begins to navigate back toward where the house might be.

"Um," Morgan squeaks out.

"I need to go help a girl," Jody says, disappearing into the dark.

"Jody, what the fuck?" Morgan calls out.

It's clear that Jody is leaving to go help Rachel, and this makes Morgan wonder if the devil was listening in on her thoughts as her feet carried her out into the woods.

"Why are you leaving me?" Morgan shrieks, stamping her bare feet.

"Go look. You'll see," Jody's voice echoes.

The spot where Jody was standing in the brush most likely contains an answer to his new distance. *Please don't be a body*, Morgan thinks to herself as she carefully navigates to her answer. *It can't be a body*. She walks closer, the pines seemingly holding back their branches so the bright moonlight can show her what the devil has prepared.

Pain shoots through Morgan in a clenching blast, then she falls backward. Not thinking, only reacting, Morgan smashes her hand across the bottom of her foot to knock away whatever bit her. The teeth sink into her hand, but she calms down slightly when the moonlight reveals that her attacker is a long thorny branch. Morgan removes the thorns from her hand, then licks the wound on her palm clean.

Looking down at the thorny branch, she sees that, at the end of the stem, is a rose.

In front of us is a long sprawling rose bush in a November bloom.

This was preparation.

Morgan needs to save a girl, so she runs back to Leeds house, leaving behind a tiny trail of blood that's as red as a rose.

LIV. E.

"The TV works," we hear Hummingbird announce, as Jody gets to the top of the stairs.

Carefully, like he was walking on a path of thorns with no shoes, Jody enters the Polaroid room.

Hummingbird is sitting in front of the TV. She's watching the static.

"Do you see something on that motherfucker, because I'm telling you right now, it's just snow. There's nothing on there. Don't turn this into some *Batman Forever* shit," Jody requests.

Hummingbird giggles, then pats the portion of floor next to her. She doesn't answer Jody's question, which means maybe this is some crazy Magic Eye thing, where a message shows up in the static. Hummingbird doesn't seem very horrified by what she's looking at; she seems entertained.

Jody decides it can't hurt to sit next to Hummingbird, so he joins his pretty friend in front of the TV, then he begins to squint to see if something will appear in the snow. Finding nothing, he asks, "And you're watching this because?"

"I like the static," Hummingbird says, then pauses, considering the repercussions of sharing a thought. When she decides it's worth mentioning, she admits, "I wish Mike was here."

Jody waits for Hummingbird to elaborate, as the static chews the statement.

"We could have him tell a weirdo story and it would be sun-up in no time. We'd just... bypass the night," Hummingbird says, starved for narrative in a house that can't decide on a pace or a tone.

"Actually," Jody says, "That Six Flags story was his only story. He wasn't joking when he said he was completely devoted to planning that shit. A lot of long, lonely nights went into the never-realized animal tree reveal of his total psychopathic rage. It's easy to discount the task because of how many people slap together a tragedy right after getting fired or dumped, but that wasn't Cliff's style. He was a hard worker- through and through- he never half-assed anything."

"Maybe you were always just talking so much that you never got to hear any of his other stories," Hummingbird says, scrunching her nose, never breaking eye contact with the static. Jody opens his mouth to go off on a rant about this careless assessment, but then realizes what would happen if he did. Hummingbird knew what she was doing when she made the comment. She could anticipate the response. How relaxing to be able to reasonably predict the future. The static becomes a sweet melody due to its unrelenting consistency. The entertainment that the TV used to provide to Hummingbird has been replaced. Flawed people confronting a surreal, carefully lit situation is Hummingbird's entire life now, and it's appearing commercial free in a massive binge watch that cannot be stopped. Entertainment has become reality. The movies she once watched, she lives. The band of boys she listened to with her best friend are now the *only* people there are to listen to.

"Rachel, are you okay?" Jody asks, staring into the stormy screen.

"Sure," Hummingbird gulps.

Carefully approaching the subject, Jody warns, "Because if you don't... modify your... coping mechanisms..."

"Jody..."

"Alright. Let me put it like this, just to give you an idea of where I'm at," Jody says, "There's always this part in a horror movie when the main girl is being chased through the woods, and she inevitably trips over a root and we scream at her, 'No. What are you doing? Get up, you stupid bitch! Are you serious? You just fucked a guy reverse cowgirl with amazing dexterity and now you can't navigate over a tree root? Run you whore!' and we aren't calling her that because of her sex stuff. I mean, the fact that she was so talented at riding made our dick and balls feel great so we would never make her feel guilty about it, we just mean whore in that way where something crazy happens and you're like, 'You whore,' almost in a sassy way, like the reverse of, 'You go, girl.'"

"Yeah?" Hummingbird says, as Jody continues to stumble like the girl he's describing.

"Well, you need to be careful because I'm screaming, 'Watch out, you dumb whore!' right now, and I almost feel like you're that character in the movie because you're not listening to my yelling."

Hummingbird sighs, "If you're trying to come on to me, this is, like, the worst-"

"-I have to show you something," Jody says. He quickly adds, "It's not my cock. Don't worry. I got my cock sucked earlier by your friend Morgan so I'm probably out of cum." Jody's smile drops, then he says, "I need to show you something outside."

"Are you incapable of bringing it inside? I'm watching TV," Hummingbird points out.

"Honestly, I'm afraid to bring it in here, plus it was about eleven hundred trees that way," Jody says, pointing toward the front yard.

"No, I'm not in the mood. We're going to be fine. If we... just... stay put?" Hummingbird says, working through her own theory.

"That's not correct," Jody says, crossing his arms. "I'm a drummer. Drummers are disposable."

"You don't expect me to believe that."

"I'm trying to save you."

"I believe that part," Hummingbird says.

"Why only that part?"

"Because you're still holding secrets. You're taking them to your grave. That's not good. A prideful Catholic man such as yourself shouldn't take anything to the grave besides his love of God."

Jody squints at the static, wondering if Hummingbird is watching a little CNN ticker listing all of Jody's secrets and all the file names of every cuckold video he's downloaded on the internet.

Jody mumbles, "Most of those videos are setups anyways. The performers aren't even really married so I'm not coveting thy neighb-"

"-Jody, what the fuck are you talking about?" Hummingbird asks.

"What are *you* talking about?" Jody volleys back.

"The lyrics, Jody. Your lyrics."

"I don't know-"

"-stop it!" Hummingbird yells, her arms thrashing at her sides, slapping the floor, "Kyle told me you wrote the lyrics, and you're still lying to me!"

"He told you that?"

"Um. Yeah?"

"When? Where?"

"Here. In this fucking prison," Hummingbird says.

"Come on," Jody says, putting a hand on Hummingbird's shoulder.

"You're not just the drummer. You're the guy who writes the lyrics to the Lies As Language songs," Hummingbird says, finally looking back to Jody.

"Psh. Not sure what the devil told you, but I would write wicked awesomer... not wicked... I mean, I would write more blessed songs. Praise Jesus."

"You wrote 'Reflection' and you wrote all the other songs," Hummingbird says.

Jody exhales, "Music is a collaborative process. You wouldn't understand. You've never written a song so you have no idea what you're talking about."

"I played with you in the living room. I know that it's a collaborative process. I understand. What I *don't* understand is why you're ashamed about one of the most impressive things you've done in your entire life."

"Psh," Jody disregards his accomplishment again.

"No. We're having this conversation."

"This is a distraction. You're just like Kyle. Hiding your-"

"-Jody, why do you insist on acting like a prick?" Hummingbird asks, in a ploy to get him to either leave or confront his true self. The eternal question is brought up for the millionth time and now it's up to Jody to provide an authentic answer.

"Is this a therapy session?" Jody asks the side of Hummingbird's head as she turns back to the TV.

"For you?" Hummingbird asks back.

"No."

"For me...." Hummingbird says, not as a question, then she admits, "I don't know, Jody."

"Because right now it seems like you're working on me, not working on yourself."

"Why don't you let anyone know about all the things you've done for Kyle? Why don't you ask for credit for your songs? Why don't you open up to me?" Hummingbird asks, in a row, her voice pitching up with each question.

"Because you shouldn't celebrate doing the right thing, Hummingbird. You just do it. That's something you learn after you do the right thing a lot. I hope you'll learn it someday, but I'm not surprised this lesson has escaped you so far," Jody says

The room has become dark in all ways possible. The moon and the TV fight the blackness.

"Look at me. Listen to me," Jody demands.

Hummingbird wipes away fresh tears, then looks away from the static, to Jody. The tears instantly reappear and Jody's tone gets softer because of their presence, as he explains, "If you do something good for someone, you shouldn't have to tell everyone about it. You shouldn't have to brag about it. The act should be enough. Kyle paid me back in grand gestures that were just as kind as the favor I performed for him. I'm here because of Kyle, and I both love him and hate him for that. Kyle is here because of me, and I both love and hate myself for that. What's there to celebrate in this type of situation? I made a decision that maximized my band's visibility. Great for me. I also led my brother to this house and we might as well dig his grave because of... No. He's walking out of here. I'll dig my own grave first."

Hummingbird reviews Jody. He doesn't look so good. He has bags under his eyes, and his beard is growing in, connecting his goatee to his sideburns. Time is passing. Jody is losing sleep, but he's trying to keep it together. Kyle was picked to sing those songs because it was best for the group. Jody doesn't look like Kyle. To Hummingbird, Jody looks like a leader, Jody looks like a hero. Hummingbird thinks about how many heroes have been forgotten because they acted like Jody. One disadvantage of being Christ-like is that your reward comes late. Hummingbird decides that she must believe in Heaven so Jody can get his reward. We're all going to get what we deserve in this house, except Jody- he'll get what he deserves in a much different house.

Jody closes his eyes and runs his hand down his goatee. He can no longer look at Hummingbird, and he can no longer look at the Polaroid wall, and he can no longer look at the TV. *Destroy the TV and find the light*, Jody tells himself. He needs to know what's powering this demon box. Maybe it's an internal battery? Maybe there's a cord running through one of the legs, straight into the floor? The energy can't be passing through the air in Leeds house.

TV is known to make slaves of man, but your average prime time hit doesn't stand a chance against the devil's numbers. Maybe since it's well documented that the devil and TV have worked together in the past, they continue to do each other favors. No matter how good or how shitty you are, favors are still an asset when it comes to accomplishing your goals.

Opening his eyes, Jody chooses what he hopes is the safest option, and he looks at the Polaroids on the wall. He does this only because he knows that he's supposed to change the channel. He knows that something will be revealed to him on the glowing screen if he peers into the snow.

The moment that Jody successfully convinces himself not to stare at the TV, he's forced to look away from the Polaroids, back to the crash of static that seems to stutter in uneven patterns. This swooping redirect is necessary because, in addition to the pictures of Behringer's victims, there are now also Polaroids of Mike and Rob on the wall.

LV. Capturing.

We rush out of the Polaroid room, trailing behind a sprinting Jody. We choose to abandon Hummingbird. Jody was wrong, an image was never intended to appear in the static because the only reason the TV was on was to shine a light onto the images on the wall.

At the bottom of the stairs, we hear a high-pitched, "Ow. Ow! Ow," coming from the bathroom. We look back up the stairs and briefly consider that Hummingbird might be in two places at once.

Jody doesn't have his weapon so he quietly makes his way to the edge of the bathroom door. A slight push sends the door creaking open. The scene is gradually revealed to us- a horizontal candle balanced on the toilet seat is dripping wax onto the floor, illuminating Morgan, who holds a bloody towel in her red hands.

"What happened? What happened?" Jody gasps, as he bursts inside the bathroom and gets down on one knee.

"You could have warned me about the prickers," Morgan says.

Jody eases to the floor, a smile on his face. "I couldn't give him the reaction," he admits, and just like that, the smile is gone again. This is the perspective that the house has created- when a person is hurt it's okay as long as it was an accident and they're still breathing. If a person is hurt because of their habitual faults, they're dead.

"Where's Rachel?" Morgan asks, knowing why she was led to the flowers.

"She's upstairs. Let's go see her," Jody responds.

"No. She's in front of that TV. I don't want to see what it wants to show us," Morgan responds.

Jody nods at this, then warns, "In that case, make sure you don't look at the wall of pictures."

"That's the last thing I want to look at. I mean, those poor kids. How disgusting that all of those snapshots show the last image ever taken of each of Behringer's little victims. I mean, they couldn't even..." Morgan trails off, unable to dwell on it further. She stands up and throws the bloody towel in the sink, then balances on the ball of her foot.

"And Mike," Jody says.

"And Mike, what?" Morgan snips harshly.

"And Mike's picture is on the wall too."

Morgan picks up her candle, then rushes out of the bathroom, her wound slapping the floor with heavy steps.

"Jody, please tell me this is one of your jokes," Morgan says, feeling his presence behind her. When she doesn't receive a response, she turns and hands Jody the candle, then waits for him to take the lead.

"Did you take any pictures in this house?" Jody asks, climbing the stairs.

"No. Did you?" Morgan asks.

"Yes, Morgan. I took some pictures and now this is my way to get everyone to go to my fucked up art show. Come on! You know if I took these pictures I would need plates of cheeses to serve to the guests as they reviewed my work, and you can be damn sure you'd have extensive catering responsibilities. I absolutely would've commissioned a pre-opening sample platter in advance because it would be downright negligent to select what to serve to my admirers without tasting it first. I'm more careful than that."

Morgan smiles as she enters the Polaroid room. She's now sure that she's still needed in this house. The smile fades from her face when she sees her best friend on the floor, staring into the static. She has to look away, and that's when she sees the Polaroids. Jody was right. This is not an art show, it's an exhibition. Morgan always wondered why the pictures on the wall weren't taken down and bagged, but now that new pictures have appeared, she understands no one can remove these images from the house, and if they manage to, the pictures will reappear, over, and over, and over again.

Slowly approaching the images that seemed to have multiplied further since he last looked at them, Jody calls out, "Wil! Kyle! Get up here." Jody is well aware that his strength is in leading, not interpreting. Remember the aqua-peoples?

"Shh," Hummingbird hisses at Jody, still staring at the TV. She doesn't want company. She wants to climb into the predictable static.

Moments later, Kyle enters the room and immediately begins his review of the pictures that prompted this meeting. The Lennard brothers stand on either side of the wall, their candles balancing out the glowing illumination that's coming from the TV.

In the new line of Polaroids on the wall, we find images of not only Mike and Rob, but also the surviving residents of Leeds house.

Kyle looks at a picture of himself- it's of him sleeping on the floor of Behringer's office.

The picture is clear, like it was taken with a flash.

The picture is close, like it was taken from a foot away.

The picture is evidence that during every moment we've spent in this house, someone was watching us, capturing us.

Jody, old enough to remember when Polaroids were more than just hipster lifestyle accessories, says, "They make a noise."

"What does?" Kyle asks.

"Polaroid cameras, when they take a picture, they burst out a bright flash and they make a noise. It's like thunder and lightning, but less booming and more mechanical sounding."

"Maybe he used an app?" Morgan suggests hopefully.

"Yeah, and then what, downloaded the photos and brought them to Kinko's?" Jody responds.

"I don't know what Kinko's is, but the name certainly fits the pictures," Morgan says, looking at a Polaroid of her sleeping by Jody's side. "The people who took these pictures are definitely a bunch of Kinkos."

Careful in his review, Kyle focuses on a picture of the headlights of the band van. The picture is symmetrically framed and taken so that the license plate is at the bottom of the white border. Whoever took this picture was standing in the middle of the road. Kyle looks close, and in the front seat of the van, he can see himself. The expression on his face currently, as well as in the picture, is a look of pure shock.

This picture was taken when that... cow... thing was dropped on the road.

Kyle sweeps his candlelight down the line of Polaroids. The events that each photograph detail have been placed in chronological order. This row of pictures is a sequential surveillance camera of choice moments that Leeds was inspired to document. The shooting, the wine, the fleeing, Mike's skinning- all of it is here in graphic detail. There's a picture of Mike's skin being peeled off his body, but before it is a picture of....

"We have to go," Kyle says, "We need to get out of this room, and close the door behind us."

"You can join Wil downstairs. We'll be up here. We won't turn away," Jody states.

This was a shot at Kyle. This was an implication that he was no longer part of the fighters and was now a bystander fleeing when the debris got too close.

Kyle springs forward and grabs his brother by the shoulders, "Turn away on this one, Jody. Listen to me, as your brother. Trust me, you're going to want to listen to me."

Jody watches a thousand involuntary tics fire in Kyle's face. Without the stagy eye makeup, Kyle looks tired, yet more intense, as he warns his brother, "These photographs will not stop, and I don't want to end up like those children. We're adults, Jody."

Breaking away, Jody returns to the last picture that Kyle had studied, and he sees an image of his best friend, Cliff, in bed with Morgan. This single picture bores under Jody's skin in both a similar and very different way from the Polaroid of the devil's cutting Mike's skin off, as Mike's mouth remains open, forever screaming in pain.

LVI. Reconnecting.

We sit on the floor of the upstairs bathroom, as Jody lies next to us and gags on tears that refuse to drop.

Suddenly, the bathroom door tremors with a *BANG-BANG-BANG*, and we look to Jody, who yells, "Fuck off!"

"Gladly," the voice on the other side of the door says.

Clearly not expecting his demand to be so willingly complied with, Jody calls out, "Do you have to go to the bathroom? Is there someone in the downstairs bathroom?"

"Nope," says the voice.

"So you were...?"

"Jody, are you going to let me in or are you going to allow me to walk away?"

Jody stands up, then rolls a couple feet of toilet paper over his bandaged hand. He looks in the mirror and uses his stubby candle to check if there's any snot in his goatee. Once he feels put together, Jody opens the bathroom door, and stares at Wil's soft, slightly embarrassed expression, and casually offers a, "Sup?"

"I heard you in here, crying like a man-bitch on that little carpet," Wil says, pointing to the bathmat.

Jody makes a bunch of noises to try and deny this, but fails, then returns to the bathmat and starts convulsing with core-trembling sobs.

Wil picks the candle up off the counter, shuts the door, then bodyblocks the two heart-hurt men inside the room.

"It's the fucking devil's house, dude. You can't expect your relationship to work out in the devil's house," is Wil's leadoff statement. This is something he's told himself ever since that night he had too much to drink.

"I know. I just have to blame it on the house," Jody says, trying to move past the humiliation and hurt. All he wants to do is reach Kyle Lennard levels of rational coolness.

"And then the van..."

Wil lets this moment hang.

"Yup, and the van blew up," Jody says, trying to make this not just about a girl. Two guys in a band getting angry about a girl is the type of cliché that Jody despises. This is Jody's "Run, you whore!" moment, oddly enough, brought on by a whore.

"You hit most of the keywords there. Rearrange them," Wil says, his hollow eyes brightening and his pale cheeks stretching to form a smile that makes him look like a relative of Leeds in the yellow light of the candle.

"The... van... blew..." Jody says quietly, then he realizes what Wil's getting at, "In our van too?"

"I just reviewed the pictures very closely," Wil says. "Looks like she only blew him."

"She blew Cliff in my van!" Jody yells.

"Oh!" Wil says, "No. Sorry about that, bud. Nope. She didn't do anything in the van with Cliff."

"Then what were you talking about?" Jody asks, swallowing a sob.

"Rob. She definitely put Rob's cock in her mouth," Wil says.

"Fuckkk!" Jody calls out, openly weeping, the tears soaking his toilet paper wrapped hand.

"Dude," Wil says, then sits down near Jody. He puts his hand on Jody's shoulder. "There's a really good chance that Mike probably didn't cum in her pussy more than once. I'm almost sure of it, pal," Wil says.

"I called dibsies!" Jody yells.

"You can't call dibsies on passion," Wil reminds him softly.

"Yes, you can. You absolutely can..."

"His dick was inside her before yours was. I think Rob actually had dibsies," Wil comments, as if reviewing the rule book. "I mean, during the portion of this hellacious trip when Morgan was gobbling our dead friend's penis, the only time you talked to her was when there was a good fat joke to be made."

"Because that's how I connect with people. I put dibsies on her by preying on her insecurities, haven't you ever flirted before?" Jody sobs.

"Oh trust me..." Wil says, dwelling on his own romantic failings for a moment.

"I'm not some angel-voiced twink or a better looking version of Edgar Allen Poe. I've been doing the best with what I have, okay?" Jody says, trying to make sure his problem seems worse than Wil's.

"Okay," Wil says, putting his hands up, "I mean, she only knew Rob for an hour at that point, I'm sure it meant nothing."

"She gave Rob a blowjob after knowing him for an hour," Jody repeats.

"She'd probably seen some YouTube videos of him so she felt like she knew him better," Wil rationalizes.

"This is insane," Jody says, his arms now wrapped around his legs.

"The only time it could have happened was after we saw that fucked up shadow thing. She was scared. She was, like, crying and scared. She needed a security blanket... a security penis?" Wil says, semi-defending a girl that he needs to be the next victim. He knows that if he keeps repeating the details, confirming Jody's worst fears, Morgan will be killed tonight for her indiscretions, which pushes his own funeral back at least 24 hours.

"She was scared?" Jody groans with a high weep, "That's your excuse for her? I got scared when I got in my motorcycle accident, but you know what I didn't do? Blow the EMT guy on the way to the hospital!"

"Well, yeah, you were supposed to remain perfectly still just in case you had a spinal injury," Wil mentions.

"No! I didn't blow him because I'm a normal fucking human being."

"I hope this isn't homophobia you're exhibiting here," Wil states, then crosses his arms.

"I really wish people here had other coping mechanisms besides putting my bandmates' dicks in their mouth. This is a real sticking point in this house. I mean.... well, they were doing the sticking, and Morgan was more getting stuck, but the whole thing is just messy- in both ways- in the emotional way and in the ejaculate way. My relationship with all of you is drowning under the weight of all your ejaculations," Jody sobs.

"Yeah. Our dead friend's ejaculate was spurted into your current girlfriend's mouth," Wil says, then thinks about the statement.

When Jody doesn't respond, Wil walks over to the toilet and begins pissing.

"Really?" Jody asks, teary eyed, moving out of the splash radius.

"Sorry, please forgive me," Wil says, then shakes his shoulders in a little dance.

"The way people are dropping around here, I need to keep the weak around as human shields, so I forgive you," Jody says warmly, but his voice gets weak again as he says, "I don't know if I can forgive her for this though."

"Break up with her," Wil says simply, then flushes the toilet.

"I can't. We live in the same house. That's messy."

"Well," Wil says, walking to the door, "You won't be together for long either way, and, yeah, things *are* about to get messy.

LVII. Face The Lack Of Music.

We lean against the banister at the top of the stairs, giving Wil room as he walks out of the bathroom then carefully shuts the door. He reaches up and presses his palm against the barrier between himself and Jody. It's a gesture of care- it's a display of concern that Jody cannot see. Wil opens his mouth, as though he's going to give some parting advice to his troubled friend, but he pauses there, wordlessly, unable to speak. Eventually, he releases a long breath, and his posture shrinks, then his hand slides off the door.

Making his way back to the wall of photographs, Wil passes the bedroom, and a, "Stop," from Hummingbird freezes him again.

"Did you fix it?" Hummingbird asks naively.

Wil looks into the bedroom and finds Hummingbird symmetrically located in the center of the door frame. A bright flash behind his eyes stuns him for a moment, and the only reaction he can provide to Hummingbird's question is a snorted laugh.

"Don't laugh, please," Hummingbird requests.

"The other reaction I could have given was the honest answer to your question, and I don't think you want that at all," Wil explains.

"I want you to answer my question," Hummingbird says definitively.

Wil stares at the scarred girl as she sits on Behringer's bed, and the vines depicted on the wallpaper behind Hummingbird begin to wilt

"The answer... to your question..." Wil begins slowly, running his hands through his greasy hair, "...is that we'll be okay, for now, but in general, are things okay? No, Hummingbird. They're not. Your friend either blew or fucked every hetero member of this house, and while I will admit, that's not a ton of people- in a span of a couple of days, given the amount of available straight cock- it's pretty gross."

"Fuck you, Wil!" Morgan screams from somewhere in the house, possibly under the covers of the bed.

"Please tell your friend that if she's going to read her to-do list, she must do so at a responsible volume," Wil says to Hummingbird.

Hummingbird makes a disgusted face at Wil, like he caused all of this.

"Ugh, more blame," Wil snarls, tired of it. "This house is filled with gloved hand-wringing, blame volleying, and hypothetical fatalistic scenarios."

"It must be easy not to care, but I don't have that luxury," we hear Morgan say.

This provokes Wil to walk into the bedroom, and growls, "Actually, Morgan. It *is* hard. It's pretty miserable to feel like this."

Morgan is the next to die. All Wil has to do is let her exist.

"How is it hard to turn a blind eye?" Morgan responds, sitting up in the bed, revealing herself, after the photographs did the same. We can finally see her. She looks terrified and tired; she's an easy victim. Her ash stained face contorts as it tries to push out words, and eventually, she finds her voice, "What's truly difficult is to stop and help. What's truly difficult is to deal with the ugly repercussions."

"I'm not going to tax myself with other people's mistakes," Wil says calmly. He needs a cigarette to keep things even.

"So who's going to save us if we're all focused on self-preservation, Wil? Imagine if everyone had your mentality; we'd start pushing each other to be next in line," Hummingbird says. This from a girl who explicitly avoids focusing on self-preservation as much as she can.

Morgan starts to say, "You are too selfish to realize that we have to-" but she's cut off when Wil asks, "-oh, I'm being selfish?" After a pregnant pause, he says, "If your theory is that we should do what's best for the remaining members of the house, then why are you still here, Morgan?"

"Stop it!" Hummingbird screams.

"You want me to go into those woods, with no cell phone?" Morgan asks quietly, "With no sense of direction? I mean, I'd be walking into the wilderness, with only a purse full of food, and I wouldn't have shelter if I got tired. We need to believe that someone will arrive and help us. We need to assume that not everyone in this world is as cold as you are."

"You're going to be waiting a long time," Wil says, his glare manic.

"Only you will be, Wil, because you dismiss everyone!" Morgan yells.

"Guess you're right about that, you're dismissed," Wil says, flicking his fingers, like their tips were glowing again and he needed to knock the ash away. "Bye-bye, Morgan."

"This is why you're not a real man!" Morgan shrieks. "A real man rushes forward, he doesn't walk away. This is why Kyle doesn't love you back!"

"Trust me, Morgan, you're going to want to walk away from this house for more reasons than one," Wil responds, his eyes going even wider.

"You need to take a look around you. You can learn a lot from someone like Jody," Morgan says, as black liquid ash tears drip down her chin.

"Jody? Jody is your idea of what a man is really like? You can find your 'real man' on the bathmat next to the toilet right now. What's it say about your judgment that your template for a real man is a guy who hasn't mentally progressed past the age of 16?"

"Maybe, in some ways, he's still a boy, but he's a man when it matters. When Hummingbird and I need to be protected, he steps forward. He doesn't hesitate. He just *does*. He's the one who grabs us and keeps us safe. He sticks his neck out time and time again, not only for us girls, but for everyone in this house, and that is probably the only reason why we're in the house and not the ground instead."

"I'm not here because of Jody. I'm here because I'm responsible for myself," Wil says, then begins to take stock of where we are right now, "Rob is gone, and Jody couldn't save him. You know why? Because Rob was a fucking junkie and he didn't care enough about himself to get off the shit much-less find a way out of this. What about Mike? That kid was so deep in his own world that I honestly believe he enjoyed what he saw unfolding here. I think that's why he stayed under that tree. When I saw Rob wearing Mike, I was relieved. I felt safer in that moment, knowing I didn't have to worry about the devil *and* Mike."

"How can you say this shit about your friends? How can you tack this sick ending onto their legacy? Nothing that happened to them is their fault," Hummingbird howls, and her tears become contagious.

"It's exactly that type of mentality that is going to reunite you with your faultless little friends," Wil says, walking out of the bedroom.

From the moment we stepped inside Leeds house, we all assumed certain roles. It's possible that Mike was chosen to open the doors because he wanted to walk into this world. He thirsted for what the cold house offered. Wil was the lighting guy during the initial search so he could illuminate tiny little patches of these rooms, but as soon as he walked away, the darkness would reclaim its territory. Wil kicked the closet door shut because he wanted to avoid what was looming. Now, every time Wil opens a door in this house, he holds his breath.

The sound of sobs escaping from Morgan, Hummingbird, and Jody travels through the dormant radiators of Leeds house, making these cries inescapable.

Tonight, the only way to find silence is to step outside.

LVIII. 50 Beats Per Second

For a girl who sinks her nails into stereotypes and tries to choke them into submission, Hummingbird sure has embraced this one. It's her personality's fault, and this is *Rachel* at work, not the Hummingbird we've grown to love. She can make this claim to ease the blame off her shoulders. Hummingbird feels like there are two people living inside of her and they both love taking vacations. One will usually cover for the other, but sometimes a scheduling mix-up will leave Hummingbird empty. When the valuable self-worth and sadistic self-hate go missing simultaneously, the void becomes a black hole, destroying matter indiscriminately. There are times when she feels both an emptiness and a bloated impurity at her core.

Hummingbird, to escape this recurring state of throbbing numbness, chooses to inflict some throbbing pain.

She's aggressively revisiting a technique she would frequently use back home. It all came about when Rachel had begged to see her father so she could have someone to talk to that knew what it was like to feel trapped, but her mother refused to travel to the prison, no matter how white collar and resort-like it was. "It's dangerous for a beautiful girl like you to go inside a men's prison," was the rationale, but Rachel knew that this was about revenge. After the fight with her mother, Rachel went into the basement and found her dad's possessions crammed into boxes. On this particular day, she poked around a box that contained, among other things, a little leather pouch. Inside the pouch, she found the safety razor her father had used to shave with. This archaic implement was typical for the type man that her father saw himself as- someone who likes to keep with tradition. He was raised to believe that you need to learn how to do things the hard way, because life is hard. He continued using the safety razor because he'd invested time in finding out the secrets of a perfect shave. Rachel briefly wondered why he would leave this essential item behind, then she remembered he went to jail, not on vacation.

Rachel picked up the safety razor and she thought about how the name was an ugly deceit, but she wanted to feel safety, and maybe the razor could provide it? Nostalgic for her father, and in possession of what felt like all the time in the world, Rachel took out a fresh razor blade out of the little box- that tiny razor coffin. She fitted the blade inside the headpiece, then she relocated herself next to the nearby faucet. Sitting on a shelf, draping her leg into the utility sink in the basement, Rachel shaved with that razor that bit down on the blade. She kept nicking herself, but she didn't stop practicing until her entire leg was finished. When it was done, she was dripping red, but she was proud. Her dad was right, she felt good after trying, and being punished for failing.

From then on, Rachel set out to do things the hard way; from then on, Rachel cut herself with her father's abandoned razor blades when the bloated emptiness arrived.

She told everyone that she didn't care what they thought, but the high school taunts of, "Go cut yourself, emo kid," would echo long after they bounced down the halls. Rachel would sit in the basement, slicing herself bloody, mumbling the insults that people spat at her.

Her legs were always shaved after she discovered the razor- this was sexy. When she got so good at shaving her legs that the nicks all but disappeared, she would cut deep horizontal lines in her wrists and ankles- this was not sexy. She had mastered the single blade shave and was left with no choice but to go adventuring for that "first feeling." The blade's smooth glide would make a pure white mark on her pale skin. She'd slide again, curious if she could get a cleaner slice by putting a little more pressure on the edge. Going over her previous mark, little puddles of red would appear, tight-roping the line.

That's how she developed her coping mechanism. Somehow her solution to the taunts at school was to do precisely what they were making fun of her for.

Stupid. Childish. Girl.

The marks on Hummingbird's body are glaringly public, but that doesn't deter her from keeping her ritual private. There was a long wait for Jody to stop crying and to leave the bathroom, but Hummingbird remained patient, knowing her release would eventually arrive.

When Jody vacates the second floor bathroom, Hummingbird listens to his footsteps, and when she's sure he's inside Behringer's writing room, she slides out of the bed and replaces Jody in the bathroom.

We sit down next to Hummingbird on a bathmat still wet with Jody's tears.

Wil is gone, but his taunts echo in Hummingbird's mind. She repeats tonight's fight in her head as she looks around the bathroom and searches for the lens of a camera. When she's totally confident that no one can see her, that she won't appear on that wall of shame, Hummingbird removes the razor blade she had stashed in her hair bun earlier in the day. She had found it sitting on top of the TV. The razor didn't come with any instructions, so Hummingbird waited patiently in front of the TV for a message to appear. She wanted to be told which person in the house had to be eliminated. She wanted to make a sacrifice to save her friends.

A sacrifice.

Hummingbird scares herself with this thought, but the fear doesn't dull the power of this possibility. She counts to ten. She still feels this way. She needs to sacrifice herself to save her friends. It's the only way. She counts to fifty. She still feels this way. She counts to one hundred. She still feels this way.

"I'll give you me, if you don't take them," Hummingbird says, then waits for a response. When she doesn't receive one, she makes good on her end of the bargain, hoping it will force Leeds to do the same.

Rachel runs the blade down her left wrist, then her right, and the blood hisses out of her like steam from a ruptured pipe.

"Eia," is the noise Rachel expels when she sees that things have gone too deep.

Hiss, her wrist responds.

Gasp, her lungs inhale.

Hhhh, her body exhales.

The blood doesn't drip. It sprays.

Rachel is in a heart hammering panic, as her blood vacates her body like it was being chased out. Desperate to slow the repercussions of her mistake, Rachel gets inside the bathtub, hoping that if she submerges her wrists in her own pooling blood, her emptiness won't empty her.

She's warm in Leeds house for the first time, as the drain feeds, hungry. The blood is being sucked down fast, but it splashes out faster.

Rachel can't keep her eyes open and she's okay with this because she doesn't want to look at what she's done.

With the tiny bit of strength she still has left, Rachel gets on her knees in the tub. On the light green tiles of the bathroom wall she spells out, with a Ouija slowness, "S-O-S-O-R-R," but she collapses into her own blood before the apology is completed.

Rachel's eyelids flutter like a Hummingbird's wings.

LIX. Being Right Sometimes Isn't Easy.

We follow Wil as he moves from room to room on the first floor of the house, searching for the end to a night that seems infinitely long. He keeps switching his lighter from his right hand to his left because it hurts to keep it lit for more than a couple seconds at a time. He uses the light to look for cigarettes, then when he clears the area, he plunges himself back into the darkness because the darkness is the only place he feels safe. As he makes his way to the mantle in the living room, a voice asks, "What are you doing?"

"Looking for a cigarette," Wil says, looking back into the void, toward where he remembers the sofa being.

"Then you're next," the voice says.

"Did I wake you up?" Wil asks. He doesn't need to light his lighter to confirm the identity of the voice.

"I'm not sleeping. I'm waiting in the dark for the devil," the smooth, calm voice says.

As always, this voice pulls the listener closer, and Wil asks, "So you can stop him or so you can help him?"

"Stop him," Kyle says, his voice unmistakable.

"So…" Wil responds, "Want to have a cigarette with me while you wait?"

"No."

"Want to have a glass of wine?" Wil asks, approaching the sofa. His knee hits the coffee table, and he quickly sits down on it to recover from the jolt. His back is to Kyle so they have the same shadowed view of the fireplace. Like boys waiting for Santa, they stare with total concentration at the brick portal.

"It wasn't supposed to end like this for us," Wil says, quietly.

"They warned us that it's supposed to end like this for us," Kyle says. He moves over on the sofa, but he knows Wil can't see this gesture.

"How do you know that? This is unnatural."

"That's also what they said. It's unnatural. When you look at anything as a concept it seems unnatural. Death is unnatural," Kyle responds, then thinks about it, "I mean, everyone dies, so death has supreme confidence because of his close-rate. Death is elevated, he's like the prince of…"

"Darkness?" Wil asks.

Kyle laughs once at the comment. This alleviates some of the tension. There's still a heaviness to the conversation, which forces Wil to ask, "You really think they warned us about this happening?"

"I do," Kyle says.

Now confident in the hopelessness of the situation, Wil stands up, then says, "Well, Mr. Math tells me that the odds are good that there are cigarettes somewhere in this big ass house, so I'm going to do some more investigating."

"Don't smoke them," Kyle begs.

"You're not my mother," Wil responds, walking toward the open front door.

"On top of the TV," Kyle calls out.

"What?"

"On top of the TV. A saw a soft pack up there," Kyle says.

"Thank you," Wil tells his friend.

Kyle doesn't want Wil to smoke, but telling him about the pack keeps the doomed boy inside the house. The cigarettes are bad, but Wil being outside is worse. Kyle needs to know where everyone is. He believes that Jody is in Behringer's office upstairs. He believes that Morgan and Hummingbird are in the bedroom. Now, Wil is headed to the Polaroid room. Kyle's other friends are in the front yard, and he needs them to stay there, for now.

While walking up the stairs, Wil listens carefully to hear if the girls are talking about him. He also prepares himself to hear Jody predictably forgiving Morgan. Neither of these scenarios play out, and Wil finds himself surrounded by silence. When he gets to the top of the stairs, he doesn't make his way into the girls' room because the thought dawns on him that Morgan, after having all that unprotected sex, could be pregnant in a house where a whore birthed the devil, and this would mean that the number of devils in this home could start catching up to the number of people. This sends Wil to the still glowing TV.

Kyle was right, a sun-bleached pack of Pall Malls sits atop the TV, and when Wil opens the pack, he finds three cigarettes. Two of the cigarettes are facing filter up, one of them is facing filter down- the "lucky." Wil takes out the lucky and lights it with his lighter, then drifts back into the hallway. He needs to be close to a water source so when his fingertips begin to burn, he can easily put them out.

With no light besides the cherry of his cigarette, Wil fearlessly walks by the girls' room, then proceeds past the closet where he saw *it*.

The door to the bathroom is wide open and Wil slides inside, literally, as the slick floor practically pulls him away from the carpeted hall. He carefully navigates, by memory, to the toilet, then lowers the lid and sits down. Kicking his feet up on the edge of the tub, sitting on his throne, Wil enjoys what feels like the perfect cigarette. He takes deep puffs. He inhales with a pure satisfaction and exhales all the bad. Everyone in this house is a drama queen. Everyone in this house is an actor chewing the scenery, fighting to make sure their screen time isn't reduced. Wil is the only normal one here. Since he's not an actor, Wil doesn't reach for the candle to his right; he prefers the total darkness so he can see if any part of him begins to light up. The terror never arrives- Wil's fingers remain intact, and his lungs don't begin to melt.

When the profoundly satisfying cigarette burns close to the filter, Wil flicks it into the tub. A snake-like hissing sends Wil fumbling for the candle to his right. The cigarette sizzled after it was tossed. Why would it sizzle? Besides the puddle on the floor, the only standing water in the bathroom is in the toilet, and Wil is sitting on the lid.

Wil lights the candle, then slowly moves it toward the tub.

The sloppy red message above Hummingbird's pale body is clear...

LX. Connected.

We jolt awake as a shovel lands on the sofa next to us.

Wil is standing by the piano, shining with sweat, smeared in red, dusted in brown.

Jody raises his head off the carpet and squints at Wil.

We hear footsteps slowly making their way down the stairs.

Kyle steps onto the green carpet, looks at Wil, looks at Jody, looks at the shovel next to us on the sofa, then asks with a pained expression, "Hummingbird?"

Wil nods.

Kyle begins drifting toward the piano bench, and Jody stands up to make sure no one grabs the shotgun. Passing his brother, Kyle sits down on the bench instead of opening it. He seems to be floating toward music to deal with losing a fan for the first time. *This* makes Kyle want to write a song, finally. He looks over at Jody and considers requesting that they collaborate on a way to get through this shit. Kyle can't replace Jody because he already has to replace his keyboardist and screamer.

We hear heavy steps on the stairs, and Jody immediately tenses up.

"Stay," Wil tells him, like a ceiling message.

Freshly showered, her hair up in a bun, Morgan steps into the living room. She smiles when she sees Kyle at the piano, and asks, "Wanna play a-" but before she can complete the question, she spots Wil. He's covered in dirt, covered in blood- and Morgan's hand goes to her mouth as she starts to retch.

"Front yard," is all Wil can say to her.

Morgan shakes her wet hair, her mouth appearing to be pried open by an unseen force. "We need to clean you off..." Morgan gasps, drooling, "we need..." she struggles to figure out what must be done.

"Morgan, go outside," Wil says forcefully.

Morgan shakes her head no.

"Go out into the front yard."

"Why?"

"To say goodbye to your friend," Wil spits.

Morgan's jaw unhinges even further. Her head drops and she bites her left arm as tears push out, creating a wet spot on her green child's sized T-shirt.

Wil turns away from Morgan, and says, "I'm sure you can guess-"

"-she was up there with you!" Morgan interrupts him, drool stringing from her mouth to her shoulder.

"And?"

"And now she's dead, she saved you, and you killed her!" Morgan yells.

Wil blinks fast, processing all of his interactions with Hummingbird to figure out when exactly she "saved" him. "I didn't kill your friend, Morgan. I found her, in the tub-"

"-no! You didn't! I just got out of the shower! I took a shower upstairs this morning and..."

"I cleaned it all up, Morgan, so you didn't have to. I... knew exactly what had to be done, after Hummingbird did what she felt had to be done," Wil says, then he has to clench his teeth so his mouth doesn't gape like Morgan's.

"How do I know you didn't do this, Wil?" Morgan asks, trembling, unable to look at Jody. She just wants Jody to hug her, but she now feels as though no one in this house loves her. She's alone again. She doesn't want to go into the yard because she imagines these boys will nail the front door shut behind her.

"You'll know I didn't hurt your friend when you go out and look at her. I left her next to the hole I dug," Wil says. He kept Hummingbird's body outside of the grave so Morgan could grieve.

"You did this," Morgan howls from the back of her throat.

"I didn't," Wil says, calmly able to maintain this metered response to Morgan's allegations because he knows what it's like to be in Morgan's place, and he remembers how much it sucks. When someone you love, someone you rely on, does something like this, you want to blame other people. It can't be the fault of that fragile person in the red bath because that person is the victim. The victim can't also be the villain. Someone must have knocked them off the shelf to cause them to crack in those places.

Morgan thinks about her conduct. She thinks about the screaming match she had with Wil last night. She thinks about Hummingbird's tears. She thinks about how she didn't console her friend because she was too concerned with her own problems.

How could someone be so terrible to a little girl?

Ms. Leeds.

She's still here and no one is bitchier to a woman than another woman.

Morgan pushes past Wil, as he asks, "Where are you going?"

"To find a big rose," Morgan tearfully responds, then walks out of Leeds House, barefoot.

LXI. On Her Back.

We follow Morgan as she searches through the pines for the rosebush. She couldn't bring herself to look at Hummingbird when she walked by the body. There's so much to do before the funeral can happen. Morgan has to make another flag, then she has to get the bouquets perfect, just like Rachel wanted. A wish granted, far too late, far too permanently.

After walking for far too long, her feet now cut and bruised, Morgan concludes that the roses have been removed. They weren't being grown in preparation for Hummingbird's funeral; they were there to announce the funeral. They've fully served their purpose, so Leeds has removed them. Morgan realizes that if she was to adorn Hummingbird's resting place in something that naturally grew in the Barrens, it would be like growing moss over her non-existent gravestone. Hummingbird doesn't need flowers, she needs something alive, something beautiful, something personal. It's essential that Hummingbird s resting place is marked so that when help comes, poor Rachel can be found and returned home. This burial is temporary, like the flowers, but the reason for the burial is permanent, like the clipping of a thorny stem.

Morgan hobbles back to the graveyard, and she focuses on the good memories of the time she spent in the Pine Barrens with her friend, Rachel. She thinks about the fun that two lost girls had in a situation that should've been unrelentingly scary and exceptionally bleak. She credits two people- Jody, and Hummingbird- with making the devil's house temporarily feel like a home.

Moving through the open front door of Leeds house, Morgan grabs a candle, then makes her way down into the basement.

Under the blanket of elevated demands, Morgan thinks to herself, *Damn it, Rachel. Why couldn't you listen to the ceiling? Why couldn't you Stay?* She thinks back to the sleepover in this cold tomb, and her heart warms as she remembers shrieking under the other blanket in the basement. *This* is precisely how Morgan hopes things will end- with everyone together again, smiling under a very different green blanket.

LXII. Cold Front.

We watch as Wil finally takes off his once-white shirt. He had kept the shirt on as a reminder, but he's unwilling to wear Hummingbird's blood. All of this makes us think about Mike, so we have to walk away.

We find Morgan, in the kitchen, as she bites the thread off a needle, then cuts the slack of red string to make sure it isn't dangling. Once she's happy with her tribute to her fallen friend, she decides that, yes, it's time to say goodbye.

We follow Morgan out of the open front door, past Jody on the porch, then into the front yard, which now doubles as a graveyard.

Kyle finishes smoothing out the dirt over Hummingbird's grave, then Morgan plants the flag in the ground. It reads, "Here Does Not Lie Rachel Vestrone," and has a little poorly drawn Hummingbird patch sewn on it. Morgan was extremely careful with the needle while making what she hopes is the final flag.

Kyle sits down next to the grave and takes off his gloves.

Morgan sits down next to the boy with the scars, and she wants to kiss his hands like she kissed Jody's, but she knows now that her kiss is toxic so she bites her tongue and wipes away a tear.

Kyle's scarred palms are placed on the sandy dirt above Hummingbird. He ignores the warmth he feels, and he stares at the back of his hands, fearing that the ground will move.

Morgan looks to the treetops, and she watches as, in a gradual flutter, a black flake falls from the sky and lands on the back of Kyle's right hand.

Kyle blinks his beautiful eyes twice to make sure that his hands are not burning from the center outward. He refused to share a cigarette with Wil last night so he should be safe. Lifting his left hand, Kyle touches the flake that landed on him, and it immediately crumbles into a black powder- the same black powder that Morgan has been using under her eyes- the same black powder that Kyle didn't need to use around his eyes because the pageantry required of the metalcore frontman was not necessary in the Barrens.

Head cocked to the heavens, Morgan announces, "It's snowing," in a state of pure wonderment that has otherwise been absent since the night of the concert. She makes this observation like she's a girl in Santa Cruz who prayed for an unlikely snowfall so her Christmas morning would mirror what she saw in the movies.

More flakes fall from a gray sky, and Jody desperately wants to run out into the black snow, but he doesn't. He stays on the porch and allows only his eyes to dance through the unlikely moment.

Careful, curious, and not that shocked that it's snowing in November in South Jersey, Kyle begins to study the color and consistency of the flakes. He crushes another flake in his palm, and instead of melting, it crumbles to soot. As calmly as he can, he says, "It's not snowing, we're being dusted with cinder."

"And I'm Cinderella," Morgan says, holding out her arms, her hair being peppered in ash.

"Look at me, Morgan. Listen to me. Do you know where cinder comes from?"

"Fire."

"Do you know where fire comes from?"

"Yeah," Morgan says, then crushes two flakes together and smudges the black char under her eyes.

"Say it so I know you understand," Kyle demands.

"Fire comes from hell," Morgan responds.

"Exactly," Kyle says, his blue eyes wild, "Now, if cinder is dropping from the sky, what's that tell you?"

"That this whole dang place is upside down?" Morgan responds.

"And?"

"And..." Morgan pauses, then she begins to follow Kyle's logic, "The fireplace, the tree, the snow... he wants his own holiday for his birthday, like he was Jesus."

Kyle and Morgan share a concerned look, then they head back toward the porch.

"Ain't this some *Silent Hill* type shit," Jody marvels to himself, as Kyle and Morgan walk past him into the house.

Kyle makes his way upstairs to wash the ash off him, and Morgan opts for the downstairs bathroom.

Returning to the sofa, to his purple blanket, Jody flops down. Desperate for an escape, he reaches under the sofa, then slides out a piece of paper, a pen, and a Behringer hardcover he had been stashing.

Fresh-faced, except for her eye makeup, Morgan walks into the living room, dragging her feet on the carpet, slowly making an approach toward Jody.

Quietly, almost to herself, Morgan says, "It's weird how, before, I kept worrying about my cell phone giving me some cancer-type disease, and now here I am just dancing in ash, smearing it all over myself, completely unafraid of the long-term repercussions of everything because I've realized I'm a short term person in every way..."

Jody doesn't respond. He doesn't tell Morgan to leave. He doesn't sigh an annoyed sigh. He just works on his project.

"Are you decoding things over there?" Morgan asks, sitting next to the boy she desperately needs to be her boyfriend still.

"Nah, just working on something," Jody says, attempting to end the conversation.

"Can I see?" Morgan asks, continuing the conversation.

Jody looks over at her with suspicion, then nods. He angles the paper toward Morgan, then searches her face for a reaction.

"Jody, is that?"

"Yes. Behold," Jody responds proudly.

Morgan studies a pencil drawing detailing the scene of a truck colliding with a tree. The momentum of the suddenly stopped vehicle has sent mustached midgets flying everywhere- some midgets are on the ground, some midgets are in the tree. Some midgets are in pieces.

"This is a very crude drawing," Morgan says, worried that the devil is giving Jody these visions. There are hundreds of B-movies where a little girl's art teacher contacts her parents, and is like, "You have to see this fucked up shit your kid is drawing." The parents show up and see that most of their daughter's charcoal sketches are of dead people and the blood looks really rushed and not very realistic so it's disappointing both on a mental health level and on an artistic level.

"Of course it's crude, I just started the drawing. Fuck. Did you walk over to El Salvador Dolly ten minutes into that stoner painting, like, 'Oh, El Salvador, that clock looks a little fucked up?'"

"No, I'm just saying it's macabre," Morgan meekly responds, verbally allowing Jody to be the alpha, but not vacating her seat on the sofa. She's willing to stay here and hash it out.

Jody looks down at his drawing, and calmly says, "This is real life and it's going to teach people a lesson. I'm not going to let another vehicle blow up due to overcrowding. This is why I'm making a monument out of that moment, like when those apes gave America The Statue of Liberty."

"I think you're misremembering the ending of *Planet of the Apes*," Kyle says, walking into the living room, toweling his face off.

"I don't mess with that movie. Any time I've seen a man fall to his knees and yell, 'You damn dirty apes,' police are handcuffing him like ten minutes later," Jody says.

"What you're planning on that page... is a monument to that crazy story you told us?" Morgan asks carefully.

"Yes. It will be an American tourist attraction. We'll put this bitch in South Texas near where it happened and people will come from miles around. It'll be like that Joshua Tree that Bono planted when he arrived in America."

"Your copper dead midget monument is the new Joshua Tree?" Morgan asks, looking for clarification.

"Better," Jody assures her.

"How are you going to get the airborne midgets to stay up there?" Morgan asks.

"That's the beauty of it, it's like these midgets were setting out to create a self-contained monument. They crashed into a tree, a tree has branches, you can hang things on branches."

"I know another guy who likes to hang things from branches," Wil says, walking into the living room. He's wearing a forest green flannel instead of his ruined, ripped, ashy, sweaty, bloody, once-white shirt. He looks like a new man, but sounds like the old one.

"Jody, this is all quite troubling," Kyle says, arching his neck to look at the drawing.

"Guess you don't understand what it's like to be American," Jody says. "No one does. There used to be a thing called patriotism. If we still had it, we sure as fuck wouldn't have a state named New Mexico."

"What would you call the state instead of New Mexico?" Kyle asks, holding in a laugh.

"I'd call it 'Still America,'" Jody says proudly, then stands up and walks to the window. He sees that the sky has cleared, so he tells his remaining friends, "I'm about to peace out this motherfucker to go pay my respects to Hummingbird before another ash storm comes," and the statement sounds just as insane as everything else Jody has said recently which puts all of this madness on an even playing field.

Kyle understands why the truck story was told the first time, and he understands why the changes have been made to the narrative. Jody had to make the story more absurd because nothing about the van being transformed into ash made sense. The lack of logic in this monument reflects the world we've found ourselves inhabiting. Jody had to tell this barely believable story about an auto accident because of those gloves on Kyle's hands. The band was Jody's way of fixing things for Kyle, and now that the band is gone, and the van is gone, this statue is being planned as a monument to Jody's perpetual attempt at righting wrongs.

Running his fingers through his wet hair, Wil asks, "Did you guys put her in the ground yet?"

"Yeah, but I still need to apologize to her," Jody says.

"I want to apologize to you first," Morgan says, standing up.

Jody stares at Morgan. He runs his bandaged hand over his beard, then he extends this same hand out to her. Morgan walks over, then presses her palm into his.

In this house, everyone will be punished for their actions so apologies may seem like a waste of precious breath, but forgiveness is a God-given weapon and Jody wields it like his mace.

LXIII. Rachel-Ann Vestrone.

"When you're born, you're born to a location. That location becomes part of you and you carry it with you everywhere you go. A location is only special because of the people- the people who built it, the people who invited you in, the people you found there. This means that the location you're carrying is forever filled with the people who made it special.

Home is home because that's where your family is, or it's where they used to be and now it's where their memory remains.

If you move, it's okay to be nostalgic, but it's foolish to think that you've completely left your old home. Whether you loved or hated where you were, it will follow you like a shadow, while boxes of who you were in that old house will remain, waiting for someone to go through them.

You can find a new house, but you have a responsibility to make that place a home. Don't turn it into a jail cell. You have to talk to those around you. You have to travel with friends, then make more friends. You have to be aware of everyone's feelings, not because they pose a threat, but because they pose a future. You have to call them on stage if they're hopping up and down, begging for your attention. You have to tell them how much they mean to you. You have to remind them of why they're great. You have to give a ride to someone who needs it. You have to refuse to let the trembling loaner stay behind in the parking lot. You have to make them feel safe. You have to make them feel at home. You have to make sure you don't black out when you're giving them directions.

I arrived in The Barrens with my friend and my favorite band, imperfect. We quickly found ourselves without the possessions that normally hold us back. This was a clean slate and it was up to us to determine what we drew on that slate. Stripped to our most basic societal trail markers, we had to band together to figure out how to survive.

When we weren't together, things got bad.

Leeds house was a new life, and I fucked it up. That angel-boy, Kyle Lennard, held me and gave me a second chance at my second chance. In the end, I was the same person in my new house that I was in the old house. What's the definition of insanity? Doing the same shit over and over and expecting a different result? I guess I went a little insane in the house. I got my one shot, and it was the best shot. It was never going to get any clearer than it was when I arrived, drunk, in the Barrens. I didn't have my phone to distract me. I had a girl that knew me completely, and boys that were working to know me- I had people who cared. I didn't have a job that I needed to wake up for. I didn't have a test I needed to study for. All I had was myself to study. All I had was myself to work on. Every time I tested myself, I failed. In typical Rachel fashion, I saved all my work until the night before it was due, and by then it was simply too late, so I was just like, "Kill me, now."

Even with all the distractions silenced, I remained inattentive.

I told myself that the new and scary place I woke up in was to blame.

Maybe the house *is* to blame, but I'm from a generation unable to accept personal fault so even if everyone in Leeds house died by their own hand, we would still deem it the Jersey Devil's fault. This mythical being, that may not even exist, can be handed the blame because it means that we're innocent.

I'm sorry if I disappointed you. There were so many complicated moments packed into our time at Leeds house. We panicked, and fought, and some of us lost the fight, and some of us threw the fight, and some of us will fight every day for the memory of those who didn't make it.

Everyone in Leeds house is stronger than I am.

Everyone in Leeds house deserves to be saved."

LXIV. Burying What Haunts You.

We watch as Jody and Morgan walk out of the shower together. We should've been on the other side of the door, but we sneaked into the upstairs bathroom to see what would happen to Morgan when she stood in a shower that only hours ago contained the lifeless body of her friend.

Anti-climatically, not much happened. The devil must be sleeping in after all his hard work last night. Maybe this couple is protected by the blessing that Jody gave Morgan as they knelt in the ashes in the front yard and prayed for their departed friends. Just as Morgan had applied the ash around her eyes, Jody applied ash to her head, in a cross. He wanted to be sure that the devil's snow was used as a tribute to Christ. *Ashes to ashes. Dust to dust. We came from dust and to dust we shall return.* This provided a hope for the resurrection, not in a zombie-like way that the Leeds devil would gladly coordinate, but instead in the miracle of Christ.

The shower washed away the cross, and the ashes circled the drain. Instead of fearing the moment, this gave Jody an idea. There are people in the house who need to be baptized.

Morgan reaches for the candle and lights it with the green lighter. In the orange glow, Jody wipes off the mirror, then stares at himself. Morgan wraps her arms around him, her heavy breasts pressing onto his back, and she says quietly, "Jody?"

"Yeah?"

"I'm glad your dick didn't get shot off by a sniper."

"Me too," Jody says, loved up in a post-shower, post-coital warmth that almost plumps up his freezing cold member, but Jody's shriveled penis reminds him of the reality of Leeds house. "What the fuck are we going to do?" he asks.

"Wil's next," Morgan says, airy, distant.

"Then?"

"Then me," Morgan sighs, looking into her own eyes.

"No," Jody refuses, breaking her grasp. "We can walk out of here."

"Not together, Jody."

"You start to believe it's hopeless and-"

"-it's hopeless," Morgan declares, like Hummingbird's blood had climbed into the cuts on her feet and began circulating in her body.

"I can save you," Jody says. He grabs Behringer's clothes off the counter and begins getting dressed. "I'm not going to let that happen," he says, now frantic.

Morgan, deadly serious, says, "If the sex doesn't get me, the lies will. If the lies don't get me, the envy will."

"Envy?" Jody responds, this one catching him off guard.

"I coveted what Hummingbird had every fucking moment I spent with her. Listen, Jody, the bullet is already out of the chamber. Please don't jump in front of it."

"I'll push you out of the way," Jody says.

"Good."

"To save you," Jody says, then walks out of the bathroom.

Morgan waits for a moment, then Jody returns and says, "You picked me out a Beastie Boys t-shirt? Really? In this house?" Jody takes off the shirt then puts it back on inside out.

"Bad joke," Morgan says, feeling what Jody must feel a thousand times a day.

"No such thing," Jody responds, then in the candlelight, he watches as Morgan gets dressed. He becomes a bodyguard again. A familiar guilt hangs in the air like the steam and dust.

"I have to make dinner," Morgan says, walking out of the bathroom. Jody trails behind her, more vigilant than ever. He'll help- with everything- until Morgan demands that he leave her alone. Jody will recommit himself to Morgan in hopes that she will return the favor. That's what's left. Ash removed. Clean slates.

Morgan enters the kitchen and immediately walks over to the sink. She opens her mouth to ask Jody what he wants for dinner, but she's interrupted by a shrill buzz that shrieks in a repeating second-long pulse.

Jody gets in an on-guard stance, ready to ward off whatever is making this tortured cry.

The noise seems to be coming from the single level portion of the house. Both Jody and Morgan follow the buzzing, their eyes and ears working in desperate tandem. When they step down into the single level portion of the house, they're both expecting to see some sort of little demon that looks like a raptor from hell.

After a quick search, we don't find any demons, but we do find the source of the noise. Morgan scrunches her nose, and Jody says, "It's a motherfucking phone." He's totally relaxed, pointing at a cream colored rotary phone on the wall. He lets out a couple hard laughs, still pointing.

"Doesn't it trouble you that this phone just randomly just showed up here?" Morgan asks.

"Does it normally trouble you when kick ass things happen in your life?" Jody asks.

"In this house? Yes," Morgan says.

"Don't answer it, Jody," Kyle pleads, appearing in the door frame between the single level portion of the house and the kitchen. "Don't answer his call."

"Well, this devil has been catching feelings this whole time when we don't respond, so I better answer his call," Jody says, over the phone's shriek. "You ever ignore a chick's call? Hell may hath no fury like a woman scorned, but it probably has a respectable amount of fury."

Morgan acts quickly, dashing in front of Jody, picking up the phone, then placing it to her ear. She leans casually on the wall, like a teenager in an 80's movie. She doesn't say hello. She waits to hear who is calling. She waits. Wil curiously saunters into the dining room, watching over Kyle's shoulder. Kyle, in the doorway, watches over Jody's shoulder. Jody, face to face with Morgan, watches her eyes.

"Okay... okay... okay..." Morgan says, shaking her head, "Yup, kill my friends... eat their hearts... make sweet love to Jody's corpse..." she lists, her eyes unblinking. A smile breaks across Morgan's face, then she admits, "I'm just fuckin' with ya, there's no one on the other end of the phone," then she hangs up the call.

Jody's eyes go wide, then a smile slides across his face until it can no longer contain his rapid fire laugh. Morgan, to ease the tension, channeled Jody, again. Her Beastie Boys joke failed upstairs, but she made another dickhead joke downstairs because she understands that laughs can kill tension.

"Let's call for help," Wil says, pushing past Kyle, stepping into the room.

Jody looks back at Wil, then asks, "So, who we gonna ca-"

"-if you say Ghostbusters, I will beat you like you're Kyle and I'm you," Wil says bitterly.

"Alright, give me someone to call, Wil," Morgan says, mad that her moment was interrupted.

Everyone tries to think of a number to call, and it's silent in the house.

"All of our numbers are in our phones," Kyle finally says, then realizes, "Call 911. They can track our location by the POTS line."

"What are we going to tell them?" Morgan asks, "Our van blew up, then our cell phones blew up, then the Jersey Devil tortured us in the wizard boy author's pedo suicide ghost house?"

Jody smiles, "That does sound like a pretty kick ass story. I bet we will make this minimum wage 911 operator's month," Jody says.

Morgan takes the phone off the hook and dials 9-1-1.

She listens on the line. One ring. Two rings.

Then someone picks up.

LXV. Pick Yourself Up.

We race through the house after Morgan.

"Where are you going?" Jody calls out, "Who answered the call?"

"I'm not staying here anymore," Morgan gulps, climbing up the stairs, almost on all fours.

Jody feels immediate relief that she chose to go up the stairs instead of out the open front door.

"I've felt like leaving too," Jody admits, continuing his pursuit onto the second floor.

Morgan quickly makes her way down the carpeted hallway until she reaches the same closet where Wil first caught a glimpse of what is infesting this house.

"No, like, I'm going home, Jody," Morgan says, throwing the closet door open, then pulling a men's tan trench coat off a hanger.

"This... is your home?" Jody says, as a question instead of a declaration.

Morgan puts the coat on, then the tail flutters behind her as she continues her preparations.

After grabbing Jody's flashlight off the dresser in Behringer's bedroom, Morgan quickly moves back down the stairs.

"If you want to go home, then we'll all search for home," Jody says, following Morgan out the front door.

"Is Rob going to help us search? No. You shot him," Morgan says over her shoulder.

"I saved Rob," Jody growls, pointing at the porch stairs as he stomps down them, "There was no chance that he could get out of here so I saved him from the hurt."

"Now, what? You're going to save me?" Morgan asks, standing next to the graves of the people that Jody couldn't save. She's skipping ahead in line and Jody's security guard manner won't allow it.

"Morgan, listen to me, we'll walk out of this together," Jody yells, but Morgan continues to walk away, alone.

"No," Morgan says over her shoulder, "Stay. Do not follow me."

"It's suicide," Jody calls out, resuming his hunt, trailing Morgan into the woods.

"Everything is, Jody. Pick your poison. We can't win this fight," Morgan yells, the coat billowing behind her.

"So you're going to give up?"

"I didn't say I was going to give up, I'm just looking at what happened. Rob- dead. Mike- dead. Hummingbird- dead," Morgan rants. We can no longer see her, we can only hear her now

"I miss them too, but I'm not taking the express to see them," Jody says, already out of breath.

"Do you realize I've known you for like a week and I can't think of a single conversation we've had where you weren't cursing?" Morgan says, not even looking back as she moves deeper into the woods.

"Fuck you. Don't try to damn me," Jody yells.

Morgan mumbles, "Great, Jody."

"I can say that and I'll be fine. You think I'm going to die over some curse words? You think you're going to die because we made love?" Jody yells at the pines.

Morgan finally stops walking, and moments later, Jody unexpectedly reaches her. Staring directly in Jody's eyes, Morgan says, "No, I'm going to die because I fucked your friend and took his virginity, and I would have fucked every other guy in this house if they weren't busy staring at each other's cocks. I'm a fucking slut, Jody."

Jody lets out a long exhale, then once he composes himself, he asks, "What did you hear on that phone?"

"It didn't connect," Morgan says, turning around, the coat tail flying up.

"Then why did you drop it, why did you leave in such a rush?" Jody asks, pursuing his girl again.

"I was frustrated that the phone was worthless."

"Why would he place it in the house if it didn't work?" Jody asks.

"To fuck with us. All of this is just to fuck with us," Morgan spits. She's not crying. She's not tired. She starts running.

As Morgan moves deeper into the woods, she begins to feel like she isn't fleeing; she feels like she's being pulled.

Jody can't keep up. He started his sprint nearly out of breath and now his run has slowed to a clomping walk.

Even after Morgan's can no longer be seen or heard, Jody, through gasps, desperately calls her name.

The Barrens swallow his girlfriend, and Jody becomes careless as he traverses the belly of the beast.

Continuing to rush forward, Jody feels branches snap under his feet and jagged sticks scrape his legs. He calls out for Morgan, but still only finds silence. He stops moving. He listens carefully, as the tranquil Barrens soundlessly laugh, until suddenly everything is leveled by a piercing clatter. From inside Leeds house, ring echoes out of the front door across the woods.

LXVI. Glowing Home.

We follow Morgan through the dark, as she walks with more purpose than she's ever had in her life. She ventures away from one of the best things that she's ever had because she managed to ruin it before she even realized she had it. Something guides her across the sandy soil, between those unflinching pines.

Morgan can only focus on what's in front of her, and she never looks back. Tree, tree, stumble, root, rock, tree, tree, stumble, root, rock, tree, tree, stumble, root, rock, tree, tree... a light?

On the floor of this sadistic stage is a foreign-yet-familiar glow. It's not a spotlight pointing down, illuminating an object, it's a beacon, pointing up, the light coming from inside the object and emanating out. Morgan walks to this impossibility, then drops to her knees and basks in its sinister glow. Carefully, she reaches out a hand, then picks up an enemy. Her fully restored cell phone glows in her palm.

This could be a trick, but it also could be a way to get back into that house because, fuck, Morgan more than anything wants to... *Stay.*

Tears blurring her view, Morgan can see a number is already entered on the healed screen of her phone. She presses down on the glass and begins the call.

Jody didn't make it in time to answer the call he was racing for, but he's next to the phone when Morgan's call arrives. He picks up the receiver, but he doesn't say, "Hello," because it's only one letter off from the origin of the call.

"Hello?" Morgan says when she hears that someone picked up.

Jody chokes back a sob when he hears who's on the other line. He holds the phone away from his face so the mouthpiece doesn't pick up his whimper. He can't begin the conversation because he doesn't want to distract Morgan to the point that she's physically vulnerable. All girls her age have a weakness for their phone. When Morgan is concerned only with her phone is when the fire of the Pine Barrens will engulf this girl who carries the torch.

"Are you there? Jody? Jody, if this is you on the other end, if somehow I've become that lucky to connect with you again, then I want to tell you... that I love you. I love you, Jody Lennard. I never wanted to hurt you, but I did. I hurt you, then I tried to hide it. I thought it would just go away. I thought I wouldn't have to admit what I did. I deserve what will happen to me, so I want to give you what you deserve... You deserve to know that, when my life flashes before my eyes, you'll be everywhere, Jody. You painted these Barrens a beautiful green. As evil and sick as our little vacation was, you always made me laugh, and even when I was too heavy, you carried me. I'm sorry that I got mad at you that night when you offered my best friend that spot on your shoulders. At that time I didn't deserve the closeness. I was ugly then. I believed I was so ugly. I knew I was so ugly. I didn't deserve to be carried. But then we found the house, and I found out who you really are. Behind those insane rants, I found a man who made me happy, Jody. Every second of attention you gave me, crude or not, it was a second that I will relive when everything passes by me, and I'll laugh at all the jokes I was too serious to enjoy when I first met you. I love you. I love you. I love you. I don't know why I couldn't tell you that in person. I guess I thought it was too early to say it, but time is so fucked up here that I became confused. It's so obvious now, but it's still not easy for me to say. It's hard to tell you exactly how I feel, but it's essential that I tell you everything in this moment. You are beautiful enough that I want the words to come from you, not Kyle. Even if you don't hear me right now, I hope this message reaches you in the pit of your being. You lost your phone, and you lost your van, you lost your band, and you lost your friends, but you never stopped searching for a way to save what you still had. Any other man in your shoes would have become bitter, but you didn't, and that was my light. That was the light we all hovered around. You are the center of that house, and I know that if you escape, you'll carry me with y-"

The line goes dead, and Jody drops the phone, then sprints to the front door.

For the first time since we stepped foot inside the house, the door frame is repaired and the front door is locked.

LXVII. (Almost) Everything Is Easier In The Light.

We stand in Behringer's writing room. It's destroyed.

The boy wizard books didn't fly off the shelves magically.

The desk didn't get flipped by some bizarre force suspending it in the air, then violently dropping it back down.

This morning, locked inside the freezing cold Leeds house, Jody fought back, but when he faced no retaliation, he found himself wondering where, and how, the inevitable payback was occurring. Maybe, while Jody was taking out his anger on this house, the devil was focused on doing the same to Morgan by skinning her, or melting her insides with his black goo. Maybe he was slashing her up and draining her dry. Maybe he had finally found a woman he could take his mommy issues out on.

Jody throws the door open, and he's met with a hall of closed doors. He walks by the bathroom and bangs on the door. He walks by the closet and bangs on the door. He walks by the bedroom and bangs on the door. He walks by the Polaroid room and he sees the door isn't latched shut. Jody gives the door a light push and we find Wil studying the Polaroid wall.

"Come on," Jody says, motioning for Wil to leave the room.

"Come where?" Wil asks.

"We're going to go find Morgan."

"You don't want to do that," Wil says, as Hummingbird's image flashes in his mind.

"Where's Kyle?" Jody asks.

"Downstairs," Wil responds, then when he sees Jody isn't moving, he walks out of the Polaroid room like a child being forced to go to church.

"What the fuck is he doing off on his own? We have to stick together," Jody says, as the two men make their way down the stairs.

"He was making you lunch. Okay? He wants to help you get over-"

"-there's nothing to get over, Wil. We don't know that something bad has happened to her."

"I'm sorry, but she called you on a cell phone that had Satan as its mobile provider, then you answered on a landline that snaked up from hell. I'm not sure if you've seen the terms on a wireless contract with the devil, but it goes for eternity and you're never eligible for an upgrade. It's almost as bad as a contract with AT&T." When Wil says this, it's not in his usual cynical growl. He's joking around. It seems that Morgan disappearing before Wil confirmed something to him. The order has shifted and surviving the night bolstered Wil's confidence, allowing him to relax.

We enter the kitchen and Kyle looks up from the stove, then says, "I made dino shaped fish sticks."

"We don't have time for your fucking fish sticks," Jody says, but the aroma of the lightly breaded fish treats hits his nose, and he pauses. He mulls over how time sensitive this mission is.

"Kyle, get those fried dinosaur shaped fishes out of the oven. We need sustenance before we go to war with the devil."

"That's probably what the dinosaurs said and now look at where they are, used as fuel for exploding vans," Wil says, and Jody redirects the negativity into purpose, "Wil. You have a task as well, get us waters."

"And what exactly are *you* going to do?" Wil asks, walking toward the fridge.

"I'm going to find a way to kill the devil," Jody says, then walks into the dining room.

Five minutes and one prayer later, the three remaining members of Lies As Language sit with a pile of dinosaur shaped breaded fish sticks in front of them.

"So, have you figured out a way to defeat the devil yet?" Wil asks, barely holding back a laugh.

"Don't worry, Jody. We're going to leave tonight. I promise you, we'll leave tonight," Kyle says.

"To where?" Wil asks, frustrated, "I'm really getting tired of the Lennard brothers' daily battle of the poorly thought out escape plans. This is like a prison movie except for no guys get to fuck each other."

"I get it," Jody says, "This whole situation is fucked up. I mean, it's not like electing-the-first-woman-president level of fucked up, but still it's pretty awful."

"That bastard devil is doing this so he can get a tiny piece of the world. He's carving out real estate," Kyle says.

Wil chomps a fish stick, and with his mouth full, asks, "Who the fuck would want the world?"

Jody nods, then agrees, "It would suck to have the world. You'd be personally responsible for Africa."

"Actually..." Wil muses. His continued existence has given him a new passion for life, and he's ready to mess with the two remaining members he's competing against for survival.

"Are you honestly considering having to deal with Africa's shit? You couldn't even manage to deal with two teenage girls," Jody says.

"I don't want the world. But you know who does? Aliens!"

"Shut up, Wil," Kyle says.

"Aliens are using this house for experiments. I bet all those kids upstairs weren't Behringer's victims... they were aliens in kid suits. Based on the picture lineup, we now know which kids are actually tiny aliens, and when we get out of this house, we'll have to punch all those kids in their faces," Wil says, then laughs to himself. When he sees that no one is on board with punching innocent children in the face on the off chance they're still alive and might be aliens, Wil makes claws with his hands, then in a nasally voice, he taunts Jody, "Give us your earth or feel the wrath of our tentacles."

Jody shakes his head, then says, "You're thinking of hentai. Hentai is where the tentacles come from."

Wil's claws turn back into black tipped fingers, then he fondles a dino-fishstick, and ponders, "Are 'hentai' spiders that climb into your eye sockets and lay babies behind your eyes, then later, your eyes explode out of your head when the babies hatch?"

"That's an oddly specific description for a guess that's so incredibly wrong," Kyle says.

"Yeah, I really bet the house on that one. So, does Hentai live behind your eyes?" Wil asks.

"In a way, yeah. Some of those images..." Jody says, then shivers.

"You just gave the devil a suggestion on a fucked up way we could die," Kyle says.

"He's already got it figured out. He doesn't need me," Wil responds, supremely relaxed.

"How did Behringer kill himself?" Kyle asks, then he feels his chest fill with a creeping horror because this is the first time that question has been asked aloud, despite the fact we've been living in the man's house for over... who knows how long.

"How did Behringer live in this house for so long, hurting all those kids and nothing happened to him? Why did the devil wait months to kill him for his behavior?" Jody asks.

Staring past Kyle, out the window, toward a point far in the backyard, Wil says, "Leeds didn't kill Behringer because of what he was doing. He killed Behringer because he decided to stop."

This ends breakfast.

Morgan is still missing.

No one is here to do the dishes.

The dirty plates go into the sink and this house takes another step toward becoming a bachelor pad.

"We need to find her," Jody tells his remaining bandmates. They don't question this, they merely nod in agreement, then get to work.

Kyle goes upstairs to get coats from the closet, since it's become significantly colder in the Barrens since Morgan left.

Wil scrawls out a note that, in four brief lines, details how he murdered his friends. This message isn't some stupid plot twist, it's a callback to a lesson that Mike taught us- if you want someone to find you in the woods, hide some bodies or start killing. Death will always earn you attention in the 24 hour news cycle. Wil has embraced this idea, and he'll pin this note to the house, then he'll deal with the repercussions later. What's the worst thing that could happen? The death penalty? At least he'll get a couple extra hours of supervised protection.

Kyle returns and hands out coats so we can prepare to face an especially cold November day. Wil puts on a black trench coat. Kyle puts on a gray peacoat. Jody puts on a blue bomber jacket with "USA" emblemized across the back in giant capital letters. Pausing for a moment, feeling like his outfit isn't complete, Jody turns around, then spots his cowboy hat atop the piano. He slowly walks across the living room, almost afraid of the piano now that Rob is dead and Morgan is missing. Without dwelling on the past, Jody picks up his hat and places it on his head.

It's time to go.

Jody Lennard, Kyle Lennard, and Wil Chapman step outside of Leeds House. They leave the front door open, just like they found it. They step off the porch. They step past the graves of Hummingbird and Mike and Rob. They notice a fourth grave, it gapes open, empty- for now. Who dug this grave? Since each man had taken his turn getting dirty in the Barrens, it was easier to assume that this was Wil just being prepared for the inevitable.

After exchanging searching glances, the boys all put their hands in their pockets and begin walking away from the open grave.

"Say goodbye to Leeds house," Jody sighs, but only once we're a safe distance from the graves.

All three men turn to review the house one last time, and that's when their search ends.

Morgan is on the roof of the house, naked, impaled on a lightning rod in the most logical and personal of places.

A flash blinds us like lightning- another picture on the wall.

The moment carries too much weight, and it's too effective.

Wil thinks about how Jody would always undercut the scary moments and sour the devil's pleasure with a questionable comment, and he says, "Oh great, now we're the family with our Halloween decorations up year round."

"We'll never get her down," Kyle realizes aloud, quietly.

Jody lowers his head until his neck is almost bent in an L shape. His hat falls onto the sandy ground and he makes no effort to pick it up.

"Jody?" Kyle asks, but he doesn't follow it up with, "Are you okay?" because the answer will be, "No."

Jody keeps his head slumped, then he begins slowly nodding, not in agreement or disagreement- this seems to be a move stolen from Rob at his worst.

After the shock eases and the acceptance gradually arrives, Jody wipes his nose, picks up his cowboy hat, then starts walking back to the house.

"Where are you going? We can't turn back. He wants us to go back," Kyle calls out.

"I'm going to get her down," Jody promises himself, "I'm not going to let her sit up there."

Wil shakes his head, then says, "She's not really sitting as much as-"

Jody turns around and charges back, his face dripping with tears, "-Wil, I will take her down and put you up there in her place, I promise you-"

"-that you're sooo offended? Chill out. You've been saying shit like that for three decades," Wil points out, arms raised, ready to redirect Jody's pain.

"If you believe that, Wil... I'm going-"

"-what Jody? You're going to go on the roof of a house whose landlord is a giant horse-bat-dragon-demon? Yeah, awesome idea! What could go wrong up there on a steeple slant?" Wil yells.

"I'm not letting her stay up there like that. That's not how she should be remembered. That's not how I remember her," Jody says, pointing aggressively at the brutal weathervane.

Kyle steps forward to present a likely reality, and asks, "What if you're knocked off?"

"We're all going to be knocked off," Jody points out, "It might as well happen as I'm saving someone from embarrassment. I... I don't want her to be remembered like that, and I want to be remembered as a guy who didn't give up, even when it was painfully obvious things were falling apart," Jody says. "He wasn't supposed to take Morgan next," he adds quietly.

"Who was supposed to be next?" Wil asks, then smiles.

"Wil. Do not," Kyle says, stepping between the two men.

Peeking his head past Kyle, Wil continues, "No, this is interesting. Elaborate. Why was Morgan not supposed to be-"

"-because you were next, you selfish fuck," Jody yells.

Holding his arms out cruciform, hopefully not in parody, Wil reminds us, "And I'm still here, in the flesh."

"You can be sure you're next," Jody says, then immediately regrets it.

"Whoa there, wishing death on someone, that's pretty mean. Maybe. You're. Next," Wil spits out, and it seems like he's enjoying this.

"Yes, it's mean, Wil, but that obviously doesn't matter because you're still here, being mean, and you're apparently fine" Jody says.

"It matters. It just doesn't matter as much as habitually being a jealous, disgusting whore-"

"-shut the fuck up," Kyle demands of Wil, then points to the woods, as though he's banishing his friend.

Still wearing a smile, Wil nods once at this command, then he starts treading into the unknown, ranting, "Well, isn't that cute. The Lennard brothers protecting each other. I guess that makes me... what? The redheaded stepchild? Or maybe, the black haired thirteenth child? Wil, the evil one. That's what this is supposed to be, right? That's what I've been made out to be since we've arrived. Am I possessed? Maybe possessed with logic. I'm smart enough to know that you don't want to be any type of kid in that fucking house, so send me into the woods; I'll gladly go."

"You aren't leaving," Kyle says.

"But I'm banished," Wil responds, his tone dripping in mock sadness.

"I was just asking you to take a step back. We're going to make sure that Jody is okay, and he won't be okay until he gives his girlfriend a proper burial," Kyle explains.

"He won't be okay if he tries to make that happen," Wil says, then laughs, "Do you think she's up there because it makes for a cool image when the film rights are sold? She's up there because the Jersey fucking Devil knows that Jody will go up on that roof to save her, and when Jody steps out on that uneven slant, he'll be helpless."

"She's not up there to set up Jody's death. She's only up there because she was an envy-filled whore," Kyle snaps back to Wil, and instantly realizes what he said, but it's too late.

A smile parts Wil's lips, then he says, "There's no arguing that, Kyle. You've convinced me."

LXVIII. Time Alone.

We wince as we watch Jody attempt to pull his girlfriend off the lightning rod. We're safe on the ground, while he's struggling on the roof. Every time he lets out a strained cry, we have to look away, not only because of the gore, but because of Jody's desperation. The look on his face is pure devastation, and the only way this absolute pain could be amplified further would be if the devil was to fly by and knock this broken man to the ground.

No devil flies above Leeds house today.

No devil appears when Jody finally gets his naked girlfriend off the metal pole.

No devil interferes when Jody attempts to navigate down the steep roof with Morgan.

No devil provides the push that causes Jody to slip.

No devil pries away Jody's fingers when Morgan's body slides from his grasp.

No devil pulls on Morgan's corpse to cause it to fall to the ground like a stone weighted rag doll.

All of this happens merely because Jody isn't capable of fixing things this time.

We scream at Jody when it appears as though he's considering jumping down after his girlfriend.

We feel relief when, sobbing, Jody navigates back to the peak of the pitched roof, then carefully drops down onto the shingles above the extended first floor.

When Jody is safely back inside, we rush up to the Polaroid room.

No one says anything, and Jody tries to get a grip, after losing it on the roof. He holds on to the wall to remain standing, and begs, "Please help me with her."

Wil nods once, and as he's leaving the room, heading toward the stairs, we see him remove a couple Polaroids from the wall. Jody intends to pursue this peculiar action further, but first he has to bury the love of his life.

LXIX. Morgan Levine.

"So we finally have a chance to talk.

I know what you must think of me.

Fat whore.

You think that, and there are probably a hundred other people that think that, too.

Before Leeds house, your ugly opinion of me would've torn me to pieces.

Once I got to Leeds house, once I got away from my phone, once I was able to isolate the boys from the TV images that programmed them, I felt hopeful.

I'm dead now, and, yeah, that sucks, but there's also the knowledge that there's someone who doesn't look at me like you do.

This entire trip started off with rejection.

I didn't want to follow Hummingbird, only because I knew I wasn't wanted in the van.

I stood there, in the cold, and I honestly thought that I wasn't ready for this journey.

It was easier to think that.

It would have been so fucking easy for me to walk back into the venue and call my parents so they could come pick me up.

That's not what happened though. One of the Lennard brothers turned around, and said, 'I want you to come with us tonight,' even after the other Lennard brother wanted to turn me away.

So, yeah, Kyle Lennard saved me.

He saved me from running away, making the same mistake I had been repeating for a while.

Feeling wanted, I crammed myself in the back of the van, then set off on a new journey.

I realize that so many girls before me had ended up in the back of a van and it was the shittiest thing to ever happen to them. Not for me though, being in that van was different, even though it ended up with the same outcome.

That night... I laughed and I shrieked and I held hands and I shivered.

We literally ran to Leeds House and that was the beginning.

It was the beginning of the real me.

At first, it was scary living inside a place that hummed with menace. There were so many moments that were creepy, but this idiot... I mean, an absolute idiot asshole fuckface led me into that house. Then he protected me. It was the first time in my life that a man acted like a man. My dad thought he was protecting me, but he was smothering me. The security in smothering is for the smotherer, not the smotheree. Jody gave me distance, but he hovered close enough to help me when I reached out a hand. Anytime I was in trouble, even if he caused the trouble, Jody would rush to my side.

I guess I started to get used to having him around.

We laughed so much.

I fucked up so much.

When I called him, in my last moments, he didn't need to say anything to me. I already knew how he felt. His actions during out time in the house made his feelings supremely clear.

So, yeah, Jody Lennard saved me so many times.

Even after I hurt him.

When the devil was dropping me onto the roof, my life flashed before my eyes. It was fast, but you know what? Jody's image flashed fifty or sixty times.

I'm glad you saw those moments because when they played back inside me, damn it, I felt invincible.

Then I died.

Now I'm wearing a crown of flowers that Jody made me. He got me off the roof, then placed me in that open grave. After he said goodbye, he placed the crown on my head. I still don't know where he found the flowers. These aren't the roses that I stepped on. These flowers do have dangerous stems with thorny barbs, but they almost look as if they were ripped from Hummingbirds tattoos.

Whatever garden Jody rushed into to get me these flowers, to me, it was Eden.

I eat too much. Too many apples I guess.

But even after my sin, he didn't abandon me.

Lies As Language was a space-metal Christian metalcore band.

The space that I shared with them was incredibly intimate and equally unforgettable.

The metal I found myself on was my own fault.

The Christ I was introduced to held out an injured hand.

The metalcore music I loved so much became an afterthought compared to the boys who created it.

Leeds house took my life, but the people inside it gave my life purpose, and I will never forget them because I stand with them.

The home I live in now is beautiful.

It's my sincere hope that you won't make the same mistakes I did, but if you do, I pray you have the type of friends that I gained while living in Leeds house."

LXX. Black Baptism.

We sit on the sofa between Wil and Kyle. Jody stands in front of us, with his spiked mace in his hands.

Lies As Language is a three man band with no fans. There are four occupied graves in the front yard reminding us that in a very short time things went from the glory days to the gory days.

Just as Hummingbird and Morgan needed the boys, Lies As Language need the girls. An artist has a very careful relationship with his fans. It's easy to fall out of the public eye so you need to remain present, but you have to make sure you don't become omnipresent. Now, when it's easier to find an illegal download link for an album than it is to make a legitimate purchase, a band has to find a dedicated audience that wants them to succeed and remain a band, together. They need to find people with both cold hard cash and a belief in music. They need to find people who connect so deeply to their words and sounds that they'll gladly hand over that green slice of paper they worked so hard for. The almighty ten dollar bill- that's what this all comes down to in the music business. Maybe that bill pays for a month of a streaming service, maybe it pays for a download, or maybe it pays for a CD.

The music that the remaining members of Lies As Language will make in the future will reinvent their image because every lyric and every note will be informed by their experiences in this house.

Some of the fans will abandon these boys.

Metalcore fans are predictable.

If a metalcore band stays the same, some fans will say, "I already bought this album, I don't need it again."

If a metalcore band evolves, some fans will say, "I miss the old band," then they'll go listen to the early stuff.

Both of these scenarios are a reality, so in the end, the band just has to follow what's driving them, and hope they don't completely lose their direction along the way.

If they want to evolve, they should evolve.

If they want to stay the same, they should stay the same.

There's no right or wrong way to continue on.

The important part- the most important part- is that they continue on.

It's essential for a band to find fans that genuinely like them, instead of collecting people who are just there for the hooks. It's required for bands to look at the fans as people, not transactions. It's imperative that both fans and artists join hands and create a chain that cannot be broken.

This was true before the stage lights burned.

This was true before Kyle reached out.

This was true before fate intervened.

We're still here, and the fans are gone.

All that's left is this, and the hissing question becomes *Is this enough?*

"Alright, faggots," Jody says, addressing his fellow survivors.

"Really?" Wil and Kyle both snarl.

"Sorry. Alright, gaylords," Jody corrects himself.

"Are you being homophobic because you think it will underscore the fact that we're both gay and therefore 'evil?'" Will asks.

"No," Jody says, shaking his head, "I bet Rock Hudson is looking down on us from heaven right now. I believe that God is love."

"Rock Hudson is dead? London Francis must be heartbroken," Kyle gasps.

"I meant Rock Hudson the person, not Rock Hudson the high energy puppy dog," Jody clarifies.

"Oh. Right. Okay, proceed, but tone down the bigotry. Not only for us, but for yourself," Kyle says.

"Okay, cocksuckers," Jody says, resetting.

"Still hateful," Wil responds.

"Cocksucker is out?" Jody asks.

"Yeah, they got Baldwin for cocksucker," Wil says.

"These cocksuckers are taking away cocksucker? That... sucks... cock," Jody responds, his outrage melting into general confusion due to his vocabulary being slowly revoked, word-by-word.

"Can you just begin the presentation you've been working on all afternoon?" Kyle asks, then he gets comfortable on the sofa and prepares to hear about a plan that he knows will make him feel even more doomed.

Jody holds up a large piece of glossy paper with magic marker writing on it, and explains, "Yes, this was a poster for one of the boy wizard movies that Grant Anders starred in, but I wrote on the back of it and blessed it so I'm pretty sure this plan won't make us die. I think we can all agree that none of us want to die. Can we agree on that?" Jody asks, and after a moment of silence he adds, "Can we verbally agree on that?"

"I don't want to die," Kyle and Wil both say simultaneously.

"Good, I also don't want to die," Jody confirms.

"So what's your plan to achieve not dying?" Wil sighs.

"I'm glad you asked that," Jody says, then he points with his spiked mace to the first handwritten bullet point on the poster. It reads, "Don't do fucked up horror movie shit."

"What does that mean?" Kyle asks in a huff.

"Did you ever see *Scream*?" Jody asks his students.

"The movie where Johnny Depp and the other guy kill everyone?" Wil asks.

"Spoilers, dude. And it was Skeet Ulrich. Skeet Ulrich kills everyone. One can only presume there was a misunderstanding after that movie came out and Skeet was jailed in real life for those fictional murders, since no one has ever seen him again, but the point is, don't be a Skeet."

"I hope these points aren't in order of importance," Kyle says.

"I only had one poster, they're in the order that my brain thought these thoughts," Jody explains. He moves his spiked mace to the second point, "Keep your fucking shoes on."

"Done," Wil says, kicking his boots up onto the table.

"This rule can be broken if you're in the shower, but you need someone to stand guard until you put your fucking shoes back on."

"Kyle, I'm volunteering to stand-"

"-that brings us to rule three," Jody says, interrupting Wil.

"No homo shit," Kyle reads, disappointed, despite knowing he shouldn't be.

"No one can fuck anyone anymore because you will die. My fiancé died that way," Jody says.

Wil lets a laugh burst out, "Your fiancé?"

"Yes, I'm pretty sure she would have married me if the devil did not murder her life."

"You knew her for like a week," Kyle points out.

"The greatest week of my life, Kyle," Jody reflects. "With one not so great day," he adds.

"A bunch of your friends were murdered that week," Kyle points out.

"I'm wearing rose colored glasses, I suppose," Jody responds, shrugs, then moves to rule four, "Pray to Jesus tons, okay?"

"So, what, are you going to baptize us in the sink?" Wil asks.

"I thought about that, but our water is probably being heated by the flames of hell so I'm assuming that during the ceremony it would turn to sludge and burn your flesh off, so I've chosen an alternate baptism for you."

"Oh no," Kyle says, shaking his head.

Jody drops the poster to the floor, then reaches down and picks up some papers. "Here you go," he says, giving both boys a handwritten questionnaire.

"Please fill this test out and I will consult with our test proctor, Jesus, as to whether your answers are correct," Jody says, providing pencils to the boys, then continuing, "This will be a true or false test. You must answer each question, no skipsies. To the left of the question is a check box; check the left box if the statement is true. On the right side of the paper is another check box; check in this right box for false. If you aren't sure of what to answer, just think WWJC?"

We look at the paper:

Question 1: Do you believe in Jesus?
Question 2: Jesus, cool guy?
Question 3: Should "Reflection" have been on the album?

"Jody, there's a question about the tracklist of our debut album on this baptism test," Kyle points out. Wil stifles a laugh.

"Yes. Please answer all questions or you will be considered an agent of the devil," Jody says.

Our eyes move down the test:

Question 4: Poor person- help them or, "Ew, gross?"

"Jody, question four can't be answered with true or false," Wil says, then laughs again.

"Wil, please don't disrupt Kyle. His soul's eternal happiness hangs in the balance. As does yours."

We continue reading:

Question 5. The devil's house is more funner than God's house?
Question 6. Santa must be destroyed by any means necessary?

"Is 6 supposed to be Santa or satan?" Wil asks.

"Sometimes it's hard to tell the difference, isn't it?" Jody responds, then raises his eyebrows.

The boys mark their answers on their baptism tests, then submit them for spiritual grading.

As Jody reviews the answers, he shakes his head, then mumbles, "One of these isn't even a true or false question. What's going on here? I mean... Wil, you marked 'Maybe,' for question 5."

"Honestly, other than the gray demon troll and the fact that all my friends have died here, this house isn't that bad," Wil says.

"God's house is better," Jody remarks.

"I've never been to God's house," Wil says.

"You might visit there soon- that's why we're filling out these tests," Jody says, then continues reading. After nodding in various vaguely disapproving ways and letting out two long sighs, Jody says, "Okay, congratulations, you both have been accepted into the kingdom of God. You may now, um, shake hands with your friend."

Wil and Kyle awkwardly shake hands.

"Maybe we should seal it with a kiss," Wil suggests.

Jody throws his papers down, protesting, "There is no kissing allowed during or after the written baptism test. Now, who the fuck knows how to make dinner?"

"We're out of fish sticks, and I don't know how to cook," Wil says.

"You lived alone," Kyle points out.

"Yeah, and I also, like, bought fast food every night."

"Okay. We can do this, come on," Jody says, moving onto his next task, keeping his mind busy on sustaining what he still has.

The boys follow Jody into the kitchen, then start opening random cabinets.

"This is going to be like every Adam Sandler movie where he has to make a meal to show he's responsible, then his girlfriend's kids just end up eating Girl Scout cookies stuck in a pile of peanut butter," Kyle says.

"That movie sounds fuckin' dope," Jody says. "Maybe since all our instruments are being played by The Beatles in hell you can start doing movies after you get outta here."

"Some of the Beatles are still alive," Kyle mentions.

"How do you know that? We've been gone for like a week, and Paul McCartney looked exactly like Grandma Lennard the last time I saw him on TV. Are you really that confident he's still alive?"

Kyle is unable to argue the uncanny likeness Sir Paul bears to Grandma Lennard.

After locating a box of Ritz crackers and a can of squeezy cheese, Jody says, "I'll be upstairs watching TV," then leaves the kitchen.

"The TV only plays static," Kyle calls out.

"Have you ever been in this house before? Fucked up shit happens all the time here. That TV is waiting to show me, like, my future or other crazy ass tortures, like reruns of *iCarly*," Jody bellows back.

After Jody thumps upstairs, Wil turns to Kyle, and says, "Your brother is either going insane, is already insane, or he's headed back up to the bathroom to cry in between shots of squeezy cheese. No matter what his deal is, we honestly need to think about what the fuck we're going to do."

"Wait it out?" Kyle says, "The sun will be down in the next half hour, which means we have no chance of making it out of the Barrens tonight."

"Wait it out? Wait it out? Everyone is dead, Kyle."

"Jody's still alive."

"Jody is upstairs. Which, by the way, violates... rule... two? Four? I'm not sure on the exact number, but the 'Don't do horror movie shit' rule is currently being broken right now by the guy who wrote the rulebook, or- you know- the rule poster. Your brother is horror movieing hard right now. He's going off on his own just like Scrambles did, and he will die up there. The worst part is, I bet he knows all of this and he's doing it on purpose," Wil says.

"I think he would have picked a more glamorous last meal than pressurized canned cheese-product," Kyle says, going back to the cabinets.

"Think about it. Wasn't he being unusually abrasive when we were doing that test?"

"That's just Jody."

"That's beyond the normal Jody. I was wrong. He wasn't calling us faggots to make sure it was clear we're gay, he was doing it to doom himself. You heard him, Jody believes that God is love. He thinks that love will save us, not doom us. Think about it. Remember that Bible quote, 'Judge not, lest ye be judged first...'"

"...my niggas."

"Whoa! Not you too! Don't start a sibling rivalry on this," Wil says, pointing at Kyle.

"That's the end of the quote. Your 'Bible quote' is from the once popular DMX song, 'Look Thru My Eyes.'"

"Okay, you got me on that one, that's a great fucking song. In the same vein, think about it, what if we assume we're burning in hell, but Jody doesn't think we deserve to be? Would he... do something... to get us out of here? Did he just perform this ceremony to save us, while he..." Wil can't finish the thought.

"Let's go upstairs," Kyle says, slamming the cabinet door.

Wil grabs a candle from the counter, then hands Kyle one as well.

Kyle and Wil make their way up the stairs, only to find Jody in the fetal position on the floor of the Polaroid room, squeezing pressurized cheese onto crackers, in between sobs.

Wil marches into the room, angry that Jody's leading man persona left with Morgan. "You're just going to cry and watch static? That's how it's going to end for you? Getting fucked to death by a horse is more glamorous than th- wait. I take that back. Never mind," Wil sits down abruptly when he remembers that the Jersey Devil, according to lore, has horse-like features. After Mike's death, the shock of a horse related terror had been expensed. After Morgan's death, sexual impalement had already been checked off this list. This means if either event was to happen again, it would be the sequel. The rules for a horror sequel are that things have to be bigger, badder, and bloodier. None of those elements appeal to Wil.

Instantly disarmed, Wil and Kyle try a different way to comfort Jody.

Menace and crying and static- this is the looping soundtrack of a hell house.

Laughing and music and sex- that's what *was* heard when this place was a home.

"I don't mean to sound like a broken record-" Kyle starts to say, but Will interrupts, "-that's what you are."

"I'm trying to-" Kyle attempts to continue, but Wil intrudes again, "-we all make noise in different ways, I was thinking about it when we were getting those vinyl copies pressed up."

"You're just now realizing you're not like us?" Jody asks, sniffling, wiping his nose on his bandage.

"I'm not like you, Jody. You're right. I'm also not like Kyle," Wil admits. "When we got the first vinyl pressing in, I was staring at the record, and I saw Kyle. Kyle is a vinyl record."

"Not you too," Kyle whines. "Please, for me, hold it together."

"No. Listen," Wil says, turning to Kyle, "The record comes in a sleeve- that's the compression glove of music. When you take it out of the sleeve, there are these grooves that have specific meaning. It's a needle running in the groove to create the sound. Not in the Rob way, but that's why you were the only one who could understand what Hummingbird's deal was. That's why you can feel all of our pulses. You act like the big brother a lot, which was the cause of your fights with Jody. Even the newest vinyl still feels old. It reminds you of your parents. What are all those old records good for now that you can fit every song you've ever heard in your pocket? It seems silly. It seems almost like a novelty, yet vinyl is the only sector of music that's booming. The imperfections make the experience. There's a safety and earnestness to vinyl."

"Where's this coming from?" Kyle asks.

"And Rob? Rob was a tape player, you know, like a cassette player," Wil continues, "It was all laid out with him on long strings, no skipping, and you had to wait for the best part by sitting through the bullshit. You had to be patient, unless you speed him up and everything would go so fast, then you'd have to stop him and make sure he hadn't passed the moment you were looking for. He was... fragile. If the tape strip snaps, you can try to fix it, but it will never be the same. There was an inconsistency- each time you listen to the tape, it could play at a different speed depending on how much juice is left in the batteries. That was Rob."

"What are you?" Jody asks, accepting this tangent because it feels warm.

"I'm a jukebox. I play what I want, until I'm given an incentive to play something else. Even if I'm given the incentive, you're still going to have to wait for me to get my shit together. I sit there, pressed against the wall, and no one stands by me, they just press my buttons, then they leave."

"Now me. What am I?" Jody asks. He's stopped crying. Wil was looking for sympathy with the jukebox comment, but the good thing about a jukebox is that it's at your mercy if you select a new song.

"And me?" Jody asks, searching for a distraction.

"Jody, you're like one of those cloud streaming services. All our songs are stored in you and there's also a lot of garbage that totally sucks stored in you as well. With you, there's almost too much available and all of the craziest, most abrasive stuff anyone can imagine is included in the package.

With music, most of the time, people will find their "guys" then they keep them. A music fan will curate a collection. With you, they don't have to pick and choose, they don't have to curate anything. They get everything, all at once, the good and the bad. You don't look like you should be in Lies As Language, but our music was stored in you. We got away with making people believe you were pretty empty for a while."

"What was Morgan?" Jody asks, feeling better.

"Morgan was a Discman. She was a little bulky. That's not me being mean, that's just me stating a fact, don't get angry. The Discman was great for a generation of kids who didn't have a phone to hide behind. There were millions of kids that took out their Discmans and they escaped for a couple tracks when high school became too much. Morgan was a friend like that. You knew that you had her in your back pocket and that if you ever needed her to make you feel better, she wouldn't disappoint."

The statement ends there. A lot of men in the house used Morgan like a CD. They clicked her on, then spun her hard. They're all dead now, and so is Morgan, but Jody remains, and he realizes that this is a problem.

"Don't forget Cliff, dude," Jody warns, stomping on a telling silence.

"I didn't forget him," Wil says, then smiles, "Mike would be a clock radio. Most of the time a clock radio is off, or playing quietly and being ignored, but when the alarm is hit, everything is drowned out by a piercing scream. You have no choice but to address the noise. If the alarm is set to the radio, suddenly you're being given information that cannot be stopped. It's the shocking news reported on the hour with a distance that feels almost disrespectful. The clock radio is part of the reason you get out of bed in the morning and... ah.... when it's gone... your day gets screwed up. You become less precise and you start feeling like you know nothing about the world. You stop feeling like you'll wake up when you need to."

We think about Wil's careful review, but the contemplative silence is interrupted by a growl, combined with a popping crackle.

The noise is coming from outside the house.

Wil rushes to the window. Night has dropped onto the Barrens, but two snaking lights cut through the fresh dark as they make their way to the house.

Wil instantly recognizes the lights of the Jeep as they peek through the trees, and he welcomes them in the same way he did the first night in the Barrens.

"It's Jack," Wil says, with Kyle watching over his shoulder, like they were watching a thrilling baseball game tied in the ninth inning and the ball was sailing toward the big yellow post. Fair or foul?

"Jack came back for us?" Kyle says, but there's still a skepticism in his voice.

"Let's go," Wil says, crushing into Kyle, then rushing toward the door. Something falls out of Wil's pocket when he makes this swift move.

Wil turns and reaches for what he dropped, but Jody steps on his hand to stop him. "I'm going to lift my foot and you're going to leave the pictures on the ground," Jody informs Wil.

"Come on, dude," Wil says, yanking his hand out from under Jody's tread. "Let's go, we're fucking free," Wil says, then pauses, and with pleading eyes he asks the Lennard brothers to join him downstairs, "Please come with me. We survived it. We're free."

"Should we get inside Jack's Jeep? What's the right decision here?" Kyle asks his brother.

"No. That Jeep will not bring us to safety," Jody says, then he bends down and picks up the Polaroids that Wil dropped.

Wil lunges forward, then redirects the conversation, "Guys, come on. Where do you think the Jeep is headed?" then he amplifies his intensity, "We're going to give up and stay in the devil's house?"

"Yes. We stay," Jody says.

"Awesome, we're taking orders from the fucking ceiling now," Wil says, turning away, unable to look Jody in the eyes.

No one moves.

"Our only option is idling in the yard," Wil declares, pointing at the window, the rumble of an engine still present in the air.

"No one has left the Barrens so far. Why would we be able to leave?" Jody asks.

"I can't stay here another day," Kyle tells Jody.

Jody doesn't move, so Kyle takes the lead, and says, "You're coming with us."

Sometimes you have to listen to the voice on the record because it's managed to survive all these years, so Jody puts the photos in his pocket, then he accepts his fate.

The three men move quickly down the stairs, then run to the predictably open front door.

The cold of the house rushes into them as they look outside and see that the Jeep is gone. The Barrens are silent.

"Fuck!" Wil screams.

Jody slams the door shut, then blocks it before anyone can step outside.

Unwilling to believe that the Jeep was able to reverse that fast out of the Barrens in the sandy soil, Wil runs to the window that faces the graveyard. He looks into the darkness, while Kyle stands back, stewing in self-hate for even considering that we might be rescued. Jody was right. Kyle realizes that the plan was to lure Wil outside. This was the devil hissing into Wil's ear, *Your chariot awaits.*

We watch Wil stay frozen at the window, searching for the reflection of the headlights, listening for the crackle of a rolling tire- but all he finds is an ever-deepening night. He takes a step back from the window, then the Lennard brothers both walk into the living room.

Wil opens his mouth to say something at the exact moment a burst of blinding light from outside flashes across his face, then slides away in the direction of the front door.

"Move!" Kyle and Jody both yell as they rush to pull Wil away from the window.

We all lie on the green carpet, breathing heavily, and we watch the window. After a minute of silence, the flashlight beam cuts clean across the dusty living room again.

"Jody. Where's your torch?" Kyle whispers.

"Morgan took it," Jody whispers back.

There's a moment of silence as we try to convince ourselves that this is Jack checking in on us. Maybe he just parked his Jeep out of sight, and now he's peering inside Leeds house to see if we're in here. Once we've reasoned out the situation, we stand up, but the silence is interrupted by the sound of shattering glass, then a thump above us shakes the house.

"We need to get out of here. We need to get to the Jeep," Wil says.

"There is no Jeep," Kyle exhales.

"Wil, I need your help with something in the kitchen," Jody says.

Wil lets a, "Tah," of a laugh out, then he begins to say, "I'm not going to-" but he's cut off when he finds that the chafing noise he's hearing is not feet sliding across the carpet on the second floor, but instead Jody rubbing together the three Polaroids he picked up.

Without a choice, Wil grants Jody an exclusive meeting. "Stay here, don't get in front of any windows, and yell like a motherfucker if we're in trouble," Jody instructs Kyle, then he walks toward the kitchen with Wil following a couple steps behind.

Kyle sits on the edge of the coffee table and looks at the scuffed toes of his black Converse. He tries not to listen in on the conversation in the kitchen, but succumbs to a palpable paranoia about Jody asking Wil for help. Something or someone has forcibly entered the house, on the second floor, and Jody is holding a secret meeting with Wil. With Morgan gone, Jody could be going crazy. With Morgan gone, Jody could be seeking to be reunited with her, and he knows Wil will do anything to keep himself from being next. Kyle can't go upstairs because he's too afraid to face whatever has arrived for him. He has to distract himself until his brother and his friend return. He decides to use prayer to ease the moment.

Inside the kitchen, the scene is not so serene.

"Big deal," Wil says in a hushed tone, "I took some pictures. I mean, I didn't *take* them. We know who took them."

"Why were these pictures on the wall?" Jody asks, holding them up so Wil can see them clearly.

"I don't fucking know," Wil says, casually.

"Then why did you try to remove them? Why did you try to hide them?" Jody asks.

"Don't get all paranoid because your fat ass dead girlfriend fucked everyone in-" Wil's statement is cut short by Jody's elbow. Jody pins Wil to a cabinet, his forearm pressing on Wil's throat, just as Mike had done upstairs, outside of the coat closet.

Jody growls, "Don't you dare say that I'm overreacting about what's happening. I watched him throw up tar from the pits of hell, then I shot him in the chest. I pulled my dead girlfriend off this house, if you think this is anything but the rational reaction..."

Wil gasps, while his legs kick in a struggle, and Jody only releases him because there's no point in killing a man who only has hours to live.

Staggering, recovering, gulping, Wil says, "I was trying to keep these pictures from you. I didn't want to show you what you did. That was because of the concussion you hammered out into Abaddon. Yes, you did that Jody. You and your brother did that."

"Impossible," Jody says.

"Is it?" Wil coughs, "The rest of the pictures on the wall have been proven to be accurate. Why would these photographs be any different?"

"Then why take them off the wall?" Jody asks, "If Kyle and I did this, why remove them? Wouldn't it keep you alive longer to have our terrible acts on display?"

"I saw how you reacted to the Morgan pictures and I was protecting you. You protect people, and I need to be protected, so I returned the favor."

"Wil," Jody says, showing him the pictures, "There are people with burns in these Polaroids. People we know. You expect me to believe I did this? I mean when I tussle, it may appear as though my arms are emitting sparks and are on fire but that's just great showmanship. It's not the reality of the situation. So what happened here?"

Wil is silent.

Jody, deathly serious, says, "I want you to know that even with these pictures no longer on the wall, no one views you as innocent because it's impossible to photograph what's wrong with you."

"And it's oh-so-easy to photograph what's wrong with you, you vulgar fuck?"

"Did you do this to Punchcunt Love?"

Wil smiles, "I'm surprised they survived to be honest, but then again, it's going to be a lower quality of life for them. I gotta admit, they do look pretty metal though."

Instead of laughing at the joke, Jody shies away. Wil studies this reaction and begins to realize that Jody wasn't trying to get a confession-he wanted to be wrong. Jody needed these photographs to be fake. He burns to believe that the men still alive in this house deserve oxygen in their lungs and a residence above ground.

"Listen to me," Jody demands, grabbing Wil again, but this time it's in a moment of sincerity, not a moment of anger. "You are dead," Jody says, looking Wil in his eyes, "You're fucking dead and you know it. You're living on borrowed time. If I didn't..." Jody looks away as his head drops and his eyes seal tightly shut.

Wil watches this contorted pause, but it's not easy. He wants to look away too, but he gives Jody his undivided attention because Wil has no direction; he needs this guidance. Wil's instinct is to rebel against Jody, but only because he looks at Jody as a father figure, in the same way Hummingbird replaced his mother.

History repeated, Hummingbird chased after him when he was hurt, and she ended up in the same crimson bath. Wil knows he can't let Jody end up like his father- it can't happen again.

"You are dead," Jody repeats again, "And you can go out like a motherfucker, or you can quietly let it happen."

Wil grits his teeth, "I'm going to fight the devil until-"

"-then let it happen," Jody interrupts, "Let him do it, and he will lose."

"I'll be dead," Wil says.

"You're dead no matter what," Jody reminds him, "But if you depart Leeds house without a fight, you might have a chance to find peace. If you go out fighting, like you've been doing so much of your life, you're going to have to keep fighting for eternity."

Wil has nothing left to look forward to.

He will never return home.

He will never perform on stage again.

He will never be with Kyle.

He must find peace.

A hug is shared.

A decision is made.

Wil walks out of the kitchen, then through the dining room. He looks out the windows that face the backyard and he's relieved to find total darkness. He walks across the living room, then looks out the front windows and finds the same. He's relieved to look to his left and see Kyle, sitting on the edge of the coffee table, illuminated by a stubby candle that's dripping wax onto his pants.

"I'm going to bed," Wil says robotically, then he walks out of the living room, toward the stairs.

"No. Wil! You can't," Kyle says, springing up, sending hot liquid wax onto his glove, "What went on in the kitchen?"

"Jody talked some sense into me," Wil says, his delivery Mike-like.

"No. No," Kyle repeats his chorus again, "Jody doesn't talk sense into people. That's not what Jody does."

"He made a persuasive argument," Wil says, sounding like a man who has given up, leaving his future up to the fates.

"What argument did he make?" Kyle whispers in the dark house.

"Kyle, go to bed," Jody says, entering the living room.

Kyle rubs his face with exhaustion. He huffs. He quickly realizes that the only escape from Leeds House is to dream.

"Let's go to bed," Kyle says, then both men walk up the stairs to confront whatever has broken into this home.

LXXI. If These Walls Could Walk.

We shiver in the Polaroid room. The house is cold and quiet, like a windless winter night has overstepped its bounds and claimed early November for itself. The broken window allows the frigid Barrens to climb inside the room and grip us with a need to equalize the inner and outer. A hint of moonlight keeps things from being pitch black, since the TV no longer works, because it doesn't have to.

After doing a full search of every room in the house, Jody and Kyle had originally agreed to stay in the Polaroid room with Wil. We still aren't sure what broke the window, or who caused the thud, but there are too many open exits in this house to cover them all without splitting up. The basement has been declared off limits because it could trap us without an escape, so the Polaroid room seemed like the best room to sleep in because it was on the second floor and it was close to the window so if the Jeep returned, hopefully we would notice the lights on the ceiling, the noise of the revving engine, the crackling on the gravel, the snarl of a beast.

The room proved to be too cold for Jody and Kyle, so they had to relocate to the first floor, but we're still here in the Polaroid room with Wil. It's uncomfortable- the outside temperature creeping in doesn't bring memories of our mother cracking the window so the fall air will put us to sleep. It feels like being locked out of our house and having to sleep in the shed, in the middle of a blizzard.

Under the extra blanket the Lennard brothers brought him, Wil curls into a ball on the floor and tries to think about anything besides the cold.

That's when he hears the noise he burns for.

Tick-Tick-Tick.

When Wil would pass out on the floor of his empty house during the winter, the *Tick-Tick-Tick* would wake him up, and it was a sign that the temperature in the house had dropped low enough that the heat was finally kicking on. It was a soothing sound that promised a warmer, more comfortable future.

After a minute of this sporadic ticking, the room feels no different. It might actually feel a little colder. The moment of warm nostalgia causes Wil to fixate on the temperature. The heater ticks again, and Wil physically feels the tick this time.

The pipes must be in danger of freezing. That's the only reason a long dormant heater would kick on. This house is completely self-aware. This ticking heater wasn't a favor for Wil, it was a precautionary measure. Leeds house must continue to stand. Its work is not done.

Wil wiggles under the blankets, hesitantly making his way toward the ticking. It's normal for heaters to tick, but it's also normal for shit that explodes to tick.

Wil reaches out his hand and finds the metal heater that runs along the wall- it's as cold and dead as the rest of the house.

Tick-Tick-Tick.

Still no heat.

Wil takes his lighter out of his pocket, then lights it. As the small flame burns, *Tick-Tick-Tick*, one.. two... three... small pebbles appear on the floor. The heater is spitting them out, like a *Flintstones* slot machine.

Wil reaches for one of the pebbles.

The heater falls quiet, like the rest of the house.

Wil studies the pebble, and when he realizes that it's not a rock, he feels a ping that he mistakes as fear. As another ping hits his back, Wil acknowledges that fear, no matter how powerful, does not physically strike you.

Facing the frozen heater, without turning around, Wil reaches back to collect what hit him. His fingers glide across the floor until he finds the tiny projectile. It feels wet when he scoops it up. Wil lights his lighter, and immediately sees that his singed fingertips are bathed in a bright red, and they're holding an adult's molar. This is certainly not a boy's tooth. This is not the remains of someone who has stepped out of a photograph on the wall. Wil moves his lighter toward the floor and sees that all around him are fractured teeth that are distinctly human and appear freshly harvested.

The teeth struck him on the back- they didn't fall out of the heater- they were bouncing off of it. Wil isn't facing whoever is tossing this gore.

Slowly, Wil turns around, and another tooth strikes him in the chest.

In the doorway is a silhouette of a man.

The flame of the lighter is burning Wil's finger, but he needs this light, and the rest of his body is frozen, so he accepts the pain.

The once-owner of the teeth steps forward. It's Jack. His chin is slathered in blood, and his face is gaunt and white.

Jack opens his mouth and shows that he only has a handful of teeth left. Wil opens his fist and drops a handful of teeth to the floor.

Tick-Tick-Tick.

Jack's mouth remains wide open, and a cold voice slides out. At no time does Jack's mouth move to make these words, his throat is merely the speaker cone for the information. *You stayed,* the voice says, then Jack closes his mangled fist and delivers a hammering punch to his own face. The bloody shell reacts to the hit by holding his jaw, then reaching into his mouth to collect another fractured tooth.

"Jack. What the fuck happened to you?" Wil asks. There's a second of complete darkness in the room as Wil slides his lighter into his other hand so that the burn on his thumb can get some relief. As he does this, he's struck with another piece of tooth.

Lighting the lighter again, Wil asks, "Leeds, is that you?" knowing that Jack is no longer inside this vessel.

Jack's gaping mouth projects out, *You were expecting a dragon?*

"Why are you doing this?" Wil asks the New Jersey Devil.

Your fault again, is the simple response, and in a smooth motion, the man who was once Jack unsheathes a hunting knife from his belt, then runs it across his own neck.

"No!" Wil screams out.

Jack's head flops back. *Your fault again,* his neck wound burps, then the slice opens wider, spraying an ugly red and black painting onto the floor.

Jack's nearly beheaded body stalks forward, creating an obvious exit out of the broken window.

Wil removes his finger from the thumb pad of the lighter, once again plunging the room into darkness. He makes an educated guess on where Jack is, then bursts forward, dodging in the opposite direction to pass him and reach the hallway. Will slips by the beast, untouched.

Once out of the Polaroid room, Wil adjusts his sprint so he stays on the second floor and isn't pushed down the stairs. He pumps his arms in the darkness toward a light emanating from Behringer's writing room. The Lennard brothers must still be awake. Jody's mace will save us.

Wil slides into the illuminated room, then seals himself inside. He presses his back to a bookshelf and puts his feet against the door.

When he looks to his left, he doesn't find the Lennards. He finds a man that he recognizes, but does not know. Next to Wil, on the floor, a book lays face down, and on the book's dust jacket is a black and white picture of the man who's sitting in the corner of the writing room.

We watch as R.F. Behringer, a past-his-prime author, sits at his large wooden desk and scribbles frantically in a notebook. A stack of novels with their spines all boasting Behringer's name sit atop the desk, almost building a protective wall around the author. A lone candle provides the light for the room.

"You're dead," Wil says, his feet still pressed against the door.

Instead of a response from Behringer, Wil hears a child laugh.

The tip of Behringer's pencil breaks from the jolt of panic that shoots through his body as he reacts to the giggle.

We hear the laugh again, louder, then numerous children laugh simultaneously.

Hi, Mr. Behringer, a young boy's voice pierces through the room, but there's no boy in the room. Slowly, the source of the voice reveals himself, stretching out from the plaster in the wall to Wil's left. The boy is bone thin. His hair is molded stiff, like a Ken doll. His movements are labored, and jerky, and frail. He's pure gray, except for those eyes. Those piercing red eyes.

Wil knows this boy. The last time they were face to face, the boy was crouched in the closet, hiding.

When Behringer sees that the boy is approaching him, he stands up bolt straight, knocking over his chair.

In his periphery, Wil sees more movement across from the windows. It's another boy stepping out of the wall. This apparition is composed of the same elements as the boy speaking with Behringer, but his features are different. This is a different boy, a separate boy. Both of these boys are victims, prisoners of the Polaroids.

Wil knows there will be more. The wall in the Polaroid room is evidence of this.

From above a bookcase, another red-eyed plaster boy begins to appear, stretching out from the wall, detaching, landing on his feet, then beginning his jerky movements toward the author.

The horror of this situation increases as yet another plaster boy begins to separate himself from the wall behind Behringer.

The Plaster Boys, as a collective, move closer to Behringer, one of them beckoning, *Let's play. We can do whatever we want. There are no parents here to stop us.*

Let's be friends, a plaster boy demands.

This will be fun, you're just going to have to trust us, another plaster boy says, then bares a gray toothy smile.

Trust us, a stocky plaster boy says in a light tone.

Trust us? a tall, skinny plaster boy asks.

Trust us, a limping plaster boy requests.

A very small plaster boy, directly behind Behringer, leans forward and whispers, *Don't trust us.*

Behringer rips open a desk drawer and searches through a pile of papers, candles, and lube. He uncovers a rope that sits at the bottom of the drawer, while boys continue to ooze out of the walls.

A plaster boy watches Behringer with the rope, and says, *We don't need toys. We'll have fun, just you and me.*

And me, another plaster boy says, separating from the wall by the bookcase.

And me, a plaster boy behind Behringer says, and this causes the old author to stumble a spin.

And me, it continues...

Quickly tying a noose, then hoisting himself on the desk, Behringer loops the rope around the rafter above his head. The plaster boys, in greater frequency, melt out of the wall, filling the room.

"I won't let you do this. I won't give you the satisfaction," Behringer announces in a cracked voice.

It feels good to make people feel good. Don't you want to make us feel good? a plaster boy asks.

Behringer steps off the desk, and his arms instantly reach up to grasp the noose that's squeezing his neck- just as the mob of plaster boys reach up and begin to tear at Behringer's flesh.

When the man that was hanging ends up as scattered pieces on the floor, one of the plaster boys turns to Wil and says, *Your fault again.*

LXXII. Wil Chapman.

"Pathetic. You sit here, in your comfortable climate-controlled cocoon, and you judge me?

How are you any better than me?

I'm dead because I sat idle, watching the world burn, only taking up action when I wanted to spit on the flames. And here you are, grasping onto your little novel, doing the exact same thing.

Ugly Wil, says the passive observer who doesn't own a mirror.

Do you remember how the problems in Leeds house started? A bunch of slack-jawed pineys got all crazed up and vilified a person to the point she birthed an amalgam of her mistakes and their hate. That sounds really familiar, doesn't it? I'm not saying you made me this way, but I felt your hate and it affected the people you followed through that house. Did you enjoy observing the carnage, you sweatpants wearing gawkers? Don't think I didn't notice you dumping your own insecurities onto me. That wine I drank? It tasted just like your disappointment. Delicious. You needed me to act the way I did, so I followed your instructions. It was easier for you to blame me than to get to know me. It was easier to hate me than to hate the person I remind you of. It was comfortable for you to believe that the worst thing in that house was a person. By making me the evil force in Leeds house, you could feel safe every time I wasn't in the room. I looked like the type of boy you're conditioned to be afraid of. That tattooed pale goth kid, dressed in a way that stands out. Ohhh, I was such an outsider. Profiling people like that makes you feel safe, doesn't it? Here's the bad guy, wearing a bad guy uniform so you know to keep away from him. Don't associate with the bad guy. Everything will be fresh pancakes and Eskimo kisses if you avoid the odd boy.

Look at you- suffocating from your need to escape, combined with your underlying fear of that final, permanent escape. You weren't mentioned in detail in this novel because you had no impact on what happened. The fact is, you could leave Leeds house whenever you wanted to, but so far, you haven't. Our deaths are entertainment to you.

What was your time outside of Leeds house like? You've been following us for days without being pulled away. Your life doesn't seem very demanding. You've made it this far in our story, but you're alive. You're doing better than I did. Awesome job. Congrats. Guess what you've won? More hours of self-loathing and desperate escapism. Better recharge your non-exploded cell phone so you don't miss the zero messages you currently have waiting for you.

I left Punchcunt burning in a car for what they did; I watched them at their most desperate. You left me in the devil's house for what I did; you watched me at my most desperate.

Now I'm going to watch you. Let's see how you like it.

If you think that my passivity in the face of awful acts is disgusting, then why did you passively read every word of this tragedy, while the same exact things are happening around you? They might not be happening in your home, but I'd be willing to wager you don't have to look far to find some examples close by.

The first time I stared one of Behringer's victims in the eyes, I realized that the worst evil doesn't come from the rude or the crude- it's the quiet and the secretive that are carrying out the devil's bidding. I jumped back and I shut that door when I saw the boy in the closet, but in that moment, I knew that no one could save me. I quickly accepted that the door would reopen again and again.

I could sense you awaiting my damnation as you followed me.

Cunty You: *He doesn't belong here. Why is he still alive?*

The fact is, I made it as far as I did because the other people on this journey were worse than me. Some of those people, you probably related to. You don't want to be one of the people Leeds house doomed, but I think you know if you were faced with that open door you wouldn't walk out of the Barrens either...

So here we are, and the question becomes, did the domino chain end with me, or are there still two dominoes ready to fall? I didn't waste time pulling Mike away from the tree because I knew he was the first domino. Mike, at his core, was filled with a more aggressive hate than I carried on my worst day. My hate was passive- I stepped over the bodies, while Mike would get down and stare into their dead eyes. Hummingbird didn't even like herself, so how could she be saved? And you knew I'd outlive the whore. That was a no-brainer. Jody seemed all surprised. I hope you weren't. Say what you want about Ms. Leeds, but her boy is a visionary when it comes to creating hurt. He's why you stayed to watch.

You're no better than me and you enjoyed watching the Jersey Devil work. Even after hearing how guilty you are for indulging in all of this, I bet you'll keep reading until the end."

LXIII. The Lennard Brothers.

We watch as Jody finishes his replica of the flags that Morgan used to make. He is getting better at it. The green blanket is getting smaller.

Jody carries out the flag and affixes it on a stick that was driven into the ground over Wil's grave.

"I don't even remember what he asked us to do for his funeral. He told us his last wish, and I was too focused on myself to even give him my attention," Kyle admits, wiping his compression glove across his forehead and only coming away dirtier for it.

Jody doesn't respond to this comment, he merely follows his brother back to Leeds house.

"It's time to pack up some supplies and walk away," Kyle says, stepping onto the porch.

We pass through the open front door, and as soon as we reach the living room, we're greeted by a pile of wine bottles on the coffee table.

"There's the rest of the blanket," Jody says, pointing to the green rags that have been stuffed into the mouths of the bottles. These are the flags for the Lennard brothers.

Jody walks over to the bottles and touches one of the rags, then brings his finger up to his nose.

"Gasoline?" Kyle asks.

Jody nods, then looks back down, and sighs, "Fuck. There's a card."

A tan envelope stands between the bottles, and in copperplate writing on the front, is the inscription, "To The Lennards."

"Don't even open it," Kyle sighs.

Jody picks up the card and opens it. As he reviews the message, he mumbles, "What the fuck is this? A riddle?"

"What's it say?" Kyle relents.

Trying not to give the words weight, Jody reads aloud, "If you burn it down, you'll never get out."

Kyle seems energized by this, "Then we'll just do it from the outside."

Jody holds up a finger. There's more. "If you bring these bottles outside, you'll never get out."

"Why put all this shit here, then tell us exactly what will happen with it?" Kyle asks. This game has become a series of inevitable conclusions and pre-decided outcomes that have a single X factor of free will.

Jody begins to pace, "Let's take an inventory of how truly fucked our shit is. We stay here, we die in a fire. We leave, we die in the woods. We have no clue how to summon a portal, so inter-dimensional travel is out of the question. Even if we find another way to go back in time, we run the risk of going too far, to that period of time where white people were killed by regular shit, like polio. I'm sorry, I'd rather die in New Jersey than get polio, and that's saying a lot. You have to keep in mind that back in the day tons of people died from polio and not just because their wheelchairs got bumped backward at a pool party."

This joke is so vivid that the slapstick image plays out in Kyle's head, and his mind chooses Audrey's pool as the setting for the polio pool party.

"That's it!" Kyle says.

"We go back in time and drown anyone who has polio? The virus is very contagious, so I-"

"-Ouija," Kyle says.

"No. It's pointless. There aren't any babes left in the house."

"I need you to make a board, like the one you used in the hot tub. We'll try to talk to Leeds through the Ouija, and maybe he can tell us what he wants. We've literally accomplished nothing while trying to solve this mystery on our own, so let's ask the man himself."

"Kyle, we don't even have a hot tub," Jody says, shaking his head.

"Do you really think it would be that hard to create a hot tub in this house? Scorching water shoots out of every tap."

"To be honest, the hot tub isn't crucial to the process, I just like looking at tits," Jody admits.

"I know. Come on," Kyle says, then he leads his brother down into the basement.

Jody rolls up the sleeves of his black hoodie, and the search for the perfect Ouija board begins. Jody, a man taught by the TV, seems to be treating this project like he's hosting his own DIY show. He brings his brother over to the pieces of scrap wood on the floor, then proceeds to explain, "You need a completely flat surface for the Ouija- that's the most important requirement. One knot, one gouge, and it's the difference between the Ouija telling you to 'diet' and the Ouija telling you to 'die.' Both of those things suck a dick, but one is a little worse than the other, so clarity is important."

Kyle finds a plank of wood that looks perfect, and Jody accepts it with an excited appreciation. "Normally, we'd cut this down a bit to make it more manageable, but with a bigger piece like this, it's more likely that we can keep it from levitating and smashing us in the face. If this board breaks our noses and causes our blood to seep into the pores of the wood, then it will bond us to the devil, which will be a pretty shitty way to spend eternity."

"That happens?" Kyle asks.

Jody looks up from the board, furrows his eyebrows, then says, "Sure as fuck it does. Why do you think the board game company makes their boards out of cardboard?"

"It's cheaper?" Kyle mumbles.

"Yeah, cheaper than dealing with lawsuits from sorry looking motherfuckers who got hit in the face with a piece of wood, then started eating babies," Jody says, then seamlessly transitions to the next step, "Okay, now we need a cipher eye."

"Oh no. What type of animal is a cipher?" Kyle asks, unwilling to make a sacrifice.

After a brief review of the surrounding area, Jody selects a triangle shaped piece of glass, then draws a circle in the center of the triangle with a Sharpie. This way, there will be no mistake about what the board is trying to tell us. "This is our cipher eye," Jody announces.

"We chose a board despite the fact that it might hit us in the face, and now we're adding a dangerous-looking piece of glass into the equation? Who's to say that your glass cursor won't shoot into my throat?" Kyle asks, his voice registering up an octave.

"Whoa, watch your terminology," Jody warns, "A cursor? Really? I think a 'curser' started all the shit in this house. Let's call it the de-cursor."

Kyle thinks about it, accessing a memory of the fat goth, and he says, "It might actually be called a planchette."

"Who the fuck is Planchette?" Jody asks.

Kyle shakes his head and finds himself wishing the Ouija was already finished so he would have someone to vent his frustrations to.

"We need to mark this bitch up," Jody says, holding the board as though he's displaying it to an audience. He takes the Sharpie out again, then says, "Now, we're still going to want to make sure that this is waterproof, even if we don't have a kick ass hot tub because my hands are going to start sweating when shit gets real," Jody says. Kyle's dirt caked compression gloves will continue to absorb any sweat that rises around his skin grafts.

"Everyone has their own preference about how to style their Ouija, but there are some basics that you must have," Jody says, like a bigoted Martha Stewart. "You're gonna want a 'Yes' and a 'No' because demons are lazy as fuck and a lot of your questions are going to have one of those two answers."

"Wait, is that also why you gave us True or False questions on our baptism test?" Kyle asks, all of this melding together.

"Angels are also lazy," Jody explains. "They'd be okay with me saying that. It's well documented in various paintings and ceilings that they're always flying around playin' fifes, instead of correcting baptism tests."

Kyle points at the board, then reviews the layout plan, "So in the middle is the alphabet, then the first 9 numbers under that?"

"Correct, and at the bottom, you put 'Goodbye' so you don't end up just playing with yourself."

"That seems kinda finite, don't these instruments of evil prefer the open door policy?" Kyle asks.

"I'm not totally sure. I think that's only in real estate. It's probably an afterlife courtesy to have a 'Goodbye' so that you know that you can conjure another demon. It reduces confusion in the demon world. Sort of like a sock on the door while you're fucking. No sock on the door- come right in and join me in conversation. Sock on the door- my dick is on 'do not disturb' status. Without the sock system it's hard to tell if you're fantasizing about someone's presence or if you're sitting with a big titted Ouijastank," Jody says.

Kyle busies himself with the board so he doesn't have to respond to his brother. He finds another Sharpie and draws a sun in the left corner and a moon in the right, next to the "Yes" and "No" respectively.

"What do you think about my additions?" Kyle asks, looking at the markings on the board.

"Very occult. I'll pray for your soul," Jody says, then brushes Kyle out of the way so he can begin the lettering.

Kyle added his personalization to the board because this has to be a collaborative project. If Jody is going to add the letters, Kyle had to add the imagery. They need to be even for the first time ever- older brother and younger brother, lead singer and drummer, accident victim and victim of the accident- all of it has to smooth out to a calm stasis. The Lennard brothers have to be so united that if the devil wants to strike one of them down, he'll have to be strong enough to take out both.

Whether this Ouija board works or not isn't important. Kyle appreciates spending time with his brother on this fall afternoon because he knows that it could be his last opportunity for a moment like this, not just with Jody, but with anyone. There's a saying that you don't know what you have until it's gone, but Kyle has lost so much recently that he can now appreciate everything in the moment.

One or both of the Lennard brothers will be dead by sunrise tomorrow.

Kyle's plan is to use the Ouija to make a request. He wants to be taken next.

Jody has always been the only one in the house with complete faith, and Kyle knows that the way to keep his brother alive is to rule out his option of becoming a martyr.

With a finished and dried Ouija board, along with a gleaming glass de-cursor, the Lennard brothers walk upstairs. Before Jody steps into the kitchen, he looks both ways, then quickly flanks to the right, making his way down the wood paneled hallway. He could have sworn that when he opened the basement door, he saw Morgan, in her raptor t-shirt, on her tiptoes, reaching for a high shelf. Jody isn't as stupid as he makes himself sound, so he refuses to entertain this mirage for more than a single stomach flipping moment.

After passing by the open front door, and the wine bottles, Jody places the board in the center of the dining room table, then the Lennard brothers take their seats. Kyle sits with his back to the backyard, Jody faces him with his back to the front yard.

"This is good. Usually, we'd be on the same side of the table to Ouija it up, but this way we can warn each other if we're about to get eaten by the Jersey Devil," Jody says.

Kyle adjusts in his chair so he has a full view of Jody's blind spots.

Jody lets out a big exhale, then looks at his brother. "Get ready to lift the veil," he says, then adds, "No homo."

Kyle shakes his head, and asks, "Who are these jokes for? It's only me and you left."

"I don't want things to change between us just because we've buried every human being we've seen since we left our gig," Jody says, as though he's doing Kyle a favor.

"We didn't bury Jack," Kyle points out.

"He's the body that we'll leave in Leeds house to get people to search for the sick fuck who could do such a thing," Jody says. "His wounds are self-inflicted, they'll see that. It might just keep us out of prison, if we escape this one."

The brothers place their hands on the glass de-cursor.

Kyle closes his eyes and waits for Jody to take the lead.

"How will you see if a devil is going to strangle me from behind with your eyes shut, dude?" Jody asks.

"I... I didn't really think that was an actual possibility," Kyle says, opening his eyes.

"That is a very real risk during Ouija, very real. How the fuck do you think they ended up selling so many of these motherfuckers? A boy uses the Ouija board. The boy gets strangled to death because his brother was closing his eyes like he was taking a fucking bubble bath. The strangled boy's brother buys his own Ouija to contact his now dead brother and apologize. The other brother gets strangled, then his parents find him, and they buy a Ouija, but the mom closes her eyes, so on and so on. It's a cycle, Kyle. You don't have to be a Ouijalogist to figure that out."

"Sorry. I'll keep my eyes open," Kyle says.

Both brothers lightly rest their fingertips on their last resort, then they begin.

"Leeds Devil, we summon you," Jody says.

"That's not even a question, that's a statement," Kyle whispers, "How's he going to respond to that? We didn't add a 'cool' section to the board."

"Leeds Devil, we've summoned you?" Jody asks the board, his voice metering up.

The de-cursor doesn't move.

Both brothers straighten their posture.

"Leeds, are you in this room?" Kyle asks. He closes his eyes for a moment. He flinches when the face from the window flashes behind his eyes.

"Did you kill my girlfriend?" Jody asks, his neck turning like it was trying to keep the words from leaving his throat.

The de-cursor moves up to the sun, indicating, "Yes."

Jody lets out a sigh, as this answer comes with a sting.

"Did she kill herself?" Kyle asks. He needs to know the truth. How responsible was Wil for the destruction of that beautiful creature?

The de-cursor moves away from the Yes, but stops at the center of the board and vibrates. It can't select Yes or No. Kyle wants to take his hands off the piece of glass, but he doesn't. He wants to close his eyes to squeeze out the tears, but he doesn't. He remains alert and makes sure that no devils are about to strangle Jody.

"If you're moving this, Kyle, I swear..." Jody says, fingers jittering like he had placed them on the back of a vibrating cell phone.

Kyle shakes his head no and grits his teeth.

"Will we walk out of Leeds House alive?" Jody asks.

The de-cursor continues trembling.

"Will we make it home, alive, to our homes in Connecticut?" Jody clarifies.

The de-cursor continues trembling.

"Will one of us make it home?" Kyle asks quickly, and both brothers' arms are pulled toward the sun. Speaking with the Leeds Devil was supposed to raise dead friends from the grave. It was supposed to cause each and every victim of Behringer to surround the house. It was supposed to create an elevator and that elevator was supposed to spill blood. A young strong-chinned boy was supposed to saw off his hand. A guy in a spray painted Shatner mask was supposed to power walk through the kitchen. A 1960's hockey goalie who sucks at swimming was supposed to bring his J Crew sweatered mom for a visit to the Pine Barrens. The walls were supposed to bleed flies, and Buffy was supposed to be fleeing pale Asian ghost children. That's how this story is supposed to end.

Instead, it ends like it began.

The Lennard Brothers will have to kick the living shit out of each other.

Four hands remain frozen on the de-cursor as both men know what must be done.

How do you kill yourself when you're totally pre-occupied with trying to stop the person who matters most in your life from killing himself? That is the final question, and it can't be answered with a 'Yes' or 'No.'

There are five flags in the yard.

Six Flags stopped a complete massacre.

Kyle's hands fly off the de-cursor, then he quickly flips the dining room table in hopes of pinning Jody to the ground. Jody, expecting this, leaps away from the toppling table, de-cursor still in his trembling hand, then he gives chase after a fleeing Kyle.

Jody has always felt that running is fucking terrible, but running a short distance, knowing that you can stop soon, is an adrenaline pumping ride.

With a clock-like predictability in a land without clocks, the front door is open and as soon as Kyle reaches it, Jody tackles him onto the stone porch.

An outsider would think that Jody was trying to kill Kyle; an insider would know Hummingbird's razors are upstairs, Mike's shotgun is in the piano bench, Wil's noose is upstairs, and the lightning rod is on the roof. Jody pushed his brother out onto the porch because, outside, there's nothing that Kyle can use to commit the ultimate sin.

Both brothers are already out of breath, not from the run, but from the crushing pressure. Kyle remains on his hands and knees, while Jody breaks away, cursing, kicking the chaise lounge on the stone porch.

The Lennard brothers look at each other and both desperately try to figure out another way for this to end.

Jody will have to kill himself for Kyle to live.

Kyle will have to kill himself for Jody to live.

Both men know that they're basing their actions on a board and a piece of glass meant to replicate a department store product that's almost exclusively consulted at tween sleepovers and used to confirm the identity of a cute boy's crush.

"You're the one who will survive," Kyle says, huffing gasps, hoping that these will be his last breaths, "Once I'm gone, Jody, run. There's nothing that can stop you."

The clouds collect in the sky to watch what's about to happen on the porch of this cursed home.

Jody has to deal with the very real fact that if he kills himself, he risks an eternity in hell, and if he doesn't kill himself, his life will become a living hell.

Jody has already lost Morgan.

Jody has already baptized Kyle.

Sensing a wavering man, Kyle, in that soothing voice from those Lies As Language songs, says, "Jody, you're the one who's going to get out of here alive."

"Why me?" Jody asks, like he had been diagnosed with a life-threatening disease. In a way, he has been, but the life being threatened is not his own.

"Because you got us here," Kyle says.

"Come on. I'm not making cliché sacrifices to the devil so that I can-"

"-no. Jody. You don't understand," Kyle says. Normally he would approach his brother to have this conversation, but Kyle feels a sincere need to keep a defined distance. "You got us here. You pushed me into the band and it was the best thing to ever happen to me. You wrote our songs and they've saved hundreds of kids. You brought Lies As Language onto that stage, and into the limelight, so you, Jody, were a man amongst boys and not because of your age." After he says this, Kyle has to look away because this review of his brother's selfless significance was something that Kyle didn't fully grasp until he verbally reviewed it just now. He realizes just how lucky he is, despite knowing that this is where it ends, on the porch of a house that has brought him so much pain. In the time leading up to arriving at this house, and while inside this house, Jody created so much good. Some of these good things, he let Kyle take the credit for. Hummingbird was valuable. Morgan was valuable. These girls taught Kyle that just because he was center stage, it doesn't mean he's always the main focus. Kyle has been living off Jody's soul, and it's time he returned the favor so that Jody can do the celebrated living he was already behind schedule to enjoy.

With experience and selflessness coloring his eternal fall, Jody says, "I'm not the one who walks away, do you know how many awful things I've said in my life?"

"A couple of curse words? That's what you think you'll be cut down here for?" Kyle asks, hoping that Leeds hears how petty a damning over saying "damn" is.

"A couple of curses trapped the New Jersey Devil here," Jody reminds Kyle.

"Curses can be broken," Kyle says, eyeing the open door.

"So can the body of a man who was unable to stop what happened here. So can the man who insisted on acting like a boy his entire life," Jody responds, condemning himself.

"You really don't see yourself like everyone else does, do you?" Kyle marvels, shaking his head as he walks toward his brother.

"I don't think I have what it takes to walk away from this," Jody admits- a confession that he truly believes.

Kyle doesn't have any plans for a life after Leeds House. Jody does. This is a sign.

"Jody, if anyone was going to get out of here, it was always going to be you. You were the one who always picked a path, or approached the stranger, or-"

"- do you want to know what I really saw that night, Kyle?"

"Which night?"

"The night I approached the man in the woods," Jody says, and the tension from the Ouija returns.

"What did you see?" Kyle asks, his voice airy, as he remembers that there was no answer to this looming question, because so many other questions gained precedence over it.

Jody steps forward, now only a foot away from his little brother, and he calmly explains, "You saw me, my approach was careful, and I made sure that my torch was directly pointed at the person. But, uh, it's weird... as I was walking, I only saw my shadow. I don't know how that works, but the person... he didn't have a shadow. The closer I got, the more alone I felt with the person. I didn't hear you, and if you were following behind me, I didn't notice. I was just moving toward this person- this being- and he got clearer and clearer as I got closer. Eventually, my shadow extended onto his black clothes, but the light stayed on his back. Then, he turned, and that electronic screech pierced out as I looked my corpse in its milky white eyes. Do you understand? When the figure turned, I faced myself."

Kyle puts his hand to his mouth and lets out rhythmic breaths that sound like "Ha, ha," but carry none of the joy and all of the uncontrollability of a laugh.

"Do you remember what he was wearing that night?" Jody asks.

Kyle shakes his head no, but not because he doesn't remember.

"Look at me!" Jody demands.

Kyle turns to his brother and reviews a now-familiar all black outfit.

"That figure was standing in the path that I'd take to get out of here, Kyle. I'm not meant to leave this house, you are."

"Wil was killed because he was gay, Jody. *I* am gay," Kyle says, trembling, unable to sever his mind from a split second image that screeched with terror and revealed the face of his dead brother.

"That's not why Wil was murdered," Jody says. He uses the words "murdered" instead of framing it as a suicide. "Wil was a narcissist. Wil was a sadist. Wil was only concerned with himself," Jody says.

"Wil was a homosexual, and he was killed because of it," Kyle screams.

"He was a sick fuck," Jody screams back. He mentions this partly to save his brother and partly in the hope that the soft, sandy soil will be pierced by a hand, as Wil rises from his grave to get revenge on Jody. The selfish fuck was certainly capable of perfectly timed entrances when he was alive, why should his death change anything?

Kyle's demeanor follows the clouds and he explains slowly, unsteadily, quivering, "There are all those angry assholes, with all those signs, and all those websites, and all those laws... against people like me, against people like Wil. So, are you really shocked, Jody? Everyone has been telling me how wrong I am, and I know you've heard them, so why are you surprised about this outcome? You always refused to believe the ugly people and their ugly ideas, and I love you for that, but Jody, stop and read the signs, I'm not walking out of the Barrens alive," Kyle says, crumbling.

"You're not making sense. Those men with those signs that say horrible shit like, 'GOD HATES FAGS,' those men are campaigning for Leeds. They're why I won't leave. God doesn't hate fags... because *God does not hate*. I clearly haven't shown you the God that I know if you believe the selfish warnings of threatened people with nothing but a poster board of misinterpretations. I know Him, Kyle, and my ugly words are the problem, not your love of a man who is waiting for you at home. No one is waiting for me at home. The people who are waiting for me are in the ground now. You haven't been paying attention to what's happening here if you think otherwise. The chips you're leveraging against yourself aren't a big enough pot for the devil to collect on."

"Jody?" Kyle rushes forward, but Jody doesn't see this because his vision is liquid.

"Yeah," Jody sniffs.

"This is the last time you and I will ever speak. One of us is going to die today. We have to be careful about what we say because anything we say could easily be our last words to each other."

Taking Kyle's words into account, Jody tells his brother, "You won't die because of who you are."

"I will."

"You're wrong."

"Listen to me. Wil came onto me. Do you understand? He died because of it, and I only lived this long because I said no!" Kyle screams, and he points at the ground because he believes that is where he belongs. "I said no and that's the reason I'm alive and it kills me!" Kyle screams, "...because I should be right where he is."

Jody shakes his head for what feels like a thousand refusals, then he verbally denies Kyle's assessment, "No. You don't deserve that fate."

"According to the rules of this game, yes, I do."

Just over Kyle's shoulder large drops of water start to fall from the sky like pearls sliding off a thousand necklaces. When this rain hits the thirsty sand, it bounces, then comes to rest atop the earth. It appears as though the rain refuses to enter this cursed ground.

"Do you want to know why Wil is dead?" Jody asks, the noise of the downpour giving the moment a surreal, dreamlike quality.

Kyle's eyes are covered by his hair, and when he slides his bangs to the side, he finds himself staring directly at three Polaroids of badly burned men.

"Wil could have saved Punchcunt, and he did nothing. So *that* is why Wil is dead, Kyle. Not because of a preference he didn't choose. Not because he was open about his feelings," Jody yells.

"You're lying so he'll take you," Kyle says.

"Tell me that we caused these injuries." Jody says, holding out the Polaroids of the men that Wil didn't bother to help.

Feeling guilty, disgusted, and disappointed, Kyle looks away. Handling the situation like Jody would, he says, "Maybe we can record a song for their benefit compilation."

"Don't be stupid," Jody says, then he lets a pause hang just long enough before adding, "There's no money in benefit records."

Kyle lets out a little laugh.

The sky streaks with dramatic, heavy, glistening rain that bounces off the sandy soil around the house, and drops onto the porch roof with a sound that almost resembles a twinkle. Jody and Kyle take a moment to review this downpour; each man looks beyond his brother and finds a turbulent world.

"Listen to me, Kyle," Jody says, grabbing his brother's shoulders. Kyle tenses, but he doesn't slip away from the grip. Jody looks in Kyle's eyes and tells him, "You will walk out of this forest because you have someone to walk back to. Everyone I was living for has been taken from me. Everyone I was here to protect is gone, so let me protect you. Let me protect my little brother. Morgan asked me why I didn't take credit for the lyrics, and the truth is, I never once considered ruining the illusion because every set we played, you gripped the mic with those fucking gloves, keeping my secret. You saved my life, so let me save yours. I'm not sure what the score is between us, but I know what the score is between myself and the devil, between us and God and, I assure you of this, God will protect you as you walk out of these Barrens because you were never able to have the life you deserved. I've had a fantastic life, Kyle. I found passion in music. I found success on the stage. I found love, multiple times, upstairs in Behringer's bed- I mean, I totally wrecked those sheets, probably forever. And I found my brother in these woods. I've lived a full life, Kyle, and you're just starting yours. I love you and I've never told you that and now that I have, I'm ready."

Jody lets go of his brother as the weather becomes static around Leeds house.

Moving past Kyle, Jody walks to the edge of the porch, transfixed by the glimmering shower. "It's glass," he marvels.

With enough heat and enough pressure, you can turn sand to glass. This storm is the only answer to the final question. Jody reaches into the pocket of his black pants, then says, "I need you to do something for me."

"Walk out of here with you?" Kyle asks.

"Please lie and tell people I was 27," Jody says, then he lifts the de-cursor and quickly runs the sharp edge of the glass across his neck. Jody makes an airy gasp, drops the de-cursor, then dark red blood begins to spit just above the collar of his hoodie.

Kyle rushes over so fast that he catches Jody on the way down. He removes the gloves from his hands, then presses his imperfect palms on his brother's neck. Short, choked sobs escape from Kyle like they were arterial spray. He pants like a dog, as two uniform trails of tears fall from his face onto Jody's. Kyle has no solution for this sudden departure. Jody would always spring into action and make the important decisions; he was the undisputed leader, with the answers, no matter how absurd they sounded. *Jody will reanimate*, Kyle tells himself because this can't be how it ends. Jody will come back to life, and Kyle will at least be able to say goodbye.

As the sound of the glass falling becomes the only noise besides Kyle's clipped sobs, certain realities announce themselves.

Jody has killed himself.

Kyle is covered in his brother's blood.

Jody is gone.

The sky still rains glass.

With each passing moment that Jody's body lies motionless, it becomes clearer to Kyle that he will have to step out into the glass rain. Two gloveless imperfect fingers press together then come to rest on Jody's wrist. A confirmation is provided that Kyle already had in his heart. He doesn't check his own wrist because he fears he will feel the same thing he felt when he made contact with Jody's still warm skin. He waits a moment for Jody to lift his head and laugh at him. He waits for the punchline to be revealed. Kyle's hands shake, as his tears fall like glass.

If we don't leave now, the glass will seal us inside the house. That will not be how this all ends. This storm begs Kyle to waste the opportunity his brother gave to him, but Kyle refuses. He lifts Jody, then with a wobbly gait, carries him to the chaise lounge.

Once Jody has been laid down, a bloodstained Kyle steps back into the house and walks quickly into the living room. Flipping open the piano bench, Kyle grabs the shotgun, then returns to the coffee table that's still covered in molotov cocktails.

Maybe the raining glass was supposed to deter Kyle from leaving.

It doesn't.

Kyle walks back out onto the porch and stares at the body of his brother, and an ever-expanding pool of red so dark it's almost black.

Kyle puts both his gloves back on, then in one hand he grips the shotgun, and with his other, he grabs his brother's leg and begins to pull him off the chaise. The strain on Kyle's body, on his heart, weakens him and at the same moment, it pushes him forward.

The glass has already fallen at such a rate that the bottom porch step has disappeared.

The moment Kyle steps into the rain of the glass, he feels small slices nick his face. He puts his hood up, then glances across the front yard, to the flags sitting atop the glass. Mike, Rob, and Hummingbird are on the left side of the yard. Morgan, Wil, and now Jody will rest on the right side.

Kyle makes his way through the glass and he accepts the cuts- like Hummingbird, like Jody. Inside his Converse, through his socks, shards of glass embed themselves into Kyle's feet, but this doesn't stop him from doing the right thing- he drags Jody, leaving a red trail, to a grave in the glass.

As he checks Jody for a pulse, one last time, the glass beats down ceaselessly on Kyle's back, and hundreds of sharp little triangles stick into the cotton hoodie.

Kyle buries his gloved hands into the razor quarry, then begins splashing the glass over his dead brother.

Once Jody is fully covered, Kyle reaches into his back pocket with his shaking, glass covered hand. The sting from the gasoline on the rag climbs Kyle's arm so fast that he half expects his veins to begin to spider a black tree up his arm.

Kyle places the piece of the green blanket over Jody's section of the front yard.

Mike once said to us, "One of these days you'll be forced to visit Six Flags and your future will change. Change isn't always something to fear."

LXXIV. Jody Lennard.

"A Eulogy for Jody Lennard.
Written by Kyle Lennard.
Nah, I'm just fuckin' around. It was written by me, Jody Lennard.
I'm 27.
Not sure if you got that.
I don't need to show you my ID.
What are you, a New Jersey State Trooper?
I'm dead. Are you really gonna harass a fuckin' dead person?
R.I.P. me. American tragedy, Jody Lennard.
You people really have no decency.
Nah, I'm just fuckin' around again. I'm not going to go all 'Wil' on you.
Speaking of fuckin', remember when you saw me fuck Morgan?
That was pretty awesome.
I usually last longer. My dick might have looked less than impressive in that poor lighting, but it was probably the house's fault. It manipulates things. Time... penis lengths... you know, typical cabin in the woods stuff.
What I'm saying is my dick usually looks more attractive. I'm not claiming it wears a bow tie and sips a martini; I'm just saying that erection I had when Morgan was reaching for that shelf was not me at my full potential.
Okay, enough about my dick, for now.
I need a favor from you. My little brother, Kyle, is still alive. He's a good guy, but he still needs to be taken care of and protected. He's also super fuckin' gay. I thought that, because he's in his early twenties, things would get a little nicer for him after high school, but he's still not totally convinced that he's okay, and I'm not convinced either. I'm not saying it's your fault that Kyle is having a tough go of it, but there are people like you whose

fault it might be. There are these people who yell a fuckload louder than Mike did on stage- people who have more hate in their heart than Wil- people filled with more self-hate than Hummingbird- people with more sexual shame than Morgan- people even more reckless with their words than I am. When I was standing on that porch with my little brother, he honestly thought he was the one who should die at Leeds house. The entire time we lived there he didn't fuck anyone, as far as I know. He might not have even jerked off. I'm not sure. I wasn't really focused on that, but I never found him flushing crusty tissues in our molten lava filled toilet.

Kyle was nice the entire time we were at Leeds house and he didn't make us feel like shitty assholes, unless we were being shitty assholes. He just tried to keep us all together. He tried to keep us all alive. He tried to get us away from the house, but we didn't listen. *He* listened though, always. Which means he heard when people told him he's evil or bad or disgusting. He's read the signs that people not so different from you hold up. All that shitty internet garbage you typed on YouTube in the comments section under our videos, my little brother was reading that.

Maybe. No. *Certainly,* I'm to blame as well, but I need you to be better than me.

I'm dead.

Do you want to be like me?

No?

Okay, well then I need you to progress beyond where I was and get to where you ought to be.

I also need you to protect my brother, like he protected me. He lifted that scalding motorcycle off me, physically and metaphorically. He saved me a thousand times. When our circle expanded, his concern for the wellbeing of others ballooned proportionally with it. So, please, stay with Kyle. I bet that you've quietly hoped he'd be the one who walks out of the Barrens. Don't drop that fondness for him once he gets out. Keep that concern alive because Kyle will have to face more demons, and he'll need rational people on his side to remind him that he's not wrong. People are going to continue to hurt Kyle, and next time he might not be able to hide his scars with gloves.

I think, if I could ask a single request of you, it's to not be a fuckin' dickhead just because someone is different than you are. Change now- if you don't, then one day you could wake up in shit ass South Jersey.

I know that some people might remember me as a selfish bigot, but I don't think my brother will.

I hope my decision makes his non-decision easier to embrace."

LXXV. Us.

We leave Leeds House.
We leave The Barrens.
We've survived.
Maybe we went on this journey with Lies As Language to avoid the very same things that would lead to our own gruesome demise in Leeds house.
We might have chosen this long path as a voluntary detour away from our own homes.
And we're allowed this freedom- it's our right. We're blessed with the free will to choose how we spend our time.
The stakes aren't as high for us. Maybe that means we'll end up like the bodies trapped in the Barrens. There's also a chance that we may not end up that way. We possess the one thing that the unfortunate victims of the Jersey Devil ran out of- time. Remember, to procrastinate is to be human, but we can't let the time we've been gifted pass in a lull of inactivity. Lies As Language, and the two girls they picked up along the way, went from strangers, to friends, to lovers, to family, to corpses- all in a couple of days.
At the end of our life, we may find ourselves trapped in a house, scrambling to repair our most severe defects.
Do we require definitive signs that time is running out just so we will change?
Do we need to see the devil before we accept God?
Is this why people are taken from us- not to cause us hurt, but to remind us, in the hardest of ways, that we are all bound by our actions, and our end can arrive at any moment?
We're fragile, we're human, we're strong.
We can change, and we must.
So go, now, fix yourself.
You still have time.

LXXVII. Kyle Lennard.

"The devil takes, so I've devoted myself to giving. If someone wants a picture, I take a picture. If someone wants me to follow them on a website,

I follow them on their website. If someone wants me to like their picture, I like their picture. I give them what they want, and this giving feels good. Every time I give, I step close to a person, and that closeness reminds them that they're here, and they're in control of their future. They recognize that they caused this thing to happen- something that makes them feel good. It gives them the confidence to seize the next opportunity they're shown. Ever since I walked out of Leeds house, I haven't lost anyone else, I've only gained friends. I'm lucky.

It was easy for me to think that I was cursed, that everyone I love will be taken from me for as long as I live, but that's not the reality.

I've been surprised by how good things are, and how happy I am.

I'm not lonely.

I'm not bitter.

I am, however, sorrowful.

A big hurt hangs around me like the dust in that cursed living room. Every time I feel a draft, my spine aches with a chill.

I'm haunted by Leeds House and everything that happened there- how I felt there- the realities I found there.

Before, I was clean shaven, but now I have a bit of a beard because whenever I pick up a razor, I think of Hummingbird. I had to get a new apartment. The old apartment didn't understand why I was gone for so long. The old apartment was worried about me. The old apartment didn't want me to start from scratch, yet I was given no choice- I was thrown out.

Without a home, I rented a van, and I drove across the country, attending basement shows that I found through posts that I read about on my new phone. When I saw someone perform that understood what is important, I took them from their band. City by city, I drove around collecting bandmates and equipment. A story that Jody made up became *my* story. I turned a lie into reality. Now, I'm telling the truth when Jody's words leave my lips. I feel Hummingbird smiling when I tell the story now.

My new band instantly caught on because of the confusion about what happened to the old band. There was this idea that I had finally "arrived" and everything up until this point was just my tumultuous journey to get here. The first gig my new band played wasn't at a local bar, it wasn't in Scott's basement, it was in Paris. My story, and the controversy surrounding the missing members of my first band didn't catch on in America, but it did catch on overseas.

I took to the air with my new band, as the physical traces of Lies As Language disappeared into thin air.

The authorities were never able to find any bodies in the Barrens. They alleged that I was on drugs. They said that I was drinking while on prescription pain medication for my burns. They said that I abandoned my friends and bandmates. I disagreed. I asked them about Punchcunt Love, but they weren't familiar with the band. They said they'd call me if they had any additional questions, then they released me. I had no choice but to flee to Paris. I wanted someone to blame me for what happened at Leeds house. The only people in America who discussed what happened with me were these blonde twins in their late 20's who told me my friends and brother are in Heaven. I didn't question them because every insane-sounding story I hear, I now believe.

In Paris, as we performed, a massive crowd moshed, and hardcore danced, and jumped, and reached out to touch me, then merely asked for pictures at the merch table. No one called me a killer. No one blamed me for what happened. The people who meant the world to me, turned out to mean very little to the world.

On stage, after our final song, I thanked the audience, and admitted, "Thank you for this second chance, but to be honest, I still feel like I'm crumbling, Paris."

LXXVIII. Leeds House.

The large, sleek tour bus that Crumbling Paris has traversed the United States in rumbles home for one final show of a tour that started in the winter and now comes to rest at the onset of another winter.

As the bus cuts across the November sunrise, most of the members of Crumbling Paris sleep in their bunks. They had played a gig last night. They had headlined. They had gone out and celebrated after the show.

Kyle isn't able to sleep, so he sits in the middle of the bus, on a bench seat that faces a long tinted window. Kyle's drive has become unrelenting, unending. He now pulses with an urge for action that doesn't accept mandatory downtime for recharging. He wants to record music. He wants to direct movies. He wants to produce TV shows. He wants to interact with people and listen to their insane stories when no one else will.

In the reflection of the glass, Kyle studies the tiny imperfections that now pepper his face. Like the pitted surface of a planet, these little scars tell the story of a less than tranquil past. Kyle still has his good looks, but he doesn't have a babyface anymore.

A trance of trees creates a green smear in Kyle's mind. He finally feels close to sleep, the repetition lulling him, then a flash bursts across the side of the bus like a Polaroid being snapped.

Kyle begins to unrelentingly repeat, "Stop. Stop. Stop!"

"Fuck. What now, Kyle?" barks Crumbling Paris' manager, Ralph Williams, as he stumbles out from the bunks.

"Stop the bus," Kyle demands, rushing toward the driver.

"Steve, don't stop the bus," Ralph bellows.

"Shut up! Shut the fuck up!" screams the band from the bunks.

Placing his gloved palm on the driver's shoulder, Kyle says, "Steve. This is the place. I need you to stop here."

Kyle looks back and sees Ralph tightening his belt, getting ready to give chase the moment Kyle gets off this bus.

Steve sinks in his seat, then says softly, "I'm sorry, Kyle. I would have taken a different route... I didn't realize..."

"You don't need to apologize. You just need to pull the bus over to the side of the road and don't let anyone out, besides me," Kyle says in his soothing voice.

The bus sighs as it comes to a gradual stop, then hisses once.

"What are you going to do? Why go back out there?" Steve asks.

"I don't know yet," Kyle says, as he makes his way down the squat staircase of the bus, then sprints out toward the woods.

Steve immediately stands up to block the exit so no one can follow, but the well-meaning bus driver is quickly mushed in the face by Ralph, who muscles by, then trains his eyes on the fleeing lead singer.

Steve stopped the bus without question because he lost his best friend in these woods. It's also the place where Kyle lost his brother. It's also where Kyle lost Lies As Language.

The bus' emergency flashers are turned on, and Steve sets out a red road flare, aware of the potential for danger this part of New Jersey has been cursed with.

Logic be damned, the tour must be stopped so that Kyle can make peace with the place that inspired Crumbling Paris' debut album.

Kyle still loves what he does, but the high he felt the night we landed in the Barrens can never be replicated.

Stomping through the fallen needles, Kyle feels the pull of Leeds house. He knows that he will never truly leave this home, and an invisible hand guides him like he was a lost child.

Walking a path that had been branded onto his brain, everything comes rushing back to Kyle in an adrenaline wave. The exhausting trek he took to escape Leeds house was the most vivid, guarded, painful walk of his entire life. The glass in his shoes and glass from the sky has left Kyle scarred. As he walks, he can feel the small pangs of pain from the pieces of glass still embedded in his heel.

The Barrens are millions of years old, so the two years that have passed since Kyle was last here serve as a mere moment in their extensive life. The area has not changed a bit. The leaves and the needles are on the ground again, and Kyle has trouble believing they were ever on the trees. The massive pines seem not rooted in the ground, but instead in hell itself. They stand identical, consistent, too large for Christmas, and thankfully free from any ornaments the New Jersey Devil might want to hang.

Ralph huffs, red-faced from the chill and his palpable anger, as he catches up to Kyle. "Get the fuck back on the bus. This is not what we need right now," Ralph yells. He's fed up and cold, but his uncomfortable shiver pales in comparison to what Kyle feels when he reaches the site of Leeds house and the home is absent, like a misplaced van, like a fleeting Cherokee.

Kyle pauses for a moment, worried that he had imagined it all. He takes one step forward and his perspective changes. A massive hole in the ground reveals itself. Walled with leaves, this dramatic dip was camouflaged until Kyle got close to the edge.

The open grave of Leeds house pulls us forward, like a whirlpool in a devil's hot spring.

Kyle reaches the precipice of the steep drop, then he bends down and wipes the leaves off the cracked foundation. Unafraid of the possibility that a giant beast could spring from the trees to knock him into the pit below, Kyle observes what remains of this cursed location. He's returned to this site a better man, a more secure man, a man assembling an assured confidence regarding his place in the world. When he was last in Leeds house, Kyle was half a man, just as those hateful "Christians" were so anxious to point out. Kyle was half a man in their eyes because he was gay, but he now knows that the half that was missing wasn't a female partner, but instead a divine partner. This was never an issue of sexual preference, it was always an issue of deceit... of ego... of lies. Those sins were washed off Kyle, in a current of blood, but at any moment, these cancers can return, so the foundation must be destroyed. This hole must be filled. This space must be forced to crumble, then it must be made level.

The flags are gone, and according to the police's search, so are the bodies. Kyle knows where the souls are, and that is a supreme comfort. In an industry where bands will happily sell their soul to make it, Kyle made it by keeping his. A soul isn't collateral for success- it's a crucial building block toward erecting the flammable structure of an achieved dream. Kyle's success is a victory, something that rivals the power of Leeds house. Just as Jody said, there's no equal to God's power, and it's also true that there's no equal to the satisfaction gained by an achieved dream. There are many small devils attempting to destroy Christ's work, but Kyle has aligned himself with a power that cannot be defeated. The internet comments don't bother Kyle anymore. There are those devilish remarks alleging that he's capitalizing off the dead, that he's stolen all of Jody's songs and didn't even write the Crumbling Paris album. There are the hurtful whispers blaming Kyle for the death of his band and his two dedicated fans, but the investigation concerning what happened was short and barely pursued. How do you find a van that's disappeared? How do you prosecute a man when there's no evidence? Where are the bodies? How did so much happen on such a short timeline? There were no clues left to provide hints about the fate of the missing. Leeds House caused the death of these people. Their lives might have been taken, their physical bodies might be gone, but their impact remains and continues to change lives.

The devil revealed himself to Kyle, volunteering proof that he exists. This was an amazing gift. The existence of the devil proves God exists as well. With belief as a brace, Kyle walked away from this evil house.

How Leeds house was demolished is not important, but the fact that this open grave remains in the Barrens is a deadly problem.

"Listen, I get it," Ralph says, "I mean, I don't get why we're standing in the middle of the woods in the creepiest part of an already creepy state, when we should be on our way to the gig, but I get what you're going through. We probably owe you this."

Kyle touches the concrete foundation with his gloved hand, then says, "I want you to destroy it. All of it."

"I don't get it, Kyle. You leave a string of hotel rooms in impeccable order, but you're going to go all rock star in the middle of nowhere? Are you trying to destroy this place as a metaphor that you're beyond playing-"

"-I'm not running from those basements. We started in a basement. That's why I can't have this here. I can't have this-"

"-maybe we could have you play a special-"

"-do you know how many people died in these woods?" Kyle asks.

Ralph grimaces, frustrated that he's found himself discussing this delusion again.

Kyle stands up and walks across the sandy dirt, then his gloved hands wrap around Ralph's shivering shoulders. Kyle's piercing eyes slice into Ralph like shards of glass, as he says, "I want you to listen to me very carefully. You will take every single cent that would have gone to me from this tour and you will find good men- the best men- to come here and remove all traces of this curse. We will spare no expense to make sure all precautions are taken."

"And what exactly do we do with the pieces?" Ralph asks, shaking off Kyle's grasp.

"Scatter them," Kyle says, looking back to the foundation.

"Listen. Who knows if your friends' bodies are even here."

"-I'm not scattering their ashes, I'm scattering pieces of a building built from solid ash."

Tired of this little therapy session, Ralph deals in facts, "Kyle, we're in the Pine Barrens. This is protected land. You can't just bring in trucks and a demo crew in here."

"Exactly. We're in New Jersey. Pay someone," Kyle says.

Ralph can't believe what he's hearing, and asks, "Do you know how hard it is to do that type of complete demolition in the middle of the woods?"

"Not very," Kyle responds.

Ralph watches as the lead singer of Crumbling Paris attempts to put things back together, and he marvels, "You are one damaged kid, you know that?"

Kyle, scars and all, is repairing himself every day.

Ralph approaches the foundation, then says, "When I get back, I want you to be ready to walk to the bus."

"Get back from where?" Kyle asks.

Ralph takes a step forward, then says, "Since the door is wide open, I might as well check out the inside of the house."

ACKNOWLEDGMENTS

God – Thank you for providing me with the talent to write this book. Without you, none of this would have been possible.

Mom & Dad – Your continued support and guidance has been more than I could ever ask for.

Vestron Video – Thank you for putting out some of the worst movies ever to exist. Without your exceptionally low standards, I never would have seen most of the movies that influenced this novel.

My Editor – Thank you for helping me shape, clarify, detoxify, and solidify this novel.

I'd also like to thank: My brother, Sean, who isn't Kyle. Jody Hill, Danny McBride, Sam Raimi, Kevin Smith, David Gordon Green, Woody Allen, Play By Play Video, Blockbuster Video, Ashley Kamerling, Bridge, Milton Bradley, Bruce Springsteen, Michaels, Hasbro, The Gary Mitchell, blessthefall, The Ruining, Six Flags, The Basement of Doom, 30 Seconds To Mars, The Used.

METALCORE

If you're curious about metalcore music, these 13 albums are the best place to start:

Devil Wears Prada - Plagues (the first metalcore album I ever bought)
This Romantic Tragedy - Reborn (my favorite metalcore/trancecore album)
Blessthefall - Awakenings (the best album from metalcore's most consistent band)
Memphis May Fire - Challenger
Scary Kids Scaring Kids - Self Titled (RIP Tyson Stevens)
Drop Dead, Gorgeous - In Vogue
Bring Me The Horizon - There Is a Hell, Believe Me I've Seen It. There Is a Heaven, Let's Keep It a Secret.
Motionless In White - Creatures
The Word Alive - Life Cycles
Miss May I – Apologies Are For The Weak
Aiden – Knives
Bullet For Pretty Boy – Revision: Revise
Escape the Fate - Dying is Your Latest Fashion

BORING LEGAL SHIT

Before you sue me about something in this book, e-mail me. I'll fix any legal issues related to this novel. Don't sue me. I live in Newark. I'm broke. What are you gonna win from me in court? My *Buffy* box set?

If you have print, ad, or editorial work in any of the major fashion magazines, my novels will always be free for you. E-mail me a link to your modeling work and I'll e-mail you a free digital copy of my novel. If you write those boring ass articles in between the editorials, you get nothing from me besides a small amount of resentment and some residual jealousy.

Feel free to post excerpts of this book on your blog, tumblr, twitter, facebook, or apartment walls. Please don't get any of this tattooed on your body. I once wanted a Thug Life tattoo. Imagine if I got my way.

If you downloaded this novel illegally... I honestly don't blame you. Paying zero dollars for a thing is way better than paying four dollars for a thing. I get it.

If you want to read more of my celebrity and fashion satire, visit: hbgwhem.tumblr.com or frejarizona.tumblr.com or tjamesreagan.com

If you're an agent and you want to represent my unpublished novels, email me at: tjamesreagan@outlook.com

ABOUT THE AUTHOR.

T/James Reagan is the author of *Famous For Nothing* and *Empire Waste*.
He currently lives in Newark, New Jersey.